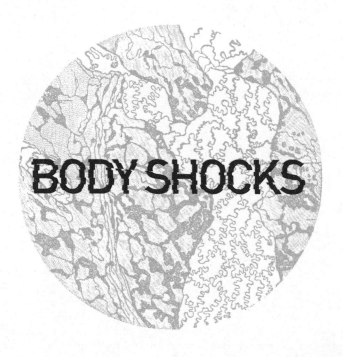

BODY SHOCKS

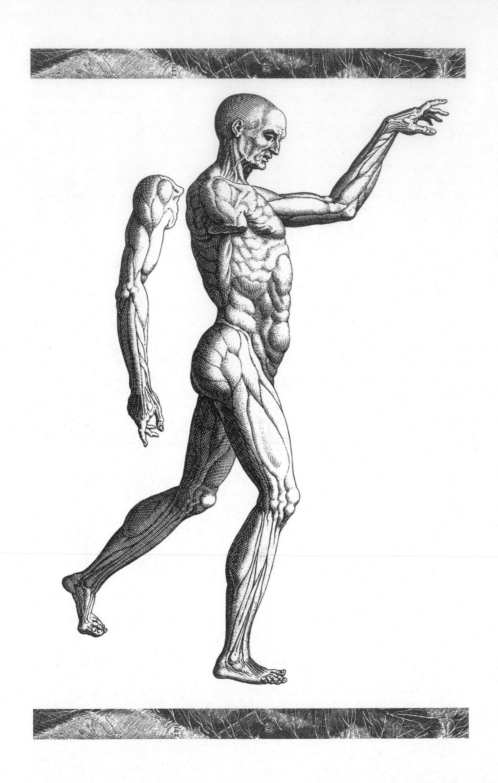

BODY SHOCKS

EXTREME TALES OF BODY HORROR

EDITED BY ELLEN DATLOW

— TACHYON —

BODY SHOCKS
Copyright © 2021 Ellen Datlow

Introduction copyright © 2021 by Ellen Datlow
Interior and cover design © 2021 by John Coulthart

Pages 379 & 380 constitute an extension
of this copyright page.

Tachyon Publications LLC
1459 18th Street #139
San Francisco, CA 94107
415.285.5615
WWW.TACHYONPUBLICATIONS.COM
TACHYON@TACHYONPUBLICATIONS.COM

Series Editor: Jacob Weisman
Project Editor: Jill Roberts

Print ISBN 13: 978-1-61696-360-6
Digital ISBN: 978-1-61696-361-3

Printed by Versa Press, Inc.

First Edition: 2021
9 8 7 6 5 4 3 2 1

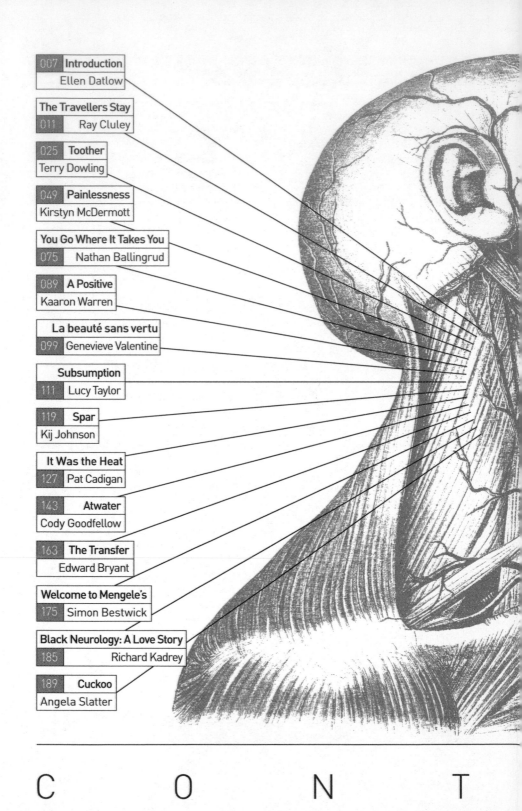

C   O   N   T

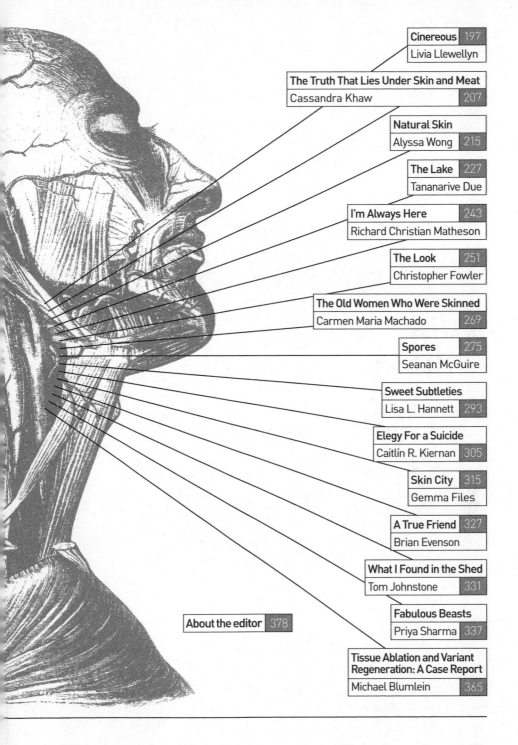

E   N   T   S

Introduction
Ellen Datlow

Body Shocks IS AN anthology of body horror. Much horror fiction is about is about damage to the body, so how is body horror different? What exactly *is* body horror?

The first use of the term was by Phillip Brophy in his 1983 article "Horrality: The Textuality of the Contemporary Horror Film." It referred to a movie subgenre that emerged in the mid-70s, most notably exemplified by David Cronenberg's *Shivers* and *Rabid* and Dario Argento's *Deep Red*. However, the theme itself has existed in text at least since Mary Shelley wrote *Frankenstein*, and has been a part of the SF/horror subgenre. "The Fly" by George Langelaan, "Who Goes There" by John W. Campbell, (also known by its movie versions *The Thing*), and "I Have No Mouth and I Must Scream" by Harlan Ellison are all examples.

Body horror has long had a strong presence in Japan. Shinya Tsukamoto's film *Tetsuo: The Iron Man*, and Katsuhiro Otomo's anime classic *Akira* blend body horror with cyberpunk. Junji Ito's *Uzumaki* and Hitoshi Iwaaki's *Parasyte* are standout manga series within the subgenre.

Gabino Iglesias provided a succinct definition of body horror in a review he wrote for the LitReactor website in 2017: "Body horror, a subgenre of horror that is also called biological horror or organic horror, refers to stories…in which the horror comes from or is based on the human body." Or, as defined by the Collins Dictionary in 2012, "in which the horror is principally derived from the unnatural graphic transformation, degeneration or destruction of the physical body."

It might be the most disturbing type of horror because it deals with the intimacy of the body's integrity being breached by intentional mutilation, accidental infestations by parasites, invasion by alien forces, degeneration, transformation, grotesquery, and pain. As Jack Halberstam, Professor of Gender Studies at Columbia University writes, body horror represents "[the] body as a locus of fear."

Of course, women have a uniquely intimate relationship with body horror, given that we bleed monthly for so much of our lives. Notable is Stephen King's *Carrie*. During her first experience of menstruation, not only is Carrie White terrified of this betrayal by her body, she's abused by the other girls in the locker room for her ignorance of this very ordinary rite of passage.

Plastic surgery can create profound horror of the uncanny valley type, as people attempt to change their bodies and faces in ways nature never intended. Implants can transform a plethora of body parts, including breasts, calves, cheeks and lips. Botox—aka the botulinum toxin—is injected into the flesh to paralyze the skin and erase wrinkles. Some people, like the infamous Bride of Wildenstein, embrace surgical transformation so deeply they end up inspiring fear and revulsion in others.

Voluntary body modifications have been practiced throughout history and across a range of cultures. Scarification and tattooing were—and still are—used by indigenous peoples to celebrate rites of passage, indicate tribal membership and strengthen the relationship to the spirit world.

Contemporary artist Fakir Musafar (the father of the Modern Primitive Movement) had his body suspended by hooks that pierced his skin, and practiced extreme corseting. Performance artist Stelarc also practiced body suspension, while Yann Brennyak, whose face sports dermal implants, has developed a new, gory technique for tattooing. These voluntary transformations—some taken to horrifying extremes—are presented to the world as art.

Is it body horror to be transformed against your will? Greek Mythology is filled with tales of hapless mortals changed into everything from birds and stones to horses and trees by the capricious gods. Cursed by envious Athena, Medusa was remade into a Gorgon with writhing snakes for hair. The sailors who served Odysseus were mutated into wild pigs by Circe, a scene that brings to mind the bone-cracking, jaw breaking man-to-beast transformation in John Landis's *An American Werewolf in London*.

The stories I've chosen to represent this subgenre of horror cover a wide range in time and subject matter. The oldest story included, "Tissue Ablation and Variant Regeneration: A Case Report," author/physician Michael Blumlein's first published story, came out in the British magazine *Interzone* in 1984. It's overtly political, expressing Blumlein's anger and outrage at the Reagan administration. It's only been reprinted a few times and as far as I can tell, has never appeared in an American anthology (it was also in Blumlein's collection, *The Brains of Rats*).

Fashion of course, has always been guilty of promoting horrific modifications to female bodies, including foot binding, neck lengthening, the use of corsets and especially the encouragement of eating disorders. So it's only natural to include a couple of stories about the extremes of fashion and transformation for the sake of beauty at any cost. Christopher Fowler's "The Look" and Genevieve Valentine's "La beauté sans vertu" each take a jaundiced view of the fashion industry.

Who isn't afraid of going to the dentist? The helplessness of sitting back in the chair, tethered down by equipment, the blind trust to allow a stranger to poke around in one's mouth with sharp objects … unsettling, to say the least. And if that poking is not consensual? Even worse. I've read several stories over the years about terrible things to do with teeth (including "On Edge" by Christopher Fowler—already represented here by his fashion monstrosity) but Terry Dowling's "Toother" is one of the most unnerving.

The stories presented here run the gamut of body horror: from back alley eyeball mods to corpse possession, fungal infestations to skinless women. Science fiction, dark fantasy, good old-fashioned horror—all present and accounted for. Not for the squeamish or faint of heart, but oh, so cathartic. A bit like picking at a healing scab; we know it should be left alone, but it's just so *satisfying* to peel back those layers and see what's hiding underneath.

Enjoy.

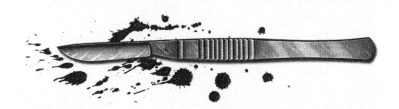

RAY CLULEY is a British Fantasy Award winner with stories published in various magazines and anthologies. Some of these have been reprinted in *Best of the Year* volumes, *Nightmares: A New Decade of Modern Horror*, as well as Steve Berman's *Wilde Stories: The Year's Best Gay Speculative Fiction*, and Benoît Domis's *Ténèbres*. He has been translated into French, Polish, Hungarian, and Chinese. His short fiction is collected in *Probably Monsters* while a second collection will soon be looking for a home. He is currently writing for Black Library's horror imprint, as well as working on his own novel. You can find out more at WWW.PROBABLYMONSTERS.WORDPRESS.COM

The Travellers Stay
Ray Cluley

By NIGHT THE motel was nameless, the stuttering fluorescence of its neon sign only a rectangular outline of where words once were. The light made the shadows of the building darker and gave moths the false hope of somewhere to go, collecting the dust from their broken wings so that a once vibrant white was now mottled and sulphurous.

By day the place fared no more favourably. The title of its sign was visible, *Travellers Stay*, but so was the fact that it needed a fresh coat of paint twenty years ago; flakes peeled like scabrous sores. In sunlight, the building behind the sign was more than a dark shape but not much more, the drab monotony of its sun-bleached walls broken only by the repetition of plain numbered doors.

When Matt arrived, the motel was neither of these places but something in between. Dusk was a veil that disguised before and after and the motel looked as good as it ever could. Anyone who came to the *Travellers Stay* came at dusk.

"We're here," Matt said. He made a slow turn and bumped gently up-down an entrance ramp. A sheet of newspaper skittered across his path as an open v, became caught on a wheel, and was turned under it twice before tearing free. He pulled into a spot between a rusting truck and a Ford that sat flat on its tyres and noticed neither. "Wake up."

Only when he cranked the handbrake did Ann stir beside him, sitting up from the pillow she'd made of her jacket against the passenger window. The denim had pressed button patterns into her forehead like tiny eyes. A sweep of her fringe and they were gone without her ever knowing they were there.

"Where are we?" Her breath was sour with sleep.

"Motel."

Ann turned to the back seat. "John, honey."

John, her teenage son, mumbled something that spilled a line of drool and woke. He wiped his chin and sat up. "What?" he said. "What?" He sniffed at the saliva drying on the back of his hand.

Matt released the steering wheel and flexed his fingers. He arched his back and shifted in his seat, eager to get out and stretch his legs.

Ann was looking around. "Here? Seriously?"

Matt ignored her.

There was a woman sitting on the porch enjoying a cigarette. She was leaning back on a chair with her feet up on the rail. She was wearing cowboy boots. Cow*girl* boots, Matt supposed. Black jeans and a vest top the same, faded gray from too many washes. The door behind her was propped open by a pack of bottled beer.

"Want me to loan you fifty?" Ann said. "She can't be any more than that."

It could have been funny from someone else, but Ann had never mastered that type of humour.

"She's not a hooker," Matt said. He was tired. His words came out the same way.

"And how would you know?"

The woman was attractive. Matt found a lot of young women were, these days. But if he felt any lust it was for the cigarette she held and the beer she drank. Hell, it was for the ease with which she did both. As he watched she brought a hand up to her mouth and inhaled lazily. She chased it with a tip of her drink.

"I *don't* know," Matt said. He got out of the car before he had to say anything else.

The woman looked his way and raised her beer in silent greeting.

"Hi," he called back. Mr Friendly.

The thump of a car door behind him. Ann.

"We'd like a room," he said to the woman.

"You sure?"

Matt looked at Ann and wondered how much of their conversation the woman might have heard.

"We're sure," Ann said. "You got any?"

Matt sensed some sort of bristling, but only from his wife. The woman in the chair merely shrugged. "Twenty or so, judging by the numbers on the doors."

"We just want one," Matt said.

"Help yourself," she said. She said it differently to most people. Got the inflections all wrong.

"Do we pay by the hour here or what?" John asked, slamming his door at the same time because he wasn't brave enough with his insult. Matt heard him, though, and he'd told him before about slamming the door. Not for the first time he wished Ann's ex had got the custody he'd apparently wanted.

Ann made a show of looking around the parking lot and beyond. It was a show Matt had seen before and it meant she was looking at how he might look at the woman.

"Just one night," he said.

"Hope so," the woman said, getting up and going inside.

That's how you do it, Matt thought, looking at John. *Chicken shit.*

Ann was looking at Matt, eyebrows raised, waiting for him to react somehow to the woman's attitude. He made a show of looking around the parking lot and beyond.

The sky had darkened to something like the colour of the woman's clothes. An occasional breeze tossed litter in small circles and swept grains of sandy dirt across the ground. From far away came the quiet noise of a passing car, a long hush of sound as if the coming night had sighed.

"We're not staying here," Ann said.

"I'm tired," he replied. It meant yes we are and I don't want to fight.

"I'll drive," said John.

"Not my car."

The woman returned with a large disk of white plastic declaring 8 in big bold black. It looked like a giant eye with twin pupils, the key dangling like a metal tear.

"Thanks," Matt said, stepping up to take it.

"Clean sheets, towels, TV." She pointed across the lot. "Vending machines are over there."

"Thanks," Matt said again. He gave the key to Ann and grabbed the bags from the trunk. John kicked at a crushed can and sent it clattering. The woman sat back in her chair and retrieved her bottle. She brought it to her mouth slowly. Swapped it for the cigarette.

"Quit staring." Ann took one of her bags from him, more for the impact of snatching it than from any desire to help. She gave the room key back to him so whatever it opened up would be his fault.

"Good night," the woman said quietly as they walked away. And in a dry tone, addressed to the floor, "Don't let the bed bugs bite."

"It's gonna be a shit hole," John said.

Matt smacked him across the back of the head with his free hand. Thought, *fuck it.*

"Hey!" John and Ann said together, John rubbing at where he'd been struck.

"Language," was all Matt said, but mostly he'd struck out because he was fed up with the boy. And there was no need to state the obvious—of course it would be a shit hole.

"You can't hit me," John said. "You're not my dad."

"Thank God."

"Matt—" Ann started.

"Sorry. I'm just tired, okay? Sorry."

He wasn't tired, though, not really. Tired of driving, and tired of taking John's crap, but not tired like he wanted sleep. In fact, what he wanted was a beer and a smoke and a few minutes on his own to enjoy both.

Ann gestured at the door. A brass 8 that was probably plastic, a peephole beneath like a dropping.

Matt fumbled with the key. The overlarge fob made it a handful. It was the old-fashioned type of key, one you turned in a lock. It turned easily enough; he could have opened the door with a toothpick. He pushed the door open.

There were whispers in there, whispers in the darkness. He reached around the frame for the light switch.

The first thing he saw when the light came on was the usual motel scenery. A large bed, nearly-white sheets tight across it with a tatty blanket on top, and a bedside table with one drawer. The drawer would have contained a bible in the old days but now probably held dried balls of gum and cigarette burns. A TV angled down from the wall so it could be seen from the twin room as well, though the door to that was closed. Somewhere there'd be a tiny bathroom that didn't have a bath.

The second thing he saw was movement as a number of cockroaches scurried for cover. Their shiny bodies glistened in the light they tried to run from. One sped for the shadows under the bed while another moved as if lost. One made straight for the open door.

John brought his foot down hard but missed. The insect dropped down between two boards of the porch.

"Beautiful room, dear," said Ann. But she went in, slinging her bag onto the bed. Fearless city girl that once was.

John went in ahead of Matt, knocking him as he passed. He said sorry as if it was an accident and Matt had to fight the urge to kick the back of his feet into a tangle that would send him sprawling to all fours.

John put the TV on and sat on the bed, looking up at a commercial.

Ann opened and closed the drawer.

"Picture's shit," John told them. He glanced at Matt and added, "Shot," as an alternative.

Matt dumped the bags and went to find the bathroom. He expected to find it between the two bedrooms.

He found it between the two bedrooms.

There was nothing there to scare away with the light. Just a sink and a toilet and a mirror. The mirror was spotted with neglect that would never wipe away. It distorted Matt's reflection, darkened his face with blotches. Someone had smeared a fingernail of snot on it.

"Nice."

He unzipped, lifted the toilet lid, and pissed, tearing a sheet of tissue to wipe the mirror with. It wasn't until he was shaking dry that he saw the cockroach turning in the bowl. Its body span in a current Matt had just made and its legs kicked at the air. It would never get out.

I know exactly how you feel.

He flushed it away, wondering how it had gotten in there in the first place.

"Matt," Ann called, "can you fix the TV?"

He glanced again at the mirror on his way out, wondering what had happened to the man he saw there.

Back when Matt smoked and drank, when he was single, when he was playing and the band was doing pretty good and could maybe one day do better, he got into a fight with a guy because the man was yelling at a woman. He did it because it was often a sure way to get laid and the woman looked good for that. Red hair, straight and long, good breasts and striking eyes. She wore a top that pushed her tits up and her eyes she showed off with subtle make up.

"The picture won't stay like it's supposed to," she said as he emerged from the bathroom. She tossed the remote onto the bed and continued pulling things from her bag. Instead of makeup, these days her eyes were lined with tiny wrinkles. She rarely looked at Matt now as she had back then. The way she looked at him now was like he was exactly the way she supposed. Her eyes still lit up when she smiled but that was less frequent, and usually because of some TV show. The first time she came her eyes had been wide and her mouth was a pretty O, as if the orgasm had startled her. He hadn't seen that for years.

Matt reached up and turned the TV off by the main switch. 'Fixed,' he said.

John muttered something Matt ignored and Ann ignored the both of them.

"I'll get some dinner," Matt said.

John threw himself onto his own bed and stretched out. "Pizza."

"He's not driving tonight," Ann told her son. She didn't use the most supportive tone.

Matt left, closing the door on both of them and resting his hands on the porch rails. He looked at the sky and saw nothing he hadn't seen a hundred times before. The words of the motel sign were invisible now, hidden in the glare of a surrounding neon rectangle. The yellow tubes looked like they'd been white once and then pissed on.

Across the lot, on the shorter length of an L shaped porch, the woman continued to smoke and drink. Occasionally she'd look at the end of what she smoked but mostly she looked at the ground.

Matt took a deep breath. He hadn't had a cigarette in six years (Ann had urged him to quit) and so he hoped for some second-hand smoke. What he smelt instead, carried to him on the dusty air, was the welcome tang of marijuana. He filled his lungs with it, slight as it was. He watched as the woman released another mouthful of smoke, wishing he was near enough to breath it in.

He went to the vending machines instead.

A couple of cockroaches, alarmed by his approach, hurried out from beneath the machine and raced past his foot, slipping under the door of room 12. Others congregated around a nearby garbage sack, bumping into each other and adjusting their course.

The vending machine offered the usual candy and chips as well as some microwave snacks, though he hadn't seen a microwave in the room. He rummaged in his pocket for money and found only a couple of folded bills. The readout told him NO CHANGE.

He'd see if the woman could help him.

She heard him coming and puffed a final time on her joint. She was stubbing it out and chasing the last toke with beer when he offered his money and said he needed change.

"Of course," she said. "Change." But she made no move to give him any. He leant closer with the cash and she took it with a sigh. She stood up and stretched, pushing out her chest in a way that was all the more alluring for being unintentional, her hands at the small of her back until it clicked. He wondered how long she'd been sitting out here. Before he could ask, or make any kind of conversation, she was stepping into the office behind her.

"For the machine?" she asked, calling it slowly. Lazily. The same way she drank her beer.

"Yeah."

She returned with a handful. "It's kinda picky with what it likes," she said, explaining all the coins.

"Great. Thanks."

She puffed her hair out of her face, brushed it aside when that didn't work. "Anything else?"

"Yes, actually. Do you have a microwave back there? Only I saw-"

"Yeah, we got one," she said, sitting again. "Just bring whatever you get and I'll nuke it." The gulp she took of her beer was an obvious goodbye.

Matt went back to the machine. He fed it coins until it served him his choices and took them back to the woman.

"Can I help you?" she asked. It wasn't like she'd forgotten seeing him already. And it was disconcertingly earnest.

"Sure," he said. "You can nuke these." He tried a smile.

"That's it?"

He wondered if she was a hooker after all.

"Er…"

She took the food from him and carried it back in, side stepping over a cockroach that sped across the floor. It turned a circle and went back the other way.

"Where you heading?" she asked, tossing the packets into the microwave. For a ridiculous moment he thought she was talking to the roach.

"Nowhere."

She looked at him, started the microwave. "You got two minutes," she said over its hum.

Matt laughed politely. "Home," he said, "Picked the boy up from his dad's, saw the in-laws. They want to give me a job."

"Not good?"

"No."

"What do you do?"

He said it for the first time in years. "I'm a musician." Words that used to impress every girl he ever said them to. Some pretended otherwise, but it always worked.

"Not any more," she said.

"What?"

"Not if ma and pa get their way."

"Oh. Yeah. Exactly."

"They just want what's best," she said. It was what Ann had told him, several times, until the drive lulled her to sleep. He'd probably end up taking the damn job.

They were quiet until the microwave dinged.

"What do *you* want?" she asked.

"I want them to leave me the fuck alone."

Matt's surprise registered only when he saw hers. She offered food that looked as plastic as its wrapping. "I meant which of these is yours?"

He took it all without specifying, muttered, "Thanks," and hurried back to his room.

He expected Ann to give him shit about how long he'd been. Wouldn't have been surprised if she'd spied on him from behind the blinds. He braced himself for it. He opened the door and went in, dropped the lukewarm food on the bed, shut the door, said, "Dinner," and then saw John.

The boy was stood in the middle of the room and at first Matt thought he was attempting some kind of prank. He wore a black cloak draped over his shoulders and had wound dark tape around his chest and waist. He flailed his arms around in cardboard tubes that he'd stretched black socks over. This was how Matt rationalised it. John's curved back was a shiny black that glistened in the room's light. Matt could see Ann's reflection in it, saw how she cowered in the corner of the room.

"Ann? What's going on?"

Ann shook her head and made wordless noise. She was rocking from side to side, looking at the thing in the middle of the room.

"John?"

He had wires sticking up from some sort of black hat. He was screeching, rubbing his extended arms up and down his legs as he crouched and then knelt. He leant forward on his elbows and brought his feet up behind where they seemed to disappear into the cape that draped him. The head wires flicked back and forth like fishing rods casting line, or like antennae. Yeah, antennae, that was it. The boy's knees opened and sprouted bristled limbs. His calves separated, spitting split shins into new feet. And still he was screeching.

Ann screeched with him. Her rocking had become easier thanks to something like a large curved shield she had on her back. Her clothes were disappearing as if melting into her skin, only to be replaced by an oil spreading from her pores. Matt watched as her breasts distended and spread into a single band of blackened flesh. He heard things cracking in her chest. Her stomach swelled then flattened and split into sections and her newly segmented body fell forward, face down to the floor. The glossy shield she wore on her back separated for a moment and shook thin wings before settling back into place. Her hair fell away as two protrusions sprouted from her head, dancing back and forth erratically as they grew. Claws burst from her palms as she reached for John. For Matt.

Matt retreated until he felt the door handle press against his back.

John was now a huddled shape the size of a suitcase. He bumped his way around the room, striking furniture and hissing. Ann was tuning tight circles on the spot.

Matt opened the door behind him and rolled around it out of the room, slamming it shut. When a cockroach fled from beneath he brought his boot down quick and hard without thinking. There was a satisfying crunch. He slid his foot back, wiping the mess into a streak. The creatures in the room were hissing and fluttering and banging into things.

Matt stepped back from the door, waiting for it to bump with an impact. The porch rail stopped him stumbling into the parking lot. He leant against it and waited.

Eventually the sounds inside subsided.

He wiped his mouth, his stubbled chin, and glanced around to see who'd been alerted by the noise.

Across from him, in a chair pushed back against the doorframe, the woman sat drinking beer. She lowered the bottle and wiped her mouth as he had done. He stared at her for a long moment before she beckoned him over.

Matt went with a quick walk that wasn't quite running, glancing back only once.

"Everything alright?" she said as he turned the corner into her section of the porch.

"My wife…"

He didn't know how to finish.

"John. He…"

She nodded, got up and went inside. By the time Matt was at her chair she had returned with another for him. She put it down beside hers and sat. "Yeah," she said. "That happens sometimes."

She gestured for him to sit. He did. When she picked up her beer, she hooked another bottle with it and passed it over.

Matt looked briefly at the bottle and took his first mouthful of real beer in five years. Ann had made him quit, or rather she bought near-beer which was the same thing. He gulped until his mouth was awash with it. It was delicious.

"How did you find this place?" said the woman.

"I just turned off the freeway. I was tired. What's happening?"

"It doesn't matter." She raised a leg and pushed against the rail to tip her chair back. She kept her foot on the rail and took another swallow of beer, leaning back in a comfortable balance. "Even if I *could* tell you."

"They're fucking cockroaches," Matt said. He'd finally pushed the words from his mouth.

"I don't think they're at the fucking stage yet," the woman said. "Gotta get used to it first."

Matt shook his head. He was calmer than he should've been, but he wasn't ready for jokes. "They *are* cockroaches?"

"Mm. Tough little critters. But then so are we, right?" She drained the last of her beer and set the bottle down with the row of other empties. From her angled position on the chair she couldn't quite set it down properly and it fell, spinning. Matt watched as it slowed to a stop, the neck pointing his way, and thought of games he'd played as a teenager.

"So the kid's not yours?" she said.

"No. God, no. He's a—"

"Cockroach." She sniggered the abrupt laugh of someone drunk. She had been looking out into the dark but faced him to say, "Sorry."

He shrugged. "I was going to say asshole."

"Like his father?"

She asked the questions without seeming to care for answers. Like they were rehearsed, or lines she knew well from a familiar movie. Matt answered her anyway with another shrug, adding, "You know, she didn't even tell me she had a kid until we'd been together a year? Can you believe that?"

The woman handed him another beer and he slapped the top off against the railing. He brought it up to his mouth so quick for the foam he hit his teeth. The woman winced for him as he gulped it down. She looked back into the darkness.

"You wanna be a rock star, huh?" she said. She smiled when she said it, looked his way so he could see it before it went. "The bright lights of fame and fortune."

"Sounds stupid now," he admitted.

They watched the moths beating themselves against the motel sign. Closer, Matt could see the words within the neon. He noticed the lack of apostrophe, *Travellers Stay*, and wondered if it was true for everyone.

"What are you doing here?" he asked her.

"Nice girl like me in a place like this?" She spat an arcing stream of beer into the parking lot. "Hiding. Deciding what I want to be. I'm allowed to do that, you know."

He held his hands up in surrender, though her tone hadn't been entirely aggressive.

The woman set her chair down and rummaged in the front pocket of her jeans for a crumpled packet of cigarettes. Matt hoped she'd offer him one and she did. When he looked inside he saw a row of ready-made joints.

"You're a musician, right?" she said, seeing his hesitation as reluctance.

He took one and gave the packet back. "It's been a long time."

She returned the pack to her jeans without taking another. "If it's your first in a while, we'll share." She pointed to where the lighter lay next to scattered cigarette butts. A couple were joints smoked down to fingertip length. Roaches, they were called, Matt remembered. This was a roach motel. He snorted a laugh.

"You gotta smoke it first," the woman said.

He glanced over at room 8 and wiped his lips dry. He sparked a flame from the lighter. The paper pinched between his fingers crackled and glowed as he sucked the flame down. He shook the lighter out, a habit he'd had long ago, and exhaled smoke in one, two, three little puffs.

"Good man," the woman said.

"Used to be." He felt light headed. It *had* been a long time. He passed the joint over.

"Thanks."

"My name's Matt."

"Amber."

A cockroach ran a straight line across the edge of the porch then turned and made for them on the chairs. Amber toed it aside gently and it hurried back the way it had come.

Matt seems to dream the sex and when he wakes he pulls her over onto him so he can watch this girl with long un-red hair fuck him again, and she does, and this time slowly, but then he's kneeling at the bedside pulling her jeans down and her panties and he realises maybe he's still drunk or still dreaming or remembering or something. He kneels at the bedside and she opens her legs to him and he stares at her sex, but this time before he can stand, plunge, enter her, before he can feel that welcoming wet warmth of a new woman, a torrent of cockroaches spills from inside, a swarm that flows from between her legs to flood the room, dropping from the bed to the floor in inky waves, scurrying over his thighs and groin and tangling themselves in the hair there. When he tries to scream, something scampers up across his neck and chin and into his mouth, bristled legs tickling his lips and tongue, wings fluttering against his teeth, and when the squat weight of it slips down his throat he wakes up gagging.

She was at the window, looking out through the blinds. The light coming in was early morning and neon. It made her look hazy.

"You can go now," she said.

She had dressed back into her jeans and vest, her arms folded over her chest and a cigarette between her fingers. He had seen that chest, kissed it, squeezed each breast. Even remembering Ann, what she had become, he felt little regret. He wanted to do it all again. He hardened under the covers thinking about it.

"I want to stay here for a while."

Outside, the motel sign flickered and blinked out.

Amber brought the cigarette to her lips and blew smoke into the weak sunlight coming in between the blinds. It curled and spread there, gray and slow. "Maybe this is my fault," she said to it.

He tried to sit up, to say something.

"No," she said. "You should go. Be a rock star or something."

He brought his arm out from under the covers to reach for her but knocked a lamp down and it smashed. He felt clumsy, like his arm was too long.

She merely glanced sidelong at him and smoked some more. "Too late," she said quietly, and pulled the cord at the window.

The blinds gathered up in a rush and bright sunlight streamed into the room, blinding him. He cried out and crossed his arms over his eyes, thinking this was the worst hangover he'd ever had until he felt how horribly bristly his flailing arms were, how slender. Maybe it wasn't a hangover, maybe he was still drunk or still dreaming or remembering or something, but oh that fucking light hurt!

He rolled from the bed, marvelling at how easy it was; there was a strange new curve to his back and, oh God, he'd seen something like it before, hadn't he? He slid into the darkness beneath the bed, the shade like cool water on his thickening skin.

She was saying something about how he'd had a chance, but it was hard to hear the words over the high noise he was making, and when she said something about his chance or choice or whatever he had no idea what she was talking about because all he could do was hiss and turn on the spot as his back split and opened and new spiny limbs burst from old ones.

I'm a moth, I'm a moth, I'm a fucking moth!

But of course he wasn't, he never had been. It was easier to hide from the light than to seek it out, easier to blame others for his lack of happiness than to risk being burned in the pursuit of it. The bed above shifted and bumped with him as he changed, but it grew more distant as he diminished and decided and became what he'd always been.

"I guess you'll stay a while," someone said. Someone who knew the way, once, but lost herself on purpose to avoid choices. She'd never be anyone or anything.

He didn't care. There were things with him beneath the bed, nudging the dust and scavenging waste. They had faces, these things. Human faces, looking down at the ground as they bumbled around. He'd never noticed them before.

He remembered, then, the one he'd crushed from room 8. Did it have a face like these? And whose face had it been?

He flexed the wings he'd never use and scurried back to his room to find out, hoping whoever he found there would accept him for what he was.

Behind him came the call of tiny voices he pretended not to understand.

TERRY DOWLING is one of Australia's most respected and internationally acclaimed writers of science fiction, dark fantasy, and horror, and author of the multi-award-winning Tom Rynosseros saga. The *Year's Best Fantasy and Horror* series featured more horror stories by Dowling in its 21-year run than by any other writer.

Dowling's horror is collected in the International Horror Guild Award-winning *Basic Black: Tales of Appropriate Fear*, the Aurealis Award-winning *An Intimate Knowledge of the Night*, and *The Night Shop: Tales for the Lonely Hours*. Other publications include his novel, *Clowns at Midnight* and *The Complete Rynosseros*. "Toother" won the Australian Shadows Award. His homepage can be found at WWW.TERRYDOWLING.COM

Toother
Terry Dowling

As Dan Truswell gave his signature three-three knock on the door in the modest hospital tower of Everton Psychiatric Facility that Friday morning, he couldn't help but glance through the second-floor window at the new sign down in the turning circle. *Everton Psychiatric Facility* it said. He'd never get used to it. That was the more politically correct name for Blackwater Psychiatric Hospital, just as words like client and guest had completely replaced patient and inmate.

"Peter, it's Dan."

Dan didn't enter Peter Rait's room, of course. That wasn't their arrangement. He just waited, looking at his reflection in the small mirror Peter kept hanging outside his door, surprised not so much by the slate grey eyes and flyaway hair but by how white that hair had become. He was fifty-nine, for heaven's sake! It was something else he'd never get used to.

Finally the door opened and Peter stood there in his pyjamas.

"Careful, Doctor Dan. That's a dangerous one."

"They all are, Peter. Carla said you've been yelling. Another nightmare?"

Peter looked tired, troubled. His black hair was tousled from sleep. "They don't usually come this often now. Harry's going to phone."

"Harry Badman?" Dear industrious Harry was two years out of his life, distanced by the usual string of promotions, secondments and strategic sidelining that marked the lives of so many career detectives in the New South Wales Police Force. "All right, Peter, so how does this dream relate?"

"Ask Harry about the teeth, Doctor Dan."

Dan thoughts went at once to the recent desecration at Sydney's Rookwood Cemetery. "Is this about—?"

"Ask him."

"What do you have, Peter?"

"I can't say till he confirms it. Ask him. He'll know."

Dan made himself hold back the rush of questions. "It's been a while."

Peter did finally manage a smile, something of one. "It has, Doctor Dan."

Dan smiled too. "Phil knows?"

"Some of it. I'll give him an update at breakfast. But it's important. Very important."

"Tell me the rest, Peter."

"I really can't."

"There are voices?"

"God, yes. But strange." Neither of them smiled at the bathos. What internal voices weren't? "They're coming over time."

Dan frowned. This was something new. "Across years?"

"The first is from the sixties."

"More, Peter."

"Let Harry start it."

You've started it! Dan almost said, but knew to hold back, just as Peter had known how much to use as a tease.

"Listen, Peter—"

"Talk later. I'll leave you two alone."

And he closed the door. Dan, of course, looked straight into Peter's mirror again, had the good grace to laugh, then headed downstairs.

Forty-nine minutes later, as Dan sat in his office reviewing the patient database, Harry Badman phoned from Sydney. There was the inevitable small-talk, the polite and awkward minimum that let them stitch up the years as best they could. Dan Truswell and Harry Badman liked one another a great deal, but their friendship had never been easy far from where their respective careers met: for Harry, pursuing the more dangerous exponents of extraordinary human behavior; for Dan, fathoming the often extraordinary reasons for it.

Finally Harry's tone changed. "I need to see you, Dan."

"It's about what happened at Rookwood last Saturday night, isn't it?"

"What have you heard?"

"What was in the news. A grave was desecrated. A recent burial." Dan said nothing about teeth. This had been one of Peter Rait's dreams after all, and it had been a while since the intense, still-young man had been "active" like this. More importantly it was Dan's way of testing Peter's special talent after all this time.

"Samantha Reid. Aged 41. Buried on Friday, dug up on Sunday sometime between two and four in the morning. Cold rainy night. No-one saw anything. The body was hauled from the coffin and left lying beside the grave."

"So, not just a grave 'tampered with,' like the papers said. Your people are good, Harry. Why the call?"

"Things were removed from the scene. I'd like your take on it."

"Stop being coy. What was 'removed'?"

"The teeth, Dan. All the teeth."

Dan had an odd rush of emotion: revulsion, fascination, the familiar numb amazement he always felt whenever one of Peter's predictions played out like this. And there was the usual excess of rationalism as if to compensate. "What do the deceased's dental records show? Were there gold fillings?"

"Dan, *all* the teeth. And it's not the first desecration. Just the first to make the news."

Dan knew he'd been slow this time, but allowed that he was out of practice too. "There were others?"

"From secluded and disused parts of the cemetery. Much older graves."

"But recent desecrations?"

"Hard to tell conclusively. Not all were reported back then. It didn't look good for the cemetery authorities. The graves were tidied up; nothing was said. We would have assumed these earlier violations were unrelated except…" He actually paused. Had the subject been less serious, it would have been comical.

"Come on, Harry. Someone's collecting teeth. What else do you have?"

"That Rattigan murder in Darlinghurst a month back. The pensioner, remember?"

"Go on."

"She wasn't strangled like the media said."

"No?"

"She was bitten to death."

Dan was surprised to find that his mouth had fallen open in astonishment. "Bitten?"

"At least two hundred times. Increasing severity."

"These could be different crimes, Harry. What makes you think they're related?"

"Teeth fragments were found in some of the wounds. Very old teeth."

But not in very old mouths, Dan realized. "Dentures made from these older desecrations?"

"Exactly."

"Surely there was saliva DNA from whoever wore them."

"No," Harry said.

Dan grasped the implications. "So, not necessarily biting as such. Someone made dentures from these older corpse teeth and—what?—killed the Rattigan woman using some sort of handheld prosthesis?"

"Spring-loaded and vicious. All we can think of. And that's *several* sets of dentures, Dan. We've traced teeth fragments back to the occupants of three older desecrations: graves from 1894, 1906 and 1911. All female. No fragments from newer teeth—"

"Too new to shatter."

"Exactly. But there could be other teeth used, from other desecrations we don't know of. There are some very old graves there; we wouldn't necessarily be able to tell. So all we have is a major fetish angle. Something ritualistic."

"My phone number hasn't changed, Harry." The accusation hung there. *You didn't call sooner!*

"You've got your life, Dan. Annie. Phil." The barest hesitation. "Peter. I didn't want to intrude."

Dan stared at the mid-morning light through his office windows and nodded to himself. "You've profiled it as what?"

"I'd rather not say. That's what this is about. Getting another take."

"Official?"

"Can be. You want the file? I'll email a PDF right now. Drive up tomorrow first thing."

"See you at the Imperial Hotel at eleven."

"See you then."

Seventeen hours later they were sitting with light beers in a quiet corner of the Imperial on Bennet Street trying to make the small-talk thing work face to face. They did well enough for six minutes before Harry put them both out of their misery.

"You got the file okay. Anything?"

Dan set down his glass. "A question first. You kept something back on the phone yesterday. You said the Rattigan woman was bitten to death."

"That's what happened," Harry said. He looked tanned, less florid than Dan remembered; in his casual clothes he could have been another tourist visiting the local wineries.

"Her teeth were taken as well, weren't they?"

Harry barely hesitated. "How'd you know?"

Dan lifted a manila folder from the seat beside him. "The results of Net searches. Know what a toother is, Harry?"

"Tell me."

"It was a vocation, to call it that, associated with body-snatching back in the eighteenth, nineteenth centuries. Back when resurrectionists—lovely name— dug up bodies to sell to medical academies for their anatomy classes. There were people who did the same to get the teeth. Sold them to dentists to make false teeth."

"Dug up corpses?"

"Sometimes. Or did deals with resurrection men already in the trade. Mostly they'd roam battlefields and take teeth from dead soldiers."

"You're kidding."

"Not when you think about it. It was much better than getting teeth from the gibbet or the grave. Ivory and whalebone were either too expensive or decayed. No enamel coating. Teeth made from porcelain sounded wrong or were too brittle. Corpse teeth were better, soldiers' teeth usually best of all, injuries permitting. Sets of authentic Waterloo Teeth fetch quite a bit these days."

"What, dentures made from soldiers who died at Waterloo?"

Dan nodded. "Fifty thousand in a single day. Mostly young men. Supply caught up with demand with battles like that. But that's the thing. There weren't many battles on that scale. Demand outstripped supply."

"You already knew this stuff?"

"Some of it. You know what I'm like. And that's quite a file you sent. I stayed up late."

Harry had his notebook on the table in front of him. He opened it and began making notes. "Go on."

"Back then there just weren't enough corpses of executed criminals or unknown homeless to satisfy the demand. Not enough from the right age or gender, even when you had poorer people selling their own teeth. Some resurrectionists began killing people."

"And these toothers did too."

"There's little conclusive evidence that I'm aware of. But that's the point, Harry. You do a job like this, you try to make sure there isn't."

"But body-snatchers can't be doing this."

"It presents that way is all I'm saying—a similar MO. If the cemetery desecrations and the Rattigan death *are* related, as the fragments suggest, we need to allow a context for it."

Harry wrote something and looked up. "So this joker could be proceeding like a modern-day toother."

Dan shrugged. "Just putting it forward, Harry. He took the Rattigan woman's teeth. Used others to kill her. So, a psychopath possibly. A sociopath definitely, probably highly organized. A latter-day resurrectionist? Not in the sense we know it. But we only have the teeth being taken and the single recent murder. I assume there are no similar cases in the CID database?"

Harry shook his head. "The usual run of biting during domestics and sexual assault. Random mostly. Nothing like this."

"Then he may be escalating; either a loner doing his own thing or someone acquainted with the old resurrectionist methodology."

Harry started writing again. "Do you have more on that?"

"Going back a hundred, two hundred years, he'd see a likely subject, get them alone and have an accomplice grab them while he slapped a pitch-plaster over their mouth and nose—"

Harry looked up. "A what?"

"A sticky mass of plaster mixed with pitch. Mostly used during sexual assault, but what some resurrectionists used too. Silenced your victim and incapacitated them. Suffocated them if that was the intention. All over in minutes."

Harry was suitably horrified. "They just held them till they expired?"

"Or did a traditional 'burking'—covered the mouth and nose with their hand till the victim asphyxiated."

"This actually happened?"

"It did. The biting takes it in a completely different direction, of course. Was the Rattigan woman drugged or bound?"

"Not that we can tell."

"That tends to suggest an accomplice. Someone to help restrain her. Do Sheehan's people have anything?"

"Just the fetish, ritual angle, Dan. A loner after trophies. It's early days. But you're taking it further, saying there could be an accomplice, someone getting the teeth for someone else—who then makes dentures and uses them to kill."

Dan glanced around to make sure that they weren't being overheard. They still had the bar virtually to themselves. "Just another possibility, Harry. Much less likely. And no conventional client. There's no economic reason for it now. It presents like that is what I'm saying."

"Okay, so either a loner or a gopher for someone who originally wanted the teeth for fetishistic reasons but is escalating. He now kills people and does the extractions himself. Focusing on females?"

"Seems that way. But until we know more, I'm still tempted to say a loner with a special mission."

Harry drained his glass and set it down on the table. "So why do a *new* grave? Why show his hand like this? Was he interrupted before he could finish? Did he *want* people to know?"

"He's fixated. He may have seen the Reid woman alive and wanted that particular set of teeth. Like in the Poe story."

Harry frowned. "What Poe story?"

"'Berenice.' A brother obsessed with his sister's teeth extracts them while she's in a cataleptic coma."

"Where do you get this stuff, Dan?"

"They're called books, Harry. But this guy is doing it for himself. And I definitely believe it's a he. He could be using the more traditional techniques."

"Drugs would be easier."

"They would. But he wants them fully conscious. So we're back to the ritual aspect you mentioned."

"That emblematic thing," Harry said.

"The what?"

"Two—three years back. That conversation we had at Rollo's. You said that people try to be more. Have emblematic lives."

Dan never ceased to be amazed by what Harry remembered from their conversations. "Emblematic? I said that?"

"Four beers. You said that. Make themselves meaningful to themselves, you said. Do symbolic things."

"Okay, well this is his thing, Harry. We can't be sure if he's following aspects of the old toother/resurrectionist MO but Sheehan's right. Given the special dentures he's made for himself, doing this has some powerful fetishistic or symbolic meaning for him. And he may have done this a lot: gone somewhere, seen a lovely set of teeth on someone, arranged to get them alone, then suffocated or bitten them and taken their teeth."

"That's horrible. You actually think he may have already done that and hidden the bodies?"

"Because of the desecrations, the older teeth being used, that's how I'm seeing it, and it may get worse." Dan thought of Peter Rait's voices. *They're coming over time.*

"How could it—ah! He may start removing the teeth while the victims are alive. And conscious?"

Dan deliberately left a silence, waiting for Harry to say it.

It took a five-count. "You think it's already got to that! But the coroner's report for the Rattigan woman showed the extractions were post-mortem."

"Harry, I think that may have been her one bit of good fortune. She died just as he was starting."

Harry shook his head. "Then we can definitely expect more."

"I'd say so. And it depends."

"On what, Dan? On what?"

"On whether it's local. Someone developing his ritual. Or if it's something international that's been relocated here."

"International?"

"Ask Sheehan to check with Interpol or whoever you guys work with now. Find case similarities. Forced dental extractions. Post- and *ante*-mortem."

"Can you come down to Sydney?"

"Phone me Monday and I'll let you know. I need to speak with someone first. You could stay around. Visit some wineries, come over for dinner tonight. Annie would love to see you."

They both knew it wouldn't go that way. Not this time. Not yet. "Sorry, Dan. I need to get going with this. Take a rain-check?"

"Roger that," Dan said.

At 2 p.m. that afternoon, Dan met with Peter Rait and Phillip Crow at a picnic table sheltered by the largest Moreton Bay Fig in the hospital grounds. Peter, thin, black-haired, pale-skinned, on any ordinary day looked a decade younger than his forty-two years, but his recent nightmares had given him an intense, peaked quality that Dan found unsettling. He sat with a manila folder in front of him.

To his left on the same bench was Phil, four years older, fair-headed, stocky, with the sort of weathered but pleasant face that Carla liked to call "old-school Australian." He looked up and smiled as Dan arrived. "Just like old times, Doctor Dan."

"It is, Phil," Dan said as he sat across from them. He had to work not to smile. Peter and Phil were his "psychosleuths," their talent pretty well dormant these last three years. Officially, both men had been rehabilitated back into society; both had elected to stay, their choice, taking accommodation and rations in return for doing odd jobs. And called it Blackwater Psychiatric Hospital, of course.

Given Peter's present state, Dan couldn't enjoy the reunion as much as he would have liked. He went straight to the heart of it.

"Peter, tell me about the voices."

Peter took two typed pages from the folder in front of him. "Here are the transcripts," he said, sounding every bit as tired as he looked.

Dan was surprised by the odd choice of words. "Transcripts? How did you manage that?"

"They keep playing over. Two different conversations now. Two different victims."

"But how—?"

"I just can, Doctor Dan, okay? It's pretty distressing. You can't know how awful it is."

Dan saw that Peter wasn't just tired; he was exhausted. "You can't stop it?"

"Giving you these might do it. Getting them out."

"Nothing else?"

"Not yet. Please, just read them."

Dan looked at the first page.

TRANSCRIPT I

[miscellaneous sounds]

[male voice / mature, controlled]

"As they say, there is the good news and the bad news."

[terrified female voice, quite young]

"What do you mean?"

"You have a choice here. The good news is that you'll wake up. All your teeth will be gone, but we'll have a relatively easy time with the extractions and you *will* wake up. You'll be alive. The alternative—you make my job difficult and you won't wake up. That's the deal."

"Why are you doing this?"

"What's it to be?"

"Why?"

"It's necessary. What's it to be?"

"There has to be a reason!"

"I'll count to three.

"Just tell me why! Please!"

"One."

"For God's sake! Why are you doing this? Why?"

"Two. Choose or I will."

"You can't expect me—"

"Three. Too late."

"No! No! I want to wake up! Please! I want to wake up!"

"All right. Just this once."

"One question."

"Go ahead."

"You could drug me and do it. Do whatever you want. Why do I even have to choose?"

"Now that's the thing. And, really, you already know why. I need you conscious for it. I may drug you at the end. Oh, dear, look. You're pissing yourself."

[sobbing]

"Why? Why? Why?"

"You're not listening. It's my thing. I need to see your eyes while I'm doing it."

"Another question."

"There always is. What is it?"

"What will you do with—with *them*? Afterwards?"

"Make a nice set of dentures. Maybe I could sell them back to you. That would be a rather nice irony, wouldn't it? Irony is quite our thing."

"What about me? Afterwards?"

"You'll wake up. Hate us forever. Go on with the rest of your life."

"But I'll wake up? I *will* wake up?"

"Make it easy for us now and, yes. You have my word."

"You're saying 'us' and 'our'."

"Oh dear. So I am."

"What's that over there?"

"I think that's enough questions."

"What *is* that?"

[sundry sounds]

[victim screaming]

[audio ends]

Dan looked up. "Peter—"

"The next one, Doctor Dan. Read the next one, please. Same male voice. Different female victim."

Dan turned to it at once.

TRANSCRIPT 2

[miscellaneous sounds]

"You're crazy!"

"I hope not, for your sake. Major dental work needs a degree of control."

"But why? Why me?"

"The usual reason. Chance. Purest hazard. You were on hand."

"Then pick someone else!"

"From someone else's viewpoint I did. But enough talk. We have a lot to do."

"Listen. Listen to me. My name is Pamela Deering. I'm a mother. I have two little girls. Emma and Grace. Aged 7 and 5. My husband's name—"

[muffled sounds]

"Ssh now, Pamela. No more bonding. We have a lot to do."

"What? What do we have to do?"

"Let's just say that your girls and hubby will have to call you Gummy instead of Mummy." [pause] "That's our little joke, Pamela."

[sobbing]

"Please. Please don't do this."

"We have to, Mu—er—Gummy. It's our thing. It won't take long."

"You're saying 'we,' 'us.' You're not alone. There's someone else."

"Tsk. How rude of me. You want to meet my associate. Over here. Try to turn your head a little more."

[sundry sounds]

"But that's not—"
[victim screaming]
[audio ends]

Dan lowered the pages. "There are two of them. He's not a loner."

"Seems that way," Peter said.

"Do you get accents at all?"

"Educated male. Educated enough. Enunciates carefully so it's hard to know. The first woman sounds English. The Deering woman sounds Australian."

"But not recent. Over time, you said."

Peter nodded. "Sixties, seventies." He gestured to include Phil, as if he were equally part of this, both of them hearing the voices. "You have to protect us, Doctor Dan."

"I always do. That comes first."

"How will you?"

"Our old method. You aren't mentioned. Any locations you give, I'll have Harry say a phonecall came in, anonymous. Someone overheard a disturbance, cries, screaming. Wouldn't give their name."

"They'll buy it?"

"Why not? It happens more and more these days. Remember, we *all* need to stay out of this."

Phil leant forward. "What happens now?"

"We have a name," Dan said. "Pamela Deering. Harry can check that out. Meanwhile, Peter—"

"I'll keep dreaming."

"You don't have to. We can give you a sedative."

"No," Peter said. "I'm doing it for them."

Dan saw the haunted look in the tired dark eyes. "We need this, Peter."

"I know."

Thirty-two cases were listed in the international database, Harry told Dan on the phone that Monday morning, different countries, different cities, different decades, though it was the sort of statistic that convinced them both that many others existed.

"They say two thousand people a year in New Guinea are killed by coconuts falling on their heads," Harry said. "How do you get a statistic like that? It can only ever be the ones you *hear* about. It's like that here. These are just the ones that came to the attention of different national authorities and have anything approximating a similar MO."

"What about the time frame, Harry?"

"Dan, we've got cases going back to the thirties and forties, even earlier. Prague. Krakow. Trieste. Bangkok, for heaven's sake! They can't be the same person. It can't be a generational thing. It doesn't work like that."

"I'd normally agree," Dan said. "But you say the MOs are similar for these thirty-two?"

"Victims bitten to death, post- or ante-mortem; the various odontologists' findings give both. Their own teeth removed before, during or after; again there's a range. Older fragments in the wounds in some instances, say, nineteen, twenty per cent."

"Harry—"

"You're not going to say a secret society. An international brotherhood of toothers."

Dan gave a grim smile. "No, but look how it presents. It's as if a very old, well-traveled sociopath has been able to find agents across a lifetime and still has at least one accomplice now, doing his dirty work. The Reid disinterment was done manually, not using a backhoe. That took a lot of effort."

"You believe this? Sheehan may not buy it."

"At this point I'm just trying to understand it, Harry. Rookwood and Darlinghurst suggest he may be local, at least for now."

"Can you come down to Sydney?"

"On Thursday. I'll be bringing Peter Rait."

Harry knew enough about Peter's gifts not to question it. "He has something?"

"For your eyes only."

"What, Dan?"

"Check if you have a missing person, a possible victim named Pamela Deering." He spelled out the name. "It could be from the sixties or seventies."

"How on earth did—?"

"Harry, you know how this has to be done. Yes or no?"

"Yes. Yes. Pamela Deering. Bring Peter with you. You got somewhere to stay?"

"I've arranged for unofficial digs at the old Gladesville Hospital on Victoria Road. There's a coffee shop on the grounds called Cornucopia. Meet us there around midday Thursday, okay?"

"Cornucopia. Got it."

"And bring a map of Rookwood Cemetery will you? The adjacent streets."

"You think he lives in the area?"

"Peter needs it."

"Done."

At a convenience store roadstop in Branxton on their drive down that Thursday morning, Peter presented Dan with a third transcript.

"You need to factor this in," was all Peter said as he handed it over. He looked more drawn than ever, as if he had barely slept the night before.

"Last night?"

"Last two nights."

"You kept it to yourself."

Peter ran a hand through his dark hair. "Look, I have to be sure, okay? I have to know that it's not—just coming from me. That I can trust it."

"And you do?"

"I'm satisfied now, Doctor Dan. I couldn't make this up."

Dan leant against the car door and read the carefully typed words.

TRANSCRIPT 3

[miscellaneous sounds]

"You're the one who took the Kellar woman. Those poor women in Zurich. You're going to take out all my teeth!"

[sounds]

"Take them out? Oh no. Not this time. Toother was very specific."

[sounds, like things being shaken in a metal box]

"Toother?"

"Yes. Your name please?"

"What difference does it make?"

"But isn't that what the experts advise? Always try to use names? Don't let them dehumanize you. My name is Paul."

"Your real name? Not Toother?"

"It'll do for today."

"Then I'll be Janice. For today. Who is Toother?"

"Why, your host, Janice-for-today. The one who taught me all I know.

Mostly he takes, but sometimes he gives."

"Gives?"

"Sometimes. I have my little hammer and my little punch, see? And you have such a full, generous mouth. Today we are going to put teeth back in. Lots and lots, see?"

[more rattling sounds]

"Big teeth. Men's teeth. We're going to call you Smiler."

[more rattling sounds]

[victim sobbing]

[victim screaming]

Dan left Peter to drowse for much of the journey south, but as they were on the bridge crossing the Hawkesbury River, he glanced aside and saw the dark eyes watching him.

"You okay?" he asked.

"Sorry for losing it back there," Peter said, as if resuming a conversation from moments before. "Things are escalating for me too. With this latest— exchange—I get something about his trophies."

Dan wished he weren't driving right then. He pulled into the low-speed lane. "You see them?"

"Just lots of—grimaces. You know, teeth without lips. It's the most terrifying thing. Bared teeth. No skin covering. Like eyes without lids. Horrible."

"Are they on shelves, in drawers, boxes, what?"

"Displayed. Arranged somehow, secretly. Nothing like smiles or grins. I just see them as bared teeth, Doctor Dan. In a private space. Sorry. It isn't much."

"Try, Peter. Whatever you get. These voices—"

"It's more than just voices. It's reciprocal now."

"Reciprocal? What does that mean?"

"It isn't just going one way. He knows I've been listening. Accessing his files. He was very angry at first, but now he's enjoying it. He's fighting back."

"How, Peter? How does he fight back?"

"Sending things, thoughts, images. They're not mine. It's more than delusions, Doctor Dan, I'm sure of it. More than my usual hypersensitivity. I just had to be sure."

"Understood. Go on."

"It's Rookwood. All those graves. I keep seeing the bodies, vulnerable, help-less, keep seeing the teeth. They're mostly all teeth, lots of dentures too. But there's such anguish. Such rage."

"Female burials?"

"Female *and* male. They're all murmuring, chattering. Some desperately wanting to be picked, calling 'Pick me! Pick me!' Others hiding. Desperately hiding. As if alive. They're not, but it's like they are for him."

"Is there a voice talking to you now?"

"*Like* a voice, Doctor Dan. *Not* a voice, but like one. I have certainties, just know things. He wants it like that."

"He's found someone he can share with. He hears the bodies calling to him you say?"

"How he sees them. Calling, begging. 'Pick me! Pick me!' Or hiding, resist-ing. Furious. Either way he sees it as liberation, sees them as all waiting to be chosen. The living victims too."

"He's *saving* them?"

"Liberating them is his word, yes. Living or dead, it doesn't matter. It just means a different method of retrieval."

"Retrieval!" Dan gave a laugh, completely without humor. "But he's in the area?"

Peter shrugged. "It's a huge cemetery, Doctor Dan. It's not called the Sleeping City for nothing. He's committed so many desecrations there. You can't begin to know. Secretly. Passionately. This is his place for now."

"Peter, I trust you completely. Just let me know what you get. Anything."

It was strange to walk the grounds of the decommissioned, largely deserted mental hospital at Gladesville later that morning. The former wards and outbuildings had been turned into offices for various governmental health services, so by day it was like a stately, manicured, museum estate. There were still vehicles in the carparks, people walking the paths, roadways and lawns, giving the place a semblance of its former life.

Dan walked those daylight roads now, glad that he wasn't doing it at night. After dark the offices and carparks were deserted, but had a strange new half-life, quarter-life, life-in-death. Instead of being left to stand as part of a vast col of blackness overlooking the Parramatta River, the old sandstone buildings and empty roads were lit, as if beckoning, urging, waiting for those willing to surrender bits of their sanity to make the place live again.

When Dan reached Cornucopia, he found Harry waiting at a table outside the café door.

"I've driven past this place a thousand times," Harry said, "and never knew how big it was. Where's Peter?"

"He sends his apologies. Said he wants to keep his mind off this for now."

"Doesn't want me asking questions," Harry said. "I can understand that."

"Harry—"

"Dan, I know how it can be for him. How it *was*. Just say hi for me."

They went in and placed their orders, then sat watching the clear autumn sky above the sandstone walls. Harry took out his notebook.

"The Deering woman went missing from a holiday house at Cottesloe Beach in 1967."

"That's Western Australia, isn't it?"

"Right. There was blood, definite signs of a struggle, but no body. And before you ask, there were no teeth fragments."

"You've been thorough."

"Now that there's international scrutiny, we have different resources available."

"What did you tell Sheehan?"

"That it came up in a missing persons keyword sweep. In the last three decades alone, there are thirty-six names of missing persons nationally where blood mixed with saliva was found at locations where each of them was last seen."

"Oral blood?"

"Right. So tell me what Peter has found."

Dan passed him the transcript folder. "Harry, you might want to finish eating first."

Dan found it hard to sleep that night. They were in separate rooms in an otherwise empty, former staff residence at the southern end of the hospital grounds, a converted single-storey brick house. It was a cool, late autumn night, pleasant for sleeping, but with all that had happened, Dan felt restless, too keenly aware of the empty roads outside and the lit, abandoned buildings, so normal, yet—the only word for it—so abnormal, waiting in the night.

The lights are on but nobody's home.

The old euphemism for madness kept coming back to him. No doubt there were security personnel doing the rounds, one, possibly more, but, just the same, there was the distinct sense that Peter and he were the only living souls in the place.

Dan kept thinking of what Peter had told him that morning, of the bodies as repositories for teeth, grimaces, smiles, lying there waiting, hiding, some calling, chattering in darkness, wanting any kind of life, others dreading such attention.

It was absurd, foolish, but Rookwood Necropolis was barely ten kilometers away, 285 hectares of one of the largest dedicated cemeteries in the world, site of nearly a million interments.

In his half-drowsing state, Dan kept thinking, too, of the old 1963 movie, *Jason and the Argonauts,* of King Aeëtes collecting and sowing the teeth from the skull of the slain Hydra, raising up an army of skeletons to combat Jason and his crew. Dan imagined human teeth being first plucked and then sown in Rookwood's older, less tended fields. If the Hydra's teeth raised up *human* skeletons, what sort of creature would human teeth raise up?

He must have fallen asleep at last, for the next thing he knew Peter was rousing him.

"Doctor Dan?" Peter said, switching on Dan's bedside light.

"Peter? What is it?"

Peter was fully dressed, his hair and eyes wild. "He's got someone! Right now. He has someone!"

Dan grabbed his watch, saw that it was 12:16 a.m. "He told you this?"

"No. But I saw anyway. He's furious that I saw."

Dan climbed out of bed, began dressing. "The reciprocal thing?"

"It backfired, yes. Showed me more than he wanted. He's so angry, but he's enjoying it too! He's still enjoying it."

"The drama. The added excitement."

"Yes. We have to hurry!"

Dan reached for his mobile. "Where, Peter? I need to call Harry."

"Good. Yes. An old factory site in Somersby Road. A few streets back from the cemetery. But I need to be there. I have to be closer, Doctor Dan. Her life depends on it."

"Those women in the transcripts—?"

"Never woke up. None of them."

"Understood."

Harry answered his mobile before Dan's call went to voicemail. He sounded leaden from sleep until Dan explained what they had. "You'll be there before I will, Dan, but I'll have two units there. Four officers. Best I can do for now. Where are you?"

"Still at the hospital. Heading out to the car. We'll need an ambulance too, Harry. The Somersby Road corner closest to the cemetery. Tell them to wait for us. No sirens."

"Right. You're sure about this, Dan?"

"Peter is."

"I'm on my way!"

"Harry, Peter stays out of it. How do we cover ourselves?"

"Anonymous tip. A neighbour heard screaming. I'll have a word with whoever turns up. Go!"

Two patrol cars and an ambulance were waiting at the corner of Somersby Road, lights off, ready. There was no sign of Harry's car yet.

"You Dr. Truswell?" an officer asked, appearing at Dan's driver-side window when he pulled up.

"Yes. Look—"

"Harry explained. I'm Senior Constable Banners. Warwick Banners. Just tell us where to go."

"It's there!" Peter said, pointing. "That building there!"

"Right. Follow us in but stay well back, hear?"

"We hear you," Dan said, and turned to Peter. "You have to stay in the car, okay?"

"I know," Peter said. "And keep the doors locked."

Dan joined the police officers and paramedics waiting at the kerb. It took them seconds to reach the building two doors down, a large brick factory-front with closed and locked roller-doors and smaller street door. The premises looked so quiet and innocent in the night, and not for the first time Dan wondered if Peter could be mistaken.

There was a single crash as the street door was forced. In moments they were in off the street, standing in utter quiet, in darkness lit by the beams of five torches.

Again it was all so ordinary, so commonplace. But Dan knew only too well how such places could be terrifying in their simplicity. He had seen the

Piggyback Killer's rooms in Newtown, such a mundane blend of walls, hallways and furniture until you opened that one door, found the two coffins. He had seen Corinne Kester's balcony view and the shed with its treacherous windows, had seen Peter Rait's own room come alive in a wholly unexpected way right there at Blackwater. Such simple, terrifying places.

This, too, was such an ordinary, extraordinary space. Who knew what it had been originally: a warehouse, a meat packing plant, some other kind of factory, but taking up the entire ground floor, large and low-ceilinged, with painted out windows and a large, windowless inner section that took up most of the back half of the premises. Given the absence of screams being reported in the neighborhood, it was very likely double brick or sound-proofed in some other way.

Dan followed the police and paramedics as they pushed through the double doors into that inner precinct. At first, it seemed totally dark. Then Dan saw that intervening pillars concealed an area off to the left lit by a dim yellow bulb. The police deployed immediately, guns ready, and crossed to it. There was no one there, just signs of where the occupant had been: a table and chair, a cupboard, a modest camp-bed with tangled bed-clothes, a hot-plate and bar fridge to one side where it all stretched off into darkness again.

Deliberate darkness. Darkness as controlled theatrical flourish, prelude to shocking revelations, precisely calculated anguish and despair.

The police led the way around more pillars. The stark white light of their torches soon found the old dentistry chair near the back wall, securely bolted to the floor, revealed the victim strapped down, alive but barely conscious, gurgling through a ruined mouth filled with her own blood.

The paramedics rushed to her aid, began working by torchlight as best they could.

Dan made himself look away, forced himself to look at what else there was in the shifting torchlight that *wasn't* this poor woman, gurgling, groaning and sobbing. He noted the straps for securing the chair's occupant, the elaborate padded clamp for holding the head, the metal tables and dental tools, other tools that had no place in dental work, the stains on the floor, dark and rusty-looking. The air smelled of disinfectant, urine and blood and something else, something sour.

An officer finally located a light switch. A single spot came on overhead, illuminating the chair and the woman, showing her ruined face and more: an array of mirrors on adjustable stands, video and audio equipment, shelves with old-style video and audio tapes, newer-style DVDs.

Souvenirs. An archive.

Dan scanned the row of audio tapes; the first were dated from the 60s.

Peter Rait's voices.

But all so mundane in a worrying sense. Though terrible to say, these were the workaday trappings of sociopaths and psychopaths the world over, how they, too, made mundane lives for themselves out of their horrific acts.

But there was a large, heavy door beyond the woman in the chair, like a rusted walk-in freezer door with a sturdy latch. Dan focused his attention on it as soon as the torch beams revealed the pitted metal surface. An exit? A hideaway? Another inner sanctum in this hellish place?

An officer approached the door, weapon ready, and pulled it back.

It was a storeroom, a small square room empty but for a large chalk-white post nearly two meters tall. The post was as round as three dinner plates, set in concrete or free-standing, it was hard to tell, but standing like a bollard, one of those removable traffic posts used to stop illegal parking, though larger, much larger, and set all over with encrustations.

Not just any encrustations, Dan knew. Sets of teeth in false mouths, fitted at different heights, randomly but carefully, lovingly, set into the white plaster, fiber-glass, concrete, whatever it was. Dentures made from real teeth, corpse teeth, teeth taken post- and ante-mortem, some of them, all of them spring-loaded and deadly!

A trophy post.

This was where Toother kept his terrible collection, displayed it for his pleasure—and, yes, for the calculated and utter terror of others.

A door slammed somewhere in the building.

The police reacted at once. The officer holding the storeroom door let it go. It was on a counterweight and closed with a resounding boom. Another shouted orders. One hurried back to secure the main entrance. The rest rushed to search the outer premises, to find other exits and locate their quarry. Footsteps echoed in the empty space.

It all happened so quickly. Dan stood listening, hoping, trusting that Peter was still out in the car, safe.

Movement close by caught his attention, brought him back. The paramedics had the woman on their gurney at last. The awful gurgling had stopped and they were now wheeling her away.

For a terrible moment, Dan was left alone with the chair under its single spot, with the tables and instruments, the archive shelves and heavy metal door, now mercifully closed.

Then there were cries off in the darkness, sounds of running, more shouting. Two gunshots echoed in the night.

Then, in seconds, minutes, however long it was, Harry was there, two officers with him.

"We got him, Dan."

"Harry. What? What's that?"

"We got him. Toother. He's dead."

"Dead?" Peter was there too, appearing out of the darkness. "You did? You really got him?"

"We did, Peter," Harry said. "He was running out when we arrived. Officer Burns and me. He was armed and wouldn't stop. Colin here had to shoot."

Dan placed a hand on Peter's arm. "No more voices?"

"No," Peter said. "No voices at all now."

"We got him, Peter," Harry said.

But Peter frowned, gave an odd, puzzled look as if hearing something, then crossed to the heavy door and pulled it back. "Harry, I don't think we did. Not this time. Not yet."

The storeroom was empty, of course.

KIRSTYN MCDERMOTT has been working in the darker alleyways of speculative fiction for much of her career. Her two novels, *Madigan Mine* and *Perfections*, each won an Aurealis Award and her most recent book is *Caution: Contains Small Parts*, a collection of short fiction published by Twelfth Planet Press. She produced and co-hosted a literary discussion podcast, The Writer and the Critic, for several years and now lives in Ballarat, Australia, with fellow writer Jason Nahrung and their two cats. Kirstyn is currently completing a creative writing PhD at Federation University with a research focus on re-visioned fairy tales. "Painlessness" won the Aurealis Award and the Ditmar Award. WWW. KIRSTYNMCDERMOTT.COM

Painlessness
Kirstyn McDermott

CHRIST, NOT AGAIN. Hard enough to sleep with the afternoon sun sleazing through the venetian blinds, the dull ache in each and every joint of her sweatsick body, and Faith groans as she rolls over to grab the bottle of water beside her bed. Blister pack of tablets beside that, antibiotics of some kind, and RelaxaTabs as well because the doctor refused to prescribe her any sort of decent sleeping pill; she takes two of each.

Natural rest, my arse.

Hard enough to sleep with the near constant vertigo and the quilt pulled right up to her chin, sweating and itching beneath it because otherwise she'll only wake up with chattering teeth and her fingernails a disturbing shade of blue.

Hard enough without *this*: the sobs and muffled shouts pressing through the shoddy townhouse wall, the nameless thumps and yesterday even the sound of smashing glass.

Faith pulls the pillow over her head but it's too hot, too close; she can't breathe properly even when she's *not* trying to smother herself. Stretches her legs instead, trying to kick the cramps from her knees, and when the shouting from next door starts up again she raises a fist for the umpteenth time to pound against the wall.

And, for the umpteenth time, stops herself at the very last second.

It might only make things worse.

No idea who her neighbours are, after all. *A single woman*, the agent's assurance during inspection, *quiet and tidy, you'll have no trouble there*—and with that now so obviously a lie, who the hell knows *what* she's moved in next door to on a fucking twelve-month lease?

The shouting ceases, gives way to sobbing. Soft, feminine cries that Faith almost can't hear and somehow that only makes it worse. So: two more

RelaxaTabs before curling tight beneath the blanket with her chin tucked close to her chest and no matter that it's harder to breathe through her congestion like that.

Harder still to sleep with what she can hear—and imagine—beyond that wall.

Between the opening screech of her neighbour's security door and the brash metallic clatter as it slams shut again, Faith shrugs into her dressing gown. Cinches the faded terrycloth belt around her waist and hop-foots it down the hall wearing just the single Ugg boot slipper because god only knows where the other one's hiding and there sure isn't any time to mount a search party. White-trash Cinderella half-tripping out her own front door and, "Hey," she calls to the woman already turning away from the letterboxes. "Hey, wait up."

Whatever she might have expected, it isn't this. Tall, much taller than Faith herself but certainly not much older, early thirties at most and even that would be pushing it. A sundress of faded sky-blue cloth, the sort of slim-hipped androgyny Faith might once have killed to possess, and something so…solid in the way she pauses, tiger-in-the-grass motionless with her face half-turned away and hidden beneath a wave of blood-bright hair.

"Can I help you?" the woman asks, blade-sharp voice with an accent too vague to place.

Faith blinks in the morning glare, one hand raised to shield her eyes. "Sorry, just wanted a word. About the…um, the…look, I'm feeling pretty crap right now and I really need to get some sleep, so…"

"I'm making too much noise."

"Well, yeah. I mean, normally—"

"Normally you wouldn't be here." The woman looks up then, looks right at her with dark eyes surrounded by even darker flesh, fist-sized bruises and a scabby-swollen cut on her lower lip, and Faith swallows, tries to find some words, any words, but the woman waves them away. "My apologies. I assumed you worked during the day. I didn't realise you were ill."

Forget about it, Faith wants to tells her, wants to ask if there is anything *she* needs like maybe a hospital or several shots of morphine maybe, but all at once it's so damn hot out here and the sunlight really is too bright, searing-white-bright like the unmarred skin on the woman's face, what little there is of it, and, *how rude, when she doesn't even know me from Adam.*

So: "I'm Faith." Right hand stuck out and trembling, and the woman regards it like a dead thing for a moment, dead or near enough. Looks at her that way too with oil-slick eyes impossibly black and shot with colours like Faith has never seen before, colours she can't even name. "Mara," the woman says.

Mara, a bassline thrumming through the sparks that jump and scratch behind her eyelids and Faith holds onto it, clutches it tighter than she clutches the frost-cold hand now closed around her own. *Do you hear that*, she says or maybe she doesn't after all.

The birds, do you hear their wings?

If ice could boil, and still stay frozen, this is how it might burn:

The seething shiver of skin on skin, on cloth, on the bare bathroom floor as she lies spread-eagled in an effort to touch absolutely nothing, or as much of it as she can. The water that ebbs around her chattering teeth, slips into her mouth despite the cool strong hands that hold up her head, long fingers curved firm around her chin when all she wants to do is slip beneath the surface and sink, sink, sink. The light that swells her skull, her bones, her guts; seeking to split her wide and spill itself into the world.

blood-fever

Barely a whisper from no one she cares to know.

Here, drink this.
Can't, I'll throw up.
You won't. Drink it.

The taste too strange, ginger and chamomile and something else that just doesn't belong, and—*oh god, oh christ*— the red plastic bucket still smelling of vomit from last time and this only makes her puke more, spasms so violent it hurts, until finally she rolls back onto the couch with a groan.

Told you I'd throw up.

The woman's smile so subtle it's almost not there at all.

Yes, and don't you feel much better for it?

Three days, Mara tells her, perched stray cat cautious on the edge of the bed. Three days since that morning when she'd passed out by the mailbox, and Faith feels nauseous all over again. Three days, which would make today what then, Saturday?

"Sunday," Mara says. "Your work called on Friday. I told them it was highly doubtful you'd be in next week but you would let them know once you were conscious again. Frankly, they didn't sound too concerned."

Unsurprising. Newbie telemarketers being more dispensable than used Kleenex, especially newbie telemarketers who were barely scratching at the lowest rung of their daily quota levels; if EzyEzcape bothered to even keep her shifts alive it would be no minor miracle. Never mind that, after almost a week without pay, if she manages to scrape together next month's rent in time, it will be the loaves and fucking fishes all over again.

"Shit." Faith tries to sit up, fails. There isn't a part of her that doesn't ache.

"I don't think you're ready for vertical," Mara observes.

"I have to go back to work tomorrow. I can't afford to be sick anymore."

Mara shrugs, do-what-you-have-to-do sort of shrug, and rises to her feet in a motion that is at once elegant and utterly final. Jaundice-faint shadow of a bruise on her cheekbone as she tucks her hair behind her ear, and only now does Faith remember.

"Hey, you said three days? That's how long I was out of it?" Frowning as the other woman nods because that can't be right, can it? Faith has had coffee table bumps take longer to fade than that and, sorry, she insists, but that *can't* that be right.

Not three days, not *only* three.

"Why would I lie?" Mara seems amused, as though this is all some elaborate game, a prank or maybe some sick-day surprise. Like maybe everyone Faith knows is huddled out in the loungeroom with party hats and sparklers and a huge hand-painted banner strung across the window: *welcome back to the world.*

"But your face…"

Words failing as Mara lifts a hand to her own cheek, fingers falling across model-smooth lips that look as though they've never even been chapped let alone left split and bleeding. "I heal fast. It has been three days." Said as though that were an eternity in itself, and her eyes are equally desolate.

Leave it alone, girl; you have no business with it.

Faith swallows, throat too dry for more than a muttered apology, and the smile Mara returns is only tooth-deep. "You seem *compos mentis* now. I'll be home all day if you need something." The square set of her jaw an unspoken challenge—*but you won't need anything*—holding Faith's gaze for a full three seconds before walking away, three long paces to the bedroom door.

Only three days.

"Wait." The woman pauses but doesn't turn round, only angles her head a little and Faith takes this acknowledgement as all she's going to get. "Thanks, okay? Thanks for taking care of me."

"There's multivitamin juice in the fridge," Mara says. "You're dehydrated and you're probably ravenous, but I wouldn't recommend solid food until tomorrow. Otherwise, you know."

A curt nod toward the red bucket in the corner, then the bedroom door closes and Mara is gone.

Friday night, and Faith sits at the kitchen table with a bottle of red wine, unopened. The same kind she left on Mara's front step a few days ago with a thank-you note scribbled in haste after her knocks went unheeded, the kind she'd once again planned to present in person, with more thanks, tonight. She'd hoped her neighbour would invite her in, that they'd crack open the bottle and drown whatever collective sorrows they managed to scrape together— which had to be quite a few—and maybe lay the foundations of something that might one day be called a friendship.

New city, new job, and Faith is lonely. Not that she would ever admit as much with a clear head, a clean bloodstream; hence the wine.

That had been the plan, anyway.

But mice and men and smothered, broken blondes, Mara isn't alone.

Faith can't hear the sounds all the way out here in the kitchen. Those same whimpers and thumps she remembers from when she was ill, sounds she'd later decided—hoped?—had been amplified by delirium, fever-swollen and exaggerated beyond all measure of reality. Until now. She picks up the cordless phone for the second time that night, index finger hovering above the 0 on the keypad.

What if Mara hates her for calling the police?

What if the boyfriend? lover? (rapist?) takes it out on Mara herself?

What if the police don't arrive in time, or even at all?

Damn it. She places the undialled phone on the table, creeps instead down the hall to the bedroom and listens by the door. Nothing, no sound at all from beyond the wall and is that a good thing or does it mean that something much worse is happening next door? Or has happened?

Bitch!

The jagged masculine snarl so loud it might be in the next room and Faith near jumps out of her skin, hands quickly at her mouth to stop the cry that rises in her throat.

But it's what comes after that finally kicks her indecisive arse into gear. The muffled sobs for him to stop, to *please just stop*, echoing in her head as she races back through the townhouse. Grabbing the wine bottle on her way—weapon? appeasement? excuse?—and then straight outside, bare feet smarting on the gravel path that joins her place with Mara's, running so fast that by the time she's pounding on the woman's front door, Faith is breathless.

A small eternity until, just as she thinks no one is ever going to answer and she's going to need that phone after all, there's a flicker of shadow over the peephole and the door opens a couple guarded inches.

"What do you want, Faith?"

Mara's eye is near-shut swollen, she's bleeding from two nasty cuts on her cheek that seem in dire need of stitches, and that's just the side of her face that Faith can see. "Are you...are you okay?"

Only the most stupid question she could have possibly asked but Mara actually smiles, thin icicle smirk accompanied by a shake of her head, that glossy red hair rippling over her face and Faith wonders how much of that colour tastes like iron right now. "I'm fine. Go home."

"You don't look fine. You look like you need help."

Mara closes her eyes and sighs, a blood-smeared hand rubbing hard against her forehead. "Faith," she says, and "listen," and then there is some scuffling behind her and the door is jerked all the way open.

He's shorter than Mara, shorter even than Faith whose eye he refuses to meet as he pushes narrow-shouldered between them, shrugging into a grey suit jacket with a peacock blue tie hanging from its pocket. Faith can see the red wedged beneath his manicured nails, the flecks of crimson on his creased white shirt.

"Phillip, wait," Mara calls out but the man doesn't even pause. Just half turns his head to mutter something which might have been *forget it* or *fuck it* or something else entirely before scuttling through the little front gate like a cockroach surprised at midnight. The hazard lights on a silver Audi flash twice as he crosses the road towards it, and within seconds the man is inside and speeding away.

"Great," Mara says. "That's just great." Sounding more resigned than angry, even though she's standing there with both hands on her hips and eyebrows drawn together in a frown that just about freezes Faith's heart. As does the blood runnelling down both her cheeks, and the sticky-wet way that black satin robe wrinkles against her ribs.

Faith swallows. "He won't be back tonight, will he?"

"God no," Mara snorts, "*He* won't be back." Then her gaze drops to the bottle of wine hanging uselessly at Faith's side and she sighs once again. Bitterdeep breath that holds all the cares of the world and then some.

"Come inside," she says, stepping back from the door. "You and me, we need to talk."

Of course she's going to look around. Mara having excused herself for a quick shower, leaving Faith to open the wine and wander through to the loungeroom, glasses in hand and bottle tucked awkward beneath her arm, and surely it doesn't hurt to look. Not that there's much to see; Spartans lived larger than this.

Big navy-blue sofa along the far wall, bare-topped coffee table and two mismatched chairs—one with a grey pinstripe fabric, and the other the kind of patchy brownish velvet you only find in the most desperate op shops or the trendiest of retro-funk café bars. Small television in one corner and a lamp standing sentry opposite, its shade almost—but not quite—the same deep blue as the sofa. But no DVDs, no CDs, no books. No little knick-knacks or photos in frames, no junk mail or shoes or shopping lists left lying around.

The only remotely personal touch, the only hint that a human being might actually inhabit this space, is the large unframed canvas hanging adjacent to the window. A stemless, scarlet rose blooming against a near black background, petals open and weeping viscous red tears onto the once-white feather floating below it. Blood tears, bloodflowers; how did that song go again, that Cure song she'd left behind in Sydney along with her night-cast wardrobe and the rest of her angst-ridden trappings? Bittersad lyrics about trust, about never really knowing who you can. The feather is soaked, bedraggled, but still curves resiliently upwards, its tip pure and unsullied, so bright against the darkness that it almost glows.

Faith runs a finger across one of the glistening droplets, and is almost surprised to find the canvas rough and dry, her skin unstained.

"A friend painted that for me. Do you like it?"

The question quietly asked, but Faith still jumps, fights the urge to hide her hand behind her back like a schoolgirl caught with cigarettes or something much worse. *Yeah*, she tells Mara, who has reappeared with showerdamp hair and a flock of bright-white butterfly stitches on both cheeks, black satin robe swapped for jeans and a sleek grey jumper. "Yeah, I like it a lot. Might have wanted to arm-wrestle you for it once upon a time."

Once upon a time, not so long ago.

"Not now?" Mara smiles, or almost smiles, as she crosses the room to claim her glass of wine from the coffee table. She sits down carefully, right in the middle of the sofa, one leg curled beneath her.

"I'm sort of starting over. You know, leaving the past behind me."

"Hmm, mysterious."

"It really isn't," Faith explains. "It's just that the people I used to hang with, my *friends* or whatever you want to call them, the whole *goth* scene"—bobbing air quotes with both hands around *that* word—"they got to be a little…poisonous."

"Goth scene?" Mara arches an exquisitely plucked eyebrow.

"You know: black clothes, eyeliner, swanning around like they *invented* depression. Like it's fucking *profound* or something."

"I know. There are goths in Melbourne too, you realise."

"Yeah, but it's not my scene down here. And anyway, I'm…"

"Over it?"

"I'm over *me*." Faith slumps into the brown velvet chair, licks the resulting splash of wine from her wrist. "I'm over who I was back there. I'm over feeling shitty every damn day, and *liking* the fact that I'm feeling shitty, and then really hating the fact that I *like* it, if any of that makes any fucking sense at all."

"Perfect sense."

Mara is good, Faith will give her that. Sitting there sipping wine and encouraging Faith to babble on about nothing like this is just some cozy girls' night in after all, like she hasn't been cut to pieces by her arsehole boyfriend or whatever variety of pondscum he happens to be.

"Listen, Mara, are you okay? Really?"

"I'm fine."

"Maybe I should drive you to hospital. Get someone to check you over, just to make sure there isn't—"

"I'm *fine*."

Her tone icier now, a note of warning clearly sounded, but Faith plunges ahead nevertheless. "You don't have to put up with that shit, Mara. You don't have to be scared of getting help either, and if you need someone to be here with you when that arsehole comes back—"

"He won't be coming back," Mara snaps. "Believe me."

"How can you be so sure? Guys like that—"

"Do you take me for an imbecile? A victim?"

Faith swallows, searching for the right words. "I'm just…concerned. I can hear stuff through the walls, you know. Stuff that doesn't sound too good."

"What you do think is happening here? Do you think that man is my *lover?* That I need to be *rescued* from him?"

The sneer in her voice unmistakable despite the peculiar accent, perhaps even because of it, and all at once Faith has had enough, has had more than enough. Feels a little like she's being kicked in the guts herself once too many times tonight and, "Oh, fuck *off.* I'm not the one sitting there with my face looking like it got pushed through a plate-glass window."

Incredibly, Mara laughs.

"This is funny? Some sad prick beats you up a couple times a week, and it's meant to be funny?"

"He's not a prick," Mara says, still smiling. "Well, he may be that, but he's also a client. Or at least he *was*—tonight was his first visit and I doubt he left with a good impression. Lasting perhaps, but not good."

"What sort of a client?" Asking even as the pennies start to tumble.

"The kind who pays for *services rendered.*"

It's not like Mara is the first prostitute Faith has ever encountered. Hell, half her former friends could be considered whores in kind, blow jobs and sleights of hand casually swapped for half a tab of speedspun bliss almost any night of the week, a gram or two of pot any given morning after.

Faith takes another mouthful of wine, its flavour grown acidic and sharp.

"Look," she says. "That doesn't matter. Just because a guy pays you, doesn't mean he gets to hurt you."

Mara shakes her head. "Sweet girl, that's what they pay me *for.*"

Except that they don't.

Pay her, definitely. Pay her enough to mean she only has to work when she wants, and can afford to be choosy about who she sees, and how often.

But they never actually *hurt* her.

The disorder has a complicated name and even more complicated diagnosis, but what it boils down to is her nervous system is defective, has been all her life. What it boils down to is she can't feel any kind of pain, can't feel extremes of hot or cold either for that matter, can't feel much more than pressure and touch.

What it boils down to is this:

Mara can be slapped and bruised and cut and burned and left broken in more ways than any human being should ever have cause to know, and none of it will hurt. All of it will heal, and most of it will heal very fast.

This makes her special.

This makes her *expensive*.

Faith hasn't bothered setting up an internet connection at home yet—no one she cares to email and too many who'll be wanting to email her—so she's McSurfing through her thirty-minute lunchbreak instead. Greasy hamburger in one hand, fritzy trackball mouse in the other, and nothing but frustration on the screen in front of her. Loads of words, masses of infocrap—googling *can't feel pain* gets her more than sixteen million results just to start with—but nothing really useful. *Sensory neuropathy* and *congenital insensitivity* and *Riley-Day syndrome* and every time a piece seems to fit, it turns out she's just been holding it upside down.

Mara doesn't fit anywhere. Not precisely.

Unless it's on one of the forbidden pages, the family-friendly blockerbots insisting she maintain a minimum safe distance.

Yet another click to bring up *congenital analgia* and maybe this is it at last: *a syndrome characterized by a global insensitivity to physical pain*. Following the links to find not a perfect fit but the best one so far, even with the short life expectancy, the high rates of undiagnosed infection, the frequency of scratched corneas, amputated fingers and tongue-tips bitten clean off in infancy. List after list of predictable injuries, obliviously accidental wounds without pain to give notice, but so what?

Maybe Mara just knows how to take care of herself.

Rattle of ice from the boy behind her who's slurping the dregs of his drink right in her ear, and Faith takes the hint. Five minutes late already and they'll dock her for that, dock her but still demand that she make up the sales, push her quota of crappy holiday deposits onto pensioners who only leave their homes every second Thursday to punch the pokies and dream of rolling over those three magic bars.

Mara has brought fruitcake. A large, moist lump of a thing that crumbles when Faith tries to cut too thin a wedge, her butter knife clearly not up to the job.

"Don't feel obliged to eat it. I didn't."

The cake left by one of Mara's clients last Christmas and Faith wonders at the type of men who take pleasure in first reducing a woman to tears and bruises and bloody wounds, and then in bringing her gifts.

"It's good, I like fruitcake. You sure you don't want a piece?"

Mara wrinkles her nose. "Thank you, no." She's only come to say there'll be company at her place tonight, from eight until ten give or take half an hour depending on how things develop. In case Faith would rather not be here.

"Thanks for the warning."

"I don't mind if you play loud music. That's what Matthew used to do."

"Who?"

"The tenant who lived here before." That midnight gaze sliding over the kitchen where the two of them sit at the wonky little table Faith picked up for twenty dollars at St Vinnies, along with three matching wooden chairs. "Not as neat as you, but better furniture."

"Right." Faith wonders just what sort of man he had really been. The bury-your-head-in-the-stereo kind, or the kind who angled for a free sample. She breaks off a sizeable corner of cake and pops it into her mouth, chews very slowly and tries to ignore the thought that emerges yet again from some sick little hollow of her mind.

Sneaking up on Mara with a needle, just to see what would happen.

Just to see if she could make her flinch.

"Come on, then," Mara says and Faith almost chokes on a chunk of mara-schino cherry. "You obviously have questions. Ask away."

The cake now dry as unbuttered toast on her tongue, too much of it to swallow quickly so Faith chews and chews, but Mara is already flicking a dismissive hand in the air. Never mind the questions, those cautious-curious inquiries posed by so many others in not so many ways. She knows them all by rote anyway, so how about they just skip straight to the answers?

The clients, these men who come to see her, they each have their reasons: sadistic power trip or erotic wish fulfillment, extreme role playing or morbid curiosity plain and unadorned. In some, the reason dwells deep below the surface, inscrutable even to themselves, and there is only the *need*, a desire pure and compulsive and absolute, that draws them to her. Some she only sees the once before they retreat ashen-faced from her door, the experience not quite what they'd expected, or else, too much more. Some are regular as the new moon. *All* of them want to hurt her; an uncommon few wish the favour returned. The clients, they're complicated.

As for Mara, it's simple. She does it for the money. And for the record, there is no sex involved; she's not that kind of whore. On occasion, for a certain kind of client, she'll use her hands to finish things off. But that service costs extra, quite a bit extra, and in any case, most of those who need it prefer to relieve themselves.

What she does, it's not about *sex*.

And never mind the soundtrack; every good girl knows how to fake it.

"So you don't get hurt?" No matter how many websites she looks at, Faith can't really get her head around this. Pain doesn't *cause* damage, it heralds it, and if someone can't feel pain, then how can they judge if they're hurt, or how badly?

"I see a specialist," Mara says. "Regular check ups."

"Does he know? How they happen, I mean, all your...injuries?"

That greyhound smile again, swift and lean and borderline dangerous. "He should do. He causes his fair share."

"Okay." Faith swallows, hard. Pushes the rest of her fruitcake away. "I'm not even gonna pretend that I understand—"

"I don't *need* you to understand," Mara cuts in sharply. "I don't even need you to care. I'm not a puzzle, I'm not something you need to solve. Or rescue. I've told you this so you know what's happening and you won't come hammering at my door again in the middle of a session and cost me a client."

"I already said I was sorry—"

"I don't need *that*, either."

The two of them glaring at each other until at last Mara pushes back her chair and gets to her feet. "I realise you're lonely, Faith. But I don't do friendship."

"Even if I paid you for it?"

A cheap shot instantly regretted, but Mara only laughs. "Even then, Faith. Especially then."

She doesn't leave. Doesn't turn on any music or even the lights. Just sits on her bed in the dark with her cheek pressed against the wall, and listens.

To nothing very much, in the end. Random sounds of movement and the occasional murmur of voices, low-key and indecipherable. Not every psycho likes his girl to scream, apparently, and Faiths wonders why she doesn't feel more relieved.

(Or less disappointed?)

Awkwardly crossed, her left leg has fallen so deeply asleep that she needs both hands to straightens it out. Heavy-numb lump of flesh below her knee, and only the vaguest sensation of pressure as she digs a fingernail into the muscle of her calf, digs hard enough to leave a little red smiley behind.

Is that what Mara feels or, rather, what she doesn't? Ever?

Faith tries to imagine what it would be like to have your whole body cocooned in this way, to have never known even the incidental pain of stubbed toes, torn fingernails and paper cuts, never mind anything more profound. Might it be so bad, if you were careful? Thinking of the reasons she left Sydney, left the people *in* Sydney, what was left of them, Faith grimaces.

Painlessness, on both sides of her skin: she could wish for worse.

Sometimes, Mara leaves a note. Little scraps of powder blue paper wedged into the screen door at eye level with a handwritten date and time, three or four days' notice for Faith to make other plans if she feels the need.

(Mostly she doesn't.)

But more often lately, it's a personal appearance, a handful words or perhaps a whole cryptic, fractured conversation about spoiled milk, lost languages, or the tribe of magpies that wander along the street each morning, spotting grubs in the nature strip and marking each passerby with a polished-marble glare.

"Friend of the crows," Faith murmurs.

"Pardon me?"

"I used to know someone who said that whenever she saw a magpie: *friend of the crows*, and she'd point two fingers at it and then back at herself. So they wouldn't dive-bomb her come spring."

"And was she?"

"What?"

"A friend of the crows."

Mara sounding so serious that Faith has to laugh. "Geez, I don't know, maybe. Never did get swooped on, not that I remember." And Mara nods, once, and turns on her heel, and that's the end of that yet again. Two steps forward, three steps back, like someone braving herself to jump from the high-dive board, and Faith wonders what it is that Mara is after. Why she can't come out and say straight up that maybe she is just as lonely as Faith, that a friend might actually be what she needs.

And yet.

There is definitely something not quite right about the woman. Not drugs or drink or any other kind of mundane madness—and Faith has known enough of these in recent times to tell—but something else she can't quite identify.

Mara is just…not right.

Middle of the night phone calls never a good thing and Faith swears loudly as she lurches from her bed, tripping on a boot and bumping her knee on the corner of the dresser on her way to the door. Three months in the townhouse and she still can't find her way in the dark, so it's a speedy zombie shuffle down the hall with arms outstretched to fumble for the loungeroom light switch while she tries to pinpoint the handset's location from its shrill, persistent ring.

Who the fuck could be calling at this hour?

No one has this number except work and her mum, and she's sworn, she's *sworn*, that no matter who turns up on her doorstep or what they say or plead or promise, she won't let them know where Faith has gone.

Of all people, she *knows* the importance of this.

The phone is under a couch cushion. Faith's stomach tightens as she presses the talk button, lifts the thing cautiously to her ear. "Hello?"

Someone breathing, or just static on a crappy line? *Hey babygirl, when you gonna come back to us?* She can almost hear Livia crooning those words, and she swallows hard. Please not her, not Liv—the one person in the whole damn world she can refuse nothing, even when those brilliant green eyes are cracked and scattered and ice-locked, or perhaps especially then—and *hello*, she says again. "Hello?"

"Faith? Faith, it's me."

"Mara?" The voice so scratchy-faint that for a second she thinks she's guessed wrong. Thinks she should hang up right now before it's too late, because she really doesn't have the strength to do this all over again, but *please* the voice whispers, *please come get me*, and her heart falls back from her mouth just a little.

"Mara, what's wrong? Where are you?"

She must have misheard, or miswritten, because Grafton Avenue only goes up to number 119 and then it's nothing but parkland. Close-huddled shrubs and knee-high grasses, with a wan yellow streetlight illuminating the sign that tries to pass this place off as *Urban Forest*. Yeah right, and Faith checks the envelope where she scribbled down the address. Definitely 141, but maybe it should be 114? Or perhaps not Grafton *Avenue*, but Street or Crescent or Road, if such a beast exists?

Unclipping her seatbelt, she reaches across for the Melways on the passenger seat and flips to the index. The interior light in the old Toyota hasn't worked for two years, so she's squinting her way through the G's when something taps at the driver side window. Little scared-mouse tap still sudden enough to startle: Mara standing out there in the night with a half-curled fist and a face bleached whiter than Faith has ever seen on someone still living, pointing at the locked rear door with her other hand, her mouth moving soundlessly beyond the glass.

Three frozen seconds before Faith finally gets her arse up and out of the car. Mara is wrapped in something that looks like a sheet, low-budget toga costume hanging in thick folds from her shoulders, the dull-dark fabric even darker in patches, and Faith doesn't want to think too much about those just yet. More concerned with getting Mara into the car, Mara who shakes her head when Faith tries to lead her around to the passenger side, who wants to lie down instead, who says she *needs* to lie down, and so Faith opens the back door and helps her crawl inside.

Even with legs loosely curled, Mara takes up almost the whole length of the seat. This tall, lean woman not so solid now, and the way she shivers in her goose-pimpled skin almost breaks Faith's heart. One bare foot sticks out from beneath the sheet with toes clenched tight, pallid little piggies turning their backs to the world, and Faith tugs a corner of the fabric over them.

"Mara, don't go to sleep on me, okay?" Leaning in and over the woman, pushing damp-matted hair from her face. "Listen, I don't know this area. Where do I go, where's the nearest hospital?"

A cobra could not have struck as quickly.

"No hospitals!" Hand closing rat-trap tight around Faith's wrist, pupils so dilated they make her whole eyes glow black, and no, she hisses again. *No hospitals.*

"Fuck that, Mara. You need—"

"No! If you even *drive past* a hospital, I swear to—" Turning her head aside as she starts to cough, brutal as broken glass, and when it's over her chin is smeared with blood. "I swear I will get out of this car. I'll get out right now, if that's what you're planning." And she almost does, pushing herself up off the seat and sliding towards the door until Faith wrestles her back down, or tries to, tells her not to be so fucking stupid but she already knows the battle is lost. No way she can take this woman anywhere against her will, and she'd bet both tits that Mara really would throw herself from a moving vehicle if she so much as *smelled* an Emergency Room sign.

"All right. All *right*, fuck!"

A long, tense moment before Mara nods and finally releases her grip. "Just get me out of here. Please."

"Where to?" Faith asks bitterly. Fresh handprint of blood on her arm and she wipes it on her shirt, navy blue fabric none the worse for such a stain. "Home to warm milk and jim-jams?"

"No, not home." Mara closes her eyes, sinks back against the cheap vinyl upholstery. "Get us onto the highway and drive south. There's a motel about twenty minutes from here."

Faith is done arguing. So when she spots the bright-lit storefront of a twenty-four hour pharmacy—*Because Your Health Shouldn't Have To Wait!*—after only a few kilometers, she doesn't even ask. Just flicks on the indicator and pulls into the near-deserted carpark. "Don't even start," she tells the rearview mirror, Mara's instantly suspicious gaze catching her own within the glass. "Unless you reckon you can put yourself back together with whatever this cruddy motel of yours has in its minibar, then I'm picking up some stuff here. That okay with you?"

Not really a question, and Mara doesn't answer it, doesn't say another word until Faith returns to the car. Two small plastic bags rustling with bandages and Dettol and surgical tape and anything else she thought might come in handy. Paracetamol too, for the headache that looms at her temples and she presses a couple of these into her palm straight away. Dry swallows and turns to flash the box at the woman in the back seat, "Don't suppose *you* want some…"

Mara's laughter splinters to a wet and ragged cough.

"Rainbows End."

"What?"

"The motel, it's called Rainbows End. Keep driving, you'll see it."

She almost didn't. Almost sped right past the place, with its tall pine trees half hiding the vacancy sign out front, and now that she's standing in the cramped reception area, she wishes she'd done just that. The night manager pushes a form across the counter and Faith hesitates for a second, pen in hand. She doesn't know Mara's last name and is reluctant to use her own because…well, just *because*, and so: *Courtney Love*, the first words that pop into her head and now nothing else will, but the man doesn't even blink when she slides the form back.

Made up name, made up address, the tariff paid with cash. Two nights in advance because otherwise they'll have to be out by ten this morning and it's already almost four, and Faith feels sick.

Sick and scared and royally pissed off.

Their twin-share room right at the end of the complex, no neighbours if the absence of cars is any indication, so thank fuck for small mercies. Faith parks at the front and gets out to open the car door for Mara, chauffeur duties never grimmer than this as her passenger extends an arm for support, stares up at her with eyes deeply shadowed but still burning bright. Tiger eyes, savage and regal, and how it must sting for Mara to have to lean against Faith like this.

Beneath the pine-sharp patina of disinfectant, the room smells of strangers and stale cigarettes. Faith helps Mara over to one of the beds, dumps the pharmacy bags beside her and then goes back to sling the *Shhh! Guest Sleeping!* sign onto the doorknob. Flimsy chain latch on the inside and she pulls that across too.

"I want some water," Mara says.

"Let's have a look at you first."

Mara shakes her head, clutches her toga-sheet with both hands. "I can look after myself." Weighty blue-green cotton like you'd find in an operating theatre, far too much of it soaked magenta by now, and Faith has well and truly had enough of this shit.

"Fuck you, then."

Four long strides to the door of the room, fishing the car keys from her pocket with one hand while the other reaches for the security chain, because this isn't her problem and never was and—

"Wait," Mara whispers. "Please." Little-girl-lost voice Faith has never heard before, little girl lost *forever*, and somehow that's more frightening than all the blood. A voice to stop her dead, and she turns to see Mara rising carefully to her feet. "Look then," Mara says, "Look if it matters so much to you." And she lets the sheet fall.

Bride of Fucking Frankenstein the first thing that comes to mind, but it's so much worse than that.

Black-bristled sutures winding their jagged way from clavicles to pelvis, vaguely Y-shaped like an autopsy incision and crowded by an ugly patchwork of cuts that could only in these circumstances be thought lesser wounds. Ribs and belly and the almost non-existent swell of her breasts all bearing the mark of knife or scalpel, some stitches torn apart and bleeding fresh, crimson rivulets to join the dark and clotted mess that cakes her body from the waist down.

"Christ."

The word little more than appalled, astonished breath, but Mara just grins. "Nothing to do with *him*," she says, as a thin trickle of blood slides down her calf and around her ankle, pools on grotty grey carpet that has seen better days—though surely not worse ones.

For an entire precarious minute, Faith just stares, car keys digging sharply into her palm. She can still leave, can still turn her back on this whole fucked-up mess and just walk away, drive away and try very hard to pretend that she never even heard the phone ring tonight, *because this is not her problem*. This is Mara's nightmare but if Faith doesn't leave right now, if she doesn't open the motel door right this second, then it will become her nightmare as well and god only knows when—or if—either of them will wake up.

Mara wobbles a little, unsteady on her feet, then half-sinks, half-falls back onto the bed. "Can I have that water now?"

And even as Faith closes her eyes, even before she takes her first resigned step towards the ensuite, a shored-up space within her cracks and splits and breaks wide open, and something far too familiar worms its way out, uncurls its long and greedy limbs, and laughs.

The scant, thin hour before dawn and Mara seems to have fallen asleep at last. Her shallow breathing has deepened, become more regular, and there's not the slightest response when Faith calls her name. No movement, no murmur, not even the semi-conscious flutter of an eyelid, but Faith thinks she'll wait little while longer just to be sure.

Wet, bloody-pink wads of cotton wool litter the floor, and a stained towel huddles at the end of the bed where Faith left it once Mara finally pushed her away. *Enough, enough for now*, after Faith finished washing the dried and crusted blood from her chest, her stomach, her ribs. Pale fists bunched in the sheet around her hips, clenching tighter when Faith tried to pull that down as well, tried to see the damage lurking below but *there's nothing*, Mara said. *Just blood from everything else*, and clean or dirty, what she really needed was rest.

The smell of antiseptic fills the room and Faith worries what Mara might look like beneath her sutured skin.

Or even just beneath the sheet.

Finally, careful to make not the smallest telltale sound, Faith slips from her bed and pads over to Mara's. She takes hold of the stained and crumpled fabric and peels it slowly back, wincing at the whispersoft crackle of dried blood as she draws it all the way to Mara's parted knees, morbid magician flourish to reveal—

Just what, it takes Faith a second or two to fathom.

Nothing left of what should be found between a woman's legs. Only several deep cuts cleaving flesh right down to the glisten of bone, vicious wounds like someone put a fucking *axe* to work, and filled with so much dried and crusted blood that Faith tastes bile rising fresh to her throat. So much blood that maybe it seems worse than it is—nothing band-aids are gonna fix, sure, but still maybe not as horrendous as she thinks either—and she forces herself to lean forward, to look closer.

Too close: not enough time to withdraw as Mara suddenly twists sideways and draws up her legs. Kicks out and catches Faith full in the chest with enough force to send her spinning across the room, winded and gasping like she's been kicked by a frightened horse. Tacky carpet beneath her hands as she lands and scuttles backwards on her arse, more than a little frightened herself now with Mara getting up from the bed and stalking naked towards her. Amazon tall and stitched together like a broken doll, a piece of her too large—too *chunky*—to be simply skin flapping open between her legs, slapping against her thigh with each determined step.

Faith barely makes it to the toilet before she throws up.

"Hey." Hands on her back, her shoulders, reaching around to pull the hair from her face. "You shouldn't have seen that, you should have trusted me. You should have listened when I said I was fine."

"You're not *fine*." Turning to find Mara with a motel towel wrapped close around her waist, greyish-white and already spotted scarlet. "Can you even see yourself, can you see what he's…*done* to you? What he's…" The image of torn, bloodied flesh still stark behind her eyes, blinding, and Faith stuffs a fist into her mouth. *Mara*, she whispers, and *oh christ*, and then *Mara* again.

They're all the words she can summon.

Mara sighs and sinks heavily to the floor, knees pressed tight together. "You don't understand, Faith. You don't even know the half of it."

The story is, last night was a game of Doctors & Nurses. More precisely, Doctors & Doctors—Mara's *specialist* friend with some friends of his own along for the ride, medical degrees decidedly optional. A room in a house done up as an operating theatre, and Mara the star attraction.

A patient who would remain fully conscious while you sliced and prodded and poked around inside her. A patient who would speak on command, who would weep or gasp or not speak at all if that's what you preferred. Eyes wide and bright and completely aware, even as you curved a hand around her heart to feel its rhythms against your awestruck palm.

Even as you stitched her closed again, your fingers sweating, trembling, inside their surgical gloves.

The story is, even this was not enough. Sex never in the contract but one of them had pulled down her bikini briefs anyway, the others circling close like leering wolves with the scent of blood thick in their nostrils. Until they forced apart her legs and saw what wasn't there.

As for what *was*, well. Nothing any of them could ever have seen before.

Simply, nothing.

Mara thinks they used a cleaver. They'd brought all sorts of tools, all kinds of implements to play with. A cleaver, or some other heavy-bladed knife.

But the story is: Mara gave far better than she ever might have gotten and by the end, not all of the blood spilled had been hers.

Not even most of it.

Faith doesn't want to know exactly what that means. What any of it means. Is only too grateful to be sent in search of the small, combination-locked suitcase Mara has left in care of the management for precisely such an occasion.

"Should have told us you was with her, love." A different man from the previous night, tall and hollow-cheeked, leaning towards Faith with both forearms flat on the counter. "She stays as long she needs, tell her. No charge."

Then, with genuine concern, "She okay, you reckon?"

And Faith, who knows nothing about anything anymore and is trying very hard to feel just the same, merely nods. "I think so. She says so."

Back in the room, Mara thanks her for the suitcase and disappears with it into the ensuite. There is the sound of the door locking and, after a few minutes, the rhythmic patter of the shower. Faith flops onto the bed—*her* bed, not the other one—and throws an elbow over her eyes to block out the morning sun now squeezing slantways through the not-so-vertical blinds.

Thoughts of Sydney crowd forward and, for the first time in a long time, she doesn't push them automatically away. Livia and Ben and all the others she left behind, one thousand kilometres worth of behind, because who knew how wide that particular vortex yawned. *We're, like, exploring Antarctica here*, someone had mused late one night. Russ, or maybe Corin, she can't recall. Wedged in her memory instead, the wired exultation in Liv's reply: *Baby, no, there's dirt and rocks and shit under there. This is the fucking Arctic circle: nothing but ice all the way down.*

Livia, raccoon eyes now perpetually smudged with day-old eyeliner, her dyed black hair overgrown with greasy blonde.

Livia, finding veins in her ankles so she can still go sleeveless in summer.

Livia, scratching herself to ruin in the search for subcutaneous life.

Faith had fled. No dramatic watershed moment, no death or overdose or even accidental injury to propel her into the harsh light of day, just waking up one winter morning with frozen toes and the even colder realisation that if she dragged herself off to Livia's that night she might never, ever find her way back home.

Four weeks at her mum's instead. Best mother in the whole damn world to keep her under lock and key like that, self-imposed house arrest in suburbia while she cleaned up, thawed out, thankful that she hadn't really even begun to plumb the sort of depths that Livia and the rest had so eagerly dived to. Surfacing from that level might have—almost certainly *would* have—been impossible. Would have been impossible regardless if she hadn't then picked up and moved to Melbourne with barely a pause for breath or the burning of all her address books. Faith had proved herself stronger than she'd thought, but no way would she ever be strong enough to close a door in Livia's face if that girl decided to come knocking.

Only now there's Mara, and Faith wonders if she doesn't have some sort of subconscious freak-compass guiding her every movement.

The ensuite door swings open, spilling forth steam, fluorescent light and someone Faith almost doesn't recognise. Mara has cut her hair, close-cropped schoolboy style slicked back from her forehead with gel or maybe just water from the shower. Dressed in black jeans and a baggy black t-shirt, she even seems to move differently. Loose-hipped, almost a swagger, with pale arms swinging by her sides as though buffeted by a careless breeze.

"Still here?" The surprise in her voice, no matter how mild, is just too much. This is impossible, *Mara* is impossible. Pain or no pain, no one gets cut open like that and walks around so effortlessly the very next day; no one gets *butchered* the way this woman has been and walks around *at all*, never mind in fucking *jeans*. Faith realises that if she wasn't so furious, so well and truly *fed up*, then she'd most likely be terrified out of her wits right now.

"What are you, Mara?" Anger definitely the preferred option, and she lets it all the way loose. "What the *fuck* are you?" Launching herself from the bed, reaching for Mara with no clear intention beyond doing some sort of violence of her own, but it hardly matters. Mara catches her wrists in hands too strong to be human, crosses them over and then pushes her away. Hard.

Faith lands on the corner of the mattress and topples straight to the floor, terror now sliding into prominence as she rubs her wrists together, so sore the bones themselves seem bruised.

Mara regards her in silence for a few seconds, then nods, as though arriving at some kind of decision. She sits down on the bed opposite, legs apart and elbows resting on her knees. "I'm not sure what I am," she says quietly, staring at a point between her bare, blue-veined feet. "You have so many stories, it becomes difficult—confusing—to hold onto the truth."

Faith swallows, not daring to move.

"I did not fall." Mara glances up, her tear-glazed eyes still sharply focused. "But neither did I choose a side. And more than that, I can't remember."

She winces, hand moving swiftly to her waist where it rubs in smooth, slow circles just below her ribs. "Not all of them doctors, then." And to Faith's wordless, uncomprehending shake of the head, "The liver, I think. Re-arranging itself to the proper position."

"But you…it looked like that hurt. *Did* that hurt?"

Mara shrugs.

"You told me you didn't…that you couldn't…" Not finishing, not wanting to finish. Not wanting to say the words to make it real, so Mara says them for her.

"I feel pain, Faith. I feel everything that's ever been done to me, while it lasts." Half a smile, half a grimace curving her thin, pale lips. "But think, would you really feel a mosquito bite if your leg had just been severed? Or would you want to feel it even more? Would you long for that bite, that almost insignificant sting, because the other pain—the loss, the *absence*—was just too unbearable?"

Faith gets to her knees, gets oh so slowly to her feet. "Mara…"

"No." Even with half a room between them, the raised hand snaps her frozen to the spot. "It's too late for *Mara* now. Whatever she had, you can have. Or not. I won't be returning to that place."

Run. Run. Run. Each beat of her heart imploring escape, but Faith can't seem to move. Finds her mouth opening instead, asking if there is something she can do, because if there is anything at all that might help—

"What can you do?" The woman that was Mara snaps. "You and your kind who know nothing but selfishness and cruelty." Rising from the bed, one hand lifting her shirt as if to illustrate the point. Jagged central incision that actually does look markedly better, even after these few brief hours—until two long fingers dig their way beneath the stitches and tug, pulling out half a dozen with a sickening wet pop. Gaping, bleeding wound in her belly big enough for a hand to slip into, and it does, emerging again scarlet and dripping and offered to Faith like a promise. "Tell me, what can any of you do?"

Faith feels the motel room door against her shoulder blades, even though she can't recall backing into it.

And the woman, the *creature* that was Mara stalks towards her, taller than ever with bitter-black eyes darker than the despair of stolen souls. "Cruel. Selfish. Arrogant beyond sufferance." But that hand, those blood-soaked fingers, are unexpectedly gentle as they caress Faith's cheek, slide down to cup her chin.

"Yet you are loved," the creature that was Mara whispers. "You are *all loved.*"

Faith can only hope the taste of salt on her lips comes from her own tears.

"Leave." The hand loosens, those terrible eyes close. "Leave now."

And for once, Faith does not need to be told a second time.

The door to Mara's townhouse stands slightly ajar, slightly crooked. Half off its hinges, Faith sees when she approaches, and inside the place the damage is worse. Furniture broken, upholstery torn. Smashed crockery and glassware turning the kitchen into a glittering minefield, and the bedroom reeking from the dozens of bottles of perfume that have been spilled onto the stripped and blood-stained mattress. In the wreck of a home still devoid of intimate possessions and personal touches, the saddest thing is the painting of the floating red rose. The canvas now cut to pieces, palm-sized scraps scattered over the loungeroom floor, and the wooden frame upon which it had been stretched cowering in a corner like some skeletal, broken-backed beast.

By her foot, a bit of canvas lies face down. *arest Mar* scrawled on its back in a small but confident hand, and Faith gets down on her knees to find the rest of the inscription. Oversized, paint-stiff jigsaw with too many blank pieces, but finally she has all the ones she needs.

For My Timeless Love, My Dearest Marguerette, who waits for no man. Arthur. New Orleans, July 1928.

And Marguerette may not be Mara. And Mara may have lied about the artwork being done for her by a friend. And Arthur, whoever he was, may have painted this canvas for a woman who did decide to wait for him after all, a woman with whom he grew old and lined, a woman who was mortal and human and who did not look up at the stars at night and remember what it was like to walk above them.

But Faith doesn't think so.

Especially when she turns the pieces of canvas over to see they show the curved, blood-draggled feather. Long and thin and silverwhite, the feather of eagle or albatross, or some other creature equally glorious and skybound and doomed.

Arthur, whoever he was, he had known.

Faiths curls up on the carpet, knees drawn close to her chest, and wonders when she'll stop crying. Don't you ever forget how strong you are, sweetheart, her mum had said. You got yourself through this, you can get yourself through anything.

But right now, all she wants is to feel Livia's arms around her, Livia murmuring meaningless shit into her ear. All she wants is not to feel the weight of a new day, the weight of new knowledge too frightening to consider except from the most oblique of angles. Never mind how she gets there.

Never mind if she never, ever finds her way out again.

You are loved, it had said, blood running down its slender wrist.

Right now, the scraps of canvas clutched in her desperate, desolate fists, Faith thinks love never burned colder than this.

NATHAN BALLINGRUD is the author of *North American Lake Monsters*, *The Visible Filth*, and the forthcoming *The Atlas of Hell*. Several of his stories are in development for film and TV. He has twice won the Shirley Jackson Award. He lives somewhere in the mountains of North Carolina.

You Go Where It Takes You
Nathan Ballingrud

HE DID NOT look like a man who would change her life. He was big, roped with muscles from working on offshore oil rigs, and tending to fat. His face was broad and inoffensively ugly, as though he had spent a lifetime taking blows and delivering them. He wore a brown raincoat against the light morning drizzle and against the threat of something more powerful held in abeyance. He breathed heavily, moved slowly, found a booth by the window overlooking the water, and collapsed into it. He picked up a syrup-smeared menu and studied it with his whole attention, like a student deciphering Middle English. He was like every man who ever walked into that little diner. He did not look like a beginning or an end.

That day, the Gulf of Mexico and all the earth was blue and still. The little town of Port Fourchon clung like a barnacle to Louisiana's southern coast, and behind it water stretched into the distance for as many miles as the eye could hold. Hidden by distance were the oil rigs and the workers who supplied this town with its economy. At night she could see their lights, ringing the horizon like candles in a vestibule. Toni's morning shift was nearing its end; the dining area was nearly empty. She liked to spend those slow hours out on the diner's balcony, overlooking the water.

Her thoughts were troubled by the phone call she had received that morning. Gwen, her three-year-old daughter, was offering increasing resistance to the male staffers at the Daylight Daycare, resorting lately to biting them or kicking them in the ribs when they knelt to calm her. Only days before, Toni had been waylaid there by a lurking social worker who talked to her in a gentle saccharine voice, who touched her hand maddeningly and said, "No one is judging you; we just want to help." The social worker had mentioned the word "psychologist" and asked about their home life. Toni had been embarrassed and enraged, and was only able to conclude the interview with a mumbled promise to schedule another one soon. That her daughter was already displaying such grievous signs of social ineptitude stunned Toni, left her feeling hopeless and betrayed.

It also made her think about Donny again, who had abandoned her years ago to move to New Orleans, leaving her a single mother at twenty-three. She wished death on him that morning, staring over the railing at the unrelenting progression of waves. She willed it along the miles and into his heart.

"You know what you want?" she asked.

"Um…just coffee." He looked at her breasts and then at her eyes.

"Cream and sugar?"

"No thanks. Just coffee."

"Suit yourself."

The only other customer in the diner was Crazy Claude by the door, speaking conversationally to a cooling plate of scrambled eggs and listening to his radio through his earphones. A tinny roar leaked out around his ears. Pedro, the short-order cook, lounged behind the counter, his big round body encased in layers of soiled white clothing, enthralled by a guitar magazine which he had spread out by the cash register. The kitchen slumbered behind him, exuding a thick fug of onions and burnt frying oil. It would stay mostly dormant until the middle of the week, when the shifts would change on the rigs, and tides of men would ebb and flow through the small town.

So when she brought the coffee back to the man, she thought nothing of it when he asked her to join him. She fetched herself a cup of coffee as well and then sat across from him in the booth, grateful to transfer the weight from her feet.

"You ain't got no nametag," he said.

"Oh…I guess I lost it somewhere. My name's Toni."

"That's real pretty."

She gave a quick derisive laugh. "The hell it is. It's short for Antoinette."

He held out his hand and said, "I'm Alex."

She took it and they shook. "You work offshore, Alex?"

"Some. I ain't been out there for a while, though." He smiled and gazed into the murk of his coffee. "I've been doing a lot of driving around."

Toni shook loose a cigarette from her pack and lit it. She lied and said, "Sounds exciting."

"I don't guess it is, though. But I bet this place could be, sometimes. I bet you see all kinds of people come through here."

"Well…I guess so."

"How long you been here?"

"About three years."

"You like it?"

"Yeah, Alex, I fucking love it."

"Oh, hey, all right." He held up his hands. "I'm sorry."

Toni shook her head. "No. *I'm* sorry. I just got a lot on my mind today."

"So why don't you come out with me after work? Maybe I can help distract you."

Toni smiled at him. "You've known me for, what, five minutes?"

"Hey, what can I say, I'm an impulsive guy. Caution to the wind!" He drained his cup in two swallows to illustrate his recklessness.

"Well, let me go get you some more coffee, Danger Man." She patted his hand as she got up.

It was a similar impulsiveness that brought Donny back to her, briefly, just over a year ago. After a series of phone calls that progressed from petulant to playful to curious, he drove back to Port Fourchon in his disintegrating blue Pinto one Friday afternoon to spend a weekend with them. It was nice at first, though there was no talk of what might happen after Sunday.

Gwen had just started going to daycare. Stunned by the vertiginous growth of the world, she was beset by huge emotions; varieties of rage passed through her little body like weather systems, and no amount of coddling from Toni would settle her.

Although he wouldn't admit it, Toni knew Donny was curious about the baby, who according to common wisdom would grow to reflect many of his own features and behaviors.

But Gwen refused to participate in generating any kind of infant mystique, revealing herself instead as what Toni knew her to be: a pink, pudgy little assemblage of flesh and ferocity that giggled or raved seemingly without discrimination, that walked without grace and appeared to lack any qualities of beauty or intelligence whatsoever.

But the sex between them was as good as it ever was, and he didn't seem to mind the baby too much. When he talked about calling in sick to work on Monday, she began to hope for something lasting.

Early Sunday afternoon, they decided to give Gwen a bath. It would be Donny's first time washing his daughter, and he approached the task like a man asked to handle liquid nitrogen. He filled the tub with eight inches of water and plunked her in, then sat back and stared as, with furrowed brow, she went about the serious business of testing the seaworthiness of shampoo bottles. Toni sat on the toilet seat behind him, and it occurred to her that this was her family. She felt buoyant, sated.

Then Gwen rose abruptly from the water and clapped her hands joyously. "Two! Two poops! One, two!"

Aghast, Toni saw two little turds sitting on the bottom of the tub, rolling slightly in the currents generated by Gwen's capering feet. Donny's hand shot out and cuffed his daughter on the side of the head. She crashed against the wall and bounced into the water with a terrific splash. And then she screamed: the most godawful sound Toni had ever heard in her life.

Toni stared at him, agape. She could not summon the will to move. The baby, sitting on her ass in the soiled water, filled the tiny bathroom with a sound like a bomb siren, and she just wanted her to shut up, shut up, just shut the fuck up.

"Shut up, goddamnit! Shut *up*!"

Donny looked at her, his face an unreadable mess of confused emotion; he pushed roughly past her. Soon she heard the sound of a door closing, his car starting up, and he was gone. She stared at her stricken daughter and tried to quiet the sudden stampeding fury.

She refilled Alex's coffee and sat down with him, leaving the pot on the table. She retrieved her cigarette from the ashtray only to discover that it had expired in her absence. "Well, shit."

Alex nodded agreeably. "I'm on the run," he said suddenly.

"What?"

"It's true. I'm on the run. I stole a car."

Alarmed, Toni looked out the window, but the parking lot was on the other side of the diner. All she could see from here was the gulf.

"Why are you telling me this? I don't want to know this."

"It's a station wagon. I can't believe it even runs anymore. I was in Morgan City, and I had to get out fast. The car was right there. I took it."

He had a manic look in his eye, and although he was smiling, his movements had become agitated and sudden. She felt a growing disquiet coupled with a mounting excitement. He was dangerous, this man. He was a falling hammer.

"I don't think that guy over there likes me," he said.

"What?" She turned and saw Crazy Claude in stasis, staring at Alex. His jaw was cantilevered in mid-chew. "That's just Claude," she said. "He's all right."

Alex was still smiling, but it had taken on a different character, one she couldn't place and which set loose a strange, giddy feeling inside her. "No, I think it's me. He keeps looking over here."

"Really, Claude's okay. He's harmless as a kitten."

"I want to show you something." Alex reached inside his raincoat, and for a moment Toni thought he was going to pull out a gun and start shooting. She felt no inclination to move, though, and waited for what would come. But instead, he withdrew a crumpled Panama hat. It had been considerably crushed to fit into his pocket, and once freed it began to unfold itself, slowly resuming its original shape.

She looked at it. "It's a hat," she said.

He stared at it like he expected it to lurch across the table with some hideous agenda. "That's an object of terrible power," he said.

"Alex—it's a hat. It's a thing you put on your head."

"It belongs to the man I stole the car from. Here," he said, pushing it across to her. "Put it on."

She did. She turned her chin to her shoulder and pouted her lips, looking at him out of the corner of her eye, like she thought a model might.

"Who are you?" he said.

"I'm a supermodel."

"What's your name? Where are you from?"

She affected a bright, breathy voice. "My name is Violet, I'm from L.A., and I'm strutting down a catwalk wearing this hat and nothing else. Everybody loves me and is taking my picture."

They laughed, and he said, "See? It's powerful. You can be anybody."

She gave the hat back.

"You know," Alex said, "the guy I stole the car from was something of a thief himself. You should see what he left in there."

"Why don't you show me?"

He smiled. "Now?"

"No. In half an hour. When I get off work."

"But it's all packed up. I don't just let that stuff fly around loose."

"Then you can show me at my place."

And so it was decided. She got up and went about preparing for the next shift, which consisted of restocking a few ketchup packets and starting a fresh pot of coffee. She refilled Crazy Claude's cup and gave him another ten packets of sugar, all of which he methodically opened and dumped into his drink. When her relief arrived, Toni hung her apron by the waitress station and collected Alex on her way to the door.

"We have to stop by the daycare and pick up my kid," she said.

When they passed Claude's table they heard a distant, raucous sound coming from his earphones.

Alex curled his lip. "Idiot. How does he hear himself think?"

"He doesn't. That's the point. He hears voices in his head. He plays the radio loud so he can drown them out."

"You're kidding me."

"Nope."

Alex stopped and turned around, regarding the back of Claude's head with renewed interest. "How many people does he have in there?"

"I never asked."

"Well, holy shit."

Outside, the sun was setting, the day beginning to cool down. The rain had stopped at some point, and the world glowed under a bright wet sheen. They decided that he would follow her in his car. It was a rusty old battle wagon from the seventies; several boxes were piled in the back. She paid them no attention.

She knew, when they stepped into her little apartment, that they would eventually make love, and she found herself wondering what it would be like. She watched him move, noticed the graceful articulation of his body, the careful restraint he displayed in her living room, which was filled with fragile things. She saw the skin beneath his clothing, watched it stretch and move.

"Don't worry," she said, touching the place between his shoulder blades. "You won't break nothing."

About Gwen there was more doubt. Unleashed like a darting fish into the apartment, she was gone with a bright squeal, away from the strange new man around whom she had been so quiet and doleful, into the dark grottoes of her home.

"It's real pretty," Alex said.

"A bunch of knickknacks mostly. Nothing special."

He shook his head like he did not believe it. Her apartment was decorated mostly with the inherited flotsam of her grandmother's life: bland wall hangings, beaten old furniture which had played host to too many bodies spreading gracelessly into old age, and a vast and silly collection of glass figurines: leaping dolphins and sleeping dragons and such. It was all meant to be homey and reassuring, but it just reminded her of how far away she was from the life she really wanted. It seemed like a desperate construct, and she hated it very much.

For now, Alex made no mention of the objects in his car or the hat in his pocket. He appeared to be more interested in Gwen, who was peering around the corner of the living room and regarding him with a suspicious and hungry eye, who seemed to intuit that from this large alien figure on her mama's couch would come mighty upheavals.

He was a man—that much Gwen knew immediately—and therefore a dangerous creature. He would make her mama behave unnaturally; maybe even cry. He was too big, like the giant in her storybook. She wondered if he ate children. Or mamas.

Mama was sitting next to him.

"Come here, Mama." She slapped her thigh like Mama did when she wanted Gwen to pay attention to her. Maybe she could lure Mama away from the giant, and they could wait in the closet until he got bored and went away. "Come here, Mama, come here."

"Go on and play now, Gwen."

"No! Come here!"

"She don't do too well around men," said Mama.

"That's okay," said the giant. "These days I don't either." He patted the cushion next to him. "Come over here, baby. Let me say hi."

Gwen, alarmed at this turn of events, retreated a step behind a corner. They were in the living room, which had her bed in it, and her toys. Behind her,

Mama's darkened room yawned like a throat. She sat between the two places, wrapped her arms around her knees, and waited.

"She's so afraid," Alex said after she retreated out of their sight. "You know why?"

"Um, because you're big and scary?"

"Because she already knows about possibilities. Long as you know there are options in life, you get scared of choosing the wrong one."

Toni leaned away from him and gave him a mistrustful smile. "Okay, Einstein. Easy with the philosophy."

"No, really. She's like a thousand different people right now, all waiting to be, and every time she makes a choice, one of those people goes away forever. Until finally you run out of choices and you are whoever you are. She's afraid of what she'll lose by coming out to see me. Of who she'll never get to be."

Toni thought of her daughter and saw nothing but a series of shut doors. "Are you drunk?"

"What? You know I ain't drunk."

"Stop talking like you are, then. I've had enough of that shit to last me my whole life."

"Jesus, I'm sorry."

"Forget it." Toni got up from the couch and rounded the corner to scoop up her daughter. "I got to bathe her and put her to bed. If you want to wait, it's up to you."

She carried Gwen into the bathroom and began the nightly ministrations. Donny was too strong a presence tonight, and Alex's sophomoric philosophizing sounded just like him when he'd had too many beers. She found herself hoping that the prosaic obligations of motherhood would bore Alex, and that he would leave. She listened for the sound of the front door.

Instead, she heard footsteps behind her and felt his heavy hand on her shoulder. It squeezed her gently, and his big body settled down beside her; he said something kind to her daughter and brushed a strand of wet hair from her eyes. Toni felt something move slowly in her chest, subtly yet with powerful effect, like Atlas rolling a shoulder.

Gwen suddenly shrieked and collapsed into the water, sending a small tsunami over them both. Alex reached in to stop her from knocking her head against the porcelain and received a kick in the mouth for his troubles. Toni shouldered him aside and jerked her out of the tub. She hugged her daughter tightly to her chest and whispered placative incantations into her ear. Gwen finally settled into her mother's embrace and whimpered quietly, turning all of her puissant focus onto the warm familiar hand rubbing her back, up and down, up and down, until, finally, her energy flagged, and she drifted into a tentative sleep.

When Gwen was dressed and in her bed, Toni turned her attention to Alex. "Here, let's clean you up."

She steered him back into the bathroom. She opened the shower curtain and pointed to the soap and the shampoo and said, "It smells kind of flowery, but it gets the job done," and the whole time he was looking at her, and she thought: So this is it; this is how it happens.

"Help me," he said, lifting his arms from his sides. She smiled wanly and began to undress him. She watched his body as she unwrapped it, and when he was naked she pressed herself close to him and ran her fingers down his back.

Later, when they were in bed together, she said, "I'm sorry about tonight."

"She's just a kid."

"No, I mean about snapping at you. I don't know why I did."

"It's okay."

"I just don't like to think about what could have been. There's no point to it. Sometimes I don't think a person has too much to say about what happens to them anyway."

"I really don't know."

She stared out the little window across from the bed and watched slate gray clouds skim across the sky. Burning behind them were the stars.

"Ain't you gonna tell me why you stole a car?"

"I had to."

"But why?"

He was silent for a little while. "It don't matter," he said.

"If you don't tell me, it makes me think you mighta killed somebody."

"Maybe I did."

She thought about that for a minute. It was too dark to see anything in the bedroom, but she scanned her eyes across it anyway, knowing the location of every piece of furniture, every worn tube of lipstick and leaning stack of life-style magazines. She could see through the walls and feel the sagging weight of the figurines on the shelves. She tried to envision each one in turn, as though searching for one that would act as a talisman against this subject and the weird celebration it raised in her.

"Did you hate him?"

"I don't hate anybody," he said. "I wish I did. I wish I had it in me."

"Come on, Alex. You're in my house. You got to tell me something."

After a long moment, he said, "The guy I stole the car from. I call him Mr. Gray. I never saw him, except in dreams. I don't know anything about him, really. But I don't think he's human. And I know he's after me."

"What do you mean?"

"I have to show you." Without another word, he got to his feet and pulled on his jeans. He was beginning to get excited about something, and it inspired a similar feeling in her. She followed him, pulling a long t-shirt over her head as she went. Gwen slept deeply in the living room; they stepped over her mattress on the way out.

The grass was wet beneath their feet, the air heavy with the salty smell of the sea. Alex's car was parked at the curb, hugging the ground like a great beetle. He opened the rear hatch and pulled the closest box toward them.

"Look," he said, and opened the box.

At first, Toni could not comprehend what she saw. She thought it was a cat lying on a stack of tan leather jackets, but that wasn't right, and only when Alex grabbed a handful of the cat and pulled it out did she realize that it was human hair. Alex lifted the whole object out of the box, and she found herself staring at the tanned and cured hide of a human being, dark empty holes in its face like some rubber Halloween mask.

"I call this one Willie, 'cause he's so well hung," said Alex, and offered an absurd laugh.

Toni fell back a step.

"But there's women in here too, all kinds of people. I counted ninety-six. All carefully folded." He offered the skin to Toni, but when she made no move to touch it he went about folding it up again. "I guess there ain't no reason to see them all. You get the idea."

"Alex, I want to go back inside."

"Okay, just hang on a second."

She waited while he closed the lid of the box and slid it back into place. With the hide tucked under one arm, he shut the hatch, locked it, and turned to face her. He was grinning, bouncing on the balls of his feet. "Okeydokey," he said, and they headed back indoors.

They went back into the bedroom, walking quietly to avoid waking Gwen.

"Did you kill all those people?" Toni asked when the door was closed.

"What? Didn't you hear me? I stole a car. That's what was in it."

"Mr. Gray's car."

"That's right."

"Who is he? What are they for?" she asked; but she already knew what they were for.

"They're alternatives," he said. "They're so you can be somebody else."

She thought about that. "Have you worn any of them?"

"One. I haven't got up the balls to do it again yet." He reached into the front pocket of his jeans and withdrew a leather sheath. From it he pulled a small, ugly little knife that looked like an eagle's talon. "You got to take off the one you're already wearing, first. It hurts."

Toni swallowed. The sound was thunderous in her ears. "Where's your first skin? The one you was born with?"

Alex shrugged. "I threw that one out. I ain't like Mr. Gray, I don't know how to preserve them. Besides, what do I want to keep it for? I must not have liked it too much in the first place, right?"

She felt a tear accumulate in the corner of her eye and willed it not to fall. She was afraid and exhilarated. "Are you going to take mine?"

Alex looked startled, then seemed to remember he was holding the knife. He put it back in its sheath. "I told you, baby, I'm not the one who killed those people. I don't need any more than what's already there." She nodded, and the tear streaked down her face. He touched it away with the back his fingers. "Hey now," he said.

She grabbed his hand. "Where's mine?" She gestured at the skin folded beside him. "I want one, too. I want to come with you."

"Oh, Jesus, no, Toni. You can't."

"But why not? Why can't I go?"

"Come on now, you got a family here."

"It's just me and her. That ain't no family."

"You have a little girl, Toni. What's wrong with you? That's your life now." He stepped out of his pants and pulled the knife from its sheath. "I can't argue about this. I'm going now. I'm gonna change first, though, and you might not want to watch." She made no move to leave. He paused, considering something. "I got to ask you something," he said. "I been wondering about this lately. Do you think it's possible for something beautiful to come out of an awful beginning? Do you think a good life can redeem a horrible act?"

"Of course I do," she said quickly, sensing some second chance here, if only she could say the right words. "Yes."

Alex touched the blade to his scalp just above his right ear and drew it in an arc over the crown of his head until it reached his left ear. Bright red blood crept down from his hairline in a slow tide, sending rivulets and tributaries along his jawline and down his throat, hanging from his eyelashes like raindrops from flower petals. "God, I really hope so," he said. He worked his fingers into the incision and began to tug violently.

Watching the skin fall away from him, she was reminded of nothing so much as a butterfly struggling into daylight.

She is driving west on I-10. The morning sun, which has just breached the horizon, flares in her rearview mirror. Port Fourchon is far behind her, and the Texas border looms. Beside her, Gwen is sitting on the floor of the passenger seat, playing with the Panama hat Alex left behind when he drove North. Toni has never seen the need for a car seat. Gwen is happier moving about on her own, and in times like this, when Toni feels a slow, crawling anger in her blood, the last thing she needs is a temper tantrum from her daughter.

After he left, she was faced with a few options. She could put on her stupid pink uniform, take Gwen to daycare, and go back to work. She could drive up to New Orleans and find Donny. Or she could say fuck it all and just get in the car and drive, aimlessly and free of expectation, which is what she is doing.

She cries for the first dozen miles or so, and it is such a rare luxury that she just lets it come, feeling no guilt.

Gwen, still feeling the dregs of sleep and as yet undecided whether to be cranky for being awakened early or excited by the trip, pats her on the leg. "You okay, Mama, you okay?"

"Yes, baby. Mama's okay."

Toni sees the sign she has been looking for coming up on the side of the road. Rest Stop, 2 miles.

When they get there, she pulls in, coming to a stop in the empty lot. Gwen climbs up in the seat and peers out the window. She sees the warm red glow of a Coke machine and decides that she will be happy today, that waking up early means excitement and the possibility of treats.

"Have the Coke, Mama? Have it, have the Coke?"

"Okay, sweetie."

They get out and walk up to the Coke machine. Gwen laughs happily and slaps it several times, listening to the distant dull echo inside. Toni puts in some coins and grabs the tumbling can. She cracks it open and gives it to her daughter, who takes it delightedly.

"Coke!"

"That's right." Toni kneels beside her as Gwen takes several ambitious swigs. "Gwen? Honey? Mama's got to go potty, okay? You stay right here, okay? Mama will be right back."

Gwen lowers the can, a little overwhelmed by the cold blast of carbonation, and nods her head. "Right back!"

"That's right, baby."

Toni starts away. Gwen watches her mama as she heads back to the car and climbs in. She shuts the door and starts the engine. Gwen takes another drink of Coke. The car pulls away from the curb, and she feels a bright stab of fear. But Mama said she was coming right back, so she will wait right here.

Toni turns the wheel and speeds back out onto the highway. There is no traffic in sight. The sign welcoming her to Texas flashes by and is gone. She presses the accelerator. Her heart is beating.

Shirley Jackson award-winner **KAARON WARREN** published her first short story in 1993 and has had fiction in print every year since. She has published five multi award-winning novels: *Slights, Walking the Tree, Mistification, The Grief Hole* and *Tide of Stone*, and seven short story collections, including the multi award-winning *Through Splintered Walls*. Her most recent novella, *Into Bones Like Oil* was nominated for the Stoker Award. "A Positive" won the Aurealis Award.

A Positive
Kaaron Warren

NOT LONG AFTER my father killed my mother, I removed him to a special home.

"I'm taking you somewhere nice, Dad. They've got big TV and lots of food."

"Why can't I stay with you?" I thought of the shit in the seams of his trousers, the smell of him. He was so helpless. Such a child.

"It's for the best."

I carried his empty suitcase to the front door.

"Got my Agatha Christie books in there?"

"Yep."

"And my photos? And my postcards? And my pyjamas?"

"All there, Dad."

I patted him. "You'll love it. I'll visit often," I said. I couldn't wait to see him settled in his new home.

The house was mine at last, and I didn't bother with a garage sale, didn't sort a thing. I called the Salvation Army and told them to take the lot. Everything. All my belongings were those of the man I used to be.

They marched up and down the stairs with load after load, and they were friendly at first, making jokes.

After a while they were dead silent, and they worked quickly.

They wouldn't look at me.

They carried out boxes of clothes, books, ornaments. Clocks and crockery. Glasses, flags, beakers, needles, syringes, stainless steel bowls, drips, magazines, photos. Papers they would burn or read. They carried out furniture.

They carried out bedspreads, sheets, towels. Toaster, fridge, TV, stereo.

"Shower curtain," I said, and they even took that. I went on inspection when they finished; they wouldn't come in.

I brought out one last armful of things; toothbrushes, soap, a hula hoop, jewellery, a bucket still crusty with blood, a pair of shoes and a teapot. I passed these over the threshold and waved my past goodbye.

It was still there, though, in the walls, the carpet, the ceiling, the smell of the place. So I hired a wallpaper stripper and a carpet remover and a floor polisher and I bought some paint and that was a full month's work for my girlfriend and me.

Then it was time to go see Dad. The pathetic little marks he'd scratched into me were gone, the memory of his light weight, too. He was always a small man. Smaller than Mum, although that made no difference to their happiness.

They married soon after they met, then spent fifteen years living the life. They never wanted kids. Kids would interfere. Kids didn't travel well or eat well and they were no good in restaurants. They cried and were dirty. They couldn't speak for years and when they finally learnt it was only to abuse you.

Mum and Dad planned to remain childless.

As I was growing up, people often said, "Were you an accident?" because Mum and Dad were so old when they had me. I eventually gathered that "accident" meant "unwanted" and truly did not want to know the answer. Thinking they were comforting me, my parents said, "No, you were the most planned baby ever," and told me why I was born. I realised then we were not a normal family; that not everyone shared blood with their father.

My parents exchanged fond glances as they told me the story of my birth. I always felt they cared about each other so much, one day they would both love me together. I was well-treated, properly schooled, impeccably fed, but the giggles and the games they saved for themselves.

"You were planned for very carefully, because your father got sick after a lifetime of being healthy. We just didn't know how to cope. We couldn't do the things we used to; he tired so easily."

"So you had me to keep you company at home," I said.

"Not quite," Mum said. "We went to so many doctors, and none of them could tell us how to bring him back to life. After weeks of tests, all they said was, 'It's middle age.' It really was a terrible time."

Dad was silent.

"So we started trying the other doctors, the ones you didn't see at hospital. Now they were a funny lot."

Dad smiled now. "They had me naked for the night air, eating raw meat to clear the toxins, swallowing byproducts I wouldn't like to discuss. And there was always the sex, of course."

"But none of it worked. He was still lethargic, so tired. He drooped about the house, driving me mad."

Mum always hated it when I was tired and weak. "Get a move on! Show some life!" she poked at me. She thought I did it on purpose.

"And then there was the doctor who made us young again," said Mum.

"And caused you to be born," said Dad.

"So you had me to keep you young?" I said.

"Yes."

"It was his blood that was the problem," Mum said. "It was old and tired. That's all. I would have given him all of mine, but we didn't match." Again, the fond smile. They sat together on their couch. I was on my chair in the corner; I had to twist to face them.

I said, "But you do match." It was one of the rare times I impressed them.

"Everything but our blood," Dad said. "My family were no use; they either had different blood or they were diseased. And the hospital wasn't interested in helping us."

I didn't know much about Dad's side of the family. There was a big fight years ago, around when I was born, and they didn't talk anymore.

"Is that why you hate them?" I said.

"One reason," Dad said. He and Mum had only ever needed each other.

"We were often at the doctor, begging him to help us," Dad said.

"Demanding, really," "Mum said. "How could we live like that, with death? We couldn't."

"Lucky you didn't die, Dad," I said. He wasn't much of a believer in luck. He always said, "Luck is what you do with your opportunities," which was okay if you got opportunities. If your parents took them all, how much luck could you expect to have?

Mum said, "The doctor told us it was a shame we didn't have a child, because it would probably have blood which wouldn't clump his. That was when the planning began."

Dad wanted a transfusion whenever I was able to provide one, so I have never been strong. As soon as I felt rich with blood, I'd be drained again. It was all they asked of me, though. I had no chores; no cleaning, cooking, visiting, politeness for me. Just that look in Dad's eye, that need, and the pain, and the life going out of me. Our special room was called the theatre. I thought that was normal, "I went to the theatre," people said, until I realised there were two kinds. I no longer boasted about having one. People only laughed, anyway.

I always knew when it was going to happen. I'd be the centre of attention, have favourite meals. We'd go for a drive one month, shopping another. I could never enjoy these special days though. I knew what was coming. And all day Dad would pinch and squeeze at me, wanting me pink and tender.

I never had an imagination, so I had nowhere to go while the transfusion was taking place. I wished the ceiling was a story book, all the cracks and lines making rabbits and bears. All I ever saw were cracks and lines. I knew them very well.

Dad liked to hum along to a bit of music in the background. I still hate anything classical. There was always that silence, between the movements, when I'd hear Dad's bad blood drip drip into the bucket, as mine was slowly entering his veins. It was perfect, that rhythm, and I imagined I could hear it over the crashing cymbals and roaring chords of Dad's favourite music.

Mum's favourite was the garden and she threw the full buckets over the flowers. I couldn't understand why she never answered when people asked her how she kept it so nice. Why didn't she tell them? So I answered for her. Just the once.

"Dad's blood," I said. I was locked in my room that day, all day, and the shock of being a bad boy kept my mouth shut for a long time. I liked it better as Mum's good boy, Dad's blood boy.

It was a private, quiet life. My pleasures came when they took their excursions. Dad would fill up, jovial and magnanimous as he took my strength, and Mum cooked my favourite casseroles and desserts for the freezer.

I was left to pretend the house was mine. Sometimes I dreamed a crash, their caravan folding in two and their blood pouring out when rescuers freed them.

And then things changed.

"Poor Old Girl needs to save her energy," Dad said, though he was the pale and shaky one. He liked to joke people thought Mum was his mother. "Old Girl," he called her. Never thought to let her have a go at me.

He lost his license, was the thing, and she'd never had hers because he did the driving. They took my pleasures away. Now, they never left the house. They sat quietly with me, listening to the blood pulsing through my veins.

Dad wanted blood every three weeks then. It got so I couldn't bear those nights at home, all three of us waiting for the others to talk, and almost the only thing we had to talk about was the next visit to the theatre.

Sometimes they discussed grandchildren as if I wasn't there. Never, I thought. I knew how they would treat a grandchild. They thought my blood was getting old. I'm not one of those types who feel better when they do the same things to the next generation of innocent children.

I began to go out at night, leaving the house without a word, slamming the door like a teenager. I wasn't sure what people did, out. I tired very easily, and would sometimes just sit in a place where there was a lot of noise, and absorb the energy.

I found there was an undertow in the city. It dragged me, without a fight, to kindred spirits. Damaged people without armour.

I went to one of those bars where people are whipped and manacled, because I knew about receiving pain. I'd been strapped down, pierced, drained, all my life, but I'd never liked it. They gave me a whip to use but I wasn't strong enough. Under the lights you could see my thin arms. It was very warm in there although I'm usually cold. You could see how many times I'd saved my father's life, a record of tracks.

Someone was impressed. It was a woman, with a black cowl over her face to cover the criss cross scars there, her body shrouded, her voice low, her fingers cool. I wouldn't take her offered drink, but allowed her into my car. I agreed to drive her home.

I stayed with her for two days. It was the longest I had been away from my parents, and I felt breathless without them.

We ate pizza and drank wine, and I told her my life. She was sickened. Sickened, a scarred woman hiding in black.

She said, "Why do you agree to it? You're an adult."

I had often tried to answer this question, alone, in the dark, thinking terrible thoughts in the middle of the night. When I was young, it had all seemed so normal; when I realised it wasn't, I was embarrassed, like an abused child, or children in a strange religion. Now, it's the guilt, mostly, and the fact that I've never lost my need for approval. They liked having me close by and I was too weak to move away. I didn't finish school, which Dad found irritating. He said intelligence was only a matter of looking and learning. They learnt how to give transfusions, didn't they, by watching? Mum going to hospital once and watching the whole thing. It was Mum who did it; Dad hated the sight of blood. He always kept his head turned away.

I didn't need a job either. They gave me plenty of money. I never wanted for anything.

"I don't know," I said.

I began to suffocate in her arms. She was draining love from me, swallowing it in breathless gulps. So I returned home.

I had never heard my father raise his voice; now he screamed, screeched, called me a killer. I said, "Who am I supposed to have killed?"

"Me, me," he said. He took my wrist and tried to lead me to the theatre.

"No," I said.

"What do you mean?" Mum said. Her face looked dark, damaged.

"I'm not giving blood anymore. I need it all for myself."

My father wailed. My mother cried. "Where were you?" Mum said.

"With my girlfriend."

My father stopped wailing to snort.

I went to my room.

Each day my mother grew fearful, my father begged and drooled, and I yearned for my girlfriend. So I went to my girl in black. I never imagined my mother was in danger. Their blood didn't match.

I stayed away for two nights. She wanted to meet my parents. I said, "Soon." We went for a drive in the country, to the old boarding house where she kept her mother and we watched her mother take a bath.

It was very quiet when I returned home. Quieter than usual; I could hear no pottering. The house seemed darker, and colder. But I could be inventing. Could be the house was the same as ever, and it was only afterwards I turned it into something else.

I found Dad lying on his bed in the theatre, waiting for his transfusion. The room smelt so very clean, compared to the world outside its walls.

Dad told me the story. He told it in a wheedling tone, he told me the truth, hoping it would make me help him.

"You hadn't been here for weeks," he said. To him, I only existed in the theatre, or when we were preparing for it. "And I was very ill. So I wanted your mother to do that one small thing for me. Just once. It's not like I ever asked her before." He led me around the house, indicating a wall, a room, making me look at nothing.

"But her blood was no good for you."

"That's what she always said. But I thought, maybe she's lying. Maybe it was always good. And when she said no, no, no, all I could see was red. She was cooking the potatoes how you like them, in case you came home, and I said I'd do it. But I saw red.

"I just scratched her, I thought, so I could see the blood, see if it was OK, but it wasn't."

And neither was she. My father wept and snuffled in a corner in the kitchen, denying what he had done, not looking at the proof before his eyes.

I had no time to prepare myself. I felt greater grief than I could have imagined; this woman had cared for me, kept me alive, kept me clean and fed.

We were always good at secrets. We took Mum's body away to the country and buried it. We were the only ones who would miss her.

Dad never got another drop of blood. He was probably addicted to it; he suffered. He seemed to get old very quickly. Was it Mum's death, or having to live with his own blood?

Dad finally paid attention to me. He followed me around like a little lamb, and I loved ignoring him. He didn't complain. He shrugged and sighed.

He became quite tender towards me, remembering things which never happened, emotions we never shared. Then one day he reminded me of the truth.

"Sometimes you just have to be patient. We had to wait those first few months while you grew your own blood, to take the place of your mother's. I didn't want anybody else's blood. Only yours." He said it casually, as if we had all been involved in the decision. I think he thought he'd talk me into going back to it.

We had a lovely time alone, Dad and I. He'd talk and I wouldn't listen. I cooked food he disliked or couldn't digest, and I locked the door of the theatre and kept the key on a nail out of his reach. I never washed him, till he hated the stink of himself. I sprayed him with after shave and perfume, toilet deodoriser, and laughed as he cringed from me.

None of it was enough.

It was never going to be enough. I wanted him used, drained, sucked out.

I took my girlfriend home to look at Dad.

We stood outside his bedroom window as the sun rose and watched him struggling from his bed to greet the day. He slept naked; I wouldn't help him into his pyjamas.

My girlfriend thought he was perfect. She helped me get the suitcase down from the cupboard, and watched from the car while I cajoled him out of the house. We laughed all the way there, her hand on my thigh. We felt committed; both our parents would be in the same home.

It brought tears to my eyes. It was only a small place, just a few mothers and fathers, ancient things; this one guilty of sexual abuse; that one of beatings; that mother nagged still, her purple tongue swollen from some unprescribed drug. My girlfriend's mother had her skin scrubbed in the bath. And scrubbed. And we could visit any time. We could watch it, stare at them, hate them even more.

I dropped him off and went to my own home. He saw something he didn't like before I left; his own greedy need perhaps, in someone else's eyes.

I said, "You'll fit right in, Dad. "They'll love you."

He fought like a demon to come back home with me.

My girlfriend and I visited often. We joked about our parents falling in love; everyone loved Dad there. The other residents and their occasional visitors. People loved to make him bleed, because he hated the sight of it. They pinned open his eyes and made him watch as they cut off a little toe and sold it to the highest bidder. They took his blood, plucked his white stringy hair, shaved his body. We watched from the gallery, my girlfriend and I, and we talked quietly about love and revenge.

You just have to be patient. You just have to wait until they're old and helpless.

Dad was in good company. One old man was daily raped and forced to perform orally. He liked it at first, I was told, but soon learned fear. A woman was hit every time she opened her mouth and sometimes when she didn't. She soon learned to bite her tongue.

In the dining room, hungry old people sat in front of food they hated. Some of it was mouldy, all of it was cold. They had to eat what was in front of them.

All the rooms were small and dark.

I felt unwonted tenderness when they let Dad wander the grounds in his nightshirt, a small figure with a painted face, laughter drawn in red around his mouth. He stroked and patted every part of his body. I imagined he was memorising it for the day it would be taken away from him completely.

GENEVIEVE VALENTINE is a novelist, comic book writer, and cultural critic.

La beauté sans vertu
Genevieve Valentine

THESE DAYS THEY use arms from corpses—age fourteen, oldest, at time of death. The couture houses pay for them, of course (the days of grave-robbing are over, this is a business), but anything over fourteen isn't worth having. At fourteen, the bones have most of the length you need for a model, with a child's slender ulna, the knob of the wrist still standing out enough to cast a shadow.

The graft scars are just at the shoulder, like a doll's arm. The surgeons are artists, and the seams are no wider than a silk thread. The procedure's nearly perfect by now, and the commitment of the doctors is respected. Models' fingertips always go a little black, tending to the purple; no one points it out.

Maria's already nineteen when the House of Centifolia picks her up. You don't want them any younger than that if you're going to keep them whole and working for the length of their contract. You want someone with a little stamina.

The publicity team decides to make England her official home country, because that sounds just exotic enough to intrigue without actually being from a country that worries people, so Maria spends six months secluded, letting her arms heal, living on a juice fast, and learning how to fire her English with a cut-glass accent.

The walk she already had, of course. That's how a girl gets noticed by an agency to start with, by having that sharp, necessary stride where the head stays fixed and the rest of her limbs seem to clatter in that careless way that makes the clothes look four times more expensive than they are. Nothing else is any good. They film the girls and map their faces frame by frame until they can walk so precisely the coordinates never move.

She's perfect from the first take. The House seeds Maria's audition video as classified amateur footage leaked by mistake so everyone gets interested, then pretends to crack down on security so people think her identity was a hidden asset and they got a glimpse of something clandestine. She becomes the industry's sixteenth most searched-for name.

Rhea, the head of the House, likes the look of her ("Something miserable in the turn of the mouth," she says with great satisfaction, already sketching). Maria does one season as an exclusive for Centifolia's fall collection that year, opening a single catwalk in a black robe weighed down with thirteen pounds of embroidery, her feet spearing the floor and her hands curled into fists. After that the press comes calling.

"The Princess of Roses and Diamonds," the *Bespoke* headline calls her, conjuring the old fairy tale in an article nobody reads. People just look at the photos. She scales the dragon statue on the Old Bridge in thousand-dollar jeans; she perches in the frame of an open window with her hair dragging in the wind like a ghost is pulling her through; she stands naked in a museum and holds a ball gown against her chest.

The photographer can't stop taking pictures of her face—half in shadow, half-hidden by her hair as the wind plays with the cuffs of her silk shirt. Her thin, borrowed wrists curve out of the arm of a coat; an earring looks as if it's trying to crawl in her ear just to be closer.

She's already very good about turning down questions without making it seem like she's actually turned them down; roses and diamonds fall from her lips. No one bothers with the interview, where she talks just as she's supposed to about the curated past Centifolia drilled into her. Six months' prep for nothing.

There's the occasional complaint, of course (from outside, always, those inside a couture house wouldn't dream of it). But it's a precision business. The models don't even suffer phantom aches from their old arms. The doctors clean up anything else that's wrong while they're in there, as a special service—faltering thyroids and kidney troubles and moles that are suspicious or unsightly. These girls are an investment; they're meant to live.

The Old Baroque Concert Hall is on the edge of town, and only the House of Centifolia's long history and Rhea's name could get anyone from the industry crowd to come out this far.

The runway snakes across most of the derelict space, weaving back in on itself in a pattern that came to Rhea in a dream—it reminded her of the journey through life, and of the detox trip she took to Austria.

The narrow walkway crosses itself at different sloping elevations to mimic the mountain trails; the oily pool sliding beneath it all reflects the muted tones of this season's collection, and pays homage to the foot-buckets of cold and hot water in the Austrian spa that drained lipids and negative thoughts from the body.

With thirty-five looks in the fall collection and six points of varying heights across which the meandering runway connects—"It's more of a maze than a trail," Rhea explains to potential choreographers, "it's very spiritual"—the timing has to be precise, but there are only two windows in which the girls are available to practice: once during the fitting the day before, and once mere hours before the show.

Three of the models have to be fired for having scheduled another show the day before this one, which makes them traitors to the House (you don't book something else without permission, rookie mistake, Rhea cuts them so fast one of them gets thrown out of a cab), and the three alternates have to be called up and fitted. It means six hours of all the girls standing in the unheated warehouse, loose-limbed and pliant as they're ordered to be for fittings, while assistants yank them in and out of outfits and take snapshots until the new assignments emerge and they're allowed to go rehearse.

The choreographer—he has a name, but no one dares use it when speaking of him, lest he appear before they've corrected their posture—thinks carefully for a long time. He paces the length of the runway, hopping nimbly from one level to the next at the intersections. He doubles back sharply once or twice in a way that looks, horribly convincingly, as if he's actually become lost and someone will have to risk breaking ranks to go get him. Then he reaches the end, nods as if satisfied, points to six places on the stage, and shouts, "The girls, please!"

There were two girls—there are always two, so one can be made an example of.

The one who was kind to an old beggar woman was gifted with the roses and diamonds that dropped from her mouth with every word; the one who refused to get water for a princess to drink spent the rest of her life vomiting vipers and toads.

As a girl, Rhea listened and understood what she wasn't being told. (It's how she climbed to the top of a couture house. Rhea hears.)

The one who was kind married a prince, and spent the rest of her life granting audiences and coughing up bouquets and necklaces for the guests. The one who refused was driven into the forest, where there was no one who wanted anything fetched, and she could spit out a viper any time she needed venom, and she never had to speak again.

The runway's barely finished. The polymer designed to look like luminous soil hasn't quite dried, and the models sink half an inch with every step. They don't mention it; their job is to walk, not to speak.

The idea is the ringing of a bell, which starts with a single tone being struck and builds in its echoes until every strike becomes a symphony. One girl will walk out first, then two closer behind one another, then four. It should build until every outfit can be seen perfectly and in full only at the first turn. The reveal is precious and fleeting, and isn't meant to last.

After that the show becomes the girls in formation like waves of sound, and the wash of the looks across the runways as they pass. Spectators, no matter where along the uneven rings of bleachers they may be sitting, should be in awe. There should always be more to look at than anyone can catch, that sense of being doomed to miss something wonderful; that's how a presentation becomes a show.

"Angry walks, quiet faces!" the choreographer calls, clapping his hands emphatically, slightly off from the beat of the music.

The first girl, an unknown from the ranks who was chosen to lead the show because her eyes are sunk so deep in their sockets that they look like diamond chips, shakes the boards with every step, trying desperately to keep her face quiet and look forward while still watching the choreographer for signs of disapproval.

The girls who follow the beat of the music get corrected—one sharp flick on the shoulder with a steel pen—by the PA as they come around the first big turn. The ones who follow the clapping are also wrong, but they don't know it until the second turn, and the assistant choreographer can't flick shoulders without knocking them into the reflecting pool, where the water has already been oiled (too early) and would cost a fortune to re-gloss before showtime.

Eventually the choreographer gives up on trying to explain the vision to a bunch of girls who can't even walk on the right beat, and he resorts to a cap gun, fired twice at each model as she passes the first turn to give her the metronome ticks of her stride. The shape of things visibly improves, but they spend another hour after that on quiet faces, because for a bunch of girls who claim they're professional, they flinch like you wouldn't believe.

Maria knows, from her real home, how you make silk. You boil the pupae and draw out the single filament of their cocoons from the steam, a pot of glistening threads with maggots roiling underneath.

There's no thread like it; it works miracles.

The action group ends up calling itself Mothers Against Objectification of Young Women. There had been some impassioned complaining early on during the drafting and ratification of bylaws and clauses that young men were also being objectified, probably, and it was important to make sure they felt included. But one of the internal factions pointed out that then the acronym would just be MAO, and the moment of patriotic consumer hesitation lasted just long enough for Young Women to reassert itself as the primary concern.

Mothers Against Objectification of Young Women pickets the House of Centifolia show; Rhea's been a target ever since Maria stood naked in the photograph with that ball gown in front of her, and there was more parking this far on the edge of town than near the tents in the city center. The different factions arrive two hours early, pile out with signs and fliers, and stand not-quite-near each other, as close to the door as security allows.

"Modesty is the greatest beauty!" they shout. "Keep your arms to yourself!" "Role models, not clothes models!" Role models of what, they never reach; the shouting cycles through to "Shame on the industry!" next from the oldest ones, and a few rugged idealists try their best to sneak in "American jobs!" in between the agreed-upon call and response.

The attendees squeal with delight, shifting their gold-leafed invitations under their arms so they can photograph the Mothers Against on the way inside. "Trust Rhea to provide immersive atmosphere before you even go through the doors," one of the reporters says into his recorder, shaking his head. "This collection is going to be such an amazing statement about the cultural position of the industry."

A group of audience hopefuls gathers to the right of the door crew, hoping they'll be allowed to sneak in and fill seats for the no-shows. A few of them— Fashion Week veterans who have done shows long enough to gauge the capacity of a venue from the outside—realize it will be standing room only, and start to cry. One tries to make a desperate run for it, and is still taking photographs of the interior as security lifts her away, her shoes dangling a few inches in the air above their shoes. She's a blogger, and her shoes are white brocade; the picture she takes of her feet floating between their feet will get the most click-thumbs of her whole Fashion Week report.

Mothers Against Objectification of Young Women gets increasingly concerned as spectators file in. Several of the young women are wearing revealing shirts that don't look at all American-made, one or two are wearing shirts cut straight down to the waist despite the risk of sunburn, and one woman is sixty if she's a day, wearing a shirt that's absolutely transparent except for the enormous middle finger appliqué carefully fastened to the front with tiny, elegant studs.

As she passes, she gives the MAOYM a single, long look through eyes that have been made up with a line of driftwood flakes along her eyebrows. It looks like two mouths full of teeth. By the time she's passed them and vanished inside, the Mothers Against have faltered so badly they have to start the chanting over from the beginning.

The Princess of Roses and Diamonds is closing out the show. It's supposed to be a wedding dress—traditionally, a wedding dress still closes runway shows, the pinnacle of womanly expectation nothing can shake—but Rhea wouldn't stoop to send a white wedding gown down the runway unless she could finally figure out how to stabilize the chalk filaments she's been working on.

Instead, the dress is carefully woven on a frame of horizontal reeds looped around Maria's body like scaffolding, laced in vertical threads of silk dyed the colors of earliest morning—nearly black, deep blue, murky gray, a sliver of gold—and not fastened. No seams, no knots; the thread is loosely looped at arbitrary heights, just waiting to slip free.

"It will fall apart," Rhea explains to her in a voice like a church, as the six assistants ease Maria into the gown and weave the entry panel closed. "It's supposed to. This is the chrysalis from which the moth emerges and takes flight. Help it."

Maria looks at the mirror, where the last two assistants are looping the final threads. Rhea's looking at the mirror too, her eyes brimming with tears, and Maria realizes this must be a masterpiece, that she must be wearing something that will be important later. It's important that this fragility turn into a pile of thread and reed hoops, because nothing beautiful lasts.

Maria's meant to go out and walk the runway until she's naked, to prove that nothing beautiful lasts.

Silk moths can't fly. It's been bred out of them for five thousand years. The adults are only needed to make more worms. Most aren't meant to live long enough to break the chrysalis; flight's an unnecessary trait.

The Princess of Roses and Diamonds swallowed blood for the rest of her life, every time she opened her mouth.

The capacity of the auditorium is four hundred seats, and fire rules are very strict this far into the old side of town, where there's God-knows-what piled up in the abandoned buildings and it takes a fire truck longer to reach you if anything goes up in flames. But by the time Rhea's show starts, they're running 476, not counting crew.

The program outlining the thirty-five looks becomes a scarce collectible (highest offer, seven hundred dollars) before the lights even go down. The guests who had their places reserved for them with a little place card hand-engraved with poured gold on a sliver of mother-of-pearl don't see one clear second of the show because of all the people standing in the aisles and blocking the view.

"Democracy Comes to Fashion," runs the headline in *The Walk* the next day, under a picture of the lead model with the pair of girls behind her closing in, the shot framed perfectly by the shoulders of two people who turn the rest of the runway into a curtain of black.

The models are terrified—half the reason the sequin jackets and metallic-thread tartans look so impressive is how roughly they're shaking—but they walk as they're meant to walk, their purpling fingers held to showcase their knuckle rings, their gazes fixed, heads steady and bodies a series of angles dressed in clothes that make one aspire, crisscrossing one another within a hairsbreadth of each other, just above the oil.

The press assumes that in such a display of transience, the pool was meant to be the primordial sea, to accent the flashes of gold in the clothes that must represent the minerals within the earth itself. Rhea never corrects them.

The music is a little tinny—sound check had been canceled in favor of the cap gun, and union techs don't sit around and wait for people who can't keep to a schedule—but the press assumes that's on purpose, too. "It's a recreation of the womb," writes *The Walk*, "in which the beginning of life itself is met with such overwhelming sensory input: music like whale song, extraordinary tartans layered over pinstripes with red flannel jutting out from underneath, a reminder of the vast amounts of blood that life requires."

The girls walk beautifully. All thirty-four of them.

Mothers Against Objectification of Young Women scatters as soon as Maria appears. They don't know why, since she's hardly violent about it. She's barely strong enough to open the doors.

There will be arguments among some of the Mothers later, and clauses put into the bylaws about when the picket line can be broken for humanitarian reasons and when they're expected to hold their ground.

She walks past them all without turning her head. She walks past the building and into the street and toward the empty cul-de-sac at the edge of the parking lot, where the field starts. With every step the threads shake loose—that walk is a killer, that walk gets the job done—and the first hoop's rattled to the asphalt before the Mothers Against have quite caught their breath.

It's not a mathematical process, of course—a labor of love never is—and a few of the hoops clack together as they slip down, only to be caught up in the dam of silk threads until she can jar them loose. She sheds everywhere, strands of silk in single filaments that shine along the ground like something from a fever dream, every color so expertly dyed it casts a halo against the asphalt as it falls. Once or twice threads catch and sink in a cluster all at once, and a hoop will clatter to the ground, so as she steps out of it she leaves behind a circled map to a place no one will ever reach.

She's naked long before everything finally goes, of course—a few hoops and some string do not a garment make, and the white knobs of her spine and of her borrowed wrists and blackened fingertips and the purple hollows at the backs of her knees are shaded by the deep blues and the strings of gold that are still left. She keeps walking without looking left or right. Once she hits the tall, muddy grass of the field and the gold-tipped heels of her shoes sink with the first step into the soft earth, she abandons them and continues barefoot, but she never breaks stride; she's a professional.

When she disappears into the woods beyond the field, there are three hoops hanging around her knees at strange angles, and a few vertical streaks of blue still holding them up.

After a long time, one of the Mothers Against says, "I suppose we should tell them."

One of the others—the oldest, the one wiping away tears—says, "I'll go."

The threads were mapped over the course of eight months. Rhea had a vision. She wanted a legacy.

She dyed each one by hand in a room in her apartment that got light like a Vermeer. She medicated to avoid sleep for a week so she could determine where every thread should start and end. She consulted a physicist the next week, to make sure she was right about the rate of tensile decay on a body in motion, just in case she had hallucinated during the original sketches. It wouldn't be perfect—Maria had a way of walking that no application of metrics could fully predict—but it would do what it had been made to do.

The team of dressers that wove Maria into the silk-thread gown spent the two weeks before the show locked in a hotel room with no outside connection and a half-wage stipend, with a PR vice president stationed outside to make sure no one from room service could ask them anything. Each dresser was given a garment map and practice threads from Rhea's dry runs. (She'd done sixty.) By the end of two weeks, they could do the whole dress in three hours. The day of, with the real thing, they wept once or twice as they worked; a miracle affects people in strange ways.

If it panics Rhea that her centerpiece and her prize model have vanished, no one ever gets wind of it. You don't become the head of a house by being easy to read. As soon as she hears what's happened, she cancels the finale and just orders the models to walk straight through the crowds in the aisles and hold rank outside. The attendees file out in pairs after that, past the gauntlet of thirty-four girls, and see what's left of Maria. There's a constellation of silk snakes, filaments disappearing into the tall grass, hoops leaving ghost marks where they fell, pale blue threads suspended in a little puddle of antifreeze.

No one claps. Some cry. The reporters shoulder-check each other and take hundreds of pictures at speeds that sound like someone wheezing.

"Did you see it?" the audience asks the picketers, and when the Mothers Against nod, the guests don't ask what it must have been like. They just shake the Mothers' hands, and shake their heads at Rhea as they would a brutal saint, and file silently past towards the city proper.

They never find Maria.

It could be foul play—she'd run from a house to which she owed at least six figures. There were consequences when a girl bolted on a contract, and Rhea would have taken the loss rather than let such an artist move under someone else's roof. Centifolia signed girls for life; casualties were a cost of doing business.

The cops don't make a particularly thorough search for Maria. If she's moved couture houses without approval it's a legal matter above their pay grade, and if she's vanished in the process it's a business matter, and they'll never find the body.

There are routine checks on the morgue from time to time, but they figure in that case the call will come in to them. She was healthy unless her arms malfunctioned, so it could be a while, and they'll know if something happened: Maria's is a face not even death could hide.

The girl who opened the show becomes a media darling. Someone at *Bespoke* decides she must have known what was wrong and had bravely decided to begin the show anyway, and it catches on. Rhea's team tells her to let them believe it. It's a good angle, and somebody's got to close out the spring show. They're working on a new image for her, maybe something with mermaids, something with ghosts; the sunken eyes, they've decided, will become her trademark. Rhea starts dying fabrics for her.

When the press goes wild for the story, and the MAOYM find themselves at the center of more attention than their clauses had ever planned for, a lot of things happen. Some just amplify their slogans regarding the right kind of woman, with the unblinking intensity television can lend someone, and get picked up for church work. Some split from all that and argue for transparency and freedom of industry, and precipitate updates to regulations in some of the major Houses.

The oldest Mother Against—the one who broke the news about Maria to an assistant who thanked her, threw up, and sprinted for Rhea—left the organization before she ever got in her car to go home.

Sometimes she drives all the way out to the edge of town and stands in the doorway of the Old Baroque, where the runway was never torn down, and looks from the runway to the trees on the far side of the field. The dye from one of the silk threads has held fast to the asphalt all this time, a dusting of gold pointing to the place between two trees where Maria disappeared.

Maybe she lives in the woods, the old woman thinks. She doesn't know why that comforts her.

The runway's going to seed. Reeds have sprouted from the oily pool, and there are beginning to be frogs, and the moss has started to grow over the sharp edges, a pool of pale blue algae skimming every imprint of a shoe.

The nail polish for spring is from Centifolia, in collaboration with Count Eleven. Out of the Vagary beauty line they design that year, the most popular by a factor of ten is the shade called The Woman Vanishes; it's a hundred dollars a bottle, and was sold out before it ever saw the inside of a store.

It's nearly black, tending a little purple. You dip your whole fingertip in it, so it looks like the blood has pooled.

LUCY TAYLOR is an award-winning author who has published seven novels and over a hundred short stories in anthologies and magazines. Her most recent work can be found in the anthologies *The Big Book of Blasphemy*, *Cutting Edge*, *A Fistful of Dinosaurs*, and *Vagabond 001, 002*, and *003*. Her Stoker Award-winning novel, *The Safety of Unknown Cities*, was recently reprinted in German by Festa Verlag Publications and is currently being translated into Russian by Poltergeist Press. Taylor lives in the high desert outside Santa Fe, New Mexico.

Subsumption
Lucy Taylor

ANIKKA HUNKERS AGAINST the empty water tank as Baris twists the lock on Salvation's inner door, two feet of reinforced concrete and steel leading to a mudroom with a twelve-foot ladder leading topside. He starts to climb.

Outside the scraping and cracking have begun again, just like last night after the generator failed. Persistent, rhythmic. Something or someone trying to get in?

"Wait!" she says.

He looks down. "What?"

"We don't know what's out there."

"You're right. But we don't have a choice." His lightly accented voice drifts down to her, pure Gujarati, and she's reminded why she loves him, his steady, calming voice and fierce black eyes, his stoic acceptance of the unimaginable. They'd met at the lab where Anikka's father worked (*works* she tells herself) in Los Alamos, New Mexico. It was Baris who'd helped them design Salvation, the name her father gave to the forty-two feet of galvanized corrugated pipe buried fifteen feet down in the mountains near Raton Pass west of Chama.

"The end has to come at some point," her father said, while he was laying out the plans for Salvation. "The only question is what form it comes in."

Lucky us, Anikka thinks, *now we've got the chance to find out*.

Outside the sounds are sharper, more invasive. Anikka looks up at Baris on the ladder. "If it's something horrible, something we can't survive, remember what you promised."

He pats the .9mm Luger on his hip. "You first. I'll be right after."

She feels absurdly comforted.

He engages the automatic lift mechanism. The camouflaged blast hatch powers open to a cacophony of snapping, creaking. Bones breaking on a torture rack, Anikka thinks.

As Baris exits, she begins to climb. A moment later, his laughter shocks her. "A tree fell across the hatch. Just branches, that's all it was!"

She exhales.

Topside, strands of hazy light filter through dusky, dog-turd clouds, but around them spread the piñon-juniper woodlands, unchanged as far as she can tell. She takes a shallow breath. Frowns. The air has an acrid taste now, a pungent smoky scent, richly fertilized soil underlain with the tang of decay. Baris sniffs cautiously, his right eye twitching as it does when he's confused.

"Smells strange," he says.

"Maybe the fires around Denver."

"Yeah. Chemicals." He mutters something in Gujurati. A prayer, Anikka thinks, and wishes they'd had time to stock the gas masks.

Once it started, there wasn't much time for anything. The first wave of bolides struck the northern hemisphere the day after Memorial Day in the States, late May of 2021. Fireballs at -14 brightness, twice as bright as a full moon, rained like missiles over huge sections of the planet, even as debate still raged whether they were rocky or metallic asteroids or something intelligent, an alien attack. No one agreed. Locked inside Salvation, while the ham radio still worked, they got news of inconceivable destruction—central Asia, Alaska, everything from Minnesota down to Mexico and east was sheeted in walls of fire hundreds of feet high.

Annika has steeled herself to emerge into a charred moonscape, the Old Earth reduced to ash and bones. What she sees now is so contrary to her expectations that her reeling brain struggles to accept it—darkly verdant hillsides thick with Ponderosa pines, junipers and aspen whose silver bark glows like polished pewter.

"How is this possible?" she gasps.

"Who knows? We got lucky. Let's find your dad."

They hoist their packs, check the compass, and head southwest toward Los Alamos. If Anikka's father's still alive, he'll be waiting for them.

A few miles on, they find a road that the topo map tells them will intersect with 285 just west of Chama. A breeze picks up. The swirling air grows dense with tiny particles. Anikka tells herself it's pollen from the golden chamisa that crowd the verge. Baris starts to cough, which is when she hears the voices. She grabs his arm, signals him to hush.

People coming.

A woman's querulous voice and then a harsh male one. Anikka can't make out the words, but she knows anguish when she hears it. They slide among the trees and crouch as a small band, four men and a woman, crests the hill. They trudge single-file, armed with rifles and AK-47's. All wear black bandannas over their mouths and noses, but for the stooped man in the lead. His bandanna is a startling green and appears to cause him pain, judging by how he shakes his head back and forth. Still he makes no effort to adjust it.

The group halts on the roadside, and a heated argument ensues—two of the men bellowing invective back and forth. A third man intervenes. Green Bandanna starts limping toward the trees, alone. The woman, young and burly and heavily tattooed, pulls out her pistol, racks the slide, and fires. Green Bandanna's head explodes into scarlet and smoke.

One of the men douses the body with accelerant and throws a match. The woman lingers a few minutes while the others leave. Then she crosses herself and follows.

Anikka and Baris whisper together and adjust their plan, taking into account the danger from other travelers. They'll avoid the roads and bushwhack whenever possible, staying within the shelter of the trees.

They make their way in silence, each stunned by the execution they've just witnessed.

Finally Anikka says, "That man they killed, he must've had plague."

"We don't know that."

"My father said first impact might not be the worst of this. He said the bolides could bring contaminants that would disperse when they hit."

"That makes it sound like there was intelligence behind this, like something or someone planned it. There wasn't, Nikka. Shit flies through space all the time. Earth just happened to get in the way."

"But they burned the body."

"Maybe he didn't deserve a decent burial. Maybe he was an enemy. Somebody from the wrong tribe."

"So already we're dividing into tribes?" The possibility makes her throat constrict. "What's that, the first step on the way to the Stone Age?"

He laughs and kisses her neck.

She rips cloth from her shirt tail to improvise bandannas. Again she laments the gas masks they forgot to stock. Other things, too. Like guava jelly and macadamia nuts and caviar and Brie. So many things she longs for now and wishes she could taste again.

Something flashes in her peripheral vision. She's just fast enough to glimpse a covey of quail, lightning fast as they dart for hiding. She permits herself a tiny gust of pleasure. She's always liked quail. Glad to see that some survived.

The afternoon looks much like morning, hazy under a parade of low-hanging clouds that pass ponderously, like tame elephants. At a pond, they purify some water and rest in the shade. Beneath the trees, Anikka notices the soil is soft and spongey, although there's no sign of recent rain. Gazing into the maze of trees, she spies an odd growth, a mottled, oval flower with a striking emerald center that appears to sprout from a juniper trunk. She blinks, trying to reconcile what she's seeing with what she's *not* seeing.

She nudges Baris.

"What is that?"

It takes him a moment to spot what she's pointing at and become concerned enough to tell her to stay there while he investigates. She goes with him, of course. And when he sucks in his breath and looks away, she studies more intently, willing herself to see something else, to realize it's just a trick of light that causes her to think the spine of the man slumped there is fused with the tree and that the outline of a juniper branch isn't visible through the papery skin of his throat.

He leans against the tree in a way that suggests sleep, except for the roots that snake around his legs and the glimpses of exposed femur that disturb the architectural balance of flesh and root system.

"It looks like the tree's absorbing him," she says, her tone replete with the awe and wonder of one who comes upon a nature god inside his leafy temple. But then the ruined legs spasm down and up, a croak issue from the mangled throat, and Anikka claps a hand across her gut and doubles over.

In a surreal display of effort, the head raises, lolls, fights to find a balance point on the engorged neck. The mouth twists and contorts, and a hand paws the eyes where thin green shoots have knit themselves among the brows and lips and lashes, handiwork of a sadistic seamstress or a darkly comic one.

"Who would do this?" Baris says as what once was human fights to breathe, and Anikka doesn't answer, not knowing how to tell him no one did anything, that this is now the nature of the world.

"We need to clear his airway," Baris says and slides his thumbs inside the corners of the man's mouth, trying to work free the obstructions. When this fails, he grabs his knife, flicks out the blade.

"No!" Anikka says.

Baris strokes the man's forehead and talks soothingly, as though what he is about to do is normal. "Don't be afraid. I'm only going to cut some of this away."

Bunches of tightly-clumped, dark needles fall to the forest floor, but so does blood—a lot of it. Anikka yells, "You're cutting him!"

The man convulses, legs kicking out as far as the roots allow, then planking, quivering, and going limp.

"What—?"

"It's part of him. Or he's part of the tree. You can't cut one without cutting the other."

He stares at the blood dripping from the blade.

"We've got to do something," Baris says, even as pliant green filaments weave shut the lashes, sewing off sight, and Anikka only understands the one kind of help they have to offer. She unholsters her Sig Rimfire and tells Baris to move away. When she fires, the air explodes with whirring, agitated life, pollen that's insectile, comet-shaped. She runs to join Baris, holding her breath as long as she can.

Now instead of staying in the trees, they search for roads. A highway's what they're hoping for but dirt will do, anything to keep some space between them and the forest.

Evening's coming on. They find a meadow wide enough to offer some distance from the trees and shed their packs, unfold their sleeping bags. Baris spots deer tracks, says they need food and there's still enough light to make a shot. He seems angry, eager to bring down a doe or a buck. Anikka, who's just shot a man to death, feels spent and sick and not keen for killing anything. She waves him off, crawls into her bag, and slips into murky sleep.

And wakes up dreaming that Baris is inside her, thrusting furiously with a cock carved from burled wood and tipped with a black stone arrow. Her twilit brain is trying to make sense of this, when she feels the warmth between her legs and smells the blood.

Baris' sleeping bag lies empty, but she pounds it with her fist, anger and panic released with every punch. Calm descends. She lies back down, unsnaps her jeans, struggles them down over her thighs. The flashlight shows pale green, six-inch stalks and a clutch of narrow, braided roots. When she runs a finger along the tips, she feels an answering quiver deep inside, a tiny tongue-flick sensation followed by an electric jolt of pain. Her breath hitches and she sinks her front teeth into the meat of her lip, clinging to the pain for sanity.

Gingerly she pinches a stem between two fingers and tugs, praying that this parasite will slide out easily, but the thing holds fast and more blood pours.

She wraps the pliant blades around her fingers, fists her hand, lets out all her breath and yanks before she can change her mind. Her vision pinpricks. She screams to keep from fainting.

If Baris heard her cry, she knows he'd come to her. Since he doesn't, she takes the gun and flashlight and moves shakily across the meadow, into the woods.

At first it's just bark and leaves and branches she sees, the junipers and piñons, regal aspen nodding in the breeze, but the farther she goes the more nuanced her sight becomes, the more adroitly she can parse the liminal thresh-old of this realm.

She wants to call out Baris's name, but remembers too vividly those melded vertebrae, the throat crammed with juniper and bits of bark and prefers to keep her silence.

Beneath her feet, lichen-furred roots protrude from loamy soil; they forge meandering, unnatural paths, contrive to cut her off. A twisted juniper, light-ning-struck and blackened, dangles grotesque seeds, each composed of five elongated rows, white beads that clink and shake. Then eyes and brain coordi-nate to give a meaning to this horror, flensed hands and tiny fingerbones, the trellis of a wrist. Root systems from surrounding trees intertwine with carpals, skulls and shanks, the basin of a pelvic girdle garlanded with ropey coils of greyish purple meat.

She shuts off the flashlight and pads from one splash of moonlight to the next, wandering these charnel-house woods with gun in hand, shuddering each time something drips from overhead.

That Baris is the most recent addition to this tableau is evidenced by his relative intactness and the still new look of his tactical jacket and barely scuffed Wolverines. His face, once so unspeakably dear to her, is now just unspeakable. She turns away, hating him for what he's done, but hating more the loss of him. Of everything.

For a moment she sways between gusts of grief and fury.

You said I'd go first. You'd be right behind.

The forest trembles, although there is no wind. She hears the mourning of an owl and wonders if animal life is somehow immune to this, if it's no accident she sees no skins or feathers, paws or fur. Perhaps the plants are sentient now and can distinguish among types of prey. Perhaps that is the point.

Baris's gun lies in the underbrush beside him. She starts to leave it, then goes back and tries to pick it up. Vines fight her for possession, but she wins this time, only to discover that the muzzle, trigger guard, and rear sight are already clogged with coarse and tangled weeds. She throws the gun away and tries to find her way back to the meadow, but her halting progress quickly becomes a gauntlet, she's lashed and buffeted, caressed and enmeshed, a spider in a flytrap.

When she stumbles, her foot becomes entangled. Within minutes whole portions of her throat and brain are being colonized. Adrenaline floods her bloodstream. Her heart syncopates, and she goes blind and deaf in seconds. Her brain waves spike, even as a deadly languor surges through her. Only at the last, when she feels the forest infiltrate every damp and puckered pore of her honeycomb skin does she recall the magic she still wields, the quick death Baris promised and denied her, and reaches for the Sig. Brings it to her head only to find her mind contains no memory of what this object is or how she is supposed to use it or why it even matters.

There are no words.

A sound builds within her and she tries to give it voice, but other life-forms own her now, the rich nutrients of her bone and blood divvied up among a million microscopic mouths as her body is repurposed for a grander destiny.

KIJ JOHNSON's short fiction has won the Hugo, Nebula, World Fantasy, and Sturgeon Awards, as well as the Grand Prix de l'Imaginaire. She is the associate director for the Gunn Center for the Study of Science Fiction at the University of Kansas, where she is also an associate professor. "Spar" won the Nebula Award for short story.

Spar
Kij Johnson

IN THE TINY lifeboat, she and the alien fuck endlessly, relentlessly.

They each have Ins and Outs. Her Ins are the usual, eyes ears nostrils mouth cunt ass. Her Outs are also the common ones: fingers and hands and feet and tongue. Arms. Legs. Things that can be thrust into other things.

The alien is not humanoid. It is not bipedal. It has cilia. It has no bones, or perhaps it does and she cannot feel them. Its muscles, or what might be muscles, are rings and not strands. Its skin is the color of dusk and covered with a clear thin slime that tastes of snot. It makes no sounds. She thinks it smells like wet leaves in winter, but after a time she cannot remember that smell, or leaves, or winter.

Its Ins and Outs change. There are dark slashes and permanent knobs that sometimes distend, but it is always growing new Outs, hollowing new Ins. It cleaves easily in both senses.

It penetrates her a thousand ways. She penetrates it, as well.

The lifeboat is not for humans. The air is too warm, the light too dim. It is too small. There are no screens, no books, no warning labels, no voices, no bed or chair or table or control board or toilet or telltale lights or clocks. The ship's hum is steady. Nothing changes.

There is no room. They cannot help but touch. They breathe each other's breath—if it breathes; she cannot tell. There is always an Out in an In, something wrapped around another thing, flesh coiling and uncoiling inside, outside. Making spaces. Making space.

She is always wet. She cannot tell whether this is the slime from its skin, the oil and sweat from hers, her exhaled breath, the lifeboat's air. Or come.

Her body seeps. When she can, she pulls her mind away. But there is nothing else, and when her mind is disengaged she thinks too much. Which is: at all. Fucking the alien is less horrible.

She does not remember the first time. It is safest to think it forced her.

The wreck was random: a mid-space collision between their ship and the alien's, simultaneously a statistical impossibility and a fact. She and Gary just had time to start the emergency beacon and claw into their suits before their ship was cut in half. Their lifeboat spun out of reach. Her magnetic boots clung to part of the wreck. His did not. The two of them fell apart.

A piece of debris slashed through the leg of Gary's suit to the bone, through the bone. She screamed. He did not. Blood and fat and muscle swelled from his suit into vacuum. Out.

The alien's vessel also broke into pieces, its lifeboat kicking free and the waldos reaching out, pulling her through the airlock. In.

Why did it save her? The mariner's code? She does not think it knows she is alive. If it did it would try to establish communication. It is quite possible that she is not a rescued castaway. She is salvage, or flotsam.

She sucks her nourishment from one of the two hard intrusions into the featureless lifeboat, a rigid tube. She uses the other, a second tube, for whatever comes from her, her shit and piss and vomit. Not her come, which slicks her thighs to her knees.

She gags a lot. It has no sense of the depth of her throat. Ins and Outs.

There is a time when she screams so hard that her throat bleeds.

She tries to teach it words. "Breast," she says. "Finger. Cunt." Her vocabulary options are limited here.

"Listen to me," she says. "Listen. To. Me." Does it even have ears?

The fucking never gets better or worse. It learns no lessons about pleasing her. She does not learn anything about pleasing it either: would not if she could. And why? How do you please grass and why should you? She suddenly remembers grass, the bright smell of it and its perfect green, its cool clean soft feel beneath her bare hands.

She finds herself aroused by the thought of grass against her hands, because it is the only thing that she has thought of for a long time that is not the alien or Gary or the Ins and Outs. But perhaps its soft blades against her fingers would feel like the alien's cilia. Her ability to compare anything with anything else is slipping from her, because there is nothing to compare.

She feels it inside everywhere, tendrils moving in her nostrils, thrusting against her eardrums, coiled beside the corners of her eyes. And she sheathes herself in it.

When an Out crawls inside her and touches her in certain places, she tips her head back and moans and pretends it is more than accident. It is Gary, he loves me, it loves me, it is a He. It is not.

Communication is key, she thinks.

She cannot communicate, but she tries to make sense of its actions.

What is she to it? Is she a sex toy, a houseplant? A shipwrecked Norwegian sharing a spar with a monolingual Portuguese? A companion? A habit, like nail-biting or compulsive masturbation? Perhaps the sex is communication and she just doesn't understand the language yet.

Or perhaps there is no It. It is not that they cannot communicate, that she is incapable; it is that the alien has no consciousness to communicate with. It is a sex toy, a houseplant, a habit.

On the starship with the name she cannot recall, Gary would read aloud to her. Science fiction, Melville, poetry. Her mind cannot access the plots, the words. All she can remember is a few lines from a sonnet, "Let me not to the marriage of true minds admit impediments"—something something something—"an ever-fixèd mark that looks on tempests and is never shaken; it is the star to every wand'ring bark...."

She recites the words, an anodyne that numbs her for a time until they lose their meaning. She has worn them treadless, and they no longer gain any traction in her mind. Eventually she cannot even remember the sounds of them.

If she ever remembers another line, she promises herself she will not wear it out. She will hoard it. She may have promised this before, and forgotten.

She cannot remember Gary's voice. Fuck Gary, anyway. He is dead and she is here with an alien pressed against her cervix.

It is covered with slime. She thinks that, as with toads, the slime may be a mild psychotropic drug. How would she know if she were hallucinating? In this world, what would that look like? Like sunflowers on a desk, like Gary leaning across a picnic basket to place fresh bread in her mouth. The bread is the first thing she has tasted that feels clean in her mouth, and it's not even real.

Gary feeding her bread and laughing. After a time, the taste of bread becomes "the taste of bread" and then the words become mere sounds and stop meaning anything.

On the off-chance that this will change things, she drives her tongue though its cilia, pulls them into her mouth and sucks them clean. She has no idea whether it makes a difference. She has lived forever in the endless reeking fucking now.

Was there someone else on the alien's ship? Was there a Gary, lost now to space? Is it grieving? Does it fuck her to forget, or because it has forgotten? Or to punish itself for surviving? Or the other, for not?

Or is this her?

When she does not have enough Ins for its Outs, it makes new ones. She bleeds for a time and then heals. She pretends that this is a rape. Rape at least she could understand. Rape is an interaction. It requires intention. It would imply that it hates or fears or wants. Rape would mean she is more than a wine glass it fills.

This goes both ways. She forces it. Her hands are blades that tear new Ins. Her anger pounds at it until she feels its depths grow soft under her fist, as though bones or muscle or cartilage have disassembled and turned to something else.

And when she forces her hands into the alien? If intent counts, then what she does, at least, is a rape—or would be if the alien felt anything, responded in any fashion. Mostly it's like punching a wall.

She puts her fingers in herself, because she at least knows what her intentions are.

Sometimes she watches it fuck her, the strange coiling of its Outs like a shock-wave thrusting into her body, and this excites her and horrifies her; but at least it is not Gary. Gary, who left her here with this, who left her here, who left.

One time she feels something break loose inside the alien, but it is immediately drawn out of reach. When she reaches farther in to grasp the broken piece, a sphincter snaps shut on her wrist. Her arm is forced out. There is a bruise like a bracelet around her wrist for what might be a week or two.

She cannot stop touching the bruise. The alien has had the ability to stop her fist inside it, at any time. Which means it has made a choice not to stop her, even when she batters things inside it until they grow soft.

This is the only time she has ever gotten a reaction she understands. Stimulus: response. She tries many times to get another. She rams her hands into it, kicks it, tries to tear its cilia free with her teeth, claws its skin with her ragged, filthy fingernails. But there is never again the broken thing inside, and never the bracelet.

For a while, she measures time by bruises she gives herself. She slams her shin against the feeding tube, and when the bruise is gone she does it again. She estimates it takes twelve days for a bruise to heal. She stops after a time because she cannot remember how many bruises there have been.

She dreams of rescue, but doesn't know what that looks like. Gary, miraculously alive pulling her free, eyes bright with tears, I love you he says, his lips on her eyelids and his kiss his tongue in her mouth inside her hands inside him. But that's the alien. Gary is dead. He got Out.

Sometimes she thinks that rescue looks like her opening the lifeboat to the deep vacuum, but she cannot figure out the airlock.

Her anger is endless, relentless.

Gary brought her here, and then he went away and left her with this thing that will not speak, or cannot, or does not care enough to, or does not see her as something to talk to.

On their third date, she and Gary went to an empty park: wine, cheese, fresh bread in a basket. Bright sun and cool air, grass and a cloth to lie on. He brought Shakespeare. "You'll love this," he said, and read to her.

She stopped him with a kiss. "Let's talk," she said, "about anything."

"But we are talking," he said.

"No, you're reading," she said. "I'm sorry, I don't really like poetry."

"That's because you've never had it read to you," he said.

She stopped him at last by taking the book from his hands and pushing him back, her palms in the grass; and he entered her. Later, he read to her anyway.

If it had just been that.

They were not even his words and now they mean nothing, are not even sounds in her mind. And now there is this thing that cannot hear her or does not choose to listen, until she gives up trying to reach it and only reaches into it, and bludgeons it and herself, seeking a reaction, any reaction.

"I fucking hate you," she says. "I hate fucking you."

The lifeboat decelerates. Metal clashes on metal. Gaskets seal.

The airlock opens overhead. There is light. Her eyes water helplessly and everything becomes glare and indistinct dark shapes. The air is dry and cold. She recoils.

The alien does not react to the light, the hard air. It remains inside her and around her. They are wrapped. They penetrate one another a thousand ways. She is warm here, or at any rate not cold: half-lost in its flesh, wet from her Ins, its Outs. In here it is not too bright.

A dark something stands outlined in the portal. It is bipedal. It makes sounds that are words. Is it human? Is she? Does she still have bones, a voice? She has not used them for so long.

The alien is hers; she is its. Nothing changes.

But. She pulls herself free of its tendrils and climbs. Out.

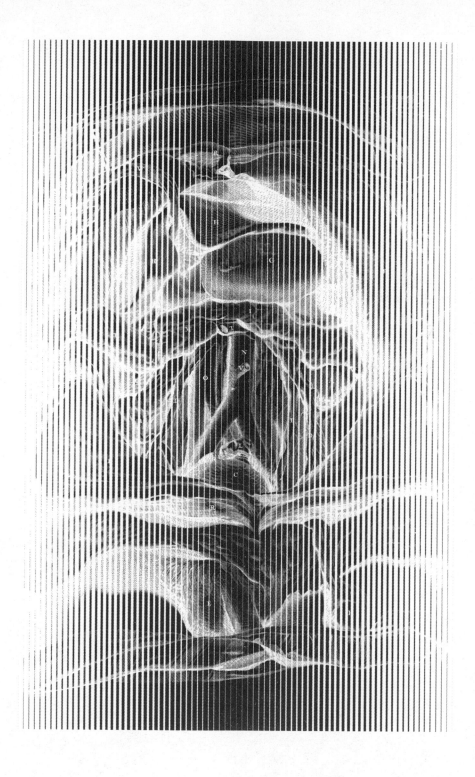

Pat Cadigan has won the Locus Award three times, the Arthur C. Clarke Award twice, the Hugo Award, and the Seiun Award. She has written twenty-one books, including one YA, two nonfiction, and several movie novelizations/media tie-ins.

In December, 2014, she was diagnosed with terminal cancer and given two years to live, but she missed that deadline. Cadigan believes it's because she was put here to accomplish a certain number of things and she is now so far behind, she can never die.

It Was the Heat
Pat Cadigan

IT WAS THE heat, the incredible heat that never lets up, never eases, never once gives you a break. Sweat till you die; bake till you drop; fry, broil, burn, baby, burn. How'd you like to live in a fever and never feel cool, never, never, never.

Women think they want men like that. They think they want someone to put the devil in their Miss Jones. Some of them even lie awake at night, alone, or next to a silent lump of husband or boyfriend or friendly stranger, thinking, *Let me be completely consumed with fire. In the name of love.*

Sure.

Right feeling, wrong name. Try again. And the thing is, they do. They try and try and try, and if they're very, very unlucky, they find one of them.

I thought I had him right where I wanted him—between my legs. Listen, I didn't always talk this way. That wasn't me you saw storming the battlements during the Sexual Revolution. My ambition was liberated but I didn't lose my head, or give it. It wasn't me saying, *Let them eat pie.* Once I had a sense of propriety, but I lost it with my inhibitions.

You think these things happen only in soap operas—the respectable, thirty-five-year-old wife and working mother goes away on a business trip with a suitcase full of navy blue suits and classy blouses with the bow at the neck and a briefcase crammed with paperwork. Product management is not a pretty sight. Sensible black pumps are a must for the run on the fast track, and if your ambition is sufficiently liberated, black pumps can keep pace with perforated wing-tips, even outrun them.

But men know the secret. Especially businessmen. This is why management conferences are sometimes held in a place like New Orleans instead of the professional canyons of New York City or Chicago. Men know the secret and now I do, too. But I didn't then, when I arrived in New Orleans with my luggage and my paperwork and my inhibitions, to be installed in the Bourbon Orleans Hotel in the French Quarter.

The room had all the charm of home—more, since I wouldn't be cleaning it up. I hung the suits in the bathroom, ran the shower, called home, already feeling guilty. Yes, boys, Mommy's at the hotel now and she has a long meeting to go to, let me talk to Daddy. Yes, dear, I'm fine. It was a long ride from the airport, good thing the corporation's paying for this. The hotel is very nice, good thing the corporation's paying for this, too. Yes, there's a pool but I doubt I'll have time to use it and anyway, I didn't bring a suit. Not that kind of suit. This isn't a pleasure trip, you know, I'm not on vacation. No. Yes. No. Kiss the boys for me. I love you, too.

If you want to be as conspicuous as possible, be a woman walking almost late into a meeting room full of men who are all gunning to be CEOs. Pick out the two or three other female faces and nod to them even though they're complete strangers, and find a seat near them. Listen to the man at the front of the room say, *Now that we're all here, we can begin* and know that every man is thinking that means you. Imagine what they are thinking, imagine what they are whispering to each other. Imagine that they know you can't concentrate on the opening presentation because your mind is on your husband and children back home instead of the business at hand when the real reason you can't concentrate is because you're imagining they must all be thinking your mind is on your husband and children back home instead of the business at hand.

Do you know what *they're* thinking about, really? They're thinking about the French Quarter. Those who have been there before are thinking about jazz and booze in go-cups and bars where the women are totally nude, totally, and those who haven't been there before are wondering if everything's as wild as they say.

Finally the presentation ended and the discussion period following the presentation ended (the women had nothing to discuss so as not to be perceived as the ones delaying the after-hours jaunt into the French Quarter). Tomorrow, nine o'clock in the Hyatt, second floor meeting room. Don't let's be too hung over to make it, boys, ha, ha. Oh, and girls, too, of course, ha, ha.

The things you hear when you don't have a crossbow.

Demure, I took a cab back to the Bourbon Orleans, intending to leave a wake-up call for 6:30, ignoring the streets already filling up. In early May, with Mardi Gras already a dim memory? Was there a big convention in town this week, I asked the cab driver.

No, ma'am, he told me (his accent—Creole or Cajun? I don't know—made it more like *ma'ahm*). De Quarter always be jumpin', and de weather be so lovely.

This was lovely? I was soaked through my drip-dry white blouse and the suitcoat would start to smell if I didn't take it off soon. My crisp, boardroom coiffure had gone limp and trickles of sweat were tracking leisurely along my scalp. Product management was meant to live in air conditioning (we call it climate control, as though we really could, but there is no controlling this climate).

At the last corner before the hotel, I saw him standing at the curb. Tight jeans, red shirt knotted above the navel to show off the washboard stomach. Definitely not executive material; executives are required to be doughy in that area and the area to the south of that was never delineated quite so definitely as it was in this man's jeans.

Some sixth sense made him bend to see who was watching him from the back seat of the cab.

"Mamma, mamma!" he called and kissed the air between us. "You wanna go to a party?" He came over to the cab and motioned for me to roll the window all the way down. I slammed the lock down on the door and sat back, clutching my sensible black purse.

"C'mon, mamma!" He poked his fingers through the small opening of the window. "I be good to you!" The golden hair was honey from peroxide, but the voice was honey from the comb. The light changed and he snatched his fingers away just in time.

"I'll be waiting!" he shouted after me. I didn't look back.

"What was all that about?" I asked the cab driver.

"Just a wild boy. Lotta wild boys in the Quarter, ma'am." We pulled up next to the hotel and he smiled over his shoulder at me, his teeth just a few shades lighter than his coffee-colored skin. "Any time you want to find a wild boy for yourself, this is where you look." It came out more like *dis is wheah you look*. "You got a nice company sends you to the Quarter for doin' business."

I smiled back, overtipped him, and escaped into the hotel.

It wasn't even a consideration, that first night. Wake-up call for six-thirty, just as I'd intended, to leave time for showering and breakfast, like the good wife and mother and executive I'd always been.

Beignets for breakfast. Carl had told me I must have beignets for breakfast if I were going to be New Orleans. He'd bought some beignet mix and tried to make some for me the week before I'd left. They'd come out too thick and heavy and only the kids had been able to eat them, liberally dusted with powdered sugar. If I found a good place for beignets, I would try to bring some home, I'd decided, for my lovely, tolerant, patient husband, who was now probably making thick, heavy pancakes for the boys. Nice of him to sacrifice some of his vacation time to be home with the boys while Mommy was out of town. Mommy had never gone out of town on business before. Daddy had, of course; several times. At those times, Mommy had never been able to take any time away from the office, though, so she could be with the boys while Daddy was out of town. Too much work to do; if you want to keep those sensible black pumps on the fast track, you can't be putting your family before the work. Lots of women lose out that way, you know, Martha?

I knew.

No familiar faces in the restaurant, but I wasn't looking for any. I moved my tray along the line, took a beignet and poured myself some of the famous Louisiana chicory coffee before I found a small table under a ceiling fan. No air conditioning and it was already up in the eighties. I made a concession and took off my jacket. After a bite of the beignet, I made another and unbuttoned the top two buttons of my blouse. The pantyhose already felt sticky and uncomfortable. I had a perverse urge to slip off to the ladies' room and take them off. Would anyone notice or care? That would leave me with nothing under the half-slip. Would anyone guess? There goes a lady executive with no pants on. In the heat, it was not unthinkable. No underwear at all was not unthinkable. Everything was binding. A woman in a gauzy caftan breezed past my table, glancing down at me with careless interest. Another out-of-towner, yes. You can tell—we're the only ones not dressed for the weather.

"All right to sit here, ma'am?"

I looked up. He was holding a tray with one hand, already straddling the chair across from me, only waiting my permission to sink down and join me. Dark, curly hair, just a bit too long, darker eyes, smooth skin the color of over-creamed coffee. Tank top over jeans. He eased himself down and smiled. I must have said yes.

"All the other tables're occupied or ain't been bussed, ma'am. Hope you don't mind, you a stranger here and all." The smile was as slow and honeyed as the voice. They all talked in honey tones here. "Eatin' you one of our nice beignets, I see. First breakfast in the Quarter, am I right?"

I used a knife and fork on the beignet. "I'm here on business."

"You have a very striking face."

I risked a glance up at him. "You're very kind." Thirty-five and up is striking, if the world is feeling kind.

"When your business is done, shall I see you in the Quarter?"

"I doubt it. My days are very long." I finished the beignet quickly, gulped the coffee. He caught my arm as I got up. It was a jolt of heat, like being touched with an electric wand.

"I have a husband and three children!" It was the only thing I could think to say.

"You don't want to forget your jacket."

It hung limply on the back of my chair. I wanted to forget it badly, to have an excuse to go through the day of meetings and seminars in shirtsleeves. I put the tray down and slipped the jacket on. "Thank you."

"Name is Andre, ma'am." The dark eyes twinkled. "My heart will surely break if I don't see you tonight in the Quarter."

"Don't be silly."

"It's too hot to be silly, ma'am."

"Yes. It is," I said stiffly. I looked for a place to take the tray.

"They take it away for you. You can just leave it here. Or you can stay and have another cup of coffee and talk to a lonely soul." One finger plucked at the low scoop of the tank top. "I'd like that."

"A cab driver warned me about wild boys," I said, holding my purse carefully to my side.

"I doubt it. He may have told you but he didn't warn you. And I ain't a boy, ma'am."

Sweat gathered in the hollow between my collarbones and spilled downward. He seemed to be watching the trickle disappear down into my blouse. Under the aroma of baking breads and pastries and coffee, I caught a scent of something else.

"Boys stand around on street corners, they shout rude remarks, they don't know what a woman is."

"That's enough," I snapped. "I don't know why you picked me out for your morning's amusement. Maybe because I'm from out of town. You wild boys get a kick out of annoying the tourists, is that it? If I see you again, I'll call a cop." I stalked out and pushed myself through the humidity to hail a cab. By the time I reached the Hyatt, I might as well not have showered.

"I'm skipping out on this afternoon's session," the woman whispered to me. Her badge said she was Frieda Fellowes, of Boston, Massachusetts. "I heard the speaker last year. He's the biggest bore in the world. I'm going shopping. Care to join me?"

I shrugged. "I don't know. I have to write up a report on this when I get home and I'd better be able to describe everything in detail."

She looked at my badge. "You must work for a bunch of real hardasses up in Schenectady." She leaned forward to whisper to the other woman sitting in the row ahead of us, who nodded eagerly.

They were both missing from the afternoon session. The speaker was the biggest bore in the world. The men had all conceded to shirtsleeves. Climate control failed halfway through the seminar and it broke up early, releasing us from the stuffiness of the meeting room into the thick air of the city. I stopped in the lobby bathroom and took off my pantyhose, rolled them into an untidy ball and stuffed them in my purse before getting a cab back to my own hotel.

One of the men from my firm phoned my room and invited me to join him and the guys for drinks and dinner. We met in a crowded little place called Messina's, four male executives and me. It wasn't until I excused myself and went to the closet-sized bathroom that I realized I'd put my light summer slacks on over nothing. A careless mistake, akin to starting off to the supermarket on Saturday morning in my bedroom slippers. Mommy's got a lot on her mind. Martha, the No-Pants Executive. Guess what, dear, I went out to dinner in New Orleans with four men and forgot to wear panties. Well, women do reach their sexual peak at thirty-five, don't they, honey?

The heat was making me crazy. No air conditioning here, either, just fans, pushing the damp air around.

I rushed through the dinner of red beans and rice and hot sausage; someone ordered a round of beers and I gulped mine down to cool the sausage. No one spoke much. Martha's here, better keep it low-key, guys. I decided to do them a favor and disappear after the meal. There wouldn't be much chance of running into me at any of the nude bars, nothing to be embarrassed about. Thanks for tolerating my presence, fellas.

But they looked a little puzzled when I begged off anything further. The voice blew over to me as I reached the door, carried on a wave of humidity pushed by one of the fans: "Maybe she's got a headache tonight." General laughter.

Maybe all four of you together would be a disappointment, boys. Maybe none of you know what a woman is.

They didn't look especially wild, either.

I had a drink by the pool instead of going right up to the hotel room. Carl would be coping with supper and homework and whatnot. Better to call later, after they were all settled down.

I finished the drink and ordered another. It came in a plastic cup, with apologies from the waiter. "Temporarily short on crystal tonight, ma'am. Caterin' a private dinner here. Hope you don't mind a go-cup this time."

"A what?"

The man's smile was bright. "Go-cup. You take it and walk around with it."

"That's allowed?"

"All over the Quarter, ma'am." He moved on to another table.

So I walked through the lobby with it and out into the street, and no one stopped me.

Just down at the corner, barely half a block away, the streets were filling up again. Many of the streets seemed to be pedestrians only. I waded in, holding the go-cup. Just to look around. I couldn't really come here and not look around.

"It's supposed to be a whorehouse where the girls swung naked on velvet swings."

I turned away from the high window where the mannequin legs had been swinging in and out to look at the man who had spoken to me. He was a head taller than I was, long-haired, attractive in a rough way.

"Swung?" I said. "You mean they don't any more?"

He smiled and took my elbow, positioning me in front of an open doorway, pointed in. I looked; a woman was lying naked on her stomach under a mirror suspended overhead. Perspiration gleamed on her skin.

"Buffet?" I said. "All you can eat, a hundred dollars?"

The man threw back his head and laughed heartily. "New in the Quarter, aintcha?" Same honey in the voice. They caress you with their voices here, I thought, holding the crumpled go-cup tightly. It was a different one; I'd had another drink since I'd come out and it hadn't seemed like a bad idea at all, another drink, the walking around, all of it. Not by myself, anyway.

Something brushed my hip. "You'll let me buy you another, wont-cha?" Dark hair, dark eyes; young. I remembered that for a long time.

Wild creatures in lurid long dresses catcalled screechily from a second-floor balcony as we passed below on the street. My eyes were heavy with heat and alcohol but I kept walking. It was easy with him beside me, his arm around me and his hand resting on my hip.

Somewhere along the way, the streets grew much darker and the crowds disappeared. A few shadows in the larger darkness; I saw them leaning against street signs; we passed one close enough to smell a mixture of perfume and sweat and alcohol and something else.

"Didn't nobody never tell you to come out alone at night in this part of the Quarter?" The question was amused, not reproving. They caress you with their voices down here, with their voices and the darkness and the heat, which gets higher as it gets darker. And when it gets hot enough, they melt and flow together and run all over you, more fluid than water.

What are you doing?

I'm walking into a dark hallway; I don't know my footing, I'm glad there's someone with me.

What are you doing?

I'm walking into a dark room to get out of the heat, but it's no cooler here and I don't really care after all.

What are you doing?

I'm overdressed for the season here; this isn't Schenectady in the spring, it's New Orleans, it's the French Quarter.

What are you doing?

I'm hitting my sexual peak at thirty-five.

"What are you doing?"

Soft laughter. "Oh, honey, don't you know?"

The Quarter was empty at dawn, maybe because it was raining. I found my way back to the Bourbon Orleans in the downpour anyway. It shut off as suddenly as a suburban lawn sprinkler just as I reached the front door of the hotel.

I fell into bed and slept the day away, no wake-up calls, and when I opened my eyes, the sun was going down and I remembered how to find him.

You'd think there would have been a better reason: my husband ignored me or my kids were monsters or my job was a dead-end or some variation on the mid-life crisis. It wasn't any of those things. Well, the seminars were boring but nobody gets that bored. Or maybe they did and I'd just never heard about it.

It was the heat.

The heat gets inside you. Then you get a fever from the heat, and from fever you progress to delirium and from delirium into another state of being. Nothing is real in delirium. No, scratch that: everything is real in a different way. In delirium, everything floats, including time. Lighter than air, you slip away. Day breaks apart from night, leaves you with scraps of daylight. It's all right—when it gets that hot, it's too hot to see, too hot to bother looking. I remembered dark hair, dark eyes, but it was all dark now and in the dark, it was even hotter than in the daylight.

It was the heat. It never let up. It was the heat and the smell. I'll never be able to describe that smell except to say that if it were a sound, it would have been round and mellow and sweet, just the way it tasted. As if he had no salt in his body at all. As if he had been distilled from the heat itself, and salt had just been left behind in the process.

It was the heat.

And then it started to get cool.

It started to cool down to the eighties during the last two days of the conference and I couldn't find him. I made a half-hearted showing at one of the seminars after a two-day absence. They stared, all the men and the women, especially the one who had asked me to go shopping.

"I thought you'd been kidnapped by white slavers," she said to me during the break. "What happened? You don't look like you feel so hot."

"I feel very hot," I said, helping myself to the watery lemonade punch the hotel had laid out on a table. With beignets. The sight of them turned my stomach and so did the punch. I put it down again. "I've been running a fever."

She touched my face, frowning slightly. "You don't feel feverish. In fact, you feel pretty cool. Clammy, even."

"It's the air conditioning," I said, drawing back. Her fingers were cold, too cold to tolerate. "The heat and the air conditioning. It's fucked me up."

Her eyes widened.

"*Messed* me up, excuse me. I've been hanging around my kids too long."

"Perhaps you should see a doctor. Or go home."

"I've just got to get out of this air conditioning," I said, edging toward the door. She followed me, trying to object. "I'll be fine as soon as I get out of this air conditioning and back into the heat."

"No, *wait*," she called insistently. "You may be suffering from heatstroke. I think that's it—the clammy skin, the way you look—"

"It's not heatstroke, I'm freezing in this goddam refrigerator. Just leave me the fuck alone and I'll be *fine!*"

I fled, peeling off my jacket, tearing open the top of my blouse. I couldn't go back, not to that awful air conditioning. I would stay out where it was warm.

I lay in bed with the windows wide open and the covers pulled all the way up. One of the men from my company phoned; his voice sounded too casual when he pretended I had reassured him. Carl's call only twenty minutes later was not a surprise. I'm fine, dear. You don't sound fine. I am, though. Everyone is worried about you. Needlessly. I think I should come down there. No, stay where you are, I'll be fine. No, I think I should come and get you. And I'm telling you to stay where you are. That does it, you sound weird, I'm getting the next flight out and your mother can stay with the boys. You stay where you are, goddamit, or I might not come home, is that clear?

Long silence.

Is someone there with you?

More silence.

I said, is someone there with you?

It's just the heat. I'll be fine, as soon as I warm up.

Sometime after that, I was sitting at a table in a very dark place that was almost warm enough. The old woman sitting across from me occasionally drank delicately from a bottle of beer and fanned herself, even though it was only almost warm.

"It's such pleasure when it cool down like dis," she said in her slow honey voice. Even the old ladies had honey voices here. "The heat be a beast."

I smiled, thinking for a moment that she'd said *bitch*, not beast. "Yeah. It's a bitch all right but I don't like to be cold."

"No? Where you from?"

"Schenectady. Cold climate."

She grunted. "Well, the heat don't be a bitch, it be a beast. *He* be a beast."

"Who?"

"Him. The heat beast." She chuckled a little. "My grandma woulda called him a loa. You know what dat is?"

"No."

She eyed me before taking another sip of beer. "No. I don't know whether that good or bad for you, girl. Could be deadly either way, someone who don't like to be cold. What you doin' over here anyway? Tourist Quarter three blocks thataway."

"I'm looking for a friend. Haven't been able to find him since it's cooled down."

"Grandma knew they never named all de loa. She said new ones would come when they found things be willin' for 'em. Or when they named by someone. Got nothin' to do with the old religion any more. Bigger than the old religion. It's all de world now." The old woman thrust her face forward and squinted at me. "What friend *you* got over here? No outa-town white girl got a friend over here."

"I do. And I'm not from out of town any more."

"Get out." But it wasn't hostile, just amusement and condescension and a little disgust. "Go buy you some tourist juju and tell everybody you met a mamba in N'awlins. Be some candyass somewhere sell you a nice, fake love charm."

"I'm not here for that," I said, getting up. "I came for the heat."

"Well, girl, it's cooled down." She finished her beer.

Sometime after that, in another place, I watched a man and a woman dancing together. There were only a few other people on the floor in front of the band. I couldn't really make sense of the music, whether it was jazz or rock or whatever. It was just the man and the woman I was paying attention to. Something in their movements was familiar. I was thinking he would be called by the heat in them, but it was so damned cold in there, not even ninety degrees. The street was colder. I pulled the jacket tighter around myself and cupped my hands around the coffee mug. That famous Louisiana chicory coffee. Why couldn't I get warm?

It grew colder later. There wasn't a warm place in the Quarter, but people's skins seemed to be burning. I could see the heat shimmers rising from their bodies. Maybe I was the only one without a fever now.

Carl was lying on the bed in my hotel room. He sat up as soon as I opened the door. The heat poured from him in waves and my first thought was to throw myself on him and take it, take it all, and leave him to freeze to death.

"Wait!" he shouted but I was already pounding down the hall to the stairs.

Early in the morning, it was an easy thing to run through the Quarter. The sun was already beating down but the light was thin, with little warmth. I couldn't hear Carl chasing me, but I kept running, to the other side of the Quarter, where I had first gone into the shadows. Glimpse of an old woman's face at a window; I remembered her, she remembered me. Her head nodded, two fingers beckoned. Behind her, a younger face watched in the shadows. The wrong face.

I came to a stop in the middle of an empty street and waited. I was getting colder; against my face, my fingers were like living icicles. It had to be only 88 or 89 degrees, but even if it got to ninety-five or above today, I wouldn't be able to get warm.

He had it. He had taken it. Maybe I could get it back.

The air above the buildings shimmied, as if to taunt. Warmth, here, and here, and over here, what's the matter with you, frigid or something?

Down at the corner, a police car appeared. Heat waves rippled up from it, and I ran.

"Hey."

The man stood over me where I sat shivering at a corner table in the place that bragged it had traded slaves over a hundred years ago. He was the color of rich earth, slightly built with carefully waved black hair. Young face; the wrong face, again.

"You look like you in the market for a sweater."

"Go away." I lifted the coffee cup with shuddering hands. "A thousand sweaters couldn't keep me warm now."

"No, honey." They caressed you with their voices down here. He took the seat across from me. "Not that kind of sweater. Sweater I mean's a person, special kinda person. Who'd you meet in the Quarter? Good-lookin' stud, right? Nice, wild boy, maybe not white but white enough for you?"

"Go away. I'm not like that."

"You know what you like now, though. Cold. Very cold woman. Cold woman's no good. Cold woman'll take all the heat out of a man, leave him frozen dead."

I didn't answer.

"So you need a sweater. Maybe I know where you can find one."

"Maybe you know where I can find him."

The man laughed. "That's what I'm say in', cold woman." He took off his light, white suitcoat and tossed it at me. "Wrap up in that and come on."

The fire in the hearth blazed, flames licking out at the darkness. Someone kept feeding it, keeping it burning for hours. I wasn't sure who, or if it was only one person, or how long I sat in front of the fire, trying to get warm.

Sometime long after the man had brought me there, the old woman said, "Burnin' all day now. Whole Quarter oughta feel the heat by now. Whole city."

"*He'll* feel it, sure enough." The man's voice. "He'll feel it, come lookin' for what's burnin'." A soft laugh. "Won't he be surprised to see it's his cold woman."

"Look how the fire wants her."

The flames danced. I could sit in the middle of them and maybe then I'd be warm.

"Where did he go?" The person who asked might have been me.

"Went to take a rest. Man sleeps after a bender, don't you know. He oughta be ready for more by now."

I reached out for the fire. A long tongue of flame licked around my arm; the heat felt so good.

"Look how the fire wants her."

Soft laugh. "If it wants her, then it should have her. Go ahead, honey. Get in the fire."

On hands and knees, I climbed up into the hearth, moving slowly, so as not to scatter the embers. Clothes burned away harmlessly.

To sit in fire is to sit among a glory of warm, silk ribbons touching everywhere at once. I could see the room now, the heavy drapes covering the windows, the dark faces, one old, one young, gleaming with sweat, watching me.

"You feel 'im?" someone asked. "Is he comin'?"

"He's comin', don't worry about that." The man who had brought me smiled at me. I felt a tiny bit of perspiration gather at the back of my neck. Warmer; getting warmer now.

I began to see him; he was forming in the darkness, coming together, pulled in by the heat. Dark-eyed, dark-haired, young, the way he had been. He was there before the hearth and the look on that young face as he peered into the flames was hunger.

The fire leaped for him; I leaped for him and we saw what it was we really had. No young man; no man.

The heat be a beast.

Beast. Not really a loa, something else; I knew that, somehow. Sometimes it looks like a man and sometimes it looks like hot honey in the darkness.

What are you doing?

I'm taking darkness by the eyes, by the mouth, by the throat.

What are you doing?

I'm burning alive.

What are you doing?

I'm burning the heat beast and I have it just where I want it. All the heat anyone ever felt, fire and body heat, fever, delirium. Delirium has eyes; I push them in with my thumbs. Delirium has a mouth; I fill it with my fist. Delirium has a throat; I tear it out. Sparks fly like an explosion of tiny stars and the beast spreads its limbs in surrender, exposing its white-hot core. I bend my head to it and the taste is sweet, no salt in his body at all.

What are you doing?

Oh, honey, don't you know?

I took it back.

In the hotel room, I stripped off the shabby dress the old woman had given me and threw it in the trashcan. I was packing when Carl came back.

He wanted to talk; I didn't. Later he called the police and told them everything was all right, he'd found me and I was coming home with him. I was sure they didn't care. Things like that must have happened in the Quarter all the time.

In the ladies' room at the airport, the attendant sidled up to me as I was bent over the sink splashing cold water on my face and asked if I were all right.

"It's just the heat," I said.

"Then best you go home to a cold climate," she said. "You do better in a cold climate from now on."

I raised my head to look at her reflection in the spotted mirror. I wanted to ask her if she had a brother who also waved his hair. I wanted to ask her why he would bother with a cold woman, why he would care.

She put both hands high on her chest, protectively. "The beast sleeps in cold. *You* tend him now. Maybe you keep him asleep for good."

"And if I don't?"

She pursed her lips. "Then you gotta problem."

In summer, I keep the air-conditioning turned up high at my office, at home. In the winter, the kids complain the house is too cold and Carl grumbles a little, even though we save so much in heating bills. I tuck the boys in with extra blankets every night and kiss their foreheads, and later in our bed, Carl curls up close, murmuring how my skin is always so warm.

It's just the heat.

CODY GOODFELLOW has written nine solo novels and three with *New York Times* bestselling author John Skipp. Two of his short fiction collections, *Silent Weapons For Quiet Wars* and *All-Monster Action,* received the Wonderland Book Award. He wrote and co-produced the short films *Stay At Home Dad* and *Clowntown: An Honest Mis-Stake.* He has also appeared in the background on numerous TV programs, as well as videos by Anthrax and Beck. He lives in Portland, Oregon.

Atwater

Cody Goodfellow

Life was not so unkind to Howell as it seemed to the world at large—it offered few surprises, and predictable rewards. Where there were explicit directions, Howell found he could go anywhere, do anything, but whenever and wherever he got lost, he found Atwater.

The first time it happened, he believed, at first, that it was as real as everything else in his life up to that point had been. On his way to a business appointment in Burbank: he'd given himself plenty of time to get there, leaving the office in Mid-Wilshire an hour ahead of the departure time on the Triple A itinerary he'd printed out the night before. After living in LA for over a year, he still did this for any place he had never driven, and kept a binder and three map books.

Traffic shut him down within sight of his office. Parked on the 101, swimming in sweat, and he suddenly, absolutely, needed to pee. He couldn't just give up and get off; it had to get better soon, but it got worse, so clusterfucked by Hollywood Boulevard that he couldn't even get through the glacial drift of traffic to the exit. Watching as the time of his appointment came and went, and he wasn't even in the Valley, yet he was committed. The southbound traffic was almost as bad. Howell left a message to reschedule with the client in Burbank. The secretary treated him like some idiot who'd tried to ride a horse into town.

Wondering which of the empty coffee cups at his feet he'd like to try peeing in, wondering why the sensible Volvo people had never tackled this crying need of the long-haul motorist, Howell crawled through the pass and into the Valley.

The 101 burst out into Griffith Park, and a blazing Catherine Wheel avalanche of sulfurous afternoon sunlight speared his brain. Cascades of shaggy green hills and shadowed black canyons lurched up to the shoulder, the wilderness under glass of the park and Howell was looking when horns sounded behind him, and the road ahead was a vacant plain.

Howell whooped with joy and stomped on the gas. The Triple A directions had wilted into pasty slime from the heat and smog and sweat from his hands, pages stuck together. The damned thing was supposed to be foolproof, distances totaled out to the hundredth of a mile, but 42.62 crept by on his trip odometer, and no Burbank Avenue. No offramp at all, and then he saw from the baffling menu of interstate and city highway junctions in the southbound lanes, that he was on the wrong freeway, and headed east to Pasadena.

No one let him out of the left lane until he'd passed under the Golden State Freeway. With a berserker roar, he kamikazed the next off-ramp and slammed on the brakes, power-sliding up a hairpin chute between blank brick walls. He skidded to a stop just short of the sign. ATWATER, it said—no population or elevation, no explanation, no Kiwanis or Lion's Club chapters. Just ATWATER.

He idled at the intersection for a good long time. No other cars came. There were no other cars. Anywhere. In the middle of LA. No cars. No pedestrians, either, and Howell waited for something, for a director to scream, "Cut!" and a crew to spill out from behind these painted murals of a ghost town to resurrect the scene he'd ruined.

On the three corners opposite the off-ramp, a 7-11, an AM/PM, and another 7-11, all abandoned, windows shattered, roofs askew and foundations cracked. All angles subtly off, and apartment buildings down the street had collapsed, crushing their ground floors or spilling their contents out into the street. All the entrances were swathed in CAUTION tape, and Condemned notices were pasted on all remaining doors. "By order of FEMA—"

The last real earthquake in Los Angeles was in 1993. Howell looked into this before taking the job and moving here. A decade later, and they never tried to rebuild? Unless it was a movie set…or something else happened here—

Imagination did nothing good for Howell. He let it go and set the Volvo rolling down the main drag.

Atwater wasn't large; he could see the same brick wall cutting across the street only a few blocks from the offramp. The whole area was walled off from the rest of the city, a pitcher plant with only one mouth, into which he'd stumbled. The sounds of the city outside were almost completely muzzled—he heard only the hushed hum of distant traffic and something like electronic wind chimes, or a Don't Walk alarm for blind pedestrians, but here, nothing moved. Fine then, he'd turn around.

A man threw himself across the hood of his car. Threw himself, those were the right words, because Howell certainly didn't hit him—

"Please," the man bleated, beating on the windshield, "please help—"

The man came around to the passenger side, and Howell hadn't locked it. He wore a navy blue suit and tie, shabby and shiny, the kind of thing an exceptionally cheap prison might parole its least promising inmates in, but he didn't look like a bum, and Howell supposed he wanted to help, so he let the man fumble it open and fall into the passenger seat. "You don't know how long I've been waiting," the man said, "for someone to come—"

"Where the hell are we? Where's everybody?"

"No onramp," the man wheezed, hauling the door shut and turning to look at Howell. "We have to go back up the off-ramp, but nobody comes in here, ever... For God's sake, let's go!"

Something buzzed past Howell's ear. He whipped his head around so fast something tore in the back of his neck, but he let out a sharp yelp and shouted, "Did you see it? You let a—let it in—" He couldn't bring himself to say the word.

Howell looked at the man's face, at gaping pores all over his face and neck, tessellated hexagons like tiny waxen mouths. Black, buzzing bullets oozed out of them. His head was a honeycomb.

"It's not as bad as it looks," the man offered, his humming hand shooting out to bar Howell in his seat. "Please just drive."

Howell shrieked. He was allergic to beestings. He was allergic to the *word* "bees." He yanked open the door and threw himself out, except the fucking seatbelt trapped him, hanging upside down in the street. His hand slapped at the button, or was it a latch. Bees swarmed and formed a beard on the man's face.

"You're making them mad," the man said, his eyes wet, nose streaming snot and furious bees drowning in it. Tiny feather-touches of agitated air played over Howell's face, the microscopic violence of thousands of wings. A homicidal halo roared around his head.

The seatbelt snapped free and Howell rolled out of the Volvo, hit the street running on all fours, out of the intersection and into the nearest shelter, the underground garage of a three-story townhouse.

He slid on his belly down the steep driveway and crawled under the gate, jammed open on a toppled Vespa scooter. The dark was his only cover, here. He had no real hope of finding help, only of hiding until the lunatic either stole his car or abandoned it, but he was not getting back in there. He'd walk out onto the freeway and hail a Highway Patrolman, he'd get out, he'd go home and never come back—

Almost nauseous now with relief, Howell unzipped and pissed in the dark.

A sound, and then another, behind him. His bladder slammed shut; his balls crawled up and wrapped around his femoral artery, legs tingled and fell into a coma. Small sounds, but distinctive, and if not threatening, then in this place they portended a myriad of things, all awful.

It was the sound of a metal tool striking a metal tray, and the sound of a miniature saw biting into something hard, and the reek of burning bone. Howell turned and sought something to hide behind as he saw how far from alone he was.

A moth-battered ceiling fixture lit up a shining steel table in the center of the empty garage. Two gaunt figures in black smocks and leather aprons hovered over it. They wore cages over their heads like old-time insane asylum alienists, or their heads were cages, for they seemed to imprison nothing but shadows.

Between them on the table lay a nude female body, painfully white, viciously thin, a naked sprawl of cruel angles and lunar planes, decoratively inked with dotted lines that encompassed the whole form. Freshly sutured cuts ran down the arms and legs, and perhaps the worst of it was that Howell saw nowhere a drop of blood.

Deftly, one of the alienists sawed down the bridge of the dead woman's nose, while the other peeled the parted skin away from the skull. Howell didn't know how long he watched; their procedures were so methodical, he got sucked into infinite minutiae, only to take a sudden, stabbing breath when suddenly, with a magician's flare, the peeler laid bare the skull and held it up.

The skull was black glass, toxic onyx ice, squealing and smoking as it met the hot, close air. The alienist dropped it into an oil drum, changed into a fresh pair of heavy rubber gloves and opened the gilded doors of a medieval reliquary on a sideboard.

The other alienist continued his master ventral incision at the jaw, laying open the fuligin rib cage, which spewed ribbons of oily vapor across the table.

Working behind, the first alienist selected a skull of ancient yellow bone from the reliquary and deftly slipped it into the hollow face, arranging the features just so, then nipping the lips of the incision together with black thread as fast as a sweatshop matron.

Cowering behind a Camaro half-propped up on cinderblocks in the mouth of the garage, Howell started to creep backwards to the gate. He'd face down the honeycombed man, or just run out onto the freeway, he'd get out of here—

When the woman on the table spoke.

"I felt that," she whimpered, and Howell was gored by the wonder in her voice, as much as by the fact that the speaker was a filleted cadaver, with two headless surgeons elbow-deep in her. He trembled, but it was thousands of misfired reflexes warring with each other as he tried to frame a reaction to this—

An alienist set a new rib cage in place and stitched it up as the other prepared to join his incision with the cleft of her groin.

Howell rushed at the cutter, screaming, "Get off her!" with his fists pounding its broad back and his mad rush tipped him so that he almost fell into it when the towering form collapsed on itself with no more resistance than an airborne shopping bag. He blundered into the edge of the table and knocked the wind out of his lungs as the alienist with the needle calmly reached for something on the tray that looked like a nail gun.

On the table, the woman looked at him. Her eyes, impossibly vast black pupils, ringed by violet irises like bone-deep bruises, drank him in and stole something he needed to breathe. "Take me," she said, "take me away—"

Howell's hand found the knife and lashed out across the table at the other alienist. The blade slashed the unresisting fabric, the black form deflated and melted into the oil-stained shadows.

Howell dropped the knife and looked for something to cover her with, trying to say, "I'll get you—get you—out—"

"What's your name, here?" she asked.

He took off his jacket and draped it over her, arms out, awkwardly trying to size her up to lift. "Um, Howell, Roger, um, Howell. Listen, are you okay to move? I saw…"

She sat up on the table and leaned into him. The exquisitely fine stitching down the center of her face creaked when she smiled and put the knife to his throat. Her other hand hustled his crotch. "I'm cured."

He looked away, but she forced him to look with her knife. "Get hard," she commanded, and tore herself open.

Her breasts, imperceptible but for her nipples, like bites from some enormous spider that lived in her bed, already swelling, seeking him out, accusing snail-eyes.

His stomach rolled and everything was hot, rushing water, drowning him. He wished he could melt and flow away through her fingers, but where he wanted it least, he swiftly became solid under the harsh ministrations of her bony hand.

Using the knife and his cock as levers, she got him up onto the table, peeled away his slacks and boxers. "Let me see you," she husked in his ear, "show me what you really are."

He couldn't melt or run away, so he just took it. Froze solid as she lowered herself onto him, cold, tight and dry, spat on the head of it and impaled herself.

Inside, she felt like anything but flesh, ground-glass needles and gnashing teeth and mortuary marble, doors within doors opening in a cold black cathedral. He thought of the operation he'd interrupted, the looted fossils of a saint swapped out for her necrotic skeleton, and in the reliquary he saw a pale yellow pelvis, untransplanted—

Spastic reflex wrapped his arms around her, protruding ribs like notches for his fingers. Her torso shook as if she was full of panicked birds, and she hissed, to him or to herself, "Take your medicine."

Shuddering, she rose up and dropped herself hard against him, and spider webs of black ice shot through his hips and into his guts. In his head, he reviewed sums, columns of expenditure figures for the projected relocation scheme his company had sent him up here to investigate. Culling them fiercely in the quiet corners of his mind, he noted two adding errors and committed them to memory, as soon as he got back to his laptop, he'd correct them—

The knife never left his throat. It sawed back and forth as she smashed herself against him, eyes rolled back, breath choppy gusts of frigid mist that grew colder with every stroke, despite the unbearable friction.

"Take it, take it," she growled in his ear, and in the cold and heat he felt he'd lost what he'd put into her, it was hers now, and she was fucking him to death with it. He could only hold on.

Her rhythm sped, stiffened, such a ferocious blur of motion that he regretted daring to open his eyes, and she screamed, "He's coming, faster, he's coming—"

The sensation spreading through him now pulled him further away from the world, fired his gut-sense that the agony of pleasure he felt was really her, taking him over. He hid from it, crying inside, please God, just let it be over—

And then it was, and his skin was slathered in cold motor oil, and she was gone. He did not look around or try to cover himself, huddled on the icy steel table in a puddle of oil and urine, shocked mute by the sudden stillness.

The ground shook.

Dust and grit sprinkled his cold, raw skin. He rolled off the table and hitched his piss-soaked pants up. He was alone in the dark. It was so quiet, he could hear the Volvo, still idling out on the street, and those faint, phantom chimes. But something else was coming, an itch in the soles of his feet, a tremor that shivered through his bowels, and he remembered what she'd said, just before she vanished.

He's coming—

A steady, subsonic rumble spread up through the floor, a silent sound of pure terrestrial protest. A whole patch of ceiling gave way, dumping plaster and shattered concrete and spark-spitting washing machines into the garage.

Howell crawled under the gate and scrambled up the driveway on all fours, uttering a weird, panicked hooting sound with each hard-fought breath. He could still hear his car, so close, he could hear the seat belt alert beeping endlessly, and the dull burble of the public radio talk show he'd tuned in on the stereo, but he could also hear voices on the street, and those chimes, growing louder, reverberating off the encircling walls of Atwater. And buzzing—

Howell hit the sidewalk and had to remind himself to get up and run to the Volvo. He saw no one around it, but the honeycomb man stood in the middle of the street, and he wasn't alone.

Another man, short, with a head like a claw hammer, and snarls of piano wire running from his arms and legs and torso to a jumbled mound of marionettes in the street behind him, like the sole survivor of some sort of street mime's massacre. A little girl stood beside them, sucking her thumb and holding a length of an impossibly long albino python, which wrapped around her so many times, showing neither head nor tail, that she might have been made out of snakes.

She pointed at Howell as he ran for his car. The honeycomb man shouted, "Wait! Take us with you!"

He said something else, but though Howell saw his mouth working, he could hear nothing but the sound of jets, a squadron of them, flying up out of the secret, hollow heart of the earth.

Behind Howell, the townhouse lurched forward and settled down into the underground garage. The apartment block behind it bulged and broke open, rooms bursting like bubbles full of abandoned human lives and flaming debris flying, and smoke and something coming through it, something that made the freaks on the street race for his car. Howell got in and slammed the door, locked it and threw the car in gear.

He screamed and threw the wheel to the right, jumping the curb and flattening a street sign. The honeycomb man spilled across the hood in a roiling cloud of bees. Howell stomped on the gas, batting the air vents shut.

The puppeteer waved at him, hurling screaming marionettes into the grill of the car. Their wooden claws gouged out his headlights and chrome and ripped off his antenna as he passed, looking, looking for the narrow niche in the wall that he'd come in through, but it was gone, the intersection with the three convenience stores was now a T-junction facing a blank brick wall.

The insanity, the injustice of it all, finally broke him. He kept going forward, but he saw nothing.

And then the ground shifted, and the car was going uphill, but he only went faster, and the wall fell away as the ground rose, as something unspeakably heavy gained on him, making a sinkhole of Atwater from which he could not hope to escape.

Howell saw the freeway. The cars were hurtling by and he was headed into their midst in the wrong direction, but he did not care. He saw only fire and black smoke in his rearview mirror, and he wrenched the wheel around as the Volvo sailed off the ragged edge of the road and over the wall, and he saw a flash of white in the mirror. He looked and saw her face, a snowflake in the collapsing furnace, and then he was over the wall, and the car's axle nearly snapped as the car hit the onramp with the wheels at a right angle, but it sailed down the dry ice-plant embankment and swerved, amid a chorus of horns, into the flow of traffic.

Howell got off at the next exit and cleaned himself up. Then he went to his appointment in Burbank.

It was some weeks before Howell could admit to himself that he wasn't going to report the incident. To tell it would make it real, declare that he believed in it, but no one would believe him. How much easier to just go on, to leave it behind, when it fit nothing else in his life but his dreams, which he never remembered, anyway. For over a year, a bad dream was all it was, and all it would ever be.

Until he got lost again.

Driving up to Sacramento, an interview for a senior accounting position with the state comptroller's office, and he would have flown, if not for the terror of handing over his life to some unseen mumbler with a bar tab in eight states. If he had been meticulous in his planning before, he was now obsessive. He bought maps and plotted his route and itinerary, and he researched Atwater, and made damned sure that nothing brought him any closer to it as he passed the junction he'd stumbled into last time.

He'd been stunned to discover it was a real place, an odd, isolated knot-hole in the haphazard sprawl of the San Fernando Valley, encircled by freeways and largely undeveloped since the early seventies, but an unremarkable, ordinary place that had suffered only a few broken windows in the last earthquake. What might have driven a more curious man mad only salved the fear he hadn't dared confront since it happened, because it confirmed that it was all a bad dream. He drove through the Valley, and passed Atwater unmolested.

He had the route folded in his lap and the GPS unit in his new Volvo told him he was in the San Joaquin Valley on the northbound 5, entering Chowchilla, but the GPS unit had no way of knowing about the truck wreck, bodies strewn across both lanes and up the scrub-brush shoulders, naked children everywhere, and all he could do was clutch the map to his breast and tell himself, you're not lost, not lost, don't look—

But they were only pigs, scattered by the impact with a truck loaded with tanks of flammable gas that came off the Chowchilla on-ramp too fast. Only a pair of highway patrol cars had arrived, the troopers hanging their heads at the waste of good bacon.

Detour signs and sawhorses with rusty orange blinking lights diverted the traffic up through Chowchilla onto the two-lane eastbound 140. Howell followed the signs through the tiny town and turned north on the 99 at the promise of eventually reaching Sacramento thereby. Remarkably, almost no other cars joined him on the detour, preferring to sit in gridlock while the dead pigs were mopped up, and he should have sneered at their stupidity, but instead, he couldn't stop wondering what they knew—

He was on the 99, he was sure of it, when it started to rain. Suddenly, he was driving through a car wash, and the GPS unit in the dash, in fact everything in the dash, blinked and went black.

He hit the windshield wipers, but they didn't work. He braked soberly to a stop, angling to the right shoulder and hitting his hazard lights, though no sign that they worked, either. He was about to call OnStar and have them send a tow truck, and he had his map out on his lap, when he saw two men step into the tiny arena of his headlights, arm in arm and grappling, legs crazily digging for traction in the slick mud.

Howell had his phone in his hand when the two men smashed their heads together and staggered back into the dark. He was pushing the number he had programmed to speed-dial the friendly OnStar operator somewhere in Bombay or New Delhi, who would use satellite imagery and impeccable, pleasingly accented English to guide him out of the storm and back to the highway, even though he was definitely not lost—

His eyes roved over the map, up the 5 to the 140 to the 99, and up the 99 past Merced, and a tiny town just off the highway, though no roads to or from it showed on the map. The town was called ATWATER.

He looked out the window. Each fighter had his hands around the other's throat, and throttled his foe for all he was worth. Faces purple and streaming in the rain, they had wrung each other half to death when one suddenly kicked the other in the gut. The injured man folded, and his attacker pressed the advantage with ruthless abandon, smashing his head again and again into the pavement.

Howell sat there watching, even after the dashboard lights came back on, and the windshield wipers gave him a clearer view.

The victor lifted the vanquished up by his head, looking deeply, longingly, into the eyes of the man he'd beaten. Then his arms tensed and he squeezed the skull, crushing it as his mouth opened wider, jaw unhinged, skin stretched, to engulf the top of the broken head between his lips. Howell's hands fumbled for the gearshift, switched on the high beams. Oblivious to the light, the victor opened his mouth still wider, hoisting his twitching enemy off his feet and forcing the body, inch by inch, into his own.

Howell reversed and floored it, headed back the way he'd come. But the road was different. Corn crowded in on both sides. He saw peaked Victorian rooftops behind the waving stalks, but knew he'd find no help there. His brain crawled out of his skull and flew above the racing Volvo. If he hadn't been so meticulous in his bathroom stops this trip, he would have voided his bladder as he screamed through the town of Atwater.

Not a single board of a building looked familiar, but he knew it was the same town.

He passed an intersection that wasn't there before, a big black sign swinging above an old wire-hung traffic light said, PENTACOST ROAD.

He passed a man dressed in his mother's skin, that still screamed and nagged in his ear; another who sweated fabulous tumors of molten gold, and fungal, crystalline growths like diamonds; an armless, legless nude woman in an eye-less rubber mask and ball-gag stuffed in her mouth, raced along side the car, borne aloft by black segmented tentacles growing from her gaping, snapping vagina.

The crumbling Victorian mansions crept closer to the road until they stran-gled it. In its death-throes, the road thrashed from left to right until a mansion blocked the road entirely, and Howell aimed for the narrow alley between the colossal house and its neighbor, but the car wedged itself into the space and refused to budge in either direction. Howell climbed over the seats and out the back.

The storm battered the land with an ever-growing din, but still he heard the somnolent music of those molten chimes, coming from everywhere and nowhere—and growing louder. He looked frantically all around, waving a flashlight in the rain-slashed dark, but still he ran full into the honeycombed man before he saw him.

Howell fell on the pavement, but rolled and aimed the flashlight at the man. His problem with the bees had gotten worse. They were bigger, the size of hummingbirds circling his head, dancing secrets to each other on his shoul-ders, the hexagonal combs like shotgun holes in his face and neck and down beneath his shirt.

"Hurry," the honeycombed man said, and the bees echoed, "she's waiting for you."

Howell backed away from the man, from his car, from his own body. There had to be a way out of this, a way to escape, to wake up—

He turned and took a long stride to run away, but there was the man who'd beaten—and eaten—his doppelganger. "Get me out of here," the man said, and fingers squirmed out of his mouth, clawed at his lips. The fighter bent over, wracked by spasms and surges of movement under his muddy white suit. He screamed, and Howell saw something thrashing in the seat of his pants, tearing away the fabric, a tail—no, a leg...

Howell backed away again, but he heard angry bees circling behind him. The man threw himself at Howell's feet, screaming so loud, so wide, Howell could see the man inside him screaming, too.

"Come on," the honeycombed man took his arm and dragged him to the porch of the mansion in the road. Cobalt blue lanterns saturated the darkness in the parlor, vertebral shadows of legions of ferns, and among them, a bed, and on it, a woman's body—

But no, it wasn't her, and had he hoped it would be? This one was enormous, a monstrous puffball belly with drained, flaccid limbs trailing away from it like the knotted fingers of surgical gloves. Sizzling wings at his back drove him closer.

"Mr. Howell," she said, and he started, because underneath all that, it was her. "I know all about you, Howell. I even know your real name. What do you know?"

"I—" he looked around, at anything but her, and he heard creaking, crackling sounds, the ferns growing up through the floor so fast they glowed, feeding on the fever-heat, the light, pouring out of her. "I don't know anything."

"You got away, but you keep getting lost, you keep coming back."

"I got away because I don't belong here. This is all some kind of—"

"A mistake?" Her breath hitched in her, like laughter, or something inside trying to escape. "You escaped because you have no imagination. You don't dream."

"I had a dream…about you, before. You—This…this is a dream—"

"This *is* a dream—" The ground rumbled. The walls shook off pictures and knickknacks. A window looking out on the street shattered, the wind and rain pried away the storm shutters. Her belly shifted and stirred. "But it's more real than where you think you came from."

Her hand shot out and caught his. He pulled away so hard he staggered into the wall, his shoulder went right through the moldy plaster. "You…did something to me. Why did you do that?"

Her face brightened. "You remember! I didn't want to give you the wrong idea, but there was no time. There's no time, now, either." Her hand caressed the turgid globe of her belly.

"I don't understand what's going on, here, but what are you?" He swallowed and choked as he realized he was most afraid that she was not real. "All of you? What happened to you?"

"You did." She convulsed, pain drawing her into a ball around her pulsating womb.

He pointed and stammered, "No, that's not mine."

"You sound like you've done this before." She shrieked and made ribbons of the sheets. Her heels dug into the mattress, kicking divots of flea-infested stuffing across the rumbling room.

Howell knew he should take her hand but was terrified of coming any closer. Her belly contorted as if it caged a wild animal, then two animals battling, then each of them began to transform to catch the other at a disadvantage. Her skin stretched out into wild formations, stalks like roots and the eyes of overripe potatoes looking for anchorage or food to fuel its runaway metamorphosis—looking for him.

Howell backed into and right through the wall. He tripped over crumbling plaster and spilled into the atrium, narrowly dodging the heavy front door swinging in the whipping wind. The rain was no longer rain. Hot ash and bits of still-flaming debris swept by his face.

The hordes of Atwater, a hundred or more of them, crowded into the cul-de-sac before the mansion. On the horizon, a blood-red sun rose and swiftly grew, for it was not rising into the sky, but rolling up the road. The horde met this sight with bestial screams and wails of despair, but they remained rooted, distracting themselves with desperate last-minute orgies, battles and suicide attempts. Though they seemed incapable of coming, killing, or dying, still they chased these forbidden states in the burning rain even as the red sun drew closer.

The chimes grew louder, a steamroller trampling a forest of tubular bells. Inside, the woman called out to him, but he was fixed to the spot.

As the sun swelled, it came clear to Howell. A towering, brazen idol, taller than the highest weathervane on any of the mansions it shouldered aside as it rolled down the street on iron-shod wheels.

A giant, saturnine head and torso, with great hands outstretched to lift its worshippers to its grinding mechanical jaws. The whole idol glowed dull red with the heat of the furnace raging inside it. All that it touched crumpled in white flames, but the hordes of freaks crowded closer, herded by cage-headed alienists with baling hooks and pikes.

The horde tortured itself, each tearing at the deformities of his or her neighbor as the heat between them came alive with light and fire. Packed closer and closer together as the idol trapped them in the cul-de-sac, they approached an ecstasy of panic, yet they meekly stepped or knelt, singly and in knots of writhing bodies, onto the spreading palms of the glowing idol.

Howell knew this was the thing from which he had averted his eyes, the last time he got lost in Atwater. When she said, "He's coming," she meant this. Now, it was too late to escape, the horde danced on his trapped car. He could go through the mansion, dive out a window on the other side and run all the way home, if he had to, but he got no further than the parlor, where the woman's ordeal was, for better or worse, nearly over.

The woman who raped him told him the thing inside her was his. He could come no closer than the hole he'd made in the wall, but he could not run away from it. Her legs jerked and wrenched impossibly akimbo, laying bare her privates, and a glimpse of something fighting its way out of her.

No one had ever asked for what she took from him. No one had ever wanted anything from him but his facility as a calculator, and so the violence with which she had taken his seed had left him curiously stronger than he'd been, before. He'd never realized how much he feared human contact, and he saw in her slitted eyes, now, how much like him she was, how loathsome the act had been for her, but how desperately necessary.

That the act had produced some offspring, here in this place that was insanity itself, was the only sane thing Howell could find to cling to.

He went to her and took her hand. He tried to soothe her with words and touch, but she seemed beyond noticing. "If you're going to be the mother of my child," he said, "I think you could at least tell me your name."

Her eyes rolled but focused on him, and in the midst of her panting seizure, she found breath to laugh at him for real. "Your *child*? Oh, Howell, you idiot—"

A rush of scalding heat raised blisters on his face, and the outer wall melted away like a tortilla under a blowtorch. Outside, all he could see was a single red eye, glowering cruel and absolute with the fires of a collapsing sun behind it, a brain that blasted all it touched to atoms. It looked full on them, now, as, all at once, the woman gave birth.

Her hand clasped his and the mountain of her belly tore open like a water-balloon smashing into a wall.

Ferns curled and turned to silver tornadoes of ash. Swamps of sweat vaporized out of the sheets. The woman's hand went slack and deflated in his grip, split open like rotten fruit. Howell's own clothes smoldered and gave off puffs of steam and smoke, but he noticed none of it.

The thing that squatted in the ruined chrysalis of the woman at first looked like nothing more than her insides, bones, muscles, guts and all, stirred and resculpted into a crude effigy of a newborn child, but it redefined itself as he watched. Swaddled in blood and shreds of uterine lining, the thing uncoiled and opened its eyes. Swollen sacs of tissue burst and unfurled into membranous wings, and Howell understood.

"Thank you," she said, her voice piping and unsteady in its new vessel, "for helping me escape. I'm sorry you won't."

The wings snapped and beat the air, shaking off slime and lifting the newborn body into the air in one swift motion. Howell ducked, then made a half-hearted attempt to catch her, but she eluded him and dove out the window, into the eye of the idol.

And then the whole house was flying sideways, and Howell had no choice but to go with it. The chiming, roaring explosion went on forever, the room rolling end over end and dancing wheels of fire all around him. And when it all stopped, he was too broken to move, but somehow, he was outside.

The brazen idol clawed at the sky, at a fleeting dart of light that was well away from its glowing grip, and the idol seemed to come unhinged inside, and all its parts simply disconnected from the others and the furnace, unleashed, spilled out waves of fire upon the hordes. Howell ran and ran and still the sound of the fire rolling, gaining, eating up the land, grew in his ears, but he kept running, in his mind calculating his speed and caloric consumption and estimated time of arrival if he just ran and ran home, if he ran to Mexico, if he just ran around the world and came back to this exact point—

Somewhere, long before he got home, he dropped in his tracks and fainted, mind and body completely spent.

And he woke up in a ditch beside the 99 just outside the town of Chowchilla, a sheriff's deputy in an orange poncho poking him in the ribs with a flashlight. "Thought you was one of them pigs," said the deputy.

He held his life together pretty well, after that, all told, and most of the time, he didn't remember his dreams.

He worked from home, toting up accounts for several small, borderline illegal companies. He did not, could not, go outside. The fear that he would get lost again, that he might lose track of the route down the street to the corner store, kept him inside. In every corner of every place he did not know as intimately as well as his own body, a doorway to Atwater waited.

And yet he kept working, eating and sleeping, because, though he did not admit it even to himself while he was awake, he hoped for something.

He lurched on through life like this for months before the dreams started to push through into work, into the blank spaces on the screen and the black pauses between commercials on TV. Her face, her wings lifting her out of the fire and into the sky. He still lived, he began to see, only because he thought she would come back.

That there might be some sign, some message to affirm that she was not just a dream, he began to seek out, but nothing came forth to save him. He looked for other Atwaters and found one, in Minnesota—"a small, friendly community which welcomes people with open arms…" said the website of the town "named for Dr. E. D. Atwater, of the land department of the St. Paul and Pacific Railroad"—but nothing to distinguish it or marry it to the others, except its name. He did searches, found people, companies, named Atwater, but nothing that resonated…until he found a listing in his old local phone book, and did a search on the computer.

Atwater Transpersonal Institute. The website gave a breezy outline of treatments, but Howell didn't read them. He looked only at the picture on the home page, of a row of couches with people lying on them, sleeping peacefully with spider webs of electrodes pasted to their skulls. He studied the woman on the nearest couch, the planed bones of her face, the black wings of hair flared out on the pastel pillow, and he got his car keys.

At the end of a quiet residential street, on the peak of a hill overlooking Presidio Park with its Spanish colonial fortress, the Atwater Institute looked like the first outpost of yet another colonization. A low, faux-adobe building huddled around a conical tower of tile and glass. It hid itself from the street behind white brick walls and eucalyptus trees, but the gates readily swung open when Howell pressed the button at the unmanned security checkpoint. He drove up the cobblestone path to the front doors, where a nurse waited. He wanted to turn around and go back home, but he forced himself to get out and walk up to her. "I think—I know a woman who is being treated here. I'd like to see her, please."

The nurse only stared, backed away and went inside, leaving the door hanging open. He followed, pausing helplessly as a valet slipped into his car and whisked it off to an underground garage.

Inside, the atrium was dimly lit by a soothing cobalt light. Banks of ferns in hanging pots softened the outlines of the room, and a soft, almost inaudible music played somewhere, an atonal carillon stirred by alien wind.

Howell wanted out, needed in. *She's here, somewhere, it's all here, it wasn't in your mind, oh God, it was all real*—

"I'll get Dr. Atwater," the nurse said, and fled the room. Howell looked at abstract pictures on the walls, at a watercolor of a man with a beehive for a head, at another of a man being strangled by marionettes with their own wires, which sprouted out of his flesh.

"Art therapy," said a voice over his shoulder. "It's not pleasant to look at, but it makes them healthier."

"What else do they do?" Howell turned and looked at the Doctor's feet. He could not look at his face, but he heard the man's reaction.

"I—my God, what're you doing here?" asked Dr. Atwater.

"You treat people with sleep therapy here, right?"

"That's correct. Maybe you—"

"I have been having bad dreams for a number of years, Doctor. About this place."

"I can't say I'm surprised. Maybe if I could show you..." Dr. Atwater beckoned him through a door into an even darker corridor. Howell followed, looking around him. The music was louder back here. Atwater said, "Binaural tones guide the treatment. Shamanic cultures know it and use them in rituals, in drumming and trance-inducing states to guide the shaman into the realm of the spirit. It's subtler than medication, and it doesn't blunt the subconscious input from the limbic system. It lets dreams become the patient's reality."

"For how long?"

"In my papers, I recommended three-day regimens over several months, but the modalities promised so much more for extreme cases, if we could only push deeper, longer. But you know all this."

Howell stopped avoiding the doctor's eyes. "Where is the woman? The one in the picture?"

Atwater opened a door, waved Howell closer. A body lay on the couch that filled the cell. Howell leapt at it, but froze.

The honeycombed man twitched and shivered on the couch. He wore mittens and restraints, but still his face was red and chafed, all facial hair plucked out from compulsive grooming.

"One of our most challenging cases. He suffers from a massive OCD complex, but in his therapy, he externalizes his disorder, manifesting it in terms he can metaphorically abolish. He's been dreaming for a month on, a week off for two years, and he's getting better."

Blinking, seeing the bees like ravens on the patient's face, Howell muttered, "No, he's not." Then, rounding on the Doctor, he demanded, "Where is she?"

He looked deep into Dr. Atwater's eyes, then, and though they were a cold blue, he saw the lambent red glow in them. His mouth made a bold pretense of smiling openness, but his brow was forked with wrathful wrinkles, and his rusty red beard formed a half-mask of flames. "I'm afraid I don't understand. Who are you looking for?"

"You know, don't you lie!" Howell flinched at his own voice, but he took hold of the Doctor's arms and pushed him back against the wall. "You were there! You tried to eat her up like all the others, but she got away from you!"

Atwater's eyes flashed, his jaw dropped. "So, you found a back door into the group… Well, that's a mystery solved, at any rate."

As if done with Howell, he made to turn away and go about his business, but Howell slammed him again into the wall. "Where is she?"

"Gone. Transferred to a private institution. Her parents might not sue. They're very wealthy, powerful people, and they were very upset when their neurotic, drug-addicted daughter came to us to be cured and emerged a full-blown schizophrenic."

"Your dream therapy fucked up her brain?"

"No, Howell, you did. She got it from you." Atwater opened another door onto darkness. "Here, I'll show you."

Howell stepped inside. A body lay on the couch, but there were many machines, a congregation of automated mourners beeping and wailing their grief and providing the only light, trees with IV dripping solutions and the atonal music of binaural chimes.

Atwater spoke into his ear in a low whisper. "He was our first extreme case. Persistent vegetative state from birth, ward of the state, we secured power of attorney before the first bricks of the Institute were laid. He was going to be my greatest triumph."

Howell approached the couch, feeling like he did in the mansion, as if he were about to ignite and combust from the heat of the idol, from the heat pouring out of the body on the couch.

"At first, he responded swimmingly, but the deeper we tried to drive into his subconscious, the more he retreated…until one day, about three years ago, he just stopped waking up. I concluded that the psychic disintegration—for that's what it looked like, to me—was a result of his distorted self-concept, his lack of imagination. But I underestimated just how powerful his imagination really was, didn't I?"

Howell tried to remember where he went to school, who his parents were, anything more than three years old, and wondered why none of it had ever mattered before. Because he was a hermetically sealed, self-contained world unto himself, and nothing outside him had ever been anything but numbers, until she forced him to touch her, and escaped—

"At the time, we never reckoned on the possibility that our patients were manifesting in a shared environment, let alone that one could escape it. When Ms. Heaton began to exhibit your symptoms, we thought it was a ploy. Ms. Heaton was very cunning, manipulative, and had attempted suicide more times than her family bothered to keep track of. We never dreamed she could contact the other patients, let alone that she might find you. But *you* found *her*."

Howell leaned closer to the sleeper, eyes roving over the only truly familiar face he'd ever known. The geography of it, seen from any angle for the first time, totally engrossed him, so that he didn't notice when Atwater locked the door and took out a syringe.

"His name is Jeremy Ogilvie, but we use code names for our patients, to protect their privacy. The nurses coined his—he used to scream at the top of his lungs whenever he was touched, so they called him the Howler."

Atwater's shadow loomed across the white desert of sheet, but Howell only leaned closer to the sleeping face.

"For so long, I've thought of you, Mr. Howell, as my only failure. It would appear that you are the only one I ever really cured."

Howell reached up and touched the mouth of the sleeping face, and smiled when its eyes opened.

EDWARD BRYANT began writing professionally in 1968 and had more than a dozen books published, including *Among the Dead*, *Cinnabar*, *Phoenix Without Ashes* (with Harlan Ellison), *Wyoming Sun*, *Particle Theory*, *Fetish* (a novella chapbook), and *The Baku: Tales of the Nuclear Age*. In the beginning he was known as a science fiction writer but gradually strayed into horror and mostly remained there until his death in 2017, writing a series of sharply etched stories about Angie Black, a contemporary witch, the brilliant zombie story "A Sad Last Love at the Diner of the Damned," and other marvelous, exceedingly dark tales.

The Transfer
Edward Bryant

SOMETHING IS NOT right.

My name is Doris Ruth MacKenzie, and I am forty-three years old. When I was a little girl, everyone around me called me Dorrie. I hated that. Nowadays, only a few friends remember—and they still call me that—but it's all right.

And then there's Jim. It's fine for Jim to call me Dorrie. I haven't loved many people, but those I *have* loved—they can do anything.

Jim? *Jim.* Where are you?

James Gordon MacKenzie has been my husband for twenty-two years. We've known each other only slightly longer than that. He's a tall man, slightly stooped, and kind. Always very kind. *And he's wearing a red mask.* Something's not right at all.

Jim? My wrists are numb. There is so much I can't touch. Behind my eyes, the pain zigzags madly. It feels like there are shards of broken glass grinding in there. I can't see anything, except what I can think of.

Jim… Where are you?

Talk to me, love.

Won't anyone speak to me? I'm talking to myself.

But I'm not going crazy. I'm *not!*

He wears a scarlet mask. It shines, glistens like—What is it I'm not seeing?

I can still feel. People always said I had empathy. Even at the beginning, when I first could frame ideas in words, I knew I could feel for others, actually *feel* others. "Equalizing potentials," my high school physics teacher said, even though he never knew what those two words actually meant to me. He was speaking of something else entirely. It was a metaphor I couldn't phrase, but I knew it fit.

"A high-pressure area's generated to the west of the Quad Cities…"

That's the practical application of my teacher's words.

Reading from the wire copy: "The low-pressure system in central Illinois is holding steady."

I'd smile again and use my breathy, little-girl voice.

"The storm's coming in fast, folks. Bring in your doggies and kitty cats. The Weather Bureau says—"

We still called it the Weather Bureau back then. It was 1963, I was twenty-three, and I was working at WWHO-TV in Aurora. I hadn't made it into Chicago yet—at least professionally—but finally I was past Peoria.

I had thought the forecast was still variable.

Oh, God. The weather report. The patterns with their smooth whorls. The transfer of energy, sometimes violently. The shapes from the contour maps swirling around me, humming monotonously, distorting all the clear, sharp angles...

At WWHO they hired me because I was cute. The station manager let me know that right away. I didn't want to go out to dinner with him, but he was very insistent, and I was hungry.

Over his medium-rare liver and onions, he said, "We'll get you the numbers. You'll be the sexiest, most watched weathergirl in the Midwest. You'll be able to write your own ticket in New York or LA, wherever you want." But first, of course, he'd have to punch my ticket in Aurora.

The smell of liver and onions and sex made me want to throw up. I said no. But it was close, dangerously so. The compulsion to touch his soul, satisfy his need, to draw near and meld with him, actually *be* him, perhaps to become even worse than he...that frightened me so much that I drew back.

I wouldn't have phrased it this way, back then, but I wanted to remain my own person.

The next night, there were messages scrawled on my weather board; they were terrible, obscene things. The Chroma-Key didn't pick them up, so only the crew and I could see them. I finished the evening news block, and then I quit. I didn't have many choices, but at least that one I could make.

So that's why I ended up in Chicago sooner than I'd expected, on the streets looking for another job; maybe I could be a weathergirl again. I don't think there are many weathergirls now. Every station has its own staff meteorologist and they usually are men. But back then, looks counted.

At least for more than they do now. I think. I haven't tried to trade on looks for a long, long time, and that's all to the good.

When I finally got a job, it was at an advertising agency on North Michigan. The company was called Martin, Metzger, and Mulcahy, and appearances certainly counted there. The men who ran the agency had a crystalline vision of how we should all look and act, whether we were at the office or not. You always represent the agency, they said. All of us had to measure up to their expectations.

It's not easy defining yourself that way, but I tried. I worked hard and did what they wanted for six months, until nearly my twenty-fourth birthday. I was a pretty good secretary. It seemed to work—I was in line for a promotion. Then I met Cody.

That's blood, isn't it? Blood, all liquid and running down—Stop it, Dorrie! Think. Remember…

My parents, my father especially, used to tell me, don't be so impressionable, Dorrie. Use your own head. But how could I do that when I used the heads of others? When I saw through their eyes and felt what they felt. And, and—

What, Dorrie? I looked back, confronted the child I was then, the person I am now.

I-I became like—No, I *became*—

Please… Damn it. Please, no, I'm me. Me, Doris MacKenzie. I am forty-three years old, though I overheard one of my neighbors at the market talking to a woman from across the street and guessing that I was in my fifties. That's as old as Jim, my husband. They didn't know I'd overheard, because there was a pyramid of paper towel rolls between us.

It's not that I mind being that old. No, it's being reminded of him. We were so much alike. My dearest, dearest. His face is so red. And it drips. Oh, Jim.

I met Cody Anderssen on my lunch break while I was walking slowly along the lakefront. At first I thought he was just another hippy. There weren't many hippies downstate in Macomb, at least none I'd ever been aware of, and certainly I'd never met one, much less talked to any. If my mother had been along, I'm sure she would have turned and walked twice as fast the other way, maybe shrieking for police at the same time. I was braver. When the freakish-looking man said, "Hi," I just kept on walking in the same measured pace.

He followed in step beside me. "You look awful nice," he said. "Will you just stop a minute and talk?"

My step faltered, and I really looked at him. He was young, perhaps even younger than I. Blue eyes—I remember those well. They were the same deep blue I sometimes saw in the winter sky above the lake. He wore a broad-brimmed leather hat and a fringed leather jacket that looked like it had been sewn at home. His goatee and long hair were blond. The hair made me feel uneasy, but the clean shine of it somehow triggered me to speak.

"You look like Buffalo Bob—"

"—Bill," he said, correcting me, apparently unamused.

I laughed. After a moment, so did he.

He told me his name and then spelled "Anderssen." "It's not so remarkable where I come from—northern Minnesota—but at least down here the *s*'s and the *e* make me something different. It's groovy."

I blinked. I wanted to ask if Cody really was his first name, but felt too shy.

At first Cody made all the conversation. He told me about leaving Minnesota and coming here, of living on the streets for months before finding a job in a pet store and an apartment he could afford. He talked about drugs, a topic that scared me. It was the question of control. "And you?" he finally said.

I talked about growing up in Macomb and hardly ever going to the city, and how, when I graduated from high school, I went against my parents and didn't enroll at Western Illinois. The first brave thing I ever did in my life was to take the bus to Peoria, then on toward Chicago.

My parents had talked so often of my striking out on my own, I thought that was what they really and truly wanted of me. The conflict made me sick for days. As ever, I stored up the tension like a battery.

But I ended up in Aurora as a weathergirl at a tiny TV station, and then immersed myself in the city.

"That's great," Cody said, and then laughed. "You oughta be a hippie too. You've got the spirit of freedom in you."

No, I didn't, but I didn't say my doubts aloud.

"It's late," I said, looking at my watch. "My lunch hour's gone. I've got to go back to the office."

"Meet me after work," said Cody. "Please?"

I stared at him. I'd never met anyone at all like this.

After work, in the mob of rush hour, I found him. The next morning, which was Saturday, I met him again and we went out to the Museum of Science and Industry and toured the coal mine. That night I accompanied him back to his apartment and lost my virginity.

And two decades later, I wish I were back in Chicago. In a different bed than where I lie now.

Two weeks later I moved into Cody's apartment. My original apartment had been larger, but I was too shy to let him move there. I kept going back to my old apartment for a month to pick up my mail. Finally Cody convinced me to tell my parents I'd moved to a nicer place. I got a post office box and hoped my folks wouldn't come visit Chicago. I told them I would come home for Christmas.

I quit my job. I wore the same kind of clothing Cody did. I let my hair grow long and straight. I started learning guitar. I used the same drugs he did. I sold the same things he did. We finished each other's sentences. We got along all right.

Cody took real delight in being special, different. It was his name, his clothes, everything. But we were both alike in so many ways now. He noticed it too.

"It's so freakin' weird," he said one night. "You and I. It's almost like looking in a mirror, except that a mirror image's reversed. You're *me*, darlin'." He shook his head.

I couldn't contradict him. Only a portion of it was wanting to be what he wished me to be. Part of it too was *being* him. I didn't know what it meant—just that it had always been so. And it worked both inside and out. Cody had an ulcer. I had an ulcer.

"I don't want you to be me," he said.

"Don't you?"

He shook his head again. "We're all free," Cody said. "It's the time of liberation."

I just stared at him. He looked back at me and finally kissed me long and hard. The gaze from his blue eyes fixed me.

"I like what I see," said Cody.

But a week later he died. I never was sure what all he took. The hardest thing I've ever done was to avoid following Cody into the abyss. It wasn't easy, but I tried to absorb the compulsion within myself.

I still had the clothing I'd brought to Chicago. I resumed my colorless, invisible presence. No more beads. No more fringe. The ulcer went away.

My name is Dorrie Mackenzie, and I'm older than that now. There are songs I can almost remember, images I can nearly recall. The portrait of Jim on my dresser at home swims into focus. But it isn't Jim. It's something I look at in my mind and then discard. Whatever it is, it can't be him. He is a pleasant, attractive man. And this thing on the dresser is, is—I don't know. It could be anything. It reminds me of the skinned head of a rabbit. I throw the image away. I will not think of it.

The dresser and the picture on it evaporate. Our house in Kansas City dissolves into fragments and then to blackness.

I see nothing. But I can listen. What I hear sounds like a man stripping away a stubborn Velcro panel.

Probably I think of that because of Jim. There is an inflatable leg-setting sleeve with Velcro seams in his bag. He's a doctor, a GP, and he even still makes occasional house calls. Takes his bag wherever he goes, even on vacation.

Vacation... See the wild beasts. Don't think about it. Red beasts. Scarlet. Dripping scarlet, shining—

Wet.

I can feel the high-pressure area all through me. My skull wants to explode. Energy flows, deepens, prepares to flood. I have so little control anymore.

Storm warning.

It was wet, raining heavily, when I met Jim. He never realized the melodramatic circumstances of how it happened. All he knew was that he happened upon a bedraggled woman trudging toward the midway point of a highway bridge over the Chicago River in the middle of a driving rainstorm. He thought I must have had automobile trouble, so he stopped to see if he could help. What he did was save my life, since I'd been planning to jump from the center of the span into the muddy current. I never let him know that. I would have turned down his offer of a ride except for his eyes. They were kind eyes, a deep liquid brown, and intelligent.

I got in his car. That was the beginning. I forgot about the attraction of the abyss, of the fatal temptation that had continued to haunt me after Cody's death.

It was love, or something similar. At least it was the need, the necessity that always tugged me toward others.

It's not that I'm a chameleon. I'm not. Transference and transformation—those are the key words. What they mean is less important than what I feel. In truth, I adapt to my environment.

It's the way I survive.

Jim and I lived in Chicago for another two years, then went to Cleveland when he was offered a good clinic position. It didn't work out as well as he'd have liked, so then it was back to Chicago. Finally we came to Kansas City, where some of Jim's medical school friends had set up a partnership and invited him in.

It was peaceful. For years, the only real conflict was my having to convince Jim that I really couldn't have children. I didn't want to tell him the truth—that I didn't want to. That was our only difference, and I think I only had the will to carry it out because he secretly, in his heart of hearts, didn't want to share his life with anyone else. At any rate, my forty-fourth birthday would be in just one more week, on the seventh; procreation was getting to be ever less of a real possibility.

For all those years, Jim urged me to be myself. It was only partially success-ful. I've stored up so much.

The forecast… Storms? Earthquake? Tidal wave? Apocalypse? I don't really know. All I do know is that my head hurts, as though the skull wants to come apart at the cranial fissures.

Jim? Touch me, stroke me, tell me things are all right. If I could just see you again.

But I would have to open my eyes.

Something I learned to notice with both Cody and Jim: it wasn't just that I came to resemble them in so many important aspects; to whatever degree, to *be* them as I was defined by each. There was always something a little extra, a lagniappe.

As they perceived me, they had what they wanted, and a little bit more.

Simple physical proximity was enough to trigger the process, closeness of bodies and souls carried it through. I discovered that sex speeded it. Sharing served as an accelerator. And trauma—

Because Jim knew many people through his work, we socialized quite a lot, and our friends sometimes remarked that we looked *so* much like each other.

Jim would allow his easy Midwestern chuckle and make a joke about the psychological studies of how so many human beings and their pets come to resemble each other. Transference.

And who was who? he'd say. Everyone would laugh.

The storm is breaking.

And here we are at the Sleepaway Motel in Bishop, California.

I will open my eyes; I *will*.

Here we are in a forsaken desert town I've never seen before and hope I never will again. Jim. Dorrie. And the new man in my life. I sound so flip only because it keeps the hysteria at bay. I had enough of trying to scream through the gag.

The heat lightning had flashed over the mountains as we checked in. One more long day to San Diego. Our first vacation in years. The Wild Animal Park on my birthday—that was Jim's promise.

We checked into the motel, that damned motel, that motel of the damned, and then—Shut up, Dorrie! There is nothing left to do. Only one thing left undone.

The knock.

Must be the manager, Jim had said. Probably didn't get a clear impression on the credit card or something.

When he unlatched the door—

Don't scream, Dorrie, don't.

—it burst open, Jim flung aside, the nameless man with the gun, the pistol, the metal dark and shining, the threat and the darkness.

It is our vacation. My birthday is in only a few days. These things don't happen to people, not to normal people, good people.

Oh, but they do, Dorrie, the man said. I know your name. Your husband—Jim?—said it before I took care of his tongue. Did you appreciate my giving him the Demerol before I worked on his face?

Not to normal people, they don't. I'm not normal.

Oh, said the man, you look normal enough to me, as normal as any other woman tied to the bed with her husband's two neckties, an Ace bandage, and a roll of gauze. Taste in ties a little conservative, eh? I figure you'll act normal enough when I get around to you. That's it. Keep your eyes open.

I am bound tightly, my shoulders hard against the headboard, my limbs stretched apart, my body open and vulnerable. I have no choice but to face Jim. He is roped upright into the wooden chair at the foot of the bed.

The weather, Dorrie. My voice now is solely in my head. The storm is breaking. The smooth contour swirls. The rain and the wind will come. If only they would rush in and cleanse—

Oh yes, Dorrie, says the man. I'm glad your husband was a doctor. Handy he brought his bag along. Saved me no end of trouble. He holds up the disposable scalpel in one hand, the mask that Jim wore in the other. No. No, Dorrie. It's not a mask at all.

The hemostats, the glittering clamps are set out on the bedspread. The fabric's pattern is designed to hide anything. But I can see the instruments. I look away from Jim to the waldo—the long, curved forceps. Beside it are the incision clips, stylized clothespins with teeth.

All told, there are three of us in the room, but in every real way, I am now alone. I begin to know with final sureness what will happen.

And yet…and yet I know I am not the person I was for all my early years. I know that somewhere inside, I do have a core that will not be bent, cannot be warped, and maybe, just perhaps, I can draw upon it.

But the forecast is bleak.

What I feel is like the pulling back of a nail from the quick of a finger. No, Dorrie, I tell myself, that is too soft, too gentle. It is more like the wrench of my heart being taken away, torn from me.

Jim's kiss was always gentle. This man's will be rough.

Jim's embrace… His touch was kind. The man's will be brutal.

When Jim entered me, it was joyfully. This man—I cannot imagine his touch. Not yet. It will tear. Burn. Like the lightning, only not clean.

The crimson, the sheen, the mask, the blood. I will say goodbye to Jim in my soul and look ahead. The man with the gun and the scalpel. I have read of killers like him and his fellows, though I didn't think people like us ever encountered them. It was always another depressing story on the news, just before the weather.

Some people win lotteries.

Jim and I—Forget that, Dorrie.

I look forward again. Storm fronts. Equalizing potentials… The man stares down at me, and is that a gentle smile? It is a smile. He holds Jim's mask in his free hand.

I think I am ready to give it up. He will possess me here on this soaked bed in the Sleepaway Motel in Bishop, California, before he pulls the trigger or pushes the blade.

His lips, shiny, part. I'll want you to wear the mask, he says, for you and me. Just for us, Dorrie. He leans down toward me.

That is when I decide.

What a surprise for him. He will comprehend the trauma of my transformation. Frankly even I do not know the extent of the power, the energy released by storm fronts colliding.

I wonder what he will encounter beyond the mask: something with horns, fangs, scales, fur? Something as bestial as only he can imagine? Or just himself enhanced? Whatever the sum, it will only be the result of his terrifying addition.

Goodbye, Jim. Farewell, love. This nameless man in the motel, regardless of how I am transformed, will get no less than he deserves.

And probably more.

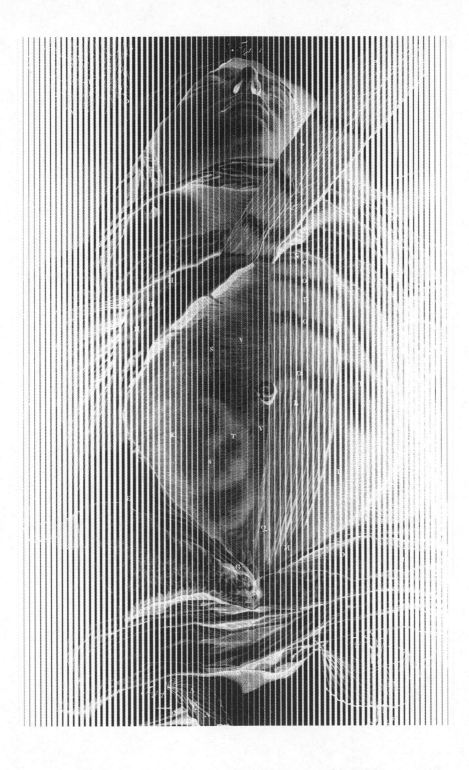

SIMON BESTWICK is the author of six novels, the novellas *Breakwater* and *Angels of the Silences,* four full-length short story collections, and two miniature ones. His short fiction has appeared in *Black Static, The Devil and the Deep,* and *The London Reader* and has been reprinted in *The Best Horror of the Year* and *Best British Fantasy 2013.* Four times shortlisted for the British Fantasy Award, he is married to fellow author Cate Gardner. His latest book is the collection *And Cannot Come Again*, recently reissued by *Horrific Tales.* He's usually to be found watching films, reading or writing, which keeps him out of mischief. Most of the time. Bestwick lives on the Wirral while pining for Wales.

Welcome to Mengele's
Simon Bestwick

ON THE SCREEN, there was a naked corpse, female, far gone in decay, face down. Behind it, a chubby balding man, middleaged, gripped its hips and buggered it. There was something horribly familiar about both figures, and it took me a moment to register what it was. When I did—

"Oh, *Jesus...*"

Even through my nausea, I had to admit that the surgeons had done a great job. Even the corpse was a dead ringer for the original.

The dozen or so necros masturbating furiously in their seats cheered, or those who were confident enough of coming did. The corpse's cheek split open and oozed pus. I grimaced and looked away.

Sharkey clapped me on the shoulder. "Come on. No worse than remixing *Candle In The Wind.*" He laughed coarsely, then caught my arm and towed me away from the open door.

We passed another two viewing rooms en route. In one, the screen showed Marilyn Monroe being gangbanged by Buddy Holly, Ritchie Valens, and the Big Bopper, with the young Elvis and John Lennon about to join in. As we passed, one of them pressed the tip of a knife to her shoulder and carved a red path down her side to her hip. Blood ran over the chinawhite skin. In the other room, the Osmonds were getting up to antics in a farmyard that I'd have otherwise thought medically impossible.

Welcome to Mengele's.

I never thought of Sharkey as the kind of guy who'd know about this kind of place, but he did.

Getting in wasn't the problem. To come calling, someone has to have told you, and they don't tell you unless they know you're their kind of client. I don't know what Mengele's look for in a client. There's one qualification that's obvious, of course, and that's money. Wads and wads of the stuff. This isn't for you if your idea of paying for it is twenty quid for a kneetrembler down the alley, that's for sure.

It was nothing to look at. A line of detacheds on a posh suburban street. Chintzy decor glimpsed through windows bordered with fronds of lace curtain. Retired majors, stockbrokers, powerdressing executives, all the trueblue backbone types with Jags and Beamers parked on their gravel driveways.

Then you come up to the fifth house on the right, crunch your way up another gravel drive and press the bell, which plays the opening bars of Beethoven's Fifth. Someone's idea of a joke. The door opens and a smiling housewife type shakes your hand, takes your coat, welcomes you inside.

Money changes hands, or at least someone's Gold Card does temporarily. And you're in. Three floors, then a basement and subbasement. Your blackest desires fulfilled on every one.

Sharkey was a mate from long ago, who'd ended up doing well for himself. Very well. One of those clawed-his-way-up-from-the-slag-heap types who'd rattle on about how he'd done it for two hours at a stretch at the slightest encouragement, like you'd never heard it before. A couple of hundred times before.

He'd been Mr MoodSwings lately. Depressed and ready to take your head off one minute, then beaming, backslapping, offering brandy and cigars and acting like the king of all the world the next. I'd been starting to feel nervous around him for a while, but I stuck with him. He was a mate.

Anyway, one night, there we'd been, Sharkey whipping out a cereal bowl full of enough snow to send Rudolph and all the reindeers airborne without Santa Claus' help and snorting it up like an industrial hoover. I turned the offer down, although I said yes to the cigars and the highpriced Napoleon VSOP or whatever it was called. We talked over old times, with me leaning forwards or backwards out of bottling range depending on which way Sharkey's pendulum was swinging at that minute. And finally Sharkey looked up, rings of white dust crusted round his snotholes, and said, "Who do you want to fuck?"

"Me?"

"Yeah, who?"

I thought about it, then mentioned his secretary, an incredibly luscious natural blonde who'd have been earning me Hail Marys from here to eternity if

I'd still been a believer. Sharkey rolled his (severely dilated) eyes and shook his head. "No, no, no. Christ, you never did have any ambition. I say *who*, I mean anybody. Anybody *ever*. Man, woman, alive, dead. *Whoever. Anybody.* Shit, pick two or three if it's a close run. Your ultimate fantasy fuck."

Well, that's a question, isn't it? I mean, I thought of his secretary because you automatically get used to that kind of thing, don't you? You let your dreams tone themselves down because it spares you the worst disappointments. And when the field's thrown wide like that—shit...

I hemmed and hawed and thought it over for a few minutes till I started seeing Sharkey's eyes rolling like the insides of tumble driers and decided I'd better get my finger out. So I took a deep breath and reeled off the rollcall for my ultimate foursome—Lauren Bacall (young) Ingrid Bergman (ditto) and from the present day, Gillian Anderson.

Sharkey nodded approval. "You're sure?" he said. "Anyone else? That's it, definitely?"

I nodded. "Yeah, why?"

He shook his head, wagged a finger naughtynaughty style and laughed. "It's a surprise. You're gonna love it."

And a couple of nights later, here we were.

Yes, it was that Mengele—Josef, the Angel of Death, performer of lunatic experiments to the strains of Wagner's *Nibelung*. The story ran that after the war, the mad doctor had carried on his obsession with twisting flesh out of shape. And it also ran that he'd had some successes. The big success had been in plastic surgery. *Plastic* being the operative word. See, there's usually a limit to what even the best surgeon can do, and how often. Sooner or later, the body—skin, muscle, bone, whichever part you're playing with—throws up the white flag and says *forget it, I give up*.

I don't know the specifics—everything about Mengele's is rumour, even its existence. You can only find out about it through friends, or the friends of friends. They can't exactly advertise. Like I said, how they decide who finds out and who doesn't is beyond me. Not that it matters right now.

Mengele linked up with a few more of the old Nazis. God knows what kind of a reunion they had, swapping mutilation stories and funny anecdotes about Himmler. But these were all medical men, the ones who'd got out before the Yanks could rescue them with Operation Paperclip or before being passed over for it and thrown to the wolves at Nuremberg or worse, the Russians. These boys all had their specialities. And when they all put their heads together…

Mengele was making headway with a process he'd come up with as an aid to his crazier experiments—trying to make arms grow out of people's backs, grafting horns onto men or dogs' heads onto women, that kind of thing. He ran up against that old brick wall, tissue rejection. He messed around with mechanical aids that connected the different bits, a kind of interface handling changeovers in blood and suchlike, but in the end it wasn't good enough for him. He wanted perfect blending between one piece and another.

His process was something to do with plasticity, protoplasms—all stuff that went clean over my head. I've got a feeling that only a maniac could have discovered it, or probably, understood it.

Whatever. What it boils down to is that with this process, tissue stretches. It literally becomes putty in your hands, whether it's flesh or bone. In that state, you can cut and twist and shape it like a sculptor, or, like clay, smooth it into another piece of tissue from something else. When the process is complete, the pieces are connected by a kind of hybrid tissue that neither piece rejects.

It was going well, but the mad doctor needed money. He was loaded as it was, of course, but he could see years of research spinning out ahead of him, and it was going to take a lot of the green stuff to sort it out. So him and his buddies hit on the perfect scam.

Want to fuck a movie star? Which one? Pick him or her from our exclusive catalogue, and if you don't find the one you're looking for, we'll create them for you. To order. Do you want them to dominate you, or has it always been your fantasy to whip and fuck Audrey Hepburn? Or whoever? Strap them down and cut off their faces to mount on your wall as souvenirs, or just because you can? You only need to ask us; we'll quote you a price.

You want them living or you want them dead? No problem. As amputees? Easy.

Movies featuring the above? Private screenings arranged at your local branch of Mengele's. At an agreed rate (usually five or six figures, and seven or eight aren't unheard of) videotapes, DVDs or, for the traditionalists, film (8 mm, 16 mm, 35 mm or even 70 mm, with and without widescreen format) are available. And with modern CGI techniques, it gets even better. The great, the good, the notsogood, alive or dead—you can have them to do with as you please at Mengele's.

Bestiality? Paedophilia? *Naturellement, Monsieur.* Down the hallways, second on your left. In the subbasement, it was (again) rumoured that some of Mengele's byblows were kept. The dogheaded. The antlered men. Arms out of backs. Whatever. Maybe it was true and maybe it wasn't. Do you *want* it to be true? As long as you've got the money, it will be. If the dogheads don't exist, they'll make 'em up just for you.

This was the ultimate brothel. You really could have anything, whoever your heart desired. And it worked. Mengele never quite got to reap the fruits of his endeavours—he got his comeuppance in some accident or other after a few more years of manufacturing refugees from Hieronymus Bosch paintings. But what he created lives on. Fantasies tailor-made, so minutely perfect you can't see the join.

As long as you don't think too hard about where the meat they're made from comes from.

There was a waiting room with half a dozen wide video screens. At the flick of a switch, you could view whatever was running in the other viewing rooms, or you could take your pick from the wall to wall collections. All sorts. Some well known—*Debbie Does Dallas, Animal Farm*—others, imports, all pretty kinky as you'd expect here, and, of course—the bulk of the display—Mengele's own homemade movies.

Production values straight out of the top drawer, of course. And the performers…well, they were all movie stars, weren't they? Or other celebrities. Although why the hell anyone would want a porn video whose star was Margaret Thatcher was beyond me. Maybe it was an S&M thing.

There was a big fancy coffee table with a glass top, onyx ashtrays, and boxes of cigars and cigarettes so fancy I'd never heard of them. A bar stocked with every kind of booze I could imagine and quite a few I couldn't. And magazines, of course, just like any other waiting room. Not that you'd be seeing the latest *Whip Gazette* while you were waiting to get your teeth drilled. And that was one of the milder ones.

It didn't give me the most erotic of feelings. You don't always want your fantasies to come true. Nothing's ever as good as the anticipation. And knowing what this place was didn't help—who set it up, and like I said, you shouldn't think about where they find the raw material…

I tried to shut it out. Shit, Sharkey meant well, didn't he? And this was supposed to be the foursome of my dreams. I tried to stop thinking about what lay under the surface, focusing instead on what it would be like to run my hands over their smooth skin, to…

And that was when the husband came in, playing host. He told Sharkey that his order was waiting in room 109, and took me up to 204.

Try to imagine it. Whoever the most attractive woman or man (or plural) you've ever seen on the small or silver screen might be. Try to imagine walking into a room and finding them waiting for you in a huge, soft bed, naked as the day they were born, with every costume and sexaid possible close at hand. They get up, come over, and they undress you, run their hands over your body and purr with delight. Then they lead you to the bed, pull back the covers, and press you down.

One of them slips you a little red pill. Within minutes you feel randier than you've ever been in your life, and harder than a telegraph pole, wetter than the sea. And they start work—hands, tongues, hot, wet holes. Just for starters.

Then you start getting down to the really good stuff. They coax and cajole you for your fantasies, laugh and giggle if you're shy and kiss and squeeze you to make you tell. And when you do, they dig out whatever odds and ends you might need in two seconds flat, and you're away again.

And it's good. It's better than you've ever known. Whatever's in that little red pill, it does the business. It never stops feeling good, and you think you can keep on going all night. Whatever it takes. It never stops feeling great.

Not even when you meet their eyes, and for a second see what's really going on at the back of them.

And then you come, and you think you'll come forever. You see light and colours and exploding stars, and it feels like the earth's blown itself apart, sending you spinning out into space, floating like a star yourself, blazing, burning bright in the icy dark. Slowly, slowly, you drift, come down, down, down, till finally the pillows and satin sheets and soft smooth flesh kiss you and slam you back into the world, leaving you surprised to find it's still here after all that.

And then the women pull the sheets tight and snug around you, all squeezing in close, pressing and rubbing together. And you drift some more.

And beside the bed, there's a fridge, humming softly and contentedly, and one of them, leans down and creaks the door to pull out a bottle of champagne, fluted glasses too. A pop, gunshot loud, as the cork flies free and ricochets off the ceiling. White foam cascades. Glasses fill, stinging your fingers with cold. You yelp. They giggle, and wrap it in a napkin to make it easier. You drink.

They feel sleepy, snuggle down in the soft, soft satin. You're not sure what to do now. Stay till someone tells you? Go back to the waiting room, or just out the door to wander your own way home, your whole life stretching desolately out before you, it seems, now this longing has been fulfilled, knowing that you'll never return. One night. A treat. Then Mengele's is always a distant memory, a tormenting one of guilt and ecstasy.

You want this night to never end, and you want it over, to get out, to go home. You swing your legs out of the bed, slither over a naked, flawless body shaped to its perfection by god knows what tortures, and reach for your trousers.

But you can't get a grip. The denim slips through your fingers. And when you try to stand up straight, your legs won't cooperate, will they? Totter across the floor a few steps. Then fall, plunge deep into the deep, thick pile of the carpet. Try to rise, but it's like fighting quicksand. The dry, ticklish scent of the carpet fills your nostrils.

The door of room 204 is swinging open. The host steps through, flanked by two hefty types I recognise without ever seeing their faces before. Know the species. Hard fuckers with muscle and no mind of their own, wanting something to do that lets them knock someone down, but no idea what. The stuff they make coppers, soldiers, and prison guards from. In this place, what do they do?

The big guys lift me up and start to carry me out. As we go through the door, just before I go under altogether, I see Sharkey in the corridor; he's having words with the management. Our genial host smiles, cigarette sticking up in its holder at a fortyfive degree angle, and reaches into his breast pocket. And money changes hands.

The torture of this place is it's so hard to die. Once, for a laugh, for someone's amusement, they shunted me and another girl together, pasted us with that tissueplasticity crap, welded us together. We clawed and fought like wild cats to rip free of one another. I gutted her to make my escape. They were taking bets on who'd do it to the other. Money changing hands again. Wads and wads of the stuff. I used to look at rolls of cash that size and burn with envy. Now the sight of it makes me sick to my stomach. They carted the girl off with her intestines trailing in the dirt. Then a couple of days later she was back on the job.

I was conscious through most of the operation; they kept me up just for the fun of it, held up a mirror to let me see them knead my face like a lump of dough, stretching and gouging before the real modelling started.

The doctors here are sick fuckers. Sometimes they'll pull and stretch someone into a sheet of pain that covers half the room, pulling the body into a huge membranous skein that they walk under, watching the veins pulse and the eyes go wide with fear in the contorted, flattenedout mask of a face as they tickle the underneath with a knife. Sometimes they do rip it, just to see. It all goes on video, of course, and whatever's left gets remodelled, put back together to use in one of the necro films.

And I thought Sharkey was a mate. No wonder he was doing so much coke; he'd been playing the stock market, a real financial smart-arse, but not smart enough. Too many eggs in one basket that turned out to be rotten through to the bottom. Out fell the eggs and smashed. Lots of lovely lolly swirling down the drain, and Sharkey looking the gutter he came from smack in the eye again. Hey, that rhymes.

So, he needed to recoup his losses. And what should he find? That Mengele's is always looking for new material—pretty selective, they are, and they tend to have a bit of a staff turnover, what with all the necros and the overenthusiastic S&M boys who want the chance to rip some beauty's body to fuck just for the experience. And he sold me to them.

A kind of backhanded compliment, I suppose. I don't know how much they paid, but I hear (rumour again, as always) the going rate usually runs to six or seven figures. Not bad for someone who never got out of the gutter Sharkey started in. Then again, I was in good nick; working in factories and scrapyards can do that, all the hammering and pushing and pulling and shifting shit honing you down to raw muscle. And clean; no illnesses, no disease—someone must have been having words with my GP. So much for the Hypocritical Oath.

They've remodelled me more times than I can remember now. It was a hell of a shock when I woke up after the first one, when I looked in the mirror and saw Marlene Dietrich looking back. Then when I looked between my legs and saw…

Still, they gave me my cock back a couple of times. I was Errol Flynn on one of them, so I got an improved model. And at least they haven't turned me into Margaret Thatcher yet.

Like I said, it's next to impossible to die here, unless they want you to. Whether *you* want to doesn't come into it. I've tried, but they can almost always bring you back. I'm prime meat; got plenty of use left in me yet. I haven't tried it since; the punishment's a spell in the subbasement wearing a dog's head and with arms growing out of your back.

But I got a stroke of luck today. It's my turn to be Princess Di this month. And guess who'll be waiting for Sharkey in room 109?

He won't know it's me, of course. Not till my fingers drive into his throat and crush his windpipe. Not till I start using my teeth to finish the job before they come and take me away to whatever death they reserve for such offenders, which will never be bad enough not to be worth the revenge.

Not till I put my bloody lips to his dying ear and tell him that however bad it is, it's no worse than that fucking remix of *Candle In The Wind*.

RICHARD KADREY is the *New York Times* bestselling author of the Sandman Slim supernatural noir series. *Sandman Slim* was included in Amazon's "100 Science Fiction & Fantasy Books to Read in a Lifetime," and is in production as a feature film. Some of Kadrey's other books include *The Grand Dark*, *The Everything Box*, *Hollywood Dead*, and *Butcher Bird*. He's also written for *Heavy Metal* Magazine, and the comics *Lucifer* and *Hellblazer*.

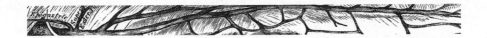

Black Neurology—A Love Story
Richard Kadrey

USING MY PULL with an acquaintance at the city morgue, I convince the attending Medical Examiner to let me watch your autopsy.

He begins with a traditional Y incision, cutting two diagonals across your upper chest until they meet at your sternum, then a single long, straight slice down to your crotch. He opens you with a crack, snapping ribs and connective tissues, laying you open and bare, more exposed than you've ever been in a lifetime of extreme exposures. I stand quietly, a little behind the Examiner, clicking away with the cheap little pocket camera I bought on the way over.

This Examiner is a true professional, experienced and respected for both his precision and the speed of his work. But now that he's opened you, he's just standing there, looking down, his head craning slowly up and down the length of you. He reaches forward and pushes a finger into your abdomen, scooping out what he finds and pressing it quizzically between his fingertips. Your body appears to be packed with a pinkish-yellow modeling clay. The Examiner makes a face and scoops out more with his hands, trying to find his way through the muck to your organs. Without warning, he lets out a little yelp and pulls back his hands. He says that he felt something move inside you. Using forceps, he reaches tentatively into you and pulls something free—a hissing rattlesnake.

After disposing of the creature in the incinerator, he examines your insides further, this time using scissors and a metal probe. He soon hits a pocket of what looks like black tar. It oozes up through the clay, darkening it. The Examiner's probe drags new things from your gut. Rosaries. Straight razors. Old bottles of laudanum and arsenic. He finds your baby teeth. Leather wrist restraints. The hand-stitched belt your daddy used on you when you needed discipline.

With his forceps, the Examiner digs into the thick clay and pulls out your heart. Instead of a fist of muscle, what he holds in the forceps is a glowing red coal, spouting a steady flame from the top and wrapped with barbed wire, like a miniature crown of thorns.

He turns and looks at me, holding up the glowing coal as if I might have an explanation. I shrug and snap a picture. "What's that?" I ask, nodding at your body. The Examiner turns to look and I reach around from behind, slicing his throat from the jugular to the carotid artery in one smooth motion, using the scalpel I stole from his instrument tray. He burbles once and I let him drop, bleeding into the cavity from which he'd extracted your burning heart. Snapping another quick photo, I run my hands down your throat, across the open halves of your chest, and along your legs, using my fingernails the way you always liked.

In the late 1990s, I read about new electronic scanning techniques that led to brain studies which revealed that our minds and bodies are all utterly unique. The neural pathways that mean pain and discomfort for some equal pleasure and contentment for others. The chemical compositions of our cerebral and spinal fluids can vary widely from person to person, perversion to perversion. Our desires are defined by our brains and our bodies are shaped by our desires. As William Blake once said, "Those who restrain desire, do so because theirs is weak enough to be restrained." The unrestrained, I wonder, watching the last of the Medical Examiner drain into you, who knows everything the unrestrained are capable of?

There's a bubbling in the bloody clay. I touch you more insistently now. Your lips. Your thighs. Your genitals. Something rises from the muck. A hand. Then an arm. Another hand beside them. I work you harder and your body begins to convulse in orgasm. You pull free from the clay, up and out of your corpse. Covered in blood and muck like an infant, you're reborn from your own body, this stranger's blood, and our overwhelming desire. You rise up to your knees, breathe into your new lungs and open your mouth, searching for your voice. Finding it, you touch my cheek and say, "I told you I'd never leave you."

I wrap you in the Examiner's lab coat and take you home.

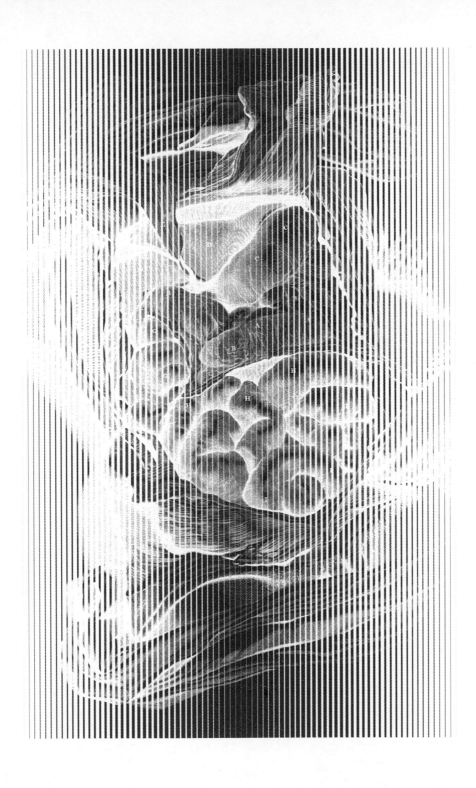

Angela Slatter is the author of the Verity Fassbinder supernatural crime series *(Vigil, Corpselight, Restoration)* and nine short story collections, including *The Bitterwood Bible and Other Recountings*. Her gothic fantasy novels, *All These Murmuring Bones* and *Morwood*, will be out from Titan in 2021 and 2022 respectively. She's won a World Fantasy Award, a British Fantasy Award, an Australian Shadows Award, and six Aurealis Awards. Her work's been translated into French, Chinese, Spanish, Japanese, Italian, Bulgarian and Russian. You can find her at WWW.ANGELASLATTER.COM, @ANGELASLATTER on Twitter, and as @ANGELALSLATTER on Instagram for photos of food and dogs that belong to someone else.

Cuckoo
Angela Slatter

THE CHILD WAS dead by the time I found her, but she suited my purposes perfectly.

Tiny delicate skin suit, meat sack, air thief.

The flesh was still warm, which is best—too hard to shrug on something in full rigor—and I crammed my bulk into the small body much as one might climb into a box or trunk to hide. A fold here, a dislocation there, a twinge of discomfort and curses when something tore, stretched just too far.

The rent was in the webbing of the right hand. Only a little rip, no matter. The sinister *manus* was my favoured choice of weapon anyway. I sat up, rolled my new shoulders—gently, carefully—then stood, rocking back slightly on legs too tender, too young to support my leviathan weight. I took a step, felt the world tilt, caught my balance before I fell and risked another tear; looked down at the single pink shoe, with its bows and glitter detail; took in the strange white cat face that ran around the hem of the pink and white dress; rubbed my miniature fingers against the dried brown stains that blotched the insides of my thigh.

The child had died hard.

The sliver of me that retained empathy ached, just a bit. But I could smell the scent of the one who'd done this, and I would follow that scent. The hunt was on, my blood was up. Time was of the essence—my presence will speed decay. I pitched my head up so my nostrils caught the evening breeze and breathed deeply, filling my borrowed lungs, so the memory would remain.

Again, I took a step, more, all steady.

Determined.

Forward.

Here's the thing: evil used to be different.

It used to be black and white. It used to be more *obvious*. Nowadays? Everyone on this planet is tainted to some degree. Once upon a time, there were villains of a memorable—perhaps even admirable—scale. But now?

Without contrast it's hard to see the differences.

I miss that—the delineation of great evil from banal nastiness.

I'd walked for two hours and the girl's legs were sore. I sighed and stepped into his front garden with its fastidiously dug flowerbeds planted with purple-red and saffron blossoms. The house was neat and tidy, a thin building running the length of the block, rather than across—I didn't need eyes to tell me that, just the child's memories. I dug around in her fading box of remembrances and found the floor plan of the house, vague as if seen in a rush. Hallway, all the doors to the left: a living room, then two more rooms, then a kitchen at the very back where he'd taken her for a glass of water. A staircase near the front door leading up: two bedrooms at the front and a bathroom at the back. The second bedroom she remembered most.

The walls had a shimmer to them, and dancing fairies were stencilled around the baseboards and just beneath the architraves. The bed was covered in a Barbie-branded duvet and so many frilly purple cushions they seemed like an eruption of fabric mumps. Shelves ran across two of the walls, burdened with My Little Ponies in every hue and style, too high for a child to reach.

And the cupboard, painted pink so it appeared as a mouth in a white face. And inside the cupboard, all those shoes, all those single left shoes, tossed in like so much refuse, as if the fetish could never be tidy. As if the inner workings would always be *messy*. Somewhere in that pile, maybe balancing precariously on the top, maybe toppled down the back, was the shoe he'd taken as she sat on the bed, before he did *anything*.

The mind began to shut down, the memories becoming the blurred white-blue of blind eyes. I clenched a hand, heard the joints crack. Time was running short.

I didn't need long.

A knock on the door, harder than intended, hurt my knuckles. I heard him moving around inside. I coiled inside the body, bracing myself against the slow wash of congealing blood and decaying organs, against the sea of human soup the child was becoming, and prepared to spring the moment I saw what I needed.

He opened the door.

Mr. Timmons gave me nothing. Nothing but a slow steady blink. His eyes shifted from the dark marks around the delicate throat, down past the bruised thighs, and lit on the bare foot.

No fear. No guilt. No remorse.

I felt sawn off at the knees. Robbed. At a loss.

He twitched a sort of smile in my direction and slowly closed the door once more.

And I didn't do a thing.

I, who once commanded legions, who fell through fire and rose again, who felt the earth shudder beneath my feet, who took into me the souls of the greatest of the worst, I…did nothing.

The woman was in the wrong place at the wrong time.

But then, aren't they all?

I'd lain quiet for ages in the alley, just the bare foot sticking out to get attention. About four in the morning, she staggered along in her high heels, saw the pale flash of flesh and stumbled over to kneel beside me. The woman leaned in and I grabbed her. I wrapped my arms around her neck and covered her mouth with one hand, pinching her nostrils shut with the fingers of the other. I held her that way until the life drained out and she released her last breath, emptying herself in a final humiliating gesture of humanity. It's easier when they're dead, they no longer have the will to fight; if you have to expend energy battling for a body, you're not in best shape for the contest to come. I stood over her and let the child's form go, unpicked myself from the rapidly putrefying corpse, then watched as it hit the asphalt heavily. It made a wet noise as the side of the face gave way on impact and the belly burst like an overripe melon.

I stayed outside for a few moments, stretching, feeling the night on what passes for my skin, just for a few moments, then did my contortionist's act and plunged into the woman. Roomier, to be sure, broad across the hips, fleshy thighs, the strange weight of breasts hanging at the chest—I cupped them, jiggled them about, found nothing to justify the fascination with them. Then I felt the fizz and buzz of alcohol in the veins, the unsteadiness of the legs, the jelly of the knees and that ache in the lower back from being pushed at the wrong angle by the height of the shoes.

I'm sorry, I said to no one in particular. I don't even know if I was. It'd been a long time since I'd expressed sentiment to anyone—anything beyond disgust and a sort of righteous boredom. I said it again, just to hear my voice, *I'm sorry. I need...*

But I didn't continue. Didn't finish. Had neither necessity nor desire to offer explanations to the dead.

I sat next to him on the park bench.

He was feeding the birds, watching all the little girls on the jungle gym, nodding, friendly, to their mothers and nannies. He didn't notice me. At least, not until his nose began to twitch. An unwashed body will garner attention sooner rather than later. His head swivelled and his eyes took me in—not that I would have been of any interest to him. He smiled and pointed towards the children as they played.

'Which one's yours?' he asked, although he must have known, couldn't have thought for a moment that my shell, still in its nightclub finery with smudged makeup and bird's-nest hair, had care of any child. He grinned slyly, as if we were in cahoots.

I turned towards him, shifted my torso, the body beginning to lose its flexibility. My clumsiness made it look as though I was showing him the woman's breasts, *presenting* them.

Disdain. Contempt. Amusement. All of these were in his face.

I raised my stolen hand and clicked its fingers. Sparks flew but didn't take. I did it again and there were flames—at first just at the tips, then they crept to engulf the hand, scorching the arm, catching quickly on the synthetic fabrics of the woman's outfit. It sped across the shoulders, split its forces and half-leapt downward, while the other continued upwards to set the bleach-blonde coif ablaze. I smiled at him from lips that curled and blackened and shrivelled back against teeth furred from no brushing.

I watched him long and hard, waiting, poised for that look, that hint, that signal.

For the light in his eyes that said he was afraid—because they're all afraid, in the end, and that's why I can take them—for the whimpering as he begged for his life.

His eyes remained dead, but for a lazy curiosity.

He stood and walked away as my body burned to a symphony of children's screams.

I followed him all the next day, incorporeal.

Vengeance has been my path for so many years. Centuries. Aeons. It's all I've known, or all I remember. I have taken what was just, from men great and ordinary, their only commonality being they had stolen lives that did not belong to them. One life or thousands unjustly snuffed out will bring my kind like a hunting hound. I have seen them all learn fear, all tremble when faced with their crimes and beg for forgiveness, more time, another chance. But this man…

There was *nothing* great about this man. There was nothing special but his refusal to *fear*.

I ventured into his house, picked through his things while he went about his daily chores. Sat on the sad mountain of shoes in the closet and wracked my brain. I heard the phone ring, and he let the answering machine get it. An official voice, tired, disinterested, left him a message, obviously used to no response, but duty-bound to follow through. I listened, then watched intently as he quite deliberately erased the recording, not bothering to take down the number or name the caller had left.

I thought I had my answer.

The smell of antiseptic was sharp enough to sting.

Soft-soled shoes squeaking on waxed floors, clangs of metal trays and bed-pans, trolleys banging through swinging doors, alarmed squeals from heart rate monitors as people died, the constant *blip* of the lesser machines, the *swoosh* of uniforms as staff hurried by.

And finally, a private room, a quiet space, oddly enough in shades of pink, a room meant for two patients but in which only one was in evidence. The bed was a striking piece of machinery, up-down-sideways buttons, the not-quite-white linen from too many washings, a curtain around it all, ostensibly for privacy, but really so no one is forced to watch someone dying.

The woman was younger than she appeared, but still older than I imagined. She looked, no matter her real age, like a crone. She was shrivelled, cannulas in both hands, tied to a battery of technology. A slit marred her throat with a tube poking through it, and a machine breathed for her. Her hair was wiry iron-grey, her face etched with lines, her eyelashes absent. Her mouth, which I imagine to have been often pursed with disapproval in life, hung slack. Saliva gathered in the deep furrows at the corner, some dried and flaking beneath the new layers of damp spittle.

I doubted she had much spirit left, no will to fight.

I touched fingers to her thin, thin chest and looked for a way in. Through the skin, through the very pores and I felt…I felt almost as if I was being pulled down as much as I was entering in. She didn't fight me as her life limped away, rather she swam around like the dregs swirled in a coffee cup and I sensed myself…contaminated.

But still, I sat the wizened carcass up, and carefully turned the machines off before I tore out probes and the sticky pads of plastic that connected us. No use causing a stir, sending a signal. It was going to be hard enough to walk the old bat out of the hospital.

I swung my blue-veined legs off the edge of the bed and gauged the distance to the door. One chunk at a time would suffice: bed to door, door to fire stairs, fire stairs to parking lot, parking lot to the end of the first block, first block to the second block, then his house halfway down that very street, not so far away.

The linoleum was cold beneath my feet.

The house was dark, but not as dark as inside the woman's head. Insistent thoughts of her son papered the walls of her memory. He was small, so small in there. So tender, so sweet, so *vulnerable*.

Ill. I felt ill.

I stood at the door to the main bedroom, watching the moonlight sheer through the curtains. I traced its trajectory to the bed. It was empty, the coverlet undisturbed. I backed away. The brittle bones in the feet seemed friable, liable to snap at any moment. The steps down the hallway, the thin tightly woven carpet, gave no comfort. The door to the princess room was ajar. I pushed it open. It did not creak as I slipped inside.

He lay flat, head thrown back, mouth open. Snores issued forth. The mountain of cushions had suffered an avalanche, and I couldn't help but trip against them as I approached. Light streamed in, hitting the sequins and glitter on the scattered squares of overstuffed fabric, throwing beams around the walls.

I drew in my own weight until the body was as light as a bird's bones, and I crawled onto the bed. My movements caused no ripple. I knelt on his chest and began to gradually let the weight loose.

His breathing became irregular; he started to struggle and soon enough he opened his eyes. Blinked to try and make out the face that hovered above his in the moonlit dark. His lids peeled back, widened in astonishment. I leaned forward, hungering for that look, that hint…

His right hand wrapped around the old woman's ankle. I glanced down as his fingers caressed the cool, corrugated flesh, tracing the ridges of ancient veins, moving upwards.

I fled. I shot out of every aperture I could find and pressed myself against the ceiling as the barely alive body slumped onto Mr. Timmons. His hand did not stop moving.

I did not cling there long. I flew through the window and fell, tumbling, to the garden beds, pressed the dirt rough against my skin, breathed deeply the fertiliser's acrid perfume. All of this felt clean compared to the contagion that seemed to still coat to me.

I stood, shaking, and slid into the clean black of night.

LIVIA LLEWELLYN's fiction has appeared in over forty anthologies and magazines and has been reprinted in multiple best-of anthologies, including *The Best Horror of the Year, Year's Best Weird Fiction*, and *The Mammoth Book of Best New Erotica*. Her short story collections *Engines of Desire: Tales of Love & Other Horrors* and *Furnace* were both nominated for the Shirley Jackson Award for Best Collection. You can find her online at WWW.LIVIALLEWELLYN.COM.

Cinereous
Livia Llewellyn

Paris
October 1799

The nails on the heels of Olympe Léon's boots are the only sounds in the silence of night's chilly end. Click click click through indigo air, like the metallic beat of a metronome's righteous heart. As always, when she sees her destination at the end of rue Saint-Martin, rising black and monolithic against the encroaching country and graying sky, her heart and feet skip beats. She thinks of each single drop of blood, spurting and squirting from the bright flat mouths of the necks, and her small calloused hands and wide bowls to catch them all. Olympe, like all the assistants, is very proud of her training, and very afraid of losing her place, very afraid of sinking back into the city's bowels, never to return. She never misses a drop.

The building has no name. It never has. Inside the courtyard, men in effluvia-stained coats scurry back and forth to one of the three large guillotines sitting on the worn packed earth. Scientists and doctors and handlers, each carrying out their part of the Forbidden Experiment. Olympe and the young assistants are forbidden to venture beyond the warren of labs and rooms on the ground floor. The rules of their mysterious, tight-knit society haven't stopped her, but after two years, she has still only seen glimpses of the eight labyrinthine stories that loom in a perfect square around the courtyard, occasionally flashes of people moving up and down the wide staircases, and the constant winking of the stairwell candle flames high above her like trapped stars in the artificial night. Most floors are reserved for research. The top two floors, merged long ago into a single high-walled prison, is where the Forbidden Experiment has taken place for over twenty years now, and only handlers are allowed inside.

Thick-limbed men swathed in heavy layers of leather and chain mail, with animal-faced masks and gloves of unyielding steel, unlock the doors to the top floor once every week, and venture into a metal bar-ceilinged warren of broken rooms and passages, untamed flora and small creeping fauna, a facsimile and perversion of the natural world, open to the elements yet contained and confined. And after a time, each handler emerges with a young boy or girl who howls and shits and pisses and bites like a wolf, a child who has had no interaction with the civilized world since birth. *Les enfants sauvages.* Some are sent to labs on the middle floors for dissection and vivisection and resurrection, some are taken to the basement levels for electrical and mechanical experiments beyond even Olympe's delicious imagination. And those tagged for the living head experiments are sent to the courtyard, to the guillotines and to her.

Olympe hangs her coat up in one holding room, and slips on her laboratory overcoat in another. She cannot describe how proud she feels when she buttons up the faded, fraying fabric. Out there in the world, there are women who read books, who study, who are scientists and doctors as much as they can be, considering women are nothing more than failed men, walking fœtuses who never developed into their full male potential. Olympe, the brothel-raised daughter of a long-dead revolutionary and a long-dead whore, is very aware she will never be one of those women, those forward-thinking academic lights of France's glorious new future, but at least she is more than what awaits her outside the double steel courtyard gates, and it never fails to thrill her. True, the great men who conduct these incredible experiments tend to recruit uneducated yet comely young women and men like herself, who don't protest when a suck or two is requested of them, but Olympe is pretty and clean and always willing to comply. And she's smart. As she grabs her copper bowls and heads into the courtyard, she thinks of the top floor, that mysterious jungle of rooms and wilderness, of the cleverly concealed panopticons inserted throughout the rotting passages and hallways from which the scientists can fully observe the enfants sauvage without interaction or detection. Thanks to her strong fingers and nimble tongue, she's been in those rooms. She's seen what goes on in the artificial wild, she's heard what the scientists say. None of the other assistants have. None of them have ambitions quite like Olympe.

Each slender wood guillotine has a name, and something of its own personality, or so Olympe would like to believe. She's worked at the bases of La Bécane and Le Massicot, both nimble and effective apparatuses, but her heart and hand belong to the swift and silent blade that descends through the center of Mirabelle. There's just something about the sharp low *whomp* of Mirabelle's heavy mouton and blade rushing through meat and bone that satisfies Olympe in a way nothing else does. Already Le Massicot has been at work—Nana is at the neck of a sauvage, her copper bowl catching the blood which will later be sent rushing through tubes and vials in some candlelit room upstairs. Étienne stands slightly behind her, one large hand on each side of the head as he holds it still and upright for display. Blood trickles and pools around his shoes. Before him three doctors crouch, touching the head lightly with calipers and other devices, taking notes as they speak in low tones. They are measuring the lingering signs of a life taken so swiftly by the blade that the head often fails to acknowledge the body's demise. Olympe has seen the eyes of severed heads blink, seen lips twitch and heard gasps and sighs. The doctors hold vials up to the mouth to catch escaping vapors, peer through pieces of glass into the gaping neck, slide lances and needles into the jelly eyes. The assistants know better than to ask what knowledge they seek, or what use they intend with it. Later, the living heads, as they are called, will be placed in large glass containers filled with viscous liquids, and join other similar containers on the fourth floor. Olympe has seen that secret, many-shelved room as well, seen the hundreds of surprised faces peering out from their amber-colored shells. She knows a good scientist must have a strong stomach and heart, but she has no real desire to return any time soon.

Mirabelle's wood frame is dull brown, the same color as Olympe's carefully pinned and bonneted hair. Lorilleaux is at his usual spot beside her, pulling worn leather gloves onto his long hands. When he clamps his fingers around the sides of each head nestling in Mirabelle's curved embrace, it's like watching a monstrous spider clamp down on its prey. An executioner stands on Mirabelle's opposite side, checking the ropes and mechanisms, giving one last polish to the blade. Sometimes the sun makes its way into the courtyard, bouncing between the windows and shining steel until it hurts to see. This morning the sky is cloudy and dull, and a fine haze floats through the air, a mixture of smoke and ash from the building crematorium and furnace fires that are never extinguished. The smell is particularly hideous today—for several weeks, an illness has steadily made its way through the sauvages, a flesh-destroying disease the doctors have yet to discover the case of or cure for, a bodily putrefaction that gives an extra tang to the feathery airborne remnants of the dead. It coats the back of their throats and settles in their chests—everyone who works outside coughs, swallows constantly, drinks water and spits out discolored globs of phlegm. Olympe stares at the blanket of clouds rolling across the squared acre of sky over her head. It looks like another courtyard, a cold and lifeless mirror of the one below. She lays her copper bowls out on the long table positioned next to the stone platform on which Mirabelle stands. There is always a small space reserved for her, at the end of all the instruments and equipment the physicians and scientists use. Today is busy—there will be three subjects from the top floor coming to each guillotine. And when Olympe isn't collecting the blood and handing it over to whoever has reserved it, she will be expected to hand instruments to those who need them, refill pens, provide fresh paper, and occasionally bring out trays of coffee and sweets. In her coat pocket, though, is her own small notebook and pencil. When time allows, she scribbles down her own set of notes, just as any good scientist would, even though she isn't quite sure how to correctly shape all the letters or spell all the words.

Lorilleaux lets out a quick gasp, and Olympe turns. Something is wrong, she realizes, and her heart skips another beat. Across the courtyard, Mirabelle's first visitor of the day approaches. A handler has one of the diseased sauvages locked in an iron jacket attached to a long pole at the back, which he uses to push the body forward—a device the handlers created when the creatures are ill, when they don't want contact with the body. The sauvage lunges and stumbles on twig-thin legs, reaches out with broken-fingered arms, as all the creatures do. But, giant strands of spittle hang from its cracked black lips, and its pallor is that of a month-old corpse, as if every particle of health had been siphoned away. And its movements are slow, Olympe notes; sluggish and confused as if fighting off a fever or waking from the too-long grip of a terrible dream. One low continual moan issues from deep within its ribcage, not the high healthy roar she's used to hearing. Around the handler and creature, physicians and scientists scurry, already throwing out theories and furiously writing down notes. One of those physicians is Marie François Xavier Bichet, favorite student to the now-deceased founder of their society, Pierre-Joseph Desault—whose own head, it is whispered, now sits blinking and gaping in some forgotten corner of the building. Bichet never appears in the courtyard unless occasion merits, unless some important discovery is about to be made.

Olympe steps to the end of the table and grabs a bowl, hugging it to her chest like a shield as the phalanx of chaos approaches. The blade rises to the top of Mirabelle, and the executioner locks the déclic and release handle into place. Lorilleaux is several meters away, on the opposite side of the table. Olympe likes his gentle disposition, but she's never seen anyone who can make a living lifting heads from dead bodies yet tremble like a girl at the sight of anything worse than a bruise. He'll never be a doctor. The handler has unlatched the pole from the metal chest plate, and another handler is removing it from the sauvage, who claws and paws at the man's mask, trying to scrap through the layers of protection to get at the flesh inside. Seconds later, the man forgotten, it swivels its head like a mad dog, snapping and biting at the soft bits of ash floating around them like dead fireflies. For what reason it does these things, Olympe cannot fathom. The men scribble faster, and Olympe reaches into her pocket, touches her little notebook as a reminder that she'll do the same thing later, when she has the chance. There is no time now, though: the first handler is maneuvering the creature's head into Mirabelle's curved base while the executioner lowers the lunette over the top of its neck. The second handler stands at the back of the bascule, holding the creatures constantly flailing legs together with one massive hand as he keeps it against the plank with another hand flat at its back. For the first time she can recall, Olympe is revolted at the sight of so much physical corruption and decay. Black and blue discolorations entirely cover the almost skeletal body, and there are perhaps a hundred shallow and deep cuts on the creature, yet no bleeding or discharge. Her lips curl slightly—it can't be possible, but it looks as if some of the vertebrae are poking out of the skin.

And now the first handler steps back, and the executioner motions them forward. Lorilleaux and Olympe take their places, she with her copper bowl to the side, and Lorilleaux with his spidery hands reaching out to clasp the creature's jerking head. He makes a wet grunt of disgust as his fingers sink into the filthy tangle of hair and soft skin. For once, Olympe can't blame him. Everyone waits. Lorilleaux buries his nose into his shoulder and violently shudders. She knows he's swallowing his own bile. Beneath his grip, the head keeps moving. Finally he lifts his own, and gives a single definitive nod. The sequence of events is practiced and swift. Once Lorilleaux nods, the executioner shouts out as he pulls the lever. Mirabelle's blade shoots down swift and straight, right through the creature's neck. Lorilleaux pulls the head away and holds it up for immediate inspection, while Olympe takes one step in and holds her copper bowl under the neck, catching as much of the blood as possible. As she holds the bowl, scientists will take samples from the flow, attempt to measure the rate, thickness and amount of drainage. It's all clockwork, performed perfectly by them every day without fail for three years. Nothing will go wrong.

Lorilleaux gives his nod. The executioner shouts out, and the head in Lorilleaux's grasp twists. The blade comes down and severs the neck—Lorilleaux drops the head, whipping away his hands as he shouts in pain. The head bounces down onto Olympe's feet, and instinctively, she drops her bowl and reaches down to grab it, her fingers outstretched like she's seen Lorilleaux's a thousand times. As her hands move down, the head turns: suddenly, there is pain, unlike anything she has felt before. An animal roar erupts from her throat, and she raises her arm, the head still attached, its teeth moving back and forth across her fingers like a miniature saw. She can feel the blood in her veins grow cold, the world turn black at the edges, and everything grow dull and murky and slow. Men surround her, using the calipers and any other instrument they can find to pry the horrible object from her body. And then it is over, and the head is gone. Olympe raises her hand to her face, steaming rivulets of red running down her palm and disappearing in the sleeves of her clothes. One finger is crooked, broken and almost torn in half at the knuckle. When she speaks, it's as if the timorous, child-like words are coming from any place other than her mouth.

—I've been bit.

Activity at the other guillotines has ceased. Olympe finds Nana at her side, guiding her across the eerily silenced courtyard to the holding rooms. Lorilleaux runs ahead, his blood-spattered boots echoing back and forth between the stone walls. The air feels too warm, and the ash, the ever-constant smell of burning flesh, the thick scratch at the back of her mouth—Olympe halts, bends over, and vomits. Bits of black spatter against her boots. A frisson of terror washes through her. Those black clots are her blood, darkened from sitting in her stomach for hours as it curdled into something else. Nana waits until she's finished, then guides her forward again, through the holding rooms and into a corner of a makeshift medical lab, where a physician is already bandaging up a sobbing Lorilleaux. He'll never be anything more than an assistant. He can't handle danger or pain. Olympe sits down, props her elbow upright against the table, and studies her finger. Already the edges of the wound are drying out, cracking slightly. Moistening a rag with her spittle, she wipes the blood away and leans in, squinting. A low moan escapes her lips, barely a feather's breath. Tiny veins of blue and black thread away from the edges of the bite marks, a network that spreads as she watches, imperceptibly slow but sure. Around the lines, the flesh blossoms in a soft pale gray. Olympe grabs a roll of clean linen and quickly begins wrapping her hand. The doctor attending Lorilleaux doesn't protest. They all know how hard she works, how quick and smart she is. Olympe takes care of herself. Several tears drop onto the cream fabric as she pins the ends tight, then rolls down her stained overcoat sleeve. She'll be fine, she tells herself as she rises from her seat, ignoring Nana's steady hand. She's going to go far.

After a few sips of water, Olympe makes her way outside and back across the courtyard to Mirabelle. Already the blood has been washed away with buckets of scalding water that sends steam curling into the air, and the remaining assistants and doctors are placing equipment into straw-filled barrows to be wheeled inside. The tracks of another wheelbarrow lead to the doors at the rear of the courtyard, where the remains will be sent first to the morgue, and then, in pieces, to other labs on other floors. Bichet and a group of the older scientists gather at the far end of the table, staring at a liquid-filled amber container set at its edge. Hair floats in the liquid like seaweed. Normally Olympe wouldn't dare approach these important men, who know her only as a pair of disembodied hands holding a blood-filled copper bowl. She sidles along the table, her uninjured hand touching the edge casually, as if it's not necessary to keep her balance. When she gets to the edge of the group, Bichet straightens, and waves her closer. The men move aside: they're making way for *her*. Little trickles of sweat run down the sides of her face. It feels like her body is pushing all the fluids out, squeezing out every last drop of moisture, to make room for the gray blossoms and the black veins.

Bichet reaches out and grabs the top of the container, twisting it around with his nimble surgeon's hands. Olympe crouches down until her chin rests on the tabletop, as though she were five again. Seaweed waves of dark hair make way for a face, bruised and contorted. The eyes are clouded over but open, and they blink, and they see Olympe. *Tête vivante*, someone whispers. Thick globs of blood stick to its lips, preserved by the fluid. Some of that blood is hers. A part of her will always be in that jar, trapped between the lips of something that is not dead or alive. The mouth opens in a soundless cry, and a piece of tooth floats out, disappearing in the waving hair. Olympe turns and runs from the table stumbling across the courtyard back to the holding rooms. Behind her, loud laughter floats and tumbles and mixes with the snowy crematory ash.

Time and the day and the ashes in the air sift past Olympe in an increasing haze of detachment and low-grade pain. She hovers near the door of the holding room, watching the handlers walk to and fro with their living cargo. None of the sauvages that they take to the guillotines are ill, as far as she can tell. Men walk back and forth between the assistants, jars and dishes and bowls filling and emptying. Heads, feet, bones, blood. A farmers' market of grotesqueries and abominations. And in the distance the fires eat away at the remains, vomiting out the ashy bits onto their heads. She stares into the distance. Her face is somewhere else. She can't feel her lips. Everyone in the courtyard coughs, hocks, spits. Something happened today that she should be weeping about, but she can't remember. She holds up her bandaged hand. The nails are black as beaded jet. They look oddly fetching.

Light gray flakes float around and against her skin. A lone idea flares to life in her mind. It's the ash. They got sick, all of them, every person and sauvage in the building, from the airborne remains of the burning dead. Olympe shivers hot and cold with the incredible scientific significance of her thoughts. All those smart men in the building, and she alone knows. She's figured it out. Life into death, into life, into death. Ouroborus. That's what the—

Nana is helping her into her scarf and coat. Is the day over already? It feels as if she only just arrived. Beyond the doors, the courtyard is pitch black, silent until tomorrow morning when the blades spring back to life. Life. Something about life. Someone walks her through the thick double gates. His face is familiar, plump and delicious. Red wet fruit in a desert. Outside, the world is quiet and calm. She hears the muted roar of the furnace far behind her, all the machinery hidden within the building that keeps it alive to gobble up all in the name of Science. Rue Saint-Martin lies before her like a dried up river, pointing a dim, insurmountable way back into Paris proper. Lights twinkle overhead in the black of night, tumble down and brush against her face. Olympe sighs. She used to remember what those are. She breathes them in as she drags her feet down the raggedy sides of the road.

A lamppost or tree trunk is at her back. When did she stop walking and sit down? The night is cold. She should feel it, but she doesn't. She should care, but.

She is going to go far.

The ash.

It was the bite, and the ash.

Olympe wills her numb fingers to begin a laborious creep through the layers of fabric, toward her notebook and pencil, though she cannot feel their progress or lack thereof. No matter, she must somehow write down her scientific observations and present them to the others in the morning, before the disease spreads further. This knowledge will be the society's salvation, its debridement, and her way out. Olympe will be taken seriously, taken under wing. Respect, at last. She will become a scholar, a doctor, a brilliant beacon of light and an example to all women of France. She stares down. Her hand is a hand that is not her hand and it is all the way on the other side of Paris or perhaps even the world and she does not know what it is at all or what it holds. At the quiet end of the street, the building stands tall and funereal against scrabbly trees and darkling sky. The river of Time rushes steadily into and through her, filling her up until all she sees and feels and hears is a great slow blanket of nothingness: and everything stops.

Disconnected images well up into her mind, images of each silky shining drop of blood out there in the dark, spurting and squirting from the bright flat mouths of open necks, and her small calloused hands and the wide bowl of her mouth to catch them all. Warm red, squirming and streaming behind the outlines of the shapes so rapidly approaching her. Bright red, to push the gray of the world away.

Cassandra Khaw is a scriptwriter at Ubisoft Montreal. Her work can be found in places like *The Magazine of Fantasy and Science Fiction*, *Lightspeed*, and *Tor.com*. She has also contributed writing to games like *Sunless Skies*, *Falcon Age*, and *Wasteland 3*.

The Truth That Lies Under Skin and Meat
Cassandra Khaw

English Breakfast, $15.20

Plump sausages laced with spice; black pudding still thick with the taste of copper; bread fried in pools of butter, mushrooms roasted in puddles of butter, baked beans soaked in grease and thinned-out tomato sauce. More butter. A bottle of sour brown sauce.

Like nothing skinny, pretty Molly would normally eat.

Meat was too triggery, Molly used to tell her friends, whenever they asked why she preferred finger-bone slivers of raw carrot to veal, heads of broccoli to lamb brains stewed in an intricate masala sauce; raw things, clean things, vegetal and bloodless. They had laughed. But it is a half-true fact.

Meat isn't triggery.

Meat *triggers*.

International phone call, £156.28

Last week, he told her everything.

Molly plucked at the seams of the armchair with her short, sharp nails until its stuffing fell out like clumps of hair and skin. Over and over, while her voice held steady and her heart thrashed in its cage of ribs.

"And you let her just…get away?"

"What else did you want me to do?"

"I don't *know*. Report her—"

"I can't. I've told you already. She has a daughter. If she goes to jail, they're going to give custody to her next of kin: her parents."

Molly felt a throb of hunger, a loosening of tendons. Under her skin, cells conspired against their veneer of humanity. "So?"

"Her parents are the reason she is the way she is, Molly. I can't—I can't do that to an innocent girl."

Molly swallowed. In her head, the words 'innocent girl' were indistinguishable from 'meat.'

"Seven years," he whispered to her. "If you're going to do anything stupid, promise me you'll wait seven years before you do anything stupid." he said and Molly said *yes, okay*, even though all of her, bone and blood and brain, ached to disobey.

Bottom-shelf whiskey, $125.50

Molly drinks in gulps, not sips, without pleasure, only an inchoate fury. The alcohol glimmers like a fire in her veins, almost enough to distract from the insurrection of her flesh, the mutiny of her marrow. Almost, but not quite.

She drains the first bottle in an hour, orders a second, a third. Halfway through the last, a man approaches, a milquetoast accountant with chins in duplicate, emboldened by booze. She does not protest his company or his conversation, nor does she argue the arm around her waist, the hand on her thigh; not even the smell of him, rank and oily with want.

At the end of the night, he says to her: "Do you want to get out of here?"

And Molly, burning inside the husk of her skin, burning with anger, burning with hate, replies: "Why not?"

Room in a two-star hotel behind the bar, free

He lays her out on the white sheets like a bride. His touch is reverent, cautious. His fingers quiver. Molly sighs as he pushes her shirt up.

For a moment, she thinks blearily of giving in, of delighting in his layered softness, his eager attention, the way his mouth, wet and hot and hungry, climbed the rungs of her ribs.

She twists fingers in his damp, thinning curls, and he moans as she pulls at him, inhumanly strong. Molly lets one small, sleek smile escape before the change eddies across her, skin and fat sloughing in ripples, dripping gore atop the sheets.

He shrieks, high and thin, even as Molly's bones rewrite themselves in the language of carnivore lusts, muscles growing long and lupine. Her skull crunches as jaws lengthen into a muzzle, and teeth into knives.

Too late, he attempts to run.

She lunges.

He screams.

Entrails, free

He is delicious, meltingly tender from a lifetime of inaction, marbled with broad strokes of fat. Better than wagyu, Molly thinks, as she cracks his sternum like an egg. Better than sex, she sighs, as she pries loose pustulant alveoli. They burst on her tongue, copper-sweet.

She nuzzles between coils of intestines, finds the cooling gelatin of his liver, slurps it down. She has missed this so much. The years, bland, thin into nothingness, replaced by the damp, salty pleasure of fresh offal.

So much better than anything else she'd tasted in these last years. Better than this human helplessness. Better than this waiting, this endless counting of the hours and the weeks and the attoseconds until she is free.

Private Investigator, $598

"She has a daughter," he says reproachfully. "An eleven-year-old girl who needs her mother."

The PI is not a bad man. Molly wouldn't have contracted him otherwise. He is merely unethical, encumbered with a vein of compassion no amount of money could drain. In a different life, he might have been a hero, a hunter, armored in whaleskin leather and dressed in blades. Not here, though. Where the law defangs, defuses, defeats any instinct but the urge to hunker down and endure.

Molly smiles, shrugs carefully. Her skin feels too tight, the ridges of her vertebrae jagged against the underside of her skin. She is afraid that if she moves too quickly, her epidermis will split, disgorging clumps of muscle and slivers of change-whetted bone, the hair of the accountant from the night before, snarled like yarn in the pit of her belly, a bezoar in infancy.

"I know."

The PI hesitates, nails digging into the sheaf of brown folders, held out like temple offerings. She can tell he is second-guessing himself, weighing the consequence of a refund, balancing this month's rent with a lifetime of guilt.

"I made a promise." she adds. "A promise to wait seven years."

He does not ask her why, or what she intends after that statute of seven. Some secrets are best left buried in the earth. Besides, there is something mythic about her proclamation, an officiousness that resonates with his intrinsic humanity, an honesty that borders on religious hypothesis. The PI, who is really a good man in a terrible world, slumps, suddenly old.

"Seven years?" he asks, and in the echoes of the words, she can hear him beg *don't hurt her, please don't hurt the girl.*

"Seven years," she lies.

iPhone 4S, $199

She calls him again, tells him about the accountant but not the detective, or her roadmap of a woman's daily rituals, demarcated by activity and hour, the photographs of a little girl with dark, thoughtful eyes.

"It was a mistake," she says, power writhing like a butterfly trapped beneath her skin.

"You *ate* him?" he whispers, incredulous. The revelation frightens him.

"The world is better without someone like him."

His riposte cuts her. "That's not up to you to say."

Molly's anger thumps against the cup of her skull, a warning she can't quite define, full of thunder, full of danger, full of rot. Her mouth thins and her blood grows hot. She runs her tongue over sharp teeth that are no longer short.

"He was just meat," she tells him, still blood-drunk, still warm from the fat she suckled from the accountant's breast. "A wastrel. No one will miss him."

"What you're doing is not right."

She chokes on his defense, on the memory of his defense, of all the times he'd prescribed life to the undeserving, of all the times he had told her to *sit, sit, stay, good girl, stay.* For a moment, she loathes him.

"It's not like I can get caught."

It is a truth. There can be no case without evidence, no arrest without a body to put on display.

"That's not the point."

Molly pauses.

"Is it because you're scared I'd hurt *her*?"

"No. It has nothing to do with that."

"Liar!" She screams, throat throbbing with the impulse to change. "It has everything to do—"

"It has everything to do with *you*. We talked about this. We talked about what the change does to—"

"You're afraid this means I'll find her and that I'll hurt her."

"No, but—"

"Yes." She thumps her fist against the wall. The concrete flakes. "Yes. It's exactly that. And I know…I know what you're going to say. You're going to tell me to think about the girl, about her daughter, about that stupid, useless child that will do nothing but grow up and consume and take and—"

"And what if she grows up to become someone compassionate, someone who understands pain, someone who changes the world, someone *worthy*?" A shivering breath. "She didn't hurt me. It wasn't right. What she did. But she didn't *hurt* me, and her daughter shouldn't suffer for this, regardless."

"That's not the point."

"No, it's *exactly* the point. This is not your story."

Molly freezes.

He continues, relentless. "This is not your story. This is mine. You understand that, right? And I am choosing to let this go. Why can't you?"

Rage blisters her vision. The phone smashes when it hits the wall, geysering electronics; motherboard shards and bits of plastic like shattered finger bones lodged in her teeth.

Kitchen knife, $5.60
She buys a dozen, even though they're nowhere near sharp enough, intended for the softest cuts, the simplest meals.

But she doesn't mind. They are only for show.

Rope, masking tape, plastic bags, $21.50
"It's a serial killer's shopping list!" The clerk laughs nervously.

Molly does not correct him.

Taxi ride, free
The money he quotes is more than she would have ever paid for a cab, but she endures the cost the way she tolerates the driver's advances. When they arrive, she devours him whole, an appetizer, a prelude.

Retribution, one relationship
She thinks about sending him an ear, a skin graft taken from a porcelain cheek, a bone strung on a loop of black rope.

She thinks about sending him a picture.

As she sits licking pancreatic juices from her fingertips, Molly thinks about many things, but mostly how much she'll miss the tobacco-warmth of his scent, the weight of his arm about her shoulders, the years that will never happen, the price of vengeance.

In the end, she does nothing at all. This was not for him, after all. This was for her.

She rolls the thought in her palm, even as she enumerates the pattern of tendons, the bouquet of veins, stretched across the floor like a warning.

"Mom?"

Molly looks up.

Dark eyes, an unlined face, hair still tangled in a cloud of restless sleep. Just a child, delicate as any other. For a moment, compassion pulls at the seams of her skin, at the despair that pinches her throat. Molly could still salvage this. She could—

Hunger judders.

She leaps.

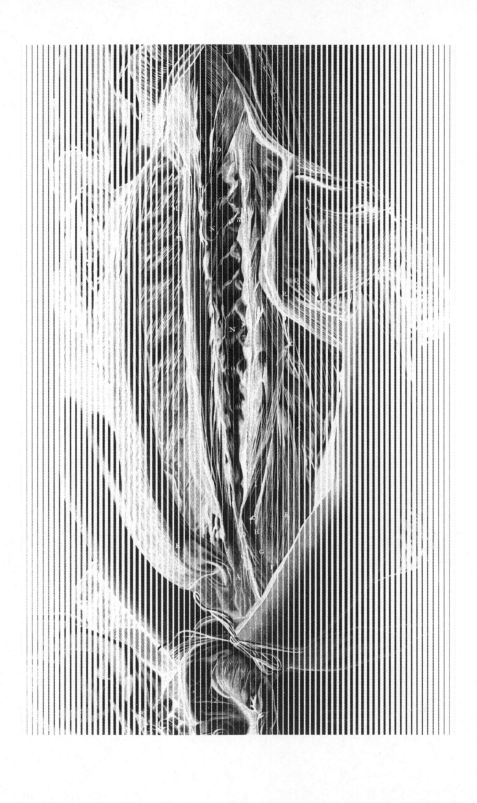

ALYSSA WONG writes fiction, comics, and games. Her stories have won the Nebula Award, the World Fantasy Award, and the Locus Award. She was a finalist for the John W. Campbell Award for Best New Writer, and her fiction has been shortlisted for the Hugo, Bram Stoker, and Shirley Jackson Awards. Her comics credits include Marvel, *Star Wars*, and *Adventure Time*. She has also written for *Overwatch* and Story and Franchise Development at Blizzard Entertainment.

Natural Skin

Alyssa Wong

As I SHRUG on my jacket, moving across the carpet as quietly as I can, my sister Xuemei pushes her blankets aside and rolls over onto her belly with a soft murmur. "Liin jie. Where are you going?"

Fuck. I glance at her across our shared bedroom, her pale skin glimmering in the near darkness. My shoes are already on; no use lying about it now. "Go back to sleep, kiddo."

"Are you going to see a surgeon?" My throat tightens and she leans forward. "Again? Ba's gonna be angry when he finds out."

"He won't be back till Tuesday. And he's not going to find out." I glare at her. "You need to stop snooping around."

"You're the one who didn't delete your browsing history." Xuemei peers at me through her curtain of black hair. She's barely more than a child, but she looks older. Her bones are changing under her skin, growing long and elegant as she shifts through puberty. In a few months she'll be taller than me. "Where are you getting the money for this?"

I start lacing up my sneakers. My phone and wallet are in my pockets already, and if I don't hurry, I'll miss my window. "Not important as long as Ba doesn't notice."

"You're too careless. What if you get hurt again?"

"He's not going to hit me."

"He's not going to hit *me*," she says. Silence stretches between us, truth stretched tight and delicate in the air. I break the quiet by zipping up my jacket, and Xuemei shakes her head. "Are you really gonna make a break for it soon?" When I nod, Xuemei reaches for my cheeks. "Good. I'll miss you."

I turn my face away from her questing fingers and push her back down onto the mattress, tucking the blanket in around her so she can't move. "Don't worry. You won't be around to miss me."

Xuemei snorts. "I wish you were going to Ottawa instead of me."

Me too. But I don't say that, leaning over to kiss her forehead and swallowing my words against her skin. "Sleep tight, kid. Don't lock the window or I won't be able to get back in."

She snuggles in, making a nest for herself. "Okay. Be safe, jie. Don't get mugged while you're out. I don't have much of the good makeup left."

I wait until my sister's breathing steadies before slipping out the window.

No one's awake to see me climb from our tiny apartment onto the fire escape, then eight stories down to the ground. Toronto winters are cold as fuck, and the frost bites at me even through my thick gloves. Fat snowflakes float down around me, covering the black, sunken drifts along the sidewalk with a new, pale skin.

Two men sit smoking on the steps of the convenience store, tobaccoed breath curling into the winter air as I cut through the deserted streets toward the nearest subway stop. I can feel their stares burrowing into my back. "Hey, sis," croaks one of the men, the stench of Hongtashan creeping along behind me. "Where are you going? It's dangerous to be out, walking all alone at night. Why don't you come keep us company?"

I slouch further into the scarf wrapped around my neck and pick up my pace, hurrying into the safety of the St. Clair station.

The Chinatown night markets six stops down the University-Spadina line are alive with business, packed with clamoring customers and shouting merchants despite the snow and the late hour. Fruit carts laden with net bags of lychee and clusters of lanzones; vendors hawking knockoff Gucci bags and Burberry scarves; racks of watches and lighters and vouchers for cheap international phone calls. Everything and anything is for sale. Cantonese batters the air and a heady, rotten scent crisps my nostrils—the smell of meat and trampled fruit, old newspapers and sweat.

As I shove my way through the milling throng, a kid dodges in front of me, kicking up dirty snow, his jacket lighting up with a dozen LED bars in alternating patterns. "How about some data infusions, jie," he says breathlessly. Plastic tubes full of synthetic blood click at his belt, alongside a sheathed, slender hypodermic needle. He's bundled up against the cold, but the stretch of skin exposed by his scarf is peppered with bandages and tiny purple specks, like mosquito bites. "Untraceable, DRM-free, nice and clean. The newest books from all your favorite authors, or maybe a package of answer keys for the standardized tests of your choice. How about it? A perfect MCAT could be your ticket to a white coat and a surgeon's degree."

I ignore him, stalking past a seafood stall; whole fishes and octopuses stare up with dead eyes from their bed of ice. I can feel my phone's edges digging into my leg with each step, the address and code stored on it burning like coals at the back of my mind. But the kid dogs my steps, weaving into my path. He's got a tacky, light-up tattoo, luminescent biopigments inked over his brow in the shape of a sun.

"Do I look like an info junkie to you?"

He has the fucking audacity to wink at me. "Ain't gotta be salty, jie. I only sell high quality, highly reputable shit. Intravenous too! Just one injection in the port of your choice and it goes straight to your brain." He fumbles in his pocket for a cord. "I'll cut you a good deal. Two of whichever bundles you want for the price of one. All the needles are sterilized and in a few days you won't even see the mark."

"I don't have a goddamn port," I say, showing him the patch sewn onto my jacket. The government emblem for Natural Status—no bodily modifications, no drugs, the basic requirements for government jobs—is stitched there in silver thread. "You're barking up the wrong tree, and you'll be lucky if I don't report you at the next police station for it."

"Bullshit." He won't get out of my way, slushing through the muck ahead of me. "Anyone can buy a jacket. You wouldn't be down here if you weren't looking for a little something extra, and you're about as Natural as a two-headed dog. Those eyelid folds are definitely fake. I can even see the scars."

Shame flares white-hot through me and my hands fly reflexively to my face. The kid goes pale when he sees my expression and he backs off, flitting into the crowd to find a new target.

It takes a few moments to stop shaking. I run my fingers carefully over my eyelids, feeling the healed incisions.

Expensive. Discreet. Almost natural.

In a few days you won't even see the mark.

But Xuemei had known that first night I'd come home from a street surgeon's clinic two years ago, had laughed at my still puffy eyes with her clear, beautiful, cruel voice and chased me around the room, trying to push her fingers into the soft tissue. *Here, Liin jiejie, I'll fix your face for you!*

True beauty recognizes its imitators. How many other people could tell? How many others I'd passed on the street tonight had known at first glance, just like my little sister? How many had seen my careful, even embroidery on my jacket patch for what it was: not machine-perfect, not government-issued, but fake, fake, fake?

The scars crawl like mealworms under my itching fingers.

I jerk my hand away before the urge to claw my eyes out gets the better of me. Mentally, I add scar cream and whitening lotion to the list of things to get before the night is over.

The night market gets dodgier the farther I go, the electric streetlamps redder and less frequent, the snowfall heavier. The address I'm looking for turns out to be a room above a murky pool hall and an acupuncturist's shop. I ring the buzzer, glancing at the tattooed, shaven-headed men gliding like sharks through the jade-colored light next door, pool sticks in hand. One catches my eye and grins, no mirth in his eyes. Despite the cold, my palms are sweating; I strip my gloves off and wipe my hands on my jeans. "Hurry up," I mutter.

"Neh yiu mut lun?" The voice through the buzzer is harsh, flat.

The words from the deep net forum flash through my head and I dig out my cellphone. *Please, please be real.* "Nei di Zhao zung ji-si?" I read, stumbling over my Cantonese. The sounds are rusty, ugly and unfamiliar in my mouth.

There's no sound but the wind, blowing frigid air in my face. "Faan uk kei," says the voice from the buzzer at last.

"No, please—" I grasp at the door. "I need to see the ji-si. Please. I have an urgent request. He's the only one who can help me."

A moment later, the lock clicks and I push my way inside.

As the elevator at the end of the dingy hall creaks slowly upward, I wonder if Xue really will miss me if I don't come home tonight, or if she'd use my disappearance to put off starting her negotiator training for another year. Baba had sent in an application for her without telling any of us, and when Xuemei's letter of acceptance had arrived, she pitched such a fit that the neighbors began to bang on our walls.

I'm doing you a favor, our baba had snapped. I'd watched them fight from the hallway door, unnoticed by both. *This is what's best for the family and what's best for you. There are people who would sacrifice everything for the chance that you have!*

Let them have it, then! she'd shouted.

Baba had slapped her across the face, shocking both of them into silence. I'd lingered by the door, unnoticed, my own dreams crumpling in my chest.

Two years prior, when I'd asked him to sign my own application, he hadn't even glanced at it. My job as the oldest daughter, Baba had told me, was to stay home and keep the household running. Someone had to keep track of the finances while he was away on his long, monthly business trips and Xue was off at school. *Don't be ridiculous*, he'd said as I'd stared at the kitchen floor. *Xuemei's much better with people than you are. And do you really expect to be successful with a face like that?*

My thumb creeps to my eyelid, but I jerk it back before I start rubbing the scars again. The eyelids had been my first surgery. The first of many mistakes, but the first of many adrenaline rushes, the deep satisfaction of watching my face take on another shape.

My reflection frowns back at me from the smudged chrome walls, mouth drawn thin. Relatives keep saying that the family resemblance between Xuemei and me has gotten stronger with age, but they're full of shit. There's nothing between us, no resemblance in her soft, pliant skin to the taut, calculated perfection of mine. Her dark, thick hair versus mine, pin-straight and flawless.

No comparison at all.

The mirrored doors slide open. A hallway with ugly, patterned blue carpet stretches before me, walls slotted with wooden doors. The third room on the left is marked *4C*. A full minute after I knock, a series of bolts shudder back on the other side, one after another. It's nearly pitch black inside the apartment; only a handful of glowing computer monitors light the rooms. With a click, a pair of naked light bulbs flare on.

The ji-si stands on the ratty carpet, shirtless but for a black sports bra, one hand on the switch and the other holding a .22 pistol. Her face, obscured by the long beak and saucer eyes of a burnished mask, is pointed at me. So is the pistol.

"You're the ji-si?" My voice is a dry croak.

"Neh yiu mut lun?" the flesh broker repeats. Her voice grates within the mask, the deep tones of a voice scrambler cutting the air.

Black market surgeon to the discreet, parts-swapper to the desperate, butcher to depraved folks who hunger for the most decadent, forbidden meats. Urban legend, miracle worker, nightmare, my first spark of hope. *She's real.*

I take a step toward her, unconsciously, and she cocks the pistol. I freeze.

"Are you fucking deaf? Or are you just stupid?" It's in English this time, languid, contemptuous. I straighten up, stare into the mirrored eyes of her mask.

"I'm here to sell," I say.

After a moment, the gun flicks down. "You're gutsy." She tucks it in the back of her sweatpants and beckons me inside. "I appreciate that."

I follow her, chest loosening.

The ji-si's voice buzzes through the apartment, distorted by the mask's metal beak. My eyes roam her body, all lean muscle and webs of scars. "There's a big blizzard coming. It's supposed to fuck up the whole city and last all night, but if the anesthesia hasn't worn off by the time the storm hits, I could put you up until morning for an extra thirty bucks." As she puts a kettle on the stove, I glance around the apartment. It's cold, almost as chilly as it was outside, and surprisingly clean. Laminated menus in oversaturated colors hang by a work desk, laying out various surgical options, accompanied by photographs of carefully preserved body parts and posed, smiling portraits. Past them is a sturdy rack of knives and surgical implements, woven through with electrical cords and plastic tubing. A long table stretches along the far wall, with a plastic sheet set up beneath. I swallow.

"I won't need to stay the night." My voice is frigid, brittle. My pulse is going crazy. *Don't crack*. "This shouldn't take too long."

The ji-si laughs, an eerie echo. "They never think so. But good surgery is about more than just hiding the seams. If you want cuts that'll heal without any of that ugly scarring, I'll need to take my time." She indicates the kettle, lit up beneath by a glowing red coil. The ice batters the windows outside. "Tea? It'll warm you up. It'll also make everything go nice and dreamy, so you won't feel a thing when the knife goes in."

I can't see her face, but I'm sure she's smirking. "No thank you," I say. "That won't be necessary."

Zhao crosses the room and we're suddenly close, too close in this tiny apartment. Her hand closes around my forearm, and I realize, for the first time, skin to skin, how little she's wearing.

"Come here. Let me get a better look at you."

She guides me onto the long table, pushing me down so that my spine touches its steel surface. Then she swings her legs up and follows me, ignoring my surprised gasp, her sneakers squeaking against the metal. "What—"

"I need to see what I've got to work with. Pretend you're at the doctor's." She's wiry but much heavier than she looks, and I can't buck her off with her weight settled on my hips. Panic rises hot in my throat, but instead of fighting, I stay very, very still.

"You have an extraordinary face," Zhao says as she rearranges my limbs, shifting my hair away from my shoulders. Her hands are clinical and calloused, but her knees press down like blades on either side of my body. When she smooths her thumbs over my cheekbones, it takes every ounce of self-control not to flinch away. Her fingers feel like they're leaving a trail of embers down my body. "Nearly all artificially constructed, from top to bottom." She glances down at the patch on my jacket and says, mockingly, "Even though you're a Natural."

A motorized handsaw hangs overhead, its cord coiled like an adder, just out of her reach. Just out of mine. I bark out a laugh, glaring at her. "Disappointed?"

"Oh no, darling. I think it's beautiful. You're a walking display of artistry, a testimony to gorgeous knifework." She sighs. "It'll be a shame to take you apart, but, well. That's what you're here for, isn't it?"

The way she says it, so reverently, her fingers lingering at the seams of old wounds, almost gives me pause. As if, perhaps, it wouldn't be such a terrible thing to be taken to pieces by this woman, to have her see what's inside. I open my mouth, but the shift of her knees makes me gasp.

"The market's been strange recently. No one knows what they want these days. Skin, of course, but it would be hard for you to walk out of here without any of that." The ji-si is humming to herself, distorted tones filtering out of her mask. Her palms skim my stomach and slide to my hipbones. "Breast, or belly? Mm, perhaps the thighs."

"Wait," I gasp. My blood is pumping so hard that I can hear it ringing in my head, and I'm not sure if it's fear or something else entirely.

"Why?" murmurs Zhao. The tip of her metal face scrapes my skin as she bends toward my neck. Its round, empty eyes glitter. "So succulent and sweet. So perfect. I could keep every one of your parts for myself, customers and profit be damned."

"Wait!" I push back on her chest. "You're wrong. I'm not here to sell any of my flesh."

Zhao pauses, the muscles in her neck tightening. Her grip on me is bruisingly hard. "Are you playing some kind of game with me, little girl?" she asks, her voice so gentle that it makes my skin prickle with fear. "You walked into my house and promised me a sale. And I intend to collect something for my coffers, whether you like it or not."

I turn my head to meet her gaze. "You'll get your money's worth," I say. "But not from me. I have a little sister." My voice catches. "And she is much prettier than I am."

Moving slowly and deliberately, I slip my wallet from my jeans' pocket and flip it open to show her the picture tucked inside. It's Xue's junior high school promotion photo. She's posed on a little stool in front of a pastel background, dressed up in her uniform-issue blouse and checked skirt, a blue bow tied loosely at her neck. Darling Xuemei, Baba's favorite, barely a teenager and already in full bloom. Doe-eyed Xuemei, all smooth, milky skin and rivers of black hair. Beautiful, natural Xuemei.

"I came here to sell her to you," I tell the ji-si. "Every last inch of her."

Zhao studies the picture for a moment, the blank eyes of her mask showing me nothing. Cold sweat beads down the back of my neck. "A little young, isn't she?" she says at last.

I wet my very dry lips. "I hear that's what people want these days."

She throws back her head with a horrible, hacking laugh that echoes through her beak. "Auctioning off your own sister? God. You're a piece of work." She looks down at me, metal face glinting in the raw, naked light. "I like you."

I stare her down. "Look at that picture and tell me she's not twice as beautiful as any of the girls on your menus. People will be clamoring for a piece of her."

The flesh broker slides her thumb over the photo. "So they will. She's almost as pretty as what I've got on the table now." She angles her beak toward me. "Tell me. If I let you go, how exactly are you planning on getting her here?"

I shake my head. "I won't. You'll have to come to me. My father's away on business, and I can drug her dinner so she'll be ready for you tomorrow night. I'll pay extra for your transportation."

Zhao studies the picture, hungry. I look away. Eyes always turn greedily toward her, but nobody ever looks at me like that. Nobody but the ji-si, warm and hard on top of me. "Will you, now. You have this all planned out."

Jealousy burns my voice hot and ugly. "I want you to take every ounce off of her, every hair, every bone. Everything. I want you to package her into little bits and make her disappear."

The ji-si rocks back on her heels, balancing over me. "My, such animosity," she murmurs. "Wherever does it come from, I wonder."

The table is cold beneath my cheek. "What does it matter? You'll get your business, and I'll get rid of mine. We both go home happy."

"I suppose that's true." Her fingers grip my chin and she turns my face toward her. "She's not going to come back if you change your mind," she says, very quietly.

I think of how Baba looks at Xuemei, how his face softens at the very sight of her. "Good," I say.

Zhao pats my cheek. I narrow my eyes at the condescension. "Nay hou duk yi, dan hai nay jun hai hou soh. No, we'll go fetch her tonight, under the cover of the storm, before the rest of the city's snowed in. I'm not about to let you waltz out of here and leave me empty-handed if your conscience decides to show up."

I don't have much choice, not with my own skin on the line. "Fine," I say. "The apartment's not far from here, anyway."

"That's what I like to hear," says the ji-si. "Come to the other table with me. Let's talk numbers."

When she climbs off me and swings to the floor, there's a strange, cold feeling in my chest I can't name. I can't tell if it's relief or disappointment.

In the end, we settle on nearly a thousand dollars: the largest sum of money I've had in my life, and more than enough to buy me a one-way plane ticket out of town. I know Zhao's cheating me, but I would take much less to be rid of her for good. One perfect little sister in exchange for a new life, a slate wiped clean.

"I'll even fix your face if you want," Zhao offers, a sly twist to her words. She turns Xue's photo over in her fingers. "Don't think I haven't noticed what you're doing. I can make you look exactly like her, if you'd like." She places the picture on the table, face down, and slides it toward me. "Think on it. Although to be honest, I like you just as you are. It suits you."

I bat her hand away. "I'll think about it," I say curtly. She just laughs at me.

Before we leave, Zhao makes me drink a shot of scorching baijiu with her. "To your fortune," she says, toasting me. "And mine. Chinese cuts are selling well. Per ounce, almost as profitable as Japanese."

To Xue, I think, looking at my bent reflection in Zhao's mask. My heart coils in me like a viper. *To beauty.*

The blizzard almost catches us on the way home, but the cab cuts through the wind and snow, its driver partitioned away behind a thick, tinted sheet of bulletproof glass.

The ji-si and I make it up the fire escape before the worst of the storm hits, but the snow has begun to fall in thick layers, making climbing difficult. The ji-si is limber, but the cold slows me more than I anticipated. I should have brought a thicker jacket.

At the landing before mine, something drapes over my shoulders. It's Zhao's long coat. "Keep up," she says. "It's going to be a long night."

I wrap the coat close and clench my jaw. I can hear her grinning at me. The coat is soft and warm, and it smells medicinal, sharp with sweat. It smells like her.

Xuemei's nightlight glows soft pink through our bedroom window. My little sister is right where I left her, tucked into bed, her hair spilling over the pillow. Her program acceptance letter rests on the desk beside her.

"Open the window," I say to the ji-si.

She already has a plastic capsule in hand, a syringe tucked between her fingers. There are teeth in her voice. "Oh no. You'll have to do that yourself."

Standing outside our room, I can't hear the sound of Xuemei's gentle, even breathing over the relentless howl of the wind. I can't hear my own. As I place my gloved palms on the window, the ji-si's jacket heavy around me, Xuemei stirs, rising halfway from the bed. Her large eyes are dazed and luminous, their spark of childish cruelty dimmed with sleep and clinging dreams.

"Last chance," says the ji-si.

On the other side of the glass, my baby sister. Inside that room, my ticket out and the face I deserve.

Xuemei mouths something. It might be my name.

I smile, feeling the scars on my eyelids stretch, and pull open the window.

TANANARIVE DUE teaches Afrofuturism and Black Horror at UCLA. The American Book Award winner, British Fantasy Award winner and NAACP Image Award recipient is the author of several novels and a short story collection, *Ghost Summer: Stories*. She is also co-author of a civil rights memoir, *Freedom in the Family: A Mother-Daughter Memoir of the Fight for Civil Rights* (with her late mother, Patricia Stephens Due). In 2013 she received a Lifetime Achievement Award in the Fine Arts from the Congressional Black Caucus Foundation. She and her husband, science fiction author Steven Barnes, co-wrote an episode of *The Twilight Zone* for CBS All Access and Jordan Peele's Monkeypaw Productions.

The Lake
Tananarive Due

The new English instructor at Gracetown Prep was chosen with the greatest care, highly recommended by the Board of Directors at Blake Academy in Boston, where she had an exemplary career for twelve years. No history of irregular behavior presaged the summer's unthinkable events.

—Excerpt from an internal memo,
Gracetown Preparatory School, Gracetown, Florida

ABBIE LAFLEUR WAS an outsider, a third-generation Bostonian, so no one warned her about summers in Gracetown. She noticed a few significant glances, a hitched eyebrow or two, when she first mentioned to locals that she planned to relocate in June to work a summer term before the start of the school year, but she'd assumed it was because they thought no one in her right mind would move to Florida, even northern Florida, in the wet heat of summer.

In fairness, Abbie LaFleur would have scoffed at their stories as hysteria. Delusion. This was Gracetown's typical experience with newcomers and out-siders, so Gracetown had learned to keep its stories to itself.

Abbie thought she had found her dream job in Gracetown. A fresh start. Her glasses had fogged up with steam from the rain-drenched tarmac as soon as she stepped off the plane at Tallahassee Airport; her confirmation that she'd embarked on a true adventure, an exploration worthy of Ponce de León's sto-ried landing at St. Augustine.

Her parents and her best friend, Mary Kay, had warned her not to jump into a real estate purchase until she'd worked in Gracetown for at least a year—*The whole thing's so hasty, what if the school's not a good fit? Who wants to be stuck with a house in the sticks in a depressed market?*—but Abbie fell in love with the white lakeside colonial she found listed at one-fifty, for sale by owner. She bought it after a hasty tour—too hasty, it turned out—but at nearly three-thousand square feet, this was the biggest house she had ever lived in, with more room than she had furniture for. A place with potential, despite its myriad flaws.

A place, she thought, very much like her.

The built-in bookshelves in the Florida room sagged. (She'd never known that a den could be called a Florida room, but so it was, and so she did.) The floorboards creaked and trembled on the back porch, sodden from summer rainfall. And she would need to lay down new tiles in the kitchen right away, because the brooding mud-brown flooring put her in a bad mood from the time she first fixed her morning coffee.

But there would be boys at the school, strong and tireless boys, who could help her mend whatever needed fixing. In her experience, there were always willing boys.

And then there was the lake! The house was her excuse to buy her piece of the lake and the thin strip of red-brown sand that was a beach in her mind, although it was nearly too narrow for the beach lounger she'd planted like a flag. The water looked murky where it met her little beach, the color of the soil, but in the distance she could see its heart of rich green-blue, like the ocean. The surface bobbed with rings and bubbles from the hidden catfish and brim that occasionally leaped above the surface, damn near daring her to cast a line.

If not for the hordes of mosquitoes that feasted on her legs and whined with urgent grievances, Abbie could have stood with her bare feet in the warm lake water for hours, the house forgotten behind her. The water's gentle lapping was the meditation her parents and Mary Kay were always prescribing for her, a soothing song.

And the isolation! A gift to be treasured. Her property was bracketed by woods of thin pine, with no other homes within shouting distance. Any spies on her would need binoculars and a reason to spy, since the nearest homes were far across the lake, harmless little dollhouses in the anonymous subdivision where some of her students no doubt lived. Her lake might as well be as wide as the Nile, protection from any envious whispers.

As if to prove her newfound freedom, Abbie suddenly climbed out of the tattered jeans she'd been wearing as she unpacked her boxes, whipped off her T-shirt and draped her clothing neatly across the lounger's arm rails. Imagine! She was naked in her own backyard. If her neighbors could see her, they would be scandalized already, and she had yet to commence teaching at Gracetown Prep.

Abbie wasn't much of a swimmer—she preferred solid ground beneath her feet even when she was in the water—but with her flip-flops to protect her from unseen rocks, Abbie felt brave enough to wade into the water, inviting its embrace above her knees, her thighs. She felt the water's gentle kiss between her legs, the massage across her belly, and, finally, a liquid cloak upon her shoulders. The grade was gradual, with no sudden drop-offs to startle her, and for the first time in years, Abbie felt truly safe and happy.

That was all Gracetown was supposed to be for Abbie LeFleur: new job, new house, new lake, new beginning. For the week before summer school began, Abbie took to swimming behind her house daily, at dusk, safe from the mosquitoes, sinking into her sanctuary.

No one had told her—not the real estate agent, not the elderly widow she'd only met once when they signed the paperwork at the lawyer's office downtown, not Gracetown Prep's cheerful headmistress. Even a random first-grader at the grocery store could have told her that one must never, ever go swimming in Gracetown's lakes during the summer. The man-made lakes were fine, but the natural lakes that had once been swampland were to be avoided by children in particular. And women of childbearing age—which Abbie LaFleur still was at thirty-six, albeit barely. And men who were prone to quick tempers or alcohol binges.

Further, one must never, *ever* swim in Gracetown's lakes in summer without clothing, when crevices and weaknesses were most exposed.

In retrospect, she was foolish. But in all fairness, how could she have known?

Abbie's ex-husband had accused her of irreparable timidity, criticizing her for refusing to go snorkeling or even swimming with dolphins, never mind the scuba diving he'd loved since he was sixteen. The world was populated by water people and land people, and Abbie was firmly attached to terra firma. Until Gracetown. And the lake.

Soon after she began her nightly wading, which gradually turned to dog-paddling and then awkward strokes across the dark surface, she began to dream about the water. Her dreams were far removed from her nightly dipping—which actually *was* somewhat timid, if she were honest. In sleep, she glided effortlessly far beneath the murky surface, untroubled by the nuisance of lungs and breathing. The water was a muddy green-brown, nearly black, but spears of light from above gave her tents of vision to see floating plankton, algae, tadpoles and squirming tiny creatures she could not name…and yet knew. Her underwater dreams were a wonderland of tangled mangrove roots coated with algae, and forests of gently waving lily pads and swamp grass. Once, she saw an alligator's checkered, pale belly above her, until the reptile hurried away, its powerful tail lashing to give it speed. In her dream, she wasn't afraid of the alligator; she'd sensed instead (smelled instead?) that the alligator was afraid of *her*.

Abbie's dreams never had been so vivid. She woke one morning drenched from head to toe, and her heart hammered her breathless until she realized that her mattress was damp with perspiration, not swamp water. At least… she *thought* it must be perspiration. Her fear felt silly, and she was blanketed by sadness as deep as she'd felt the first months after her divorce.

Abbie was so struck by her dreams that she called Mary Kay, who kept dream diaries and took such matters far too seriously.

"You sure that water's safe?" Mary Kay said. "No chemicals being dumped out there?"

"The water's fine," Abbie said, defensive. "I'm not worried about the water. It's just the dreams. They're so…" Abbie rarely ran out of words.

"What's scaring you about the dreams?"

"The dreams don't scare me," Abbie said. "It's the opposite. I'm sad to wake up. As if I belong there, in the water, and my bedroom is the dream."

Mary Kay offered nothing except a warning to have the local Health Department come out and check for chemicals in any water she was swimming in, and Abbie felt the weight of her distance from her friend. At one time, she and Mary Kay understood each other better than anyone, seeing past each other's silences straight to their thoughts, and now Mary Kay had no idea of the shape and texture of Abbie's life. No one did.

All liberation is loneliness, she thought sadly.

Abbie dressed sensibly, conservatively, for her first day at her new school.

She had driven the two miles to the school, a red-brick converted bank building in the center of downtown Gracetown, before she noticed the itching between her toes.

"LaFleur," the headmistress said, keeping pace with Abbie as they walked toward her assigned classroom for the course she'd named Creativity & Literature. The woman's easy, Southern-bred tang seemed to add a syllable to every word. "Where is that name from?"

Abbie wasn't fooled by the veiled attempt to guess at her ethnicity, since it didn't take an etymologist to guess at her name's French derivation. What Loretta Millhouse really wanted to know was whether Abbie had ancestry in Haiti or Martinique to explain her sun-kissed complexion and the curly brown hair Abbie kept locked tight in a bun.

Abbie's itching feet had grown so unbearable that she wished she could pull off her pumps. The itching pushed irritation into her voice. "My grandmother married a Frenchman in Paris after World War II," she explained. "LaFleur was his family name."

The rest was none of her business. Most of her life was none of anyone's business.

"Oh, I see," Millhouse said, voice filled with delight, but Abbie saw her disappointment that her prying had yielded nothing. "Well, as I said, we're so tickled to have you with us. Only one letter in your file wasn't completely glowing…"

Abbie's heart went cold, and she forgot her feet. She'd assumed that her detractors had remained silent, or she never would have been offered the job.

Millhouse patted her arm. "But don't you worry: Swimming upstream is an asset here." The word *swimming* made Abbie flinch, feeling exposed. "We welcome independent thinking at Gracetown Prep. That's the main reason I wanted to hire you. Between you and me, how can anyone criticize a…creative mind?"

She said the last words conspiratorially, leaning close to Abbie's ear as if a creative mind were a disease. Abbie's mind raced: The criticism must have come from Johanssen, the vice-principal at Blake who had labeled her argumentative—*a bitch*, Mary Kay had overheard him call her privately, but he wouldn't have put that in writing. What did Millhouse's disclosure mean? Was Millhouse someone who pretended to compliment you while subtly putting you down, or was a shared secret hidden beneath the twinkle in her aqua-green eyes?

"Don't go easy on this group," Millhouse said as when they reached Room 113. "Every jock trying to make up a credit to stay on the roster is in your class. Let them work for it."

Sure enough, when Abbie walked into the room, she faced desks filled with athletic young men. Gracetown was a co-ed school, but only five of her twenty students were female.

Abbie smiled.

Her house would be fixed up sooner than she'd expected.

Abbie liked to begin with Thomas Hardy. *Jude the Obscure*. That one always blew their young minds, with its frankness and unconventionality. Their other instructors would cram conformity down their throats, and she would teach rebellion.

No rows of desks would mar her classroom, she informed them. They would sit in a circle. She would not lecture; they would have conversations. They would discuss the readings, read pages from their journals, and share poems. Some days, she told them, she would surprise them by playing music and they would write whatever came to mind.

Half the class looked relieved, the other half petrified.

During her orientation, Abbie studied her students' faces and tried to guess which ones would be most useful over the summer. She dismissed the girls, as she usually did; most were too wispy and pampered, or far too large to be accustomed to physical labor.

But the boys. The boys were a different matter.

Of the fifteen boys, only three were unsuitable at a glance—bird-chested and reedy, or faces riddled with acne. She could barely stand to look at them.

That left twelve to ponder. She listened carefully as they raised their hands and described their hopes and dreams, watching their eyes for the spark of maturity she needed. Five or six couldn't hold her gaze, casting their eyes shyly at their desks. No good at all.

Down to six, then. Several were basketball players, one a quarterback. Millhouse hadn't been kidding when she'd said that her class was a haven for desperate athletes. The quarterback, Derek, was dark-haired with a crater-sized dimple in his chin; he sat at his desk with his body angled, leg crossed at the knee, as if the desk were already too small. He didn't say "uhm" or pause between his sentences. His future was at the tip of his tongue.

"I'm sorry," she said, interrupting him. "How old did you say you are, Derek?"

He didn't blink. His dark eyes were at home on hers. "Sixteen, ma'am."

Sixteen was a good age. A mature age.

A female teacher could not be too careful about which students she invited to her home. Locker-room exaggerations held grave consequences that could literally steal years from a young woman's life. Abbie had seen it before; entire careers up in flames. But this Derek…

Derek was full of possibilities. Abbie suddenly found herself playing Millhouse's game, noting his olive complexion and dark features, trying to guess if his jet-black hair whispered Native American or Latino heritage. Throughout the ninety-minute class, her eyes came to Derek again and again.

The young man wasn't flustered. He was used to being stared at.

Abbie had made up her mind before the final bell, but she didn't say a word to Derek. Not yet. She had plenty of time. The summer had just begun.

As she was climbing out of the shower, Abbie realized her feet had stopped their terrible itching. For three days, she'd slathered the spaces between her toes with creams from Walgreens, none helping, some only stinging her in punishment.

But the pain was gone.

Naked, Abbie raised her foot to her mattress, pulling her toes apart to examine them…and realized right away why she'd been itching so badly. Thin webs of pale skin had grown between each of her toes. Her toes, in fact, had changed shape entirely, pulling away from each other to make room for webbing. And weren't her toes longer than she remembered?

No *wonder* her shoes felt so tight! She wore a size eight, but her feet looked like they'd grown two sizes. She was startled to see her feet so altered, but not alarmed, as she might have been when she was still in Boston, tied to her old life. New job, new house, new feet. Her new feet represented a logical symmetry that superseded questions or worries.

Abbie almost picked up her phone to call Mary Kay, but she thought better of it. What else would Mary Kay say, except that she should have had her water tested?

Instead, still naked, Abbie went to her kitchen, her feet slapping against her ugly kitchen flooring with unusual traction. When she brushed her upper arm carelessly across her ribs, new pain made her hiss. The itching had migrated, she realized.

She paused in the bright fluorescent lighting to peer down at her rib cage, and found her skin bright red, besieged by some kind of rash. *Great,* she thought. *Life is an endless series of challenges.* She inhaled a deep breath, and the air felt hot and thin. The skin across her ribs pulled more tautly, constricting. She longed for the lake.

Abbie slipped out of her rear kitchen door and scurried across her back yard toward the black shimmer of the water. She'd forgotten her flip-flops, but the soles of her feet were less tender, like leather slippers.

She did not hesitate. She did not wade. She dove like an eel, swimming with an eel's ease. *Am I truly awake, or is this a dream?*

Her eyes adjusted to the lack of light, bringing instant focus. She had never seen the true murky depths of her lake, so much like the swamp of her dreams. Were they one and the same? Her ribs' itching turned to a welcome massage, and she felt long slits yawn open across her skin, beneath each rib. Warm water flooded her, nursing her; her nose, throat and mouth were a useless, distant memory. Why hadn't it ever occurred to her to breathe the water before?

An alligator's curiosity brought the beast close enough to study her, but it recognized its mistake and tried to thrash away. But too late. Too late. Nourished by the water, Abbie's instincts gave her enough speed and strength to glide behind the beast, its shadow. One hand grasped the slick ridges of its tail, and the other hugged its wriggling girth the way she might a lover. She didn't remember biting or clawing the alligator, but she must have done one or the other, because the water flowed red with blood.

The blood startled Abbie awake in her bed, her sheets heavy with dampness. Her lungs heaved and gasped, shocked by the reality of breathing, and at first she seemed to take in no air. She examined her fingers, nails and naked skin for blood, but found none. The absence of blood helped her breathe more easily, her lungs freed from their confusion.

Another dream. Of course. How could she mistake it for anything else?

She was annoyed to realize that her ribs still bore their painful rash and long lines like raw, infected incisions.

But her feet, thank goodness, were unchanged. She still had the delightful webbing and impressive new size, longer than in her dream. Abbie knew she would have to dress in a hurry. Before school, she would swing by Payless and pick up a few new pairs of shoes.

Derek lingered after class. He'd written a poem based on a news story that had made a deep impression on him; a boy in Naples had died on the football practice field. *Before he could be tested by life*, Derek had written in his eloquent final line. One of the girls, Riley Bowen, had wiped a tear from her eye. Riley Bowen always gazed at Derek like the answer to her life's prayers, but he never looked at her.

And now here was Derek standing over Abbie's desk, on his way to six feet tall, his head bowed with shyness for the first time all week.

"I lied before," he said, when she waited for him so to speak. "About my age."

Abbie already knew. She'd checked his records and found out for herself, but she decided to torture him. "Then how old are you?"

"Fifteen." His face soured. "'Til March."

"Why would you lie about that?"

He shrugged, an adolescent gesture that annoyed Abbie no end.

"Of course you know," she said. "I heard your poem. I've seen your thoughtfulness. You wouldn't lie on the first day of school without a reason."

He found his confidence again, raising his eyes. "Fine. I skipped second grade, so I'm a year younger than everyone in my class. I always say I'm sixteen. It wasn't special for you."

The fight in Derek intrigued her. He wouldn't be the type of man who would be pushed around. "But you're here now, baring your soul. Who's that for?"

His face softened to half a grin. "Like you said, when we're in this room, we tell the truth. So here I am. Telling the truth."

There he was. She decided to tell him the truth too.

"I bought a big house out by the lake," she said. "Against my better judgment, maybe."

"That old one on McCormack Road?"

"You know it?"

He shrugged, that loathsome gesture again. "Everybody knows the McCormacks. She taught Sunday school at Christ the Redeemer. Guess she moved out, huh?"

"To her sister's in Quincy?" The town shared a name with the city south of Boston, the only reason she remembered it. Her mind was filled with distraction to mask strange flurries of her heart. Was she so cowed that she would leave her house in a mess?

"Yeah, Quincy's about an hour, hour and a half, down the 10…" Derek was saying in a flat voice that bored even him.

They were talking about nothing. Waiting. They both knew it.

Abbie clapped her hands once, snapping their conversation from its trance. "Well, an old house brings lots of problems. The porch needs fixing. New kitchen tiles. I don't have the budget to hire a real handyman, so I'm looking for people with skills…"

Derek's cheeks brightened, pink. "My dad and I built a cabin last summer. I'm pretty good with wood. New planks and stuff. For the porch."

"Really?" She chided herself for the girlish rise in her pitch, as if he'd announced he had scaled Mt. Everest during his two weeks off from school.

"I could help you out, if...you know, if you buy the supplies."

"I can't pay much. Come take a look after school, see if you think you can help." She made a show of glancing toward the open doorway, watching the stream of students passing by. "But you know, Derek, it's easy for people to get the wrong idea if you say you're going to a teacher's house..."

His face was bright red now. "Oh, I wouldn't say nothing. I mean...anything. Besides, we go fishing with Coach Reed all the time. It's no big deal around here. Not like in Boston, maybe." The longer he spoke, the more he regained his poise. His last sentence had come with an implied wink of his eye.

"No, you're right about that," she said, and she smiled, remembering her new feet. "Nothing here is like it was in Boston."

That was how Derek Voorhoven came to spend several days a week after class helping Abbie fix her ailing house, whenever he could spare time after football practice in the last daylight. Abbie made it clear that he couldn't expect any special treatment in class, so he would need to work hard on his atrocious spelling, but Derek was thorough and uncomplaining. No task seemed too big or small, and he was happy to scrub, sand, and tile in exchange for a few dollars, conversation about the assigned reading, and fishing rights to the lake, since he said the catfish favored the north side, where it was quiet.

As he'd promised, he told no one at Gracetown Prep, but one day he asked if his cousin Jack could help from time to time, and after he'd brought the stocky, freckled youth by to introduce him, she agreed. Jack was only fourteen, but he was strong and didn't argue. He also attended the public school, which made him far less a risk. Although the boys joked together, Jack's presence never slowed Derek's progress much, so Derek and Jack became fixtures in her home well into July. Abbie looked forward to fixing them lemonade and white chocolate macadamia nut cookies from ready-made dough, and with each passing day she knew she'd been right to leave Boston behind.

Still, Abbie never told Mary Kay about her visits with the boys and the work she asked them to do. Her friend wouldn't judge her, but Abbie wanted to hold her new life close, a secret she would share only when she was ready, when she could say: *You'll never guess the clever way I got my improvements done*, an experience long behind her. Mary Kay would be envious, wishing she'd thought of it first, rather than spending a fortune on a gardener and a pool boy.

But there were other reasons Abbie began erecting a wall between herself and the people who knew her best. Derek and Jack, bright as they were, weren't prone to notice the small changes, or even the large ones, that would have leaped out to her mother and Mary Kay—and even her distracted father.

Her mother would have spotted the new size of her feet right away, of course. And the odd new pallor of her face, fishbelly pale. And the growing strength in her arms and legs that made it so easy to hand the boys boxes, heavy tools or stacks of wooden planks. Mary Kay would have asked about the flaky skin on the back of her neck and her sudden appetite for all things rare, or raw. Abbie had given up most red meat two years ago in an effort to remake herself after the divorce tore her self-esteem to pieces, but that summer she stocked up on thin-cut steaks and salmon she could practically eat straight from the packaging. Her hunger was also *voracious*, her mouth watering from the moment she woke, her growling stomach keeping her awake at night.

She was hungriest when Derek and Jack were there, but she hid that from herself.

Her dusk swims had grown to evening swims, and some nights she lost track of time so completely that the sky was blooming pink by the time she waded from the healing waters to begin another day of waiting to swim. She resisted inviting the boys to swim with her.

The last Friday in July, with only a week left in the summer term, Abbie lost her patience.

She was especially hungry that day, dissatisfied with her kitchen stockpile. Gracetown was suffering a record heat wave with temperatures hovering near 100 degrees, so she was sweaty and irritable by the time the boys arrived at five-thirty. And itching terribly. Unlike her feet, the gills hiding beneath the ridges of her ribs never stopped bothering her until she was in her lake. She was so miserable, she almost asked the boys to forget about painting the refurbished back porch and come back another day.

If she'd only done that, she would have avoided the scandal.

Abbie strode behind the porch to watch the strokes of the boys' rollers and paintbrushes as they transformed her porch from an eyesore to a snapshot of the quaint Old South. Because of the heat, both boys had taken their shirts off, their shoulders ruddy as the muscles in their sun-broiled backs flexed in the Magic Hour's furious, gasping light. They put Norman Rockwell to shame; Derek with his disciplined football player's physique, and Jack with his awkward baby fat, sprayed with endless freckles.

"Why do you come here?" she asked them.

They both stopped working, startled by her voice.

"Huh?" Jack said. His scowl was deep, comical. "You're paying us, right?"

Ten dollars a day each was hardly pay. Derek generously shared half of his twenty dollars with his cousin for a couple hours' work, although Jack talked more than he worked, running his mouth about summer superhero blockbusters and dancers in music videos. Abbie regretted that she'd encouraged Derek to invite his cousin along, and that day she wished she had a reason to send Jack home. Her mind raced to come up with an excuse, but she couldn't think of one. A sudden surge of frustration pricked her eyes with tears.

"I'm not paying much," she said.

"Got *that* right," Derek said. Had his voice deepened in only a few weeks? Was Derek undergoing changes too? "I'm here for the catfish. Can we quit in twenty minutes? I've got my rod in the truck. And some chicken livers I've been saving."

"Quit now if you want," she said. She pretended to study their work, but she couldn't focus her eyes on the whorls of painted wood. "Go on and fish, but I'm going swimming. Good way to wash off a hot day."

She turned and walked away, following the familiar trail her feet had beaten across her back yard's scraggly patch of grass to the strip of sand. She'd planned to lay sod with the boys closer to fall, but that might not happen now.

Abbie pulled off her T-shirt, draping it nonchalantly across her beach lounger, taking her time. She didn't turn, but she could feel the boys' eyes on her bare back. She didn't wear a bra most days; her breasts were modest, so what was the point? One more thing Johanssen had tried to hold against her. Her feet curled into the sand, searching for dampness.

"It's all right if you don't have trunks," she said. "My back yard is private, and there's no harm in friends taking a swim."

She thought she heard them breathing, or maybe the harsh breaths were hers as her lungs prepared to give up their reign. The sun was unbearable on Abbie's bare skin. Her sides burned like fire as the flaps beneath her ribs opened, swollen rose petals.

The boys didn't answer; probably hadn't moved. She hadn't expected them to, not at first.

One after the other, she pulled her long legs out of her jeans, standing at a discreet angle to hide most of her nakedness, like the Venus de Medici. She didn't want them to see her gills, or the rougher patches on her scaly skin. She didn't want to answer questions. She and the boys had spent too much time talking all summer. She wondered why she'd never invited them swimming before.

She dove, knowing just where the lake was deep enough not to scrape her at the rocky floor. The water parted as startled catfish dashed out of her way. Fresh fish was best. That was another thing Abbie had learned that summer.

When her head popped back up above the surface, the boys were looking at each other, weighing the matter. Derek left the porch first, tugging on his tattered denim shorts, hopping on one leg in his hurry. Jack followed, but left his clothes on, arms folded across his chest.

Derek splashed into the water, one polite hand concealing his privates until he was submerged. He did not swim near her, leaving a good ten yards between them. After a tentative silence, he whooped so loudly that his voice might have carried across the lake.

"Whooo-HOOOOO!" Derek's face and eyes were bright, as if he'd never glimpsed the world in color before. "Awesome!"

Abbie's stomach growled. She might have to go after those catfish. She couldn't remember being so hungry. She felt faint.

Jack only made it as far as the shoreline, still wearing his Bermuda shorts. "Not supposed to swim in the lake in summer," he said sullenly, his voice barely loud enough to hear. He slapped at his neck. He stood in a cloud of mosquitoes.

Derek spat, treading water. "That's little *kids*, dumbass."

"Nobody's supposed to," Jack said.

"How old are you, six? You don't want to swim—fine. Don't stand staring. It's rude."

Abbie felt invisible during their exchange. She almost told Jack he should follow his best judgment without pressure, but she dove into the silent brown water instead. Young adults had to make decisions for themselves, especially boys, or how would they learn to be men? That was what she and Mary Kay had always believed. Anyone who thought differently was just being politically correct. In ancient times, or in other cultures, a boy Jack's age would already have a wife, a child of his own.

Just look at Mary Kay. Everyone had said her marriage would never work, that he'd been too young when they met. She'd been vilified and punished, and still they survived. The memory of her friend's trial broke Abbie's heart.

As the water massaged her gills, Abbie released her thoughts and concerns about the frivolous world beyond the water. She needed to feed, that was all. She planned to leave the boys to their bickering and swim farther out, where the fish were hiding.

But something large and pale caught her eye above her.

Jack, she realized dimly. Jack had changed his mind, swimming near the surface, his ample belly like a full moon, jiggling with his breast stroke.

That was the first moment Abbie felt a surge of fear, because she finally understood what she'd been up to—what her new body had been preparing her for. Her feet betrayed her, their webs giving her speed as she propelled toward her giant meal. Water slid across her scales.

The beautiful fireball of light above the swimmer gave her pause, a reminder of a different time, another way. The tears that had stung her in her backyard tried to burn her eyes blind, because she saw how it would happen, exactly like a dream: She would claw the boy's belly open, and his scream would sound muffled and far away to her ears. Derek would come to investigate, to try to rescue him from what he would be sure was a gator, but she would overpower Derek next. Her new body would even if she could not.

As Abbie swam directly beneath the swimmer, bathed in the magical light fighting to shield him, she tried to resist the overpowering scent of a meal and remember that he was a boy. Someone's dear son. As Derek (was that the other one's name?) had put it so memorably some time ago—perhaps while he was painting the porch, perhaps in one of her dreams—neither of them yet had been tested by life.

But it was summertime. In Gracetown.

In the lake.

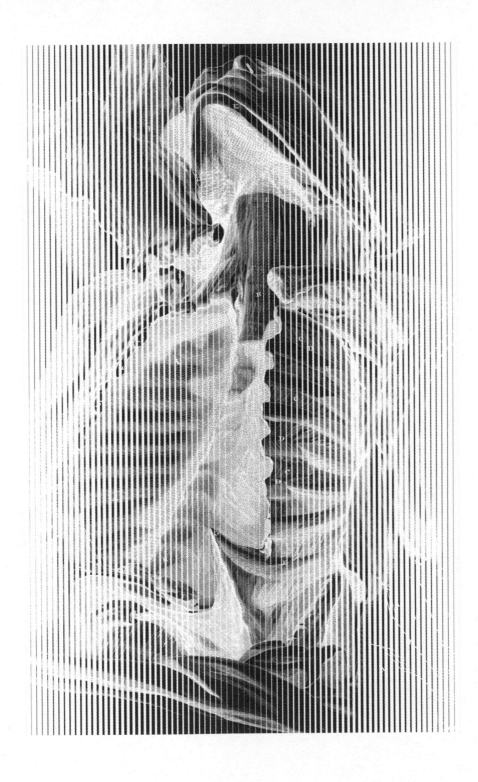

RC Matheson is a #1 bestselling author and screenwriter/producer *The New York Times* calls "…a great horror writer." He has created, written, and produced acclaimed TV series, mini-series and films, including cult favorite *Three O'clock High* and Stephen King's *Battleground* which won two Emmys. Matheson has worked with Steven Spielberg, Tobe Hooper, Nicholas Pileggi, Joe Dante, Roger Corman, Mel Brooks and many others. He has adapted novels by Dean Koontz, Whitley Strieber, Roger Zelazny, Stephen King, H.G. Wells and George R. R. Martin for film. Matheson's short stories appear in his collections, *Scars And Other Distinguishing Marks*, *Zoopraxis*, *Dystopia*, and 130 anthologies, including many *Best of the Year* volumes. His novels include *Created By* and *The Ritual of Illusion*. Matheson is a professional drummer and studied privately with CREAM's Ginger Baker.

I'm Always Here
Richard Christian Matheson

"I'm always here,
please never cry.
You may refuse,
you might ask why

One life as two,
two lives as one.
I am your rose,
you are my sun."

5:47 PM

DADDY IS STILL. He stuck himself and he's sleeping bad. Blowtorching; fevered. His veins blister and rush. All the rust and suffering is going for his throat. He twists and moans, soaking in nightmares. It'll hit Baby soon. His dyed hair is crepe black on white, casket skin.

I've been on the road with them for three days.

I picked up the tour in LA as it slid slow and sensual across America, coming up that Gibson-neck heartland and making people feel again. Be alive again.

All the major venues, SRO. Critical raves. Brilliant this, brilliant that. "…wonderment." "…perfection." "…horror." I covered Elvis in '76 through his Australian/Japan tour for the *Stone*, and it feels the same. Powerful, out of control.

Sacred.

Nashville is close. Light quilts feed the ground; warm veins. I hit PLAY and walk over to sit beside Daddy and Baby.

"How you feelin' Baby? Can we talk a little more?"

We've already laid down five hours' worth. Scholling. Family. Bones. We keep our voices low. Daddy talks in his sleep. She stares out the Lear's swim-mask window, cradles freckled fingers. Nods.

"Let's get a little more into some history. I've read you and Daddy met when you were thirteen…"

She fingers her 7 Up. Slips a delicate finger into hollowed cube, watches it melt; a momentary ring.

"I was just a little girl."

Her blonde hair smells like apples. I tell her and she smiles. Her voice is soft. Gentle.

"I used to listen to Daddy sing when I was a kid. Had all his records. HE was all that made me happy." Her accent is Kentucky; a calming sound. "My folks drank heavy, argued heavy. It was violent. Real violent."

Her expression falls somewhere to its knees and weeps helplessly even though it barely changes. She looks at me, sad and happy.

"Daddy sang like an angel. Sounded a little like Hank Williams. I wore out every album I had. Learned to sing harmony that was perfect with him." She whispers. "We're not talking too loud are we? He has to sleep."

Daddy moans a little. The coral bed inside his nervous system cuts him. Baby strokes his brow, kisses it.

"Okay, Daddy," she whispers. "I'm here. I'm always here."

I smile.

Baby nods, gently hums the melody to "I'm Always Here," and I remember hearing the haunting ballad when I was losing my marriage; drowning. It soared with mournful, aching confession and always made me cry.

"I loved that song first time I heard Daddy sing it. That's when I knew for sure I'd do anything for him." She looks off. "Literally anything."

The Lear is slashing clouds and they bleed grey. We'll be landing in Nashville in ten minutes. Daddy and Baby go on at eight-thirty, right after the Oak Ridge Boys. I have orchestra pit, dead center. *Rolling Stone* wants it all from up close. The faces. The music.

The poignant impossibility.

"After Daddy won the Grammy for best album in '81, it all started going bad. We've all heard about his marriage failing, money troubles. Why did he lose it all?"

I'm already tinkering with the header for the piece. But it needs work. Something that plays with "seamless." I'm not happy with it.

Baby shades a palm over tired eyes; a priest closing the lids on a dead face. She thinks back, seeing the photo album that always hurts, the one that's always half-open; memories bound and trapped. A phrase occurs to me: "terrible questions, sad answers." From one of Daddy's early songs, "Being Left Ain't Right."

"…drugs. All kinds. Daddy's still fighting it. It's hard for him. He's so sensitive." She takes his sleeping hand as a nightmare wraps him in barbed wire. "But more than that. I guess you'd really have to call it loneliness. From the deepest part of himself. First time I managed to get backstage and talk to Daddy, I could see his eyes were like…wounds. It was more than being an addict. It was…" She licks girlish lips. "I don't know, the despair. I suppose. Everybody he cared about was gone. His heroes. His family. They'd all left, abandoned him."

She sipped more of the 7 Up. Wiped her soft mouth with a "DADDY AND BABY '88 TOUR" napkin.

"I wanted to be there for him. So…"

"So, you followed him."

"Yes."

"Everywhere?"

"Yes."

"Like a groupie?"

"People said it. I never was that. I was his friend. His mother. Later, it's true…his lover."

I pull out a cassette, Baby and Daddy's first album, MOTHER AND LOVER. Baby takes it, feels it in her curious, childlike hands.

"He dedicated all the songs to me. 'Course the biggest was…"

"…'I'm Always Here.'"

"'I'm Always Here,' yes. It was our biggest seller until the new album. But you can never feel the same as the first one. The thrill."

We've gotten to the hard part.

About the procedure.

I choose words carefully, watching her features for reaction, as if staring at a radar screen, checking for impending collisions.

"The question is…very personal."

"It's all right. Go ahead."

"…did it hurt?"

She smiles the way some people do when they're in terrible pain.

"Yes, it was extremely painful. After, that is. It hadn't been done before. But the doctor was reassuring…he'd been researching…in the same area of… procedure."

"Only in reverse."

"That's right."

"How long did it take?"

"Almost two days. Thirty-seven hours."

She laughs a little. "You're probably wondering how I talked Daddy into it, right? Most folks wonder that."

She grows serious, once again.

"When I met him, he told me he had nothing left and nowhere to go. He was sick. Owed money to agents, promoters, the government…it was awful."

"And he was ill."

"That's why he finally agreed. The doctors said he would die. He was weak. His whole body was like…a crumbling statue. It was just a matter of time." Her voice becomes loving, confessional. "I had to help. No one else cared like me."

I check through my notes. Lawsuits. Divorce papers, bankruptcy bullshit. The guy's life hit the wall at a hundred, and the windshield cut him into bloody, monthly payments that were impossible.

"He was dying. You have to understand. This giant talent laying in the hospital bed like some frail…child. The man I'd loved since I was a little girl. I gave blood, organs…whatever they needed."

"It wasn't enough." I was reading from an article in *Newsweek's* "Medical Breakthroughs" page. Couple years back.

She shakes her head. No, it wasn't enough.

The Lear starts down at a crash angle. I kill the tape recorder, return to my seat, click my belt on. I glance over and see Baby talking softly into Daddy's ear, combing his hair with maternal fingers. She kisses his colorless hand and I see he's speeding, sweating; tissues beyond repair.

It starts to hit Baby as the jet lands, and she cries on Daddy's shoulder like a little girl, a faint agony tearing her in half.

9:15 PM

Scalpers are getting rich.

The guy behind me is standing and stomping. "Yeah, Baby, we *luuvvv* you, hon!"

I turn when he whistles. He's some six-pack crammed into a fat Stetson, and he's clapping and whooping it up along with the rest of the screaming Grand Ole Opry.

My photographer is Green Beret, squat-crawling across the footlights like they were landmines. He's snapping Nikon slices of Daddy and Baby taking bows.

They're dressed in sparkly, Country Western outfits that cost over ten thousand dollars. I asked them at their Marriott penthouse, when they were dressing for tonight's show; a story I can't begin to convey.

By then, I will tell you, Baby was completely high. But it doesn't hit her as hard as Daddy. His system swallows most of it. She told me after the pain subsides, she feels numb and giddy. Sometimes paranoid.

Daddy told her he was doing his best to cut the stuff off. Leave it. Drive past it, like a hideous accident you never wanted to see.

But it'll take a few more months. Their doctors are furious. Everyone is trying to understand. Baby helps them when they see the love she has for Daddy.

Baby said it was worth it for her to wait.

A dozen rosy kliegs bouquet on the empty stage and, as the two step into its calming circle, they thank the crowd; bow more. Baby smiles.

Daddy looks serious, deeper; sadder.

Then, he softly touches the guitar strings at his waist and a radiant chord begins the trance. The audience feels it. I feel it. My photographer, changing film, stops moving, stares up at the stage.

Daddy starts to sing a low, suffering lullaby and Baby joins him, a foamy, background harmony. He sings his half; looking into her eyes.

"I need to tell you,
I would've died.
To say it outright
should bruise my pride.

But without your love
to feed my life.
without your heart,
at my side....
Honey, it's all for nothing."

I look around and see tears fill a thousand eyes as Baby twists her head to look at Daddy. They sing the chorus together, as if cutting themselves open and mixing their blood.

> *"I'm always here,*
> *please never cry.*
> *You may refuse,*
> *You might ask why*
> *One life as two,*
> *two lives as one.*
> *I am your rose,*
> *you are my sun."*

The melody is slow, beautiful; feeling.

The notes are inevitable and Baby's smile is a twenty-year-old Madonna looking at her perfect child. As they sing, their separate bodies now joined as one, which feeds Daddy, he is singing pure and strong like the old days. Like when he got up there with Hank Williams and Merle Haggard and Carl Perkins and knocked everybody dead.

How the surgeon was able to fuse their two bodies, allowing Baby's younger, healthier fluids and strength to nurture Daddy's ailing flesh, has been discussed on talk shows, analyzed on news shows, lampooned on comedy shows. It's shocking and touching to people. Repugnant and life affirming. Everybody has a reaction.

I found it a hideous misuse of medical technique when I first heard about it. A grotesque immorality. Before I'd met Baby and Daddy. Until I saw the love she felt for him and the total dependency he couldn't hide, no matter how strong or renown he once was. Bathed in the warmth of her giving and her love, he had returned to being a child, carried not in her womb but outside it.

The lights have dimmed to a single spot, and Daddy and Baby are singing a cappella, staring into one another's eyes; lovers, friends, mother and child.

> *"I'm always here,*
> *please never cry.*
> *You may refuse,*
> *you might ask why."*

Throughout the Ole Opry House, couples are embracing, looking in silhouette like countless Daddy's and Baby's, joined in unguarded vulnerability. As I look around, I fight remembering how wonderful it was to be in love and hold my wife close when we were going strong.

I look up and see Daddy, and he's smiling for the first time all day. Baby whispers she loves him, as the crowd screams for more, and I suddenly notice how alone I feel.

"One life as two,
two lives as one.
I am your rose,
you are my sun."

The applause swirls around me and I start to cry, wanting so bad to be close to someone again.

CHRISTOPHER FOWLER is the multi award-winning author of nearly fifty novels and short story collections, including the acclaimed Bryant & May mysteries. His novels include *Roofworld*, *Spanky*, *The Sand Men*, and *Hell Train*, plus two volumes of memoirs, *Paperboy* (winner of the Green Carnation Prize), *Film Freak*, and *The Book of Forgotten Authors*. In 2015 he won the CWA Dagger In The Library for his body of work. His latest novel is *The Lonely Hour*. He lives in London and Barcelona, and blogs every day at WWW.CHRISTOPHERFOWLER.CO.UK.

The Look
Christopher Fowler

I never wanted to be a model.

I wanted to be *the* model.

He only picks one for each season. And after he picks her, nothing is ever the same again. He sees a special quality in a girl and draws it out. Then he presents it to the world. If you're picked, everything you do is touched with magic. You don't become a star, you become a legend. Ordinary people are awed by your presence. It's as if you've been marked by the hand of God.

As far back as I could remember, I wanted to be the girl he picked.

I got off to a bad start. I wouldn't concentrate on lessons at school. I didn't study late into the night. I hung out with my girlfriends, discovered boys, fell for their lies, fell out with my parents just before they did the same with each other. I had a best friend, a girl called Ann-Marie who lived across the street. Ann-Marie had a weight problem and wore these disgusting dental correctors, and overwashed her hair until it frizzed up and it looked like she'd stuck her tongue in an electric socket, but she helped me out with my homework, and it made me look good to walk beside her when we were out together. She hung around with me because she was seriously screwed up about her looks, and nobody wanted to be around her. It sounds cruel but the lower her self-esteem fell, the more mine rose.

I come from nothing, just faceless ordinary people. My mother would hate me saying that, but it's true. We lived in a rented flat on the tenth floor of a rundown apartment block in a depressing neighbourhood. I had no brothers or sisters, and my father went away years ago. My mother was never around because she worked all the time. Any humour, any life, any joy she had once been able to summon up had been scuffed away by her angry determination to maintain appearances. Nobody in my family ever had any money, or anything else. But I was aware from an early age that I had something. I had the Look. And I knew it.

Kit Marlowe says there's a moment in everyone's life when they have the right look. It may only last for just a single night. It may last for a season. Once in a rare while, it lasts a whole year. The trick is knowing when it's about to happen and being ready for it. I was ready.

I was so fucking ready.

I should tell you about Kit Marlowe, as if you don't already know. His first London collection freaked people out because he used a blind girl as his model, and everyone thought she was going to fall off the catwalk, which was really steep, but she didn't because she'd been rehearsing for an entire year. She wore these really high stilettos, and tiny skirts like Japanese Kogals, and hundreds of silver-wire bracelets. He has more than one model, but the others always stay masked in black or white muslin so that nothing detracts from the one he has selected to bear the Look for his collection.

He had one model who performed in his show under hypnosis. The clothes she modelled were actually stitched onto her, right through the flesh. Her veil was sewn to her forehead, her blouse held tight by dozens of tiny silver piercings that ran across her breasts. Even her boots were held on by wires that passed through her calves. I read an interview with her afterwards in which she stated that she hadn't felt a thing except total faith in Kit Marlowe. But not all of his designs were that extreme. Many of them were simple and elegant. That was the thing; you never knew the kind of look he would go for next.

Kit Marlowe got kicked out of school and has no qualifications. He's a natural. He says he learned everything he needs to know from television. He's larger than life. I guess I first heard about him when I was eight or nine and started collecting photographs of his models. I don't know how old he is. He began young, but he may even be in his thirties by now. He's a guru, a god. He changes the way we look at the world. His clothes aren't meant to be worn by ordinary people, they're there to serve a higher purpose, to inspire us. I used to study the pictures in amazement. I never saw anything he did that didn't surprise me. Some of it was grotesque and outlandish, but often it had this timeless, placeless beauty.

It was Ann-Marie who first pointed out the strange quality he brought to his models. We were sitting in a McDonald's waiting for my father to give us a lift home, studying a magazine filled with pictures from his Paris show, and she showed me how he mixed stuff from different eras and countries, so there'd be like, seventies' Indian beadworked cotton and fifties' American sneakers and eighties' Japanese skirts. But he combines everything with his own style, and in the presentation he'll throw in a wild card, like using a Viennese choir with African drummers and Latino house, the whole sound mixed together by some drum 'n' bass Ibiza DJ, and he'll set the whole event in something like a disused Victorian swimming pool, making all these fashion gurus trek miles out into the middle of nowhere to view his collection.

Once he showed his fashion designs on this video installation in New Jersey, setting monitors all around a morgue, where he ran footage of his clothes dressed on real corpses, teenagers who had died in car crashes. Then his model of the season came out from between the monitors with her masked team, all in blood-spattered surgical gowns, which they tore open to reveal the new season's outfits. It was so cool, dealing with social issues through fashion like that.

Kit Marlowe only designs for women. He says it's all about being extraordinary. He searches out girls who have something unique, and what he searches for completely changes every season. He never uses anyone older than nineteen. He says until that age we behave with a kind of animal instinct that is lost as we grow older. His models come from all over the world. He's used a Russian, a Hungarian, a Tunisian, a Brazilian, a Korean and an American as well as English girls, all of them complete unknowns. He just plucks them out of small towns. They give up their old lives for him, and he gives them new ones. He rechristens them. He gives them immortality.

One model to reveal the Look was a girl he called Acquiveradah. She was from St. Petersburg, seventeen, a little over six feet tall, very skinny and odd-looking, parchment-white skin with pale blue veins, and she wore mothwing purple gowns in gossamer nylon that showed her body in incredible detail. The Look was instantly copied by chain stores, who messed it up to the point of parody by adding layers of cheap material underneath. I remember her being interviewed. She said that meeting with Kit Marlowe had brought her violently alive for the first time, and yet the experience was 'like being stroked on the cheek with a butterfly wing'. She looked so ethereal I thought she was going to float away from the camera lens and up into the sun.

Kit has a special look of his own, too, but the details change constantly. Long hair, cropped hair, shades, goatee, facial tattoos, piercings, none of the above. He puts on weight and loses it according to the clothes he chooses for the season. Some likes and dislikes remain throughout his transformations. He likes unusual girls, particularly Eastern Europeans who can't speak English but who express themselves with their bodies. He loves to court controversy because he says it gets people talking about clothes. He's always being linked to gorgeous girls, and he openly admits that he has sex with his models. Kit says that understanding their sexuality helps him to uncover the Look. He likes strong women. He prefers fiercely textured fabrics and colours, silver, crimson, black and green. He laughs a lot and jokes around on camera, except when he's discussing his own creations. Then he's deadly serious. He owns houses all over the world but lives in France. He's physically big (although he might be short, it's hard to tell) and from some angles he has a heavy chin, except last year when he lost a lot of weight. He hates phonies and hype. He says his designs reflect the inner turbulence of the wearer. He explains how his clothes create chromatic harmonisations of the spirit. I filled an entire book with his sayings, and that was just from last season's interviews. It was Ann-Marie who heard about him coming to our town. He'd shown his collections outside London before, but never as far North as this. I wanted to see the show so badly. Of course it was invitation only, and I had no way of getting my hands on one. But we could at least be somewhere close by.

I was very excited about this. I knew that just to be near him would be to sense the future. Kit Marlowe is always ahead of the game. It's like he's standing on a chair searching the horizon while the rest of us are on the ground looking at each other like a bunch of morons. He never tells the press what the Look is going to be, but he drops hints. There were rumours going around in the style press that he was planning a range of computerised clothing; that he was going to combine microchip circuitry with the most basic fabrics and colours. But nobody really knew what that meant or what he was up to, and if they did they weren't saying.

Sometimes we went clubbing at the weekend. I would dye my hair blond while my Dad's girlfriend was out at work on Friday night, then dye it back before school on Monday. Ann-Marie and I figured that if we couldn't get into the show we could maybe get into his hotel and catch sight of him in the lobby afterwards, but it wasn't as easy as it sounded. He was staying near the station in this converted Victorian church covered with gargoyles, a cool place with headset dudes in floor-length black coats guarding the doors. Ann-Marie was smart, though. She figured we needed escorts otherwise we'd never get into the building, so we bribed these friends of Ann-Marie's brother who were going into the centre of town for the weekend. They sold insurance and wore off-the-peg suits and looked respectable, so we dressed down to match them, only I wore another set of clothes underneath. Ann-Marie couldn't because she was heavy enough already, and wasn't bothered anyway, but I wanted to be noticed. I was ready for it. I had the Look. My time was now.

The show was mid-afternoon, and we figured he'd come back and change before going to a party. We had a pretty tight lock on his movements because he gave so many interviews and loved talking to the press; all you had to do was piece everything together and you had the entire trip plan. This was probably how the guy who killed John Lennon managed it, just by gathering news of his whereabouts and drawing all the timelines together. It's pretty easy to be a stalker if you're single-minded. But I wasn't a stalker. I just wanted to be touched by the hand of God. Kit Marlowe says if you're strong about these things, you can make them happen.

It was one of those days that didn't look as though it would get light at all and was mistily raining when we reached the hotel. There was a sooty slickness on the streets that seemed left over from the area's coal-mining past, and the traffic was creeping forward through the gloom like a vast funeral procession. We were stuck in a steamed-up Ford with the insurance guys, getting paranoid about the time, and they were fed up with us because we hadn't stopped talking for the last hour.

"He's never going to make it through this," said Ann-Marie, but the rain was good because we could wear our hoods up, and the doormen wouldn't think we were teenage hookers or street trash. Once we had made it safely into the hotel lobby, we ditched the boring insurance guys and they went off to some bar to get drunk. We knew that Kit Marlowe was staying on the seventh floor because he had this superstitious thing about sevens (a fact disclosed in another wonderfully revealing interview) but when we went up there, we couldn't tell which suite he'd taken. I thought there would be guards everywhere but there was no security, none at all, and I figured that maybe the hotel didn't know who he was. We couldn't cover both sides of the floor from a single vantage point, so we split up, each taking a cleaner's cupboard. Then we waited in the warm soapy darkness.

Every time I heard the elevator ping, I stuck my head out. This went on for ages, until the excitement was so much that I fell asleep. The next thing I knew,

Ann-Marie was shaking me and hissing in my ear. I wondered what the hell her problem was, and then what the hell she was wearing.

"I found the maid's uniform on one of the shelves, I thought it would make me look less conspicuous," she explained.

"Well, it really doesn't, Ann-Marie. Pink's not your colour, and certainly not in glazed nylon with white piping. You look like a marshmallow."

"Take a look down the corridor."

"Ohmigod." A group of people was coming straight towards us. I ducked back in. "How do I look?"

"Take your coat off. Give it to me." Ann-Marie held out her arms. I was wearing an ensemble I had invented from cuttings of every Kit Marlowe collection. Obviously I couldn't afford the materials his designers used so I had come up with equivalents, adding a few extra details like plastic belts and sequins. It was a look that was very ahead of its time, and I knew he'd love it the moment he saw it.

I took a few quick breaths, not too many in case I started to hyperventilate, then stepped out of the cupboard. A man and a woman were talking quietly. They looked like a couple of Kit Marlowe's PR consultants or something. They dressed so immaculately in grey suits, black tees, trainers, and identical haircuts that they looked computer-generated. Behind them was Acquiveradah, a drifting wraith in some kind of green silk-hooded arrangement. I had forgotten how long and white her arms and neck were, how strangely she moved. She looked like she'd been deep-frozen and only half thawed. Kit Marlowe was at her side (quite a lot shorter than I expected), dressed in a shiny black kaftan-thing. I could see from here that his buttons were silver crucifixes, and every time he passed under one of the corridor spotlights they shone onto the walls. It was as though he was consecrating the hotel just by walking through it.

I realised at this point that I was standing right in the middle of the passage, blocking their way. I felt Ann-Marie tugging at my sleeve, but I was utterly mesmerised. I tried to hear what they were saying. Acquiveradah sounded angry. She and Kit were speaking hard and low. Something about changing dates, deadlines, signing it, moving it, being in Berlin. Oh, God, Berlin's so damned cold, she was complaining, like it was a big chore going there. And then they stopped.

They stopped because I was standing in their way like a fool, staring with my mouth open.

"What the fuck's going on?" Kit Marlowe himself was speaking, actually speaking. "Who's this? Did somebody order a singing telegram?" He was talking about me. Time slowed down. My skin prickled as he stepped forward through his PR people.

"Who are you?"

I knew I had to answer. "I'm—" But I realised I had made an incredibly stupid mistake. I had concentrated so hard on the Look that I had never invented a name for myself. "I'm—" I couldn't think of anything to say. I didn't want to tell him my real name because it's so ordinary, but I couldn't make one up on the spot. Behind him, Acquiveradah started hissing again. Kit held up his hand for silence and continued to stare.

"You, I like what you're wearing."

I closed my hanging mouth, not daring to move. This was the moment I had waited all of my life for.

"Tell me something."

I tried to breathe.

"Do they give you a choice?"

What was he talking about?

"I don't suppose so. Hotels only care about their guests, right? Everyone else gets the universal look. Staff are treated the same anywhere in the world." He wiped his nose on the back of his hand, and looked to one of the PRs for approval. "Right? I never thought of that, but it's true, right?" The PRs agreed enthusiastically. "It's a universal look."

I could see him. I could hear him. But I couldn't piece together what he was saying. Not until I followed his eyeline and saw that he was talking past me. Talking to Ann-Marie. She was standing behind us near the wall, beside a trolley filled with little bottles of shampoo, conditioner and toilet rolls. She was wearing the maid's uniform, and I saw now how much it suited her. It was perfect, like she worked here. But also, like she was modelling it.

"It's a look,' Kit fucking Marlowe was saying, "I don't know if it's the Look, but it's certainly a look. Come here, darling."

"Kit, for God's sake," Acquiveradah was saying, but he was reaching out to Ann-Marie and drawing her into his little group. My supposed best friend walked right past me into their spotlight, mesmerised, and I felt my eyes growing hot with tears as the scene wavered. Moments later they were gone, all of them, through a door that had silently opened, swallowed them and closed.

I was numb. Left behind in the empty corridor. I couldn't move. I couldn't go anywhere. Ann-Marie had our return money in her bag.

Then the door opened again, and Acquiveradah backed out. I could hear her making excuses to Kit. (Something about "from my room"—something like "in a few minutes".) I can't remember what she said, but I knew she was telling him lies. She moved awkwardly toward me and placed a cold hand on my shoulder. She was stronger and more purposeful than she looked.

"I have to talk to you, little girl. In here." She ran a swipe card through the door behind me and pushed me into the room. For a moment I was left standing in the dark while she fumbled for a light switch. In the fierceness of the mirrored neon that flicked on around the suite she looked hard and old, nothing like her photographs. There was something else about her appearance I found odd, a lopsidedness that skewed her features and gave her a permanent stare, like she'd only partially recovered from a stroke. "Sit down there." She indicated the edge of the bed. I pushed aside a tray of barely touched food and some empty champagne bottles, and sat. "Does your friend really want to model?"

I found my voice. "I never thought she did."

"A lot of girls act like that. It's a secret of successful modelling, not looking like you care whether you'll ever do it again. The moment you try too hard it shows. I can take it or leave it, they say. The world's top models spend their entire lives telling everyone they're giving it up next season, it's all bullshit. What they mean is, they're frightened they won't cut it next time. Nobody holds the Look for long. I'll ask you again; does she really want to model?"

I tried to think. "I guess she does. She wants to be liked."

"Fine, then we'll leave it. I don't know what will happen. He's been—well, let's say he's not thinking clearly after a show, and he may change his mind, but he may not, and if you see your friend again you should at least be able to tell her what she's in for. Most of them have no idea." She was talking in riddles, pacing about, trying to light a joint. "Look at me, I'm a good example. I had no idea what this sort of thing involved." She pulled up the hem of her hooded top and exposed her pale stomach. "I was the wrong shape, too wide here. They took out my bottom three ribs on both sides, here see?" Her pearlised finger-nails traced a faint ridge of healed stitches, the skin puckered like cloth. "I had my stomach stapled. Some of my neck removed and pinned back. My cheek-bones altered. Arms tucked. Eyes lifted. The graft didn't take at first and my left eye turned septic. It was removed and replaced with moulded plastic. You can't tell, even close up. It photographs the same because I always wear a full contact in the other one to match the texture." She drew on the joint, glancing anxiously at the door. "They removed fat from my ass, but I was still growing and my body started shedding it naturally, and I lost what I didn't have, so now it's very painful to sit down. I can feel the tops of my femurs rubbing, ball and socket scraping bone. Oh don't give me that look, fashion always hurts. Christ, they used to tighten the foreheads of Egyptian girls to prevent their skull-plates from knitting. Chinese foot-binding, ever hear of that?" I shook my head. "And athletes, they train so hard as kids that it stunts their growth, they give up any semblance of normal life for their careers, it's just what you have to do to get to the top and most people aren't prepared to do it, that's why they remain mediocre. You have to put yourself out, a long way out. It's pretty fucking elementary."

"I can't imagine that Kit Marlowe would allow that sort of thing to—"

"Exactly, you can't imagine. You don't get it, do you? There is no Kit Marlowe, he's a corporation, a conglomerate, he's jeans and music and vodka and cars and clothing stores, he's not an actual person. There's always a front-man, someone the public can focus on but he's not real. He's played by some-body different nearly every season. I assume most people recognise that in some fundamental way."

"But the fashions. His vision. The Look."

"Whoever's in place for this collection just follows the guidelines. 'Kit Marlowe' is a finder. This one picked your friend, but she's the third person he's picked in the last two days. They all have to be submitted to a hundred fucking committees before they get any further. The fabrics people never agree with the drinks people, the car people want older role models, and everyone hates the music people."

I had been trying hard not to cry, but now I couldn't stop my eyes from welling over. "The Look,' I said stupidly. 'He said anyone could…"

"It's not about a look, you little idiot, it's about being young. That's all you need to be. Young. Gap-toothed, cross-eyed, bow-legged, brain-damaged, whatever. If you're young you can wear anything, razorblades, pieces of jagged glass, shit-covered rags—and believe me you'll have to do that while they're all experimenting—you'll still look good because you're so incredibly fucking young. And if there's really a look, something that pleases every sponsor, then you're photographed in it and you do a few catwalks. And then it all goes away. Fast. People are like fruit; they don't stay fresh long before everyone knows they're damaged. That's all the Look is. Anyone should be able to figure it out."

"But what happens after that? Don't the models go to the press and describe how they've been—"

"Been what, exactly? Been given shitloads of money and fame and set up for life? Nobody makes you sign, honey, it's a choice, pure and simple. You get a contract and you honour your side of the deal, like any other job. The only thing is if any of the surgical stuff goes wrong, I mean badly wrong, you're fucked because they've got good legal people."

"But the people who interview Kit Marlowe, they must see that he changes—"

"They see what they choose to see. Ask yourself who employs them. Who owns the magazines they write for, the networks they broadcast for. You've got to think bigger, kid." She looked at her watch. "Shit, I have to get back. If you see your friend again, you'll have to make the choice. Do you give her a friendly word of warning, or not bother? After all, she looks like she forgot about you pretty quickly." The sour smile that crossed her face actually cracked her makeup.

"I don't believe any of this," I heard myself saying angrily. "You've lost it and you don't want anyone younger to get their turn. You're jealous of her, that's all."

Acquiveradah sighed and threw the remains of her joint onto a plate of torn-apart fruit. She stood there thinking. A fly crawled around the edge of a champagne flute. "All right." She dug into the pocket of her green hooded jacket, brought out another card, and held it up before me. "Go to room 820, on the next floor. Take a look, but don't touch their skin, you understand? Don't do anything girly, like screaming. Not that I suppose you'll wake them, because by now they'll be so fast asleep that the place could burn down and they wouldn't feel it. Oh, hang on." She went into the bathroom and came back out with a pair of nail-scissors. "Use these to get a good look. Then think about your friend. And leave the entry-card in the room when you leave."

I left the room and ran off along the corridor on wobbly legs. I knew if I got in the elevator I would take it straight back down to the ground floor, so I took the stairs instead. I found room 820 easily. The corridor was silent and deserted. I ran the swipecard through the lock and slowly pushed the door open. I couldn't see anything because the blinds were drawn and the lights were off. Besides, I guessed it was dark outside now. I stood in the little passage by the room's mirrored wardrobes, unable to leave the diamond of light thrown from the corridor. I listened and heard breathing, slow steady breathing, from more than one body. I could smell antiseptic. I tried to recall the room layout from the floor below. The lights had to be somewhere to my right. I reached out my hand and felt along the wall. Several switches were there. I flicked them all on.

The room had two beds, and someone was asleep in each of them. The pale cotton hoods they always wore in the shows were still stretched across their features. They continued to breathe at the same steady pace, and did not seem disturbed by the lights.

I walked over to the nearest one and bent closer. I could vaguely make out her features under the hood, which was held on tight with a plastic drawstring. I remembered the nail-scissors Acquiveradah had given me, and realised what she had intended me to do. I inserted the points just above the fastened collar and began to cut open the hood.

I found myself looking at the girl who had been hypnotised and pierced for the Kit Marlowe collection three seasons ago. The piercings had left terrible scars across her face, raised lumps of flesh as hard as pebbles, as red and sore as tumours. There were fresh crusts of blood around her ears, as though her skin had still not learned to cope with the demands being made upon it. Her teeth had been replaced by perfect white china pegs, neatly driven through gum and bone, but the gums had turned black and receded. I reached out my hand. I just wanted to see that she was real. I touched her cheek and felt the waxy flesh dent beneath my fingertips. When I removed my hand, the indentations remained, as though her skin was infected.

When I saw that she wasn't going to move, I pulled back her lower lip and saw lines of thick black stitches running around the base of her jawline. I could only imagine that after her turn in the spotlight this poor thing had agreed to stay on as one of the backing models, even though her face would never again be seen. Could fame do that, leave you so hungry for more that you would choose to stay, whatever your new situation might be?

I bent over her until our noses almost touched. The opened muslin hood lay around her face, framing it so that she looked like a discarded birthday gift. One of her eyes was closed. Hardly daring to breathe, I lifted the eyelid. There was a large glass marble in the socket, the kind boys used to play with at school.

I couldn't bring myself to look at the other model. Who knew what fresh horrors I might find? I was still thinking about it when the body beneath my hand moved and sat up. I think I screamed. I know I left that antiseptic-reeking room and shot out into the corridor as though I was running across hot coals. I was more confused than frightened. When I saw that Miss Three-Seasons-Ago wasn't coming after me, I tried to gather my thoughts. I wanted to help Ann-Marie but I badly wanted to leave, and the indecision froze me. At last I decided to try and find the way back. I went to the stairs and ran down to the floor where I had last seen her. The corridor was so silent and empty I could have been inside an Egyptian tomb. I found the door that Kit and his team had closed on me. It was still shut. I stopped in front of it, staring stupidly at the gilded number, willing it to open, praying that it would open.

And then it did.

The PR pair came out. The woman looked at me and smiled. "I guess you're waiting for your little friend," she said, as if talking to a stupid child. "She can't see you right now. She's busy."

"What are you doing to her?"

"Don't worry, she's enjoying herself. Now, I think you'd better go on home."

"I can't. She's got my money."

The woman sighed and pulled a wad of notes from inside her jacket. "Take this and just go away, okay?" She pushed a roll of bills into my hand. Behind her, the hotel door shifted open slightly, and I caught a glimpse of the room inside. It was very brightly lit. Ann-Marie had no clothes on. She was sitting in a chair looking very fat and white, and there was something sticking out of her, protruding from between her legs. It looked like a long steel tube with a red rubber bulb on one end. She was smiling and looking up at the ceiling, then suddenly her whole body began to shake. Somebody kicked the door shut with a bang.

I closed my fist over the money and ran, out into the night and the rain.

The rest of the evening was awful. I had to hitch home, and this creepy lorry-driver kept staring at my tits and making suggestions. I think he got the wrong idea because of the way I was dressed. Ann-Marie lived with her drunk mother and her stupid stoner brother. I called at their house, but no-one was at home. They were never at home. Anyway, they weren't expecting her back for another day.

I talked to Ann-Marie's mother later, and she showed me the letter, about how her little girl was dropping out of school because she had a modelling contract and was moving to London to become a star. Her family, such as it was, certainly didn't seem too bothered. They were pleased she was going to bring in some money. I guess my own happiness for Ann-Marie had something to do with being glad that I wasn't in her place. She was missed in class for a couple of weeks, and that's about all. She wasn't the kind of person you noticed, whereas I was. Maybe that was why she'd been chosen.

Anyway, when the next season's collection was announced, I received an invitation. The thing was printed on a sheet of pressed steel that nearly slashed the tops off my fingers when I opened the envelope. By this time I was planning to leave home and start media studies at the local college. I went down to London and located the venue, a disused synagogue somewhere behind Fleet Street. Once again, it was raining. I'd decided to play it safe and wear plain black jeans and a tee shirt. To tell the truth, I was growing out of dressing like a Kit Marlowe wannabe, but I was still eager to find out how Ann-Marie had fared in her new career. We were served fancy cocktails in a burnished iron antechamber, then ushered into the main salon.

A few wall-lights glowed dimly. Only the deep crimson outline of the cat-walk could be discerned in the gloom. As we took our seats, the room was abuzz with anticipation. A single spotlight illuminated a plump young man standing motionless at the foot of the runway.

Kit Marlowe surveyed his dominion with satisfaction. He waited for everyone to settle, lightly patted the back of his waxed hair, and beamed. "Ladies and gentlemen," said a voice emanating from the speakers around us as Kit moved his lips, "I'd like to thank you for coming out from the West End in such foul weather, and I hope you'll find your efforts well rewarded. Welcome to my collection. This year the Look honours someone very special, someone we all know but never fully acknowledge. This Kit Marlowe season, ladies and gentlemen, is dedicated to the ordinary working girl. She is all around us, she is in all of us, a part of the machinery that fills our lives. She is the spark that ignites and powers the engines of society. She is Andromeda, and this is her Look."

We realised that the figure speaking before us was an animatronic manne-quin. As the overhead voice pulsed away into silence, it collapsed into the floor, and brilliant red walls of laser light rolled up to create a virtual room in space.

Along the catwalk and stepping into this lowering box of fractal colour came a figure that could not be recognised as Ann-Marie. She looked like every girl you ever saw serving behind a counter or a trolley, like all of them yet none of them. Her outfit was that of a streamlined, futuristic servant, but as the electronic soundtrack grew in pitch and volume something happened to the clothes she was wearing. They changed shape, refolding and refitting into different patterns on her body, empowering her, transforming her from slave to dominatrix. I later discovered that every item modelled in the show was manipulated by computer programs, interacting with silicon implants in the fabrics that tightened threads and changed tones. Kit Marlowe had invented digital fashion. The entire room burst into spontaneous applause.

Behind Ann-Marie moved two eighties-throwback robot girls, their heads encased in shiny foil-like fabrics. I wondered if one of them was a mutilated, ageing Acquiveradah. Lights dazzled fiercely and faded. The sonic landscape created a vision of primitive mechanisation tamed and transformed by the all-powerful electron. When I looked again, Ann-Marie had changed into a different outfit. She performed all her changes onstage, dipping within the spinning vectors of hard light, aided by the micro-circuitry in her clothes. Or rather, *their* clothes, the creations that had resulted from the findings of so many secret focus groups, research and development teams, marketing and merchandising meetings. What 'Kit Marlowe' had succeeded in doing was gaining access to the birth-point of the creative process.

As the show reached its zenith the room erupted, and stayed in a state of perpetual arousal through the hammering climactic flourishes of the performance. I'd like to think that the audience applause was spontaneous, but even that was doubtful.

I saw her after the show. My ticket admitted me to a party for special buyers. I queued for the cloakroom, queued for the VIP lounge, queued to pay my respects to the new star. Waited until she was standing with only one or two people, and moved in on her. I couldn't bring myself to call her 'Andromeda', nor could I call her Ann-Marie because she wasn't the Ann-Marie I knew any more. There was something different about her eyes. She had little markings carved into the actual ball of each eye, as though the pupils had been scored with a scalpel and filled with coloured ink.

"Eye tattoos," she explained when I asked. "They're going to be big."

Her eyelashes had been shaved off and her mouth artificially widened somehow, the lips collagen-implanted and reshaped. She still had heavy breasts, but now she had a waist. And great legs. I had never seen her legs before tonight. She was wearing a body-stocking constructed in the kind of coarse material you saw on African native women, but the fabric glowed in faint cadences, like the pulse of someone between dreams and wakefulness.

"How does it do that?" I asked.

"The material has microscopic mirroring on one facet of the thread. It twists slightly to the rhythm of my heartbeat," she explained.

"Jesus, couldn't it electrocute you?"

"The voltage is lower than that required to run the average pacemaker. Don't worry, I'm better than fine." She spoke as if she had learned her reply from a script, and I guess she had. I looked down at her hands. She had no fingernails. There were just puckers of ragged flesh where her nails had been.

"I'm glad you could come. It means a lot. I wondered if you'd ever forgive me."

"I'm not sure I have. Your mum says you never write any more."

"I don't know what I'd say to her. I send money, of course. She wouldn't approve if I told her half of what happens around here. I mean, it's great and everything, but—"

"But what? Can we have a drink together?"

Ann-Marie looked around guiltily. "I'd love to have a drink, but I'm not allowed. The first few weeks were rough, but I feel a lot more centred now. You wouldn't believe the eating and exercise regime."

The Ann-Marie I knew would never have used a word like 'centred'. I was hungry for answers. I wanted to know what went on behind the hotel doors. I went to touch her and she flinched. "All models have to work out," I told her, "but there's more to it than that, isn't there?"

She gave me her patented blank look. Her eyes went so unfocused she could have been watching a plane land.

"Come on, Ann-Marie, I know."

"Well, I admit," she said softly, "there's a downside, a real downside. I wish we could talk more. I miss you."

"I just want to know if you're happy," I asked. "Tell me you made the right choice."

"I don't know. They took out a length of my gut. Stripped my veins and tried to recolour them. They tried out some piercings at the top of my legs and attached them to the flesh on the backs of my arms, but it wasn't a good look. If I eat the wrong things I start bleeding inside. They tried little mirrors instead of my fingernails but my system rejected them. They were going to run fine neon wires under my skin to light me up, but their doctor said it would be too dangerous for me to move around with so much electric cable in me. I won't tell you what they wanted to do to me down below. There are other things going on that you wouldn't—"

Suddenly a tiny LED on her collar blinked, just once, so briefly that I later wondered if I imagined it. Ann-Marie's face paled. The fine wire collar around her neck automatically tightened, cutting into her skin, closing off her throat and the carotid artery in her neck. A vein throbbed angrily at her temple. Liquid began to pool in the bay of her mouth. The bodysuit closed more tightly around her as its circuitry came alive. She could barely find the air to speak. A second later the spasm ended, and the collar released itself to its preset diameter.

"I have to go now," she whispered hoarsely, her eyes searching my face as if trying to memorise my features for some future recollection. She turned away, stiffly walking back to her keepers. I figured she was miked up, and wondered if that was the first time they had been called upon to jerk her lead. But for now, Ann-Marie was gone. Andromeda returned to her celestial enclosure of light, away from the mundane world, into the mists of mythology.

I understood then what she had surrendered to keep the Look.

The terrible truth is, I would still have changed places with her for a taste of that life, just for a chance to be someone, to look down upon dreary mortals from the height of godhood. I would have done anything—I would still do anything—to get a second chance. To have Kit Marlowe look at me and smile knowingly. To let his people experiment with my body until they were happy no matter how much it hurt, and I would smile back at them through the stitches and the blood and the endless tearing pain. I would surrender everything.

Because nothing can ever take away the power of the Look. To be adored is to become divine. All your life is worth its finest moment. And when at last you fall from grace, you still have eternity to remind you of that time.

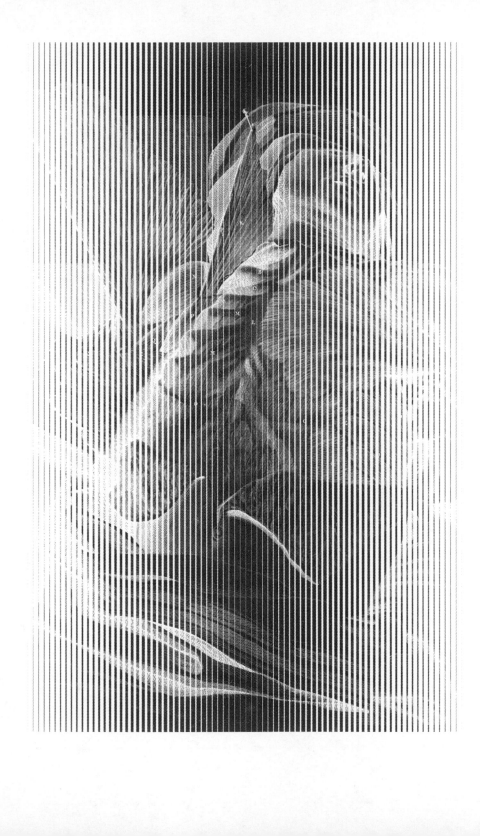

CARMEN MARIA MACHADO is the author of the bestselling memoir *In the Dream House* and the short story collection *Her Body and Other Parties*. She has won the Bard Fiction Prize, the Lambda Literary Award for Lesbian Fiction, the Brooklyn Public Library Literature Prize, the Shirley Jackson Award, and the National Book Critics Circle's John Leonard Prize. In 2018, the *New York Times* listed *Her Body and Other Parties* as a member of "The New Vanguard," one of "15 remarkable books by women that are shaping the way we read and write fiction in the 21st century."

Her essays, fiction, and criticism have appeared in *The New Yorker, The New York Times, Granta, Conjunctions, McSweeney's Quarterly Concern, Best American Science Fiction & Fantasy, Best American Nonrequired Reading*, and elsewhere. She is the Writer in Residence at the University of Pennsylvania and lives in Philadelphia with her wife.

The Old Women Who Were Skinned
Carmen Maria Machado

THERE ONCE WERE two sisters, close in age, who had been birthed and loved and became stooped and wise and were now old women together. They lived in a house in a courtyard surrounded by a tall stone wall, meant to keep out most children and all men, though starlings made their nests in the boughs of the elms.

One day, the king—an old man himself—was walking by the wall when he heard the lilting voices of the sisters, who had become accomplished singers over their long years. He listened for a while, his eyes narrowed with contentment, and then ambled his way to a small gap in the mortar.

"What sweet creatures sing behind these walls?" he asked. Both sisters scrambled for the gap, but the first sister—a little taller, with slightly longer legs—got there first.

"We have always been here, your highness," she said, her voice gravelly at its edge.

"Show me," the king said.

So the first sister slipped her finger into the gap. She felt the king's breath puff on her skin, and then his lips enveloped it.

The thrill she felt! Out of sight, the king's mouth was wet and tight—like probing her own sex—and she felt a kick of desire as he suckled her fingertip as if it were a nipple. At the edge of the pull and draw was a nip of teeth, and she moaned. Excited by this, the king bit down and drew blood, which excited him further. It was all he could do to not loose himself from his clothes.

"My young maiden," he said. "My blushing, tender girl. Come to my bed-chamber tonight. I wish to be your first, to barricade past your maidenhead."

The sisters laughed silently behind their hands, for they had rid themselves of their maidenheads long ago. But then the first sister said, sweetly, "My king, you may have any part of me you wish. I will be there tonight."

And then the king was gone. The first sister withdrew her finger and examined the bite marks at their tip. Before she departed, she had the second sister gather up her extra skin and pin it tightly behind her back, so that she might appear young as the king believed her to be.

That night, the first sister arrived at the castle beneath a cloak, and was whisked upstairs by staff as silent as dolls. From outside his bedchamber door, she said, "My love, I am afraid of fire. Please put out your candles before I enter."

From within, she heard the hiss of a snuffed flame.

The door opened.

In the silt of the shadows they made love. Afterwards, as she glowed with sensation, the first sister wished him to see her as she really was. She wanted his pleasure to come from her stomach and thighs and breasts, not those of some imaginary creature. And so in the darkness, she stood, and unpinned her skin. She struck a match and laid it to the candle's wick.

The king, horrified by her shape, leapt from the bed. He shoved her toward the window, and then out of it. "Please, please," she begged as he pried her fingertips from the ledge. He did not even stay to watch her fall.

The first sister plummeted down, and down, but just before she struck the ground, she became tangled in the branches of a tree. Its thorns hooked into the soft folds of her body. She screamed and cried and hung there like a tanning hide.

It was then that a group of fairies passed by. They laughed at the old woman in the tree, bare and slick and weeping. Her humiliation was intoxicating to them as wine.

Fairies are very indulgent, self-satisfied creatures, and their meddling knows no ends. And so one of them waved his finger and the first sister dropped to the earth. She lay on the cool soil, afraid to move. The fairies walked off, and she heard their voices long after they'd disappeared into the night. Her tears dried and left streaks of salt behind.

When the first sister finally stood up, she felt strange—no longer sore, and supple as a reed. She ran her hands over her body, apple-firm and smooth. Her flesh was young again.

The second sister waited for the first sister to return. They had shared lovers throughout their long lives, and as soon as they were together again, the second sister knew that she would learn the secrets of the king's pleasure, and take her own in turn.

But when the night thinned into dawn, and then day, and the first sister did not return, the second sister left their home to find her. She walked along the wall and through the door and out into the bright world. All she found near the castle was a beautiful young maiden, sitting naked beneath a tree.

"Excuse me," said the second sister, "I don't mean to trouble you, but have you seen—"

It was then that she recognized her sister's eyes, hazel as her own.

The first sister looked at the second sister with horror. Had her own skin hung in such a way? Had she been so shriveled, so loose, so ancient? She could barely remember.

"What's happened to you?" the second sister asked.

"This is the skin that was beneath," the first sister said. She closed her eyes and shook her head, as if disagreeing with herself. She tried to explain again. "This is my true skin."

The second sister reached out and touched the first sister's jaw. It was downy and soft as a newborn fawn. They had not had skin like that since they were young women together. "You're gone," she said. "Sister, you've left me behind."

The first sister pulled her face away. "I'm sorry," she said. She stood and walked back toward the castle, to find the king.

The second sister walked to town and located a barber. "Take my skin," she said. She handed him a coin.

"Take it off?" he said.

She handed him a second coin.

He shrugged. He dragged his razor up and down a leather strap, and then held it up for inspection. The blade-edge caught the morning light.

It was like the sweet, briny bite of sugar against an open nerve; then, like being dropped into the sun.

The second sister continued to live even after the barber hung her skin from his window, and then sold it to a bookbinder. But with no flesh to contain her body, the wet meat of her muscle and the roping of her tendons were on full display. Bits of dust and soil clung to her damp organs. She often woke to the sensation of mice scrabbling beneath her breastbone, of skittering cockroaches rounding her eye. On the rare occasion when she ventured beyond the wall, mothers would bend down to their children and point at her. "See?" they would say. "This is what happens when you worry about your looks. Such is the price of vanity." She spent the remainder of her life wiping crumbs from her joints and crevices, tears draining through her body like raindrops sliding down a windowpane.

As for the first sister, there are many stories about how she ended up trawling the earth for her old skin. In the first, the king died, and when she went to find her sister, she discovered a dead, shucked corpse in a chair by their old fireplace, and she clutched the body and wept and wept. In another, the king tired of her, and their old home was vacant and lined with dust, and soon she found herself wandering the land alone.

No matter the story, one thing is the same: she missed her old skin. She felt vulnerable without its age and warmth, like a fox pelt silver with time, and its power of concealment. This taut, ageless woman, her skin gleaming like dew clinging to stem and petal, with a mouth like a pitted cherry, was never left alone. Wherever she went, men followed with their hands and cocks and voices, their hungers and wants and desires. They trampled and pursued.

She hunted down the fairies. She demanded they return her skin to her, and when they laughed and refused, she pulled their heads from their bodies like dandelions. In this way, she walked and searched until the end of her days. Her grief never abated, and when she died and should have become part of the soil, she remained unchanged and immutable as wax.

She is there still, if you know where to look.

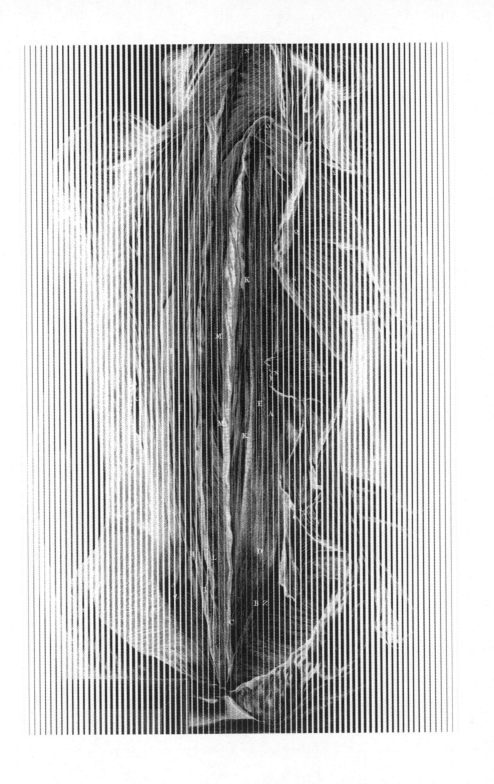

Seanan McGuire lives, works, and occasionally falls into swamps in the Pacific Northwest, where she is coming to an understanding with the local frogs. She has written a ridiculous number of novels and even more short stories. Keep up with her at www.seananmcguire.com. On moonlit nights, when the stars are right, you just might find her falling into a swamp near you.

Spores
Seanan McGuire

June 2028

Something in the lab smelled like nectarine jam. I looked up from the industrial autoclave, frowning as I sniffed the air. Unusual smells aren't a good thing when you work in a high-security bio lab. No matter how pleasant the odor may seem, it indicates a deviance from the norm, and deviance is what gets people killed.

I straightened. "Hello?"

"Sorry, Megan." The round, smiling face of one of my co-workers—Henry, from the Eden Project—poked around the wall separating the autoclave area from the rest of the lab. His hand followed, holding a paper plate groaning under the weight of a large wedge of, yes, nectarine pie. "We were just enjoying some of Johnny's harvest."

I eyed the pie dubiously. Eating food that we had engineered always struck me as vaguely unhygienic. "Johnny baked that?"

"Johnny baked it, and Johnny grew it," Henry said, beaming. "The first orchard seeded with our Eden test subjects has been bearing good fruit. You want a slice?"

"I'll pass," I said. Realizing that I was standing on the border of outright rudeness, I plastered a smile across my face and added, "Rachel's planning something big for tonight's dinner. She told me to bring my appetite."

Henry nodded, his own smile fading. It was clear he didn't believe my excuse. It was just as clear that he would let me have it. "Well, we're sorry if our festivities disturbed you."

"Don't worry about it." I gestured to the autoclave. "I need to unpack this before I head out."

"Sure, Megan," he said. "Have a nice evening, okay?" He withdrew, vanishing around the cubicle wall and leaving me comfortably alone. I let out a slow breath, trying to recover the sense of serenity I'd had before strange smells and coworkers disrupted my task. It wasn't easy, but I'd had plenty of practice at finding my center. Less than thirty seconds later, I was unpacking hot, sterile glassware and getting my side of the lab ready for the challenges of tomorrow.

Project Eden was a side venture of the biotech firm where I, Henry, and several hundred others were employed. Only twenty-three scientists, technicians, and managers were appended to the project, including me, the internal safety monitor. It was my job to make sure the big brains didn't destroy the world in their rush toward a hardier, easier to grow peach, or an apple that didn't rot quite so quickly after it had been picked. On an official level, I was testing the air and lab surfaces for a committee-mandated parts per million of potential contaminants. On an unofficial level, I spent a lot of time sterilizing glassware, wiping down surfaces, and ordering new gloves, goggles, and lab coats.

It was work that could have been done by someone with half my education and a quarter of my training, but the pay was good, and it gave me an outlet for the compulsions that had kept me out of field biology. Besides, the hours were great. I didn't mind being a glorified monkey if it meant I got to work in a good, clean lab, doing work that would genuinely better the world while still allowing me to quit by four on Fridays.

The team was still celebrating and eating pie when I finished putting the glassware away and left for the locker room. I hadn't been kidding about Rachel telling me to save my appetite. It had been a long day, and I wanted nothing more than to spend an even longer night with my wife and daughter.

Rachel was in her studio when I got home. She had a gallery show coming up, and was hard at work on the pastels and impressionistic still lifes that were her bread and butter. I knocked on the wall to let her know I was there and kept walking toward the kitchen. It was her night to cook—that part was true— but that didn't mean I couldn't have a little snack before dinner. The Farmer's Market was held on Tuesday afternoons. I had worked late Tuesday night, but I knew Rachel and Nikki had gone shopping, and Rachel had the best eye for produce. Whatever she'd brought home would be delicious.

The fruit bowl was in its customary place on the counter. I turned toward it, and froze. A thick layer of grayish fuzz covered its contents, turning them from a classicist's ideal still life into something out of a horror movie. "Rachel!" I shouted, not moving. It was like the information my brain had was too jarring to fully process. It would take time for all of me to get the message. "There's something wrong with the fruit!"

"You don't have to shout, I'm right here." My wife stomped into the kitchen, wiping her hands on the dishtowel she'd been using to clean her paintbrushes between watercolor overlays. She had a smudge of bright pink dust on one cheek, making her look like a little girl who'd been experimenting with her mother's cosmetics. I fell in love with her all over again when I saw that perfect imperfection.

That was the best thing about being married to my best friend, as I'd been telling people for the past fifteen years: I got to fall in love with her every day, and no one ever thought I was being weird. Sometimes normalcy is the most precious gift of all.

I didn't get the chance to tell Rachel about the fruit. Her eyes followed my position to its logical trajectory. It was almost a relief when she recoiled the same way I had, her upper lip curling upward in atavistic disgust. "What did you do?" She turned toward me, scowling. "This was all fresh when we brought it home yesterday."

I blinked at her. "What do you mean, what did I do?" I asked, feeling obscurely offended. "I can't make fruit go off just by looking at it."

"Well, then, did you bring something home from the lab?" She stabbed her finger at the gray-washed contents of the bowl. "This isn't right. I examined this fruit myself. There was nothing wrong with it."

"You got this from the farmer's market, right?" She was right about the age of the fruit: I remembered her bringing it home and dumping it into the bowl, and it had looked fine then. I'd even been thinking about how nice those peaches would taste with some sharp cheddar cheese and a bottle of artisanal hard cider. I wouldn't have done that for moldy fruit. I wouldn't have made it to the office without sterilizing the entire room.

Rachel frowned. "Yes, we did."

"There you go." I picked up the whole bowl, holding it gingerly to avoid any contact with the gray scum, and walked it over to the trash can. The decay had progressed far enough that the bowl's contents made an unpleasant squishing noise when I dumped them out. I wrinkled my nose and put it in the sink, resisting the urge to toss it into the trash with the fruit instead. "Something went bad and set off a chain reaction."

Rachel wasn't listening. She wrinkled her nose at the place where the bowl had been sitting, and before I could say anything, she ran her finger through the circle of gray fluff marking its footprint. "This crap is on the table, too. We're going to need disinfectant."

"I'll disinfect the table," I said, swallowing a jolt of panic. "Go wash your hands."

Rachel frowned. "Honey, are you having an attack?"

"No." Yes. "But this stuff reduced a bowl of fruit to sludge in less than eighteen hours. That doesn't make me feel good about you getting it on your hands." I glared at the gray circle. Rachel's finger had cut a clean line through it, showing the tile beneath. "Please. For my sake."

"Megan, you're scaring me."

"Good. Then you'll use extra soap."

"You're such a worrywart," she said, a note of affectionate exasperation in her voice. She kissed my cheek and was gone, flouncing back into the hall, leaving me alone with the faint scent of rotten fruit.

I looked at the circle for a moment longer, and then turned to the sink. I was going to need a lot of hot water.

Fungus is the great equalizer.

We give bacteria a lot of credit, and to be fair, life as we know it *does* depend on the tiny building blocks of bacteria. They allow us to digest food, recover from infections, and eventually begin the process of decaying back into the environment. But the truly heavy lifting of the decaying process comes from fungus. Fungus belongs to its own kingdom, separate from animals and vegetables, all around us and yet virtually ignored, because it's not as flashy or exciting as a cat, dog, or Venus flytrap.

There are proteins in mushrooms that are almost identical to the ones found in mammalian flesh. That means that every vegetarian who eats mushrooms instead of meat is coming closer than they would ever dream to their bloody hunter's roots. With so many things we've cataloged but don't understand, how many things are there that we don't know yet? How many mysteries does the kingdom of the fungus hold?

Rachel—after washing her hands to my satisfaction—had gone to pick up our daughter from cheerleading practice. Nikki was in the middle of one of her "dealing with either one of my mothers is embarrassing enough, I cannot handle them both" phases, which would normally have aggravated me. Tonight, I took it as a blessing. Having them both out of the house made it easier for me to go through the kitchen and systematically bleach, disinfect, and scrub every surface the fruit might have touched to within an inch of its life.

Rachel's immediate "what did you do" response wasn't unjustified. I worked in a lab full of biotech and geniuses, after all; it wasn't unreasonable to blame me when something went awry. But that was why I was always so *careful*. Didn't she see that? Nothing from the lab ever entered our home. I threw away two pairs of shoes every month, just to cut down the risk that I would track something from a supposedly clean room into our meticulously clean home. Whatever this stuff was, it couldn't be connected to Project Eden. It just didn't make any sense.

When I was done scrubbing down the counters, I threw the sponges I'd used into the trash on top of the moldy mess that had been a bowl of nectarines and apples—the mold had continued to grow, and was even clinging to the plastic sides of the bag—and hauled the whole thing outside to the garbage bin.

I was on my knees on the kitchen floor, going through my third soap cycle, when Rachel and Nikki came banging through the front door, both shouting greetings that tangled together enough to become gloriously unintelligible, like an alphabet soup made of my favorite letters. "In here!" I called, and continued scrubbing at the linoleum like I'd get a prize when I was finished. I would, in a way. I would get the ability to sleep that night.

Footsteps. I looked up to find them standing in the kitchen doorway, and smiled my best "no, really, it's all right, this isn't an episode, it's just a brief moment of irrational cleanliness" smile. It was an expression I'd had a lot of practice wearing. The elbow-length rubber gloves and hospital scrubs probably didn't help. "Hi, guys. How was practice?"

Nikki frowned, which was almost a relief. There had been a lot of eye-rolling and stomping lately, which wasn't fun for anyone except for maybe her, and I wasn't even certain about that. Having a teenager was definitely a daily exercise in patience. "Mom, why are you scrubbing the kitchen floor? It's not Thursday."

I'd been braced for the question. I still cringed when it was actually asked. There was a weight of quiet betrayal behind it—nights when I'd missed my medication without realizing it and wouldn't let her eat until I'd measured every strand of dry spaghetti and placed it in a pot of boiling, previously bottled water; days spent searching through the women's department at Target for the only bras that had no structural or cosmetic flaws. Years of living with my OCD had left her gun-shy in a way neither Rachel nor I could have predicted when we decided to have a baby.

Nikki looked so much like me at her age, too. That was part of the terror. Nikki was sixteen, and that was roughly the age I'd been when my symptoms had really begun to solidify. Had she managed to dodge the bullet of her genetics, or was she going to start washing the skin off of her hands any day now? No one knew. No one had any way of knowing.

"Remember I told you about the fruit from the farmer's market going off?" asked Rachel, coming to my rescue as she had so many times before. "That mold was nasty. It needed to be cleaned up before we'd be able to cook in here again."

Nikki glanced to the trash can, which was so clean it gleamed. "All this over a little mold?"

"It wasn't a little mold," I said. I was starting to feel like I should have taken a picture of the trash before taking it outside. That stuff had been growing at a rate that made me frankly uncomfortable, and for more reasons than just my OCD. I might be obsessed with cleanliness, but that didn't make me immune to the allure of a scientific mystery. Mold that grew at that kind of rate was mysterious to be sure.

If it were legal to burn trash in our neighborhood, I would have already been looking for the matches.

"Uck," said Nikki: her final word on the matter. She backed out of the doorway and announced, "I'll be in my room," then turned to prance away, flipping her hair theatrically. Rachel watched her go, waiting until the characteristic sound of a door being slammed confirmed Nikki's retreat to her room. Only then did Rachel turn back to me, rolling her eyes. I managed to stifle my laughter.

"You're where she gets the stomping around and slamming doors, you know," I accused, resuming my scrubbing. "My little drama queens."

"I had to contribute something," Rachel said. There was a worried note in her voice. I glanced up to see her leaning in the doorway, arms folded, frowning as she watched me. "Honey…is this really about the mold? You can tell me if you're having a bad night. I just need to know."

I shook my head and went back to work. "I'm fine, honestly. I took my medication, and I'm not having trouble breathing." Asthma-like symptoms were often my first warning of a serious attack. "I just *really* didn't like the looks of that mold, and I don't want to risk it being carried through the house on our shoes. I already scrubbed down the table and the trash can."

"Mmm-hmm." From Rachel's tone, I could tell that she was debating whether or not to believe me. "What about the fridge?"

The smell of the bleach was soothing. I kept scrubbing. "The fruit never went into the fridge. I did a basic check for mold or signs of spoilage, found none, and left it alone. You can check if you want, as soon as I'm done with the floor."

"I will, you know."

"I know." I dropped the sponge into my bowl of sudsy water and stood, stripping off my gloves. I threw them into the trash and turned to find Rachel still looking at me with concern. I offered her a tired smile. "I'm sort of counting on it. What do you want to do for dinner?"

"How do you feel about spaghetti?" The question was neutral enough, but I understood its intent. Spaghetti was one of my triggers, and had been since Nikki was a baby. If I could tolerate irregular pasta, I wasn't having an attack.

"Spaghetti sounds great," I said. "Do you want me to go get some tomatoes from the garden?"

"That would be wonderful."

"Be right back." I stepped out of the kitchen, my bare feet feeling slightly tacky from the bleach, and kissed her cheek before starting for the back door. The floor was clean. The mold was gone. It was a beautiful evening, and it was going to be an even more beautiful night.

Rachel's spaghetti was, as always, fantastic. She had a real gift with the sauce, managing to combine basic ingredients in a way that was nothing short of magic to me. I could work up complex solutions in the lab, I could synthesize impossible things, but ask me to brown some ground turkey and I was lost. Even Nikki, who had been making vague noises about watching her weight—worrisome, given how slim she was and how often OCD was connected to eating disorders—ate a serving and a half.

Dessert would have been a fruit tart, had everything gone as planned. In the absence of the fruit, we had ice cream—pear sorbet for me, Ben and Jerry's coffee with chunks for Rachel and Nikki—while we talked about our days. As always, Nikki was happy to listen to Rachel talk about painting, and began interrupting with facts about her own infinitely interesting life as soon as I started talking about what I'd been working on back at the lab. I thought about getting offended, and settled for smiling and stealing half of Nikki's ice cream while she was distracted. Rachel's job was more interesting to hear described: she created art, something that could be seen and touched and immediately understood without years of education and practical experience. All things being equal, I'd rather hear about Rachel's job, too.

All in all, it was a pretty peaceful night at home. No, that's not right. Once I shut away the dread that still lingered in the pit of my stomach over the gray mold in the kitchen, it became a *perfect* night. It was just flawed enough to be real, and so real I wanted to repeat it over and over again for the rest of my life. If I could have had that night a hundred times, I would have been able to die a happy woman.

That's the trouble with perfect nights: No matter how good they are, you only ever get to live them once.

It was a work night for me and a school night for Nikki, and both of us were in bed by ten. Rachel joined me an hour or so later. I woke up when she pressed a kiss into the hollow of my throat, her lips practically burning my skin. She snuggled close, and we both dropped down into dreamland, where everything was safe and warm and nothing could ever hurt us, or change our perfect little world.

I woke to the sound of Rachel whispering my name, over and over again. "Megan," she said, her voice tight with some arcane worry. "Megan, wake up, please, I need you to wake up now. *Please.*" It was the panic in that final plea that did me in, yanking me straight through the layers of sleep and back into our bedroom. There was a strange, dusty scent in the air, like something left in the back of an airless room for a long time without being disturbed.

"Rachel?" I sat upright, reaching for the lamp on my side of the bed. Light would make things better. Monsters didn't thrive in the light.

"No! Don't turn it on." The panic that had woken me was even stronger now. "Megan, I...I need you to take Nikki and go next door. Call the paramedics when you get there, but don't turn on the light."

"What?" I squinted into the darkness. Rachel was sitting on the far edge of the bed. I could see her silhouette in the light coming through the open bathroom door. "Honey, what's wrong? Did you hurt yourself? Let me see."

"Oh, no." She laughed, but the panic wasn't gone. It laced through her laughter, turning it jagged and toxic. My heartbeat slowed for a moment, and then sped up as my own panic bloomed. "You don't want to see, Megan, all right? You don't want to see, and I don't want you to see, so please, just go. Get Nikki and go."

"I'm not going to do that. Honey, what's wrong?" And then, God help me, I turned on the light.

Rachel was wearing her favorite nightgown, the blue satin one with the popped and faded lace flowers around the neckline. Her back was to me and her hair was loose, hanging to hide her face from view. As I watched, she sighed so deeply that her entire body seemed to sag, the delicate tracery of her spine pressing hard against her skin.

"I should have known you'd turn on the light," she said, and twisted to face me.

I didn't gasp or recoil. I wish, looking back, that I could say I'd been a better person than that, but the truth is that I was too stunned to do anything but stare silently, trying to make sense of the single gray mitten that she had pulled over her left hand, or the patch of pale gray felt that she had glued to the corner of her left eye. Then she blinked at me, and the strands of mold clinging to her eyelashes wavered in the breeze, and my denial snapped like a broken branch, leaving me holding nothing but splinters. Before I knew it, I was standing with my back against the wall, as far from her as I could get without actually fleeing the room.

Now I understood the dry, dusty smell. It wasn't old paper or a forgotten library book. It was mold, living, flourishing mold, feasting on the body of my wife.

My throat was a desert. It didn't help that Rachel—my beautiful Rachel, who should have been the one panicking, if either one of us was going to—was looking at me with perfect understanding, like she hadn't expected any other reaction, yet still couldn't blame me for following the nature she'd always known I was slave to. She blinked again, and I realized to my horror that the sclera of her left eye was slightly clouded, like something was beginning to block the vitreous humor. Something like the spreading gray mold.

"I must have had a cut on my hand," she said. "I thought I'd scrubbed hard enough, but I guess I was wrong. And then I rubbed my eye in my sleep...maybe that's a good thing. The itching woke me up. So we can go to the hospital and they can do whatever it is you do when you get a...a fungal infection, and then it'll all be okay. Right? I just have to go to the hospital. Right?" There was a fragile edge to her words, like she was standing very close to the place where reason dropped away, leaving only a yawning chasm of blackness underneath.

She looked so sad. My girl. My wife. The woman I had promised to have and to hold, in sickness and in health, amen. And I couldn't make myself go to her. I tried—no one will ever know how hard I tried—but the muscles in my legs refused to work, and the air in my lungs refused to circulate until I was stepping backward into the doorway, away from the dry, dusty smell of mold growing on human flesh.

"I'll call the hospital," I said, and fled for the hall.

Nikki woke when the ambulance pulled to a stop in front of our house, flashing lights painting everything they touched bloody red. "Mom?" She appeared on the stairs, holding her robe shut with one hand and squinting through the curtain of her hair. "What's going on?"

I forced myself to smile at her. The EMTs already had Rachel outside. They'd taken one look at her and swung into action with a speed that impressed even me, producing gloves and sterile masks and anything else they could use to keep themselves from coming into contact with her skin. Even then they'd touched her as little as possible, guiding her with words, not hands, casting anxious looks at each other and then back at me as they moved. I understood their concern, but there was nothing I could do about it. I couldn't even force myself to follow them. The dry mold smell filled our bedroom, almost solid in its presence. I wanted to bleach the whole place, *would* have bleached the whole place, except that I knew Rachel's treatment might depend on being able to examine the spot where she'd been infected.

"Rachel's not feeling so well," I said. "I'm going to follow her to the hospital as soon as they call and tell me it's all right. I was going to come up and make sure that you were awake before I went."

Nikki's eyes got very wide and round. "You're going to leave me here?"

"No, I'm going to ask Mrs. Levine from next door to keep an eye on you." I didn't want to leave her alone in the house, but even more, I didn't want to take her to the hospital. Not until we knew what the *thing* on Rachel's arm was, and whether it was contagious.

It had to be contagious. It had been on the fruit, and then it had been on the table, and Rachel had touched the residue on the table; just touched it, nothing more than that. If this stuff wasn't contagious, she had been exposed at the same time as the fruit, and Nikki—

Sudden terror seized me. "Honey," I said, fighting to keep my voice level, "are you feeling all right?"

Nikki's eyes got even wider. "Why? Is it food poisoning? My stomach feels fine."

"No, it's not food poisoning. Hold on." I flicked on the light, illuminating the hall and stairs in a harsh white glow. Nikki squinted at me, looking affronted. I would worry about her sensibilities later. "Show me your hands."

"What? Mom—"

"*Show me your hands.*" I was using the tone Rachel always called "OCD voice"—and she wasn't kidding, exactly, even if she used the label to soften my admittedly violent reactions, turning them into something that wouldn't frighten people who weren't as used to me as she was.

Nikki had grown up with my quirks and issues. She stopped arguing and held her hands out for me to inspect. They were spotlessly clean, with short, close-clipped fingernails that had been manicured with a simple clear coat. Most importantly, there was no mold on them. I swallowed the urge to tell her to disrobe, to prove that she wasn't infected. Things weren't that bad. Things weren't going to *get* that bad. I wouldn't let them. I couldn't help her if I let them. I had to hold onto control with both hands, because if I lost it—

If I lost it, I was going to lose everything. For the first time in my life, the sense of impending doom that followed me around might actually have weight.

"Mom, what's going on?" Her voice shook a little as she pulled her robe tight around herself once more. "Where are they taking Rachel?"

"I told you. To the hospital." I turned to look at the front door, and then at the open door to our bedroom. "Go upstairs. You can get online if you want, but I don't want you down here until I've cleaned up a little." Any mold that was in our bedroom could stay; I could sleep on the couch. But the kitchen? The dining room? My fingers itched, and I rubbed them together to reassure myself that it was just the urge to clean, and not a sign of contamination.

"Okay," said Nikki meekly, and turned and fled back to her room, where she could barricade the door against me and my insatiable need to scrub the world.

Rachel's hand. Rachel's beautiful, delicate hand. Completely obscured by clinging gray.

I turned and walked straight for the closet where we kept the bleach.

———

The hospital called a little after five a.m., four hours after they had loaded Rachel into the back of an ambulance and left me alone with a contaminated house and a teenage daughter who refused to come out of her room. The gray mold had been growing on Rachel's latest picture, almost obscured by the pastel loops and swirls. I'd stopped when I found it, standing and staring transfixed at the delicate swirls it cut through the color. There was something strangely beautiful about it. It was hardy, and alive, and finding sustenance wherever it could. Even in pastels.

It was eating the last thing my wife had touched before she came to bed and woke me up pleading for help. I had thrown the picture in the trash and was in the process of bleaching the studio walls when the phone rang. My gloves were covered in bleach. I answered anyway. I didn't trust the receiver. "Hello?"

"May I speak to Megan Riley?"

"Speaking." It felt like my insides had been bleached along with the walls. *Please don't be calling to tell me that she's gone*, I prayed. *Please, please, don't be calling to tell me that she's gone.*

"Your wife, Rachel Riley, was admitted shortly after one o'clock this morning. She's resting comfortably, but I have some questions for you about her condition."

Relief washed the bleach away. "So she's all right?"

There was an uncomfortable pause. "I don't want to mislead you, Ms. Riley. Her condition is very serious. Anything you can tell us would be a great help."

I closed my eyes. "She came into contact with a strange gray mold that was growing on some fruit in our kitchen around five o'clock yesterday afternoon. She woke me up shortly after one with the same mold growing on her hand and eye. Judging by how advanced it was, I would estimate that it had been growing since the afternoon, and had only reached a visible stage after she went to bed. She said that it itched."

"Have you, or has anyone else in your home, come into contact with this mold?"

Yes. I've been chasing it through my house, murdering as much of it as I can find. "No, although I've poured a lot of bleach on it," I said. "My teenage daughter is here with me. She hasn't touched any of the mold, and she's clean. I didn't sterilize our bedroom. I thought you might need to examine some of the stuff growing in a relatively natural way."

There was a pause before the doctor asked, "Do you have anyone who can look after your daughter for a short time, Ms. Riley? You may want to come to the hospital."

"Is Rachel all right?"

"Her condition is stable for the moment."

We exchanged pleasantries after that, but I didn't really hear or understand them. When the doctor ended the call I hung up, opening my eyes and leaning against the counter with all my weight on the heels of my hands. My gaze fell on the sink, and on the fruit bowl, which I had scrubbed until my hands were raw before going to bed the night before.

A thick layer of gray mold was growing in the bottom.

I relaxed as soon as Nikki and I stepped into the cool, disinfectant-scented lobby of the hospital. Nothing could take away from the sense of cleanliness that pervaded this place, not even the people sitting in the chairs nearest to the admission window, waiting for their turn to see the doctor.

Nikki was wearing her robe over a pair of jeans and a pilled sweatshirt that she should have thrown away at the end of the winter. It swam on her petite frame, making her look smaller and even more fragile. I resisted the urge to put an arm around her, offending her teenage pride and making her reject me. Instead, I walked to the open window, waited for the receptionist to acknowledge me, and said, "Megan and Nikki Riley. We're here to see Rachel Riley?"

Her eyes went wide with comprehension and something that looked like fear. "Please wait here," she said, before standing and vanishing behind the dividing wall. I stepped back, rubbing my chapped hands together and wishing I didn't feel quite so exposed. Something was wrong. I knew it.

"Ms. Riley?"

Nikki and I turned to the sound of our last name. A door had opened behind us, and a doctor was standing there, looking weary and worried, wearing booties and a plastic hair cap in addition to the expected lab coat and scrubs. I stepped forward.

"I'm Megan Riley," I said.

"Good. I'm Dr. Oshiro. This must be Nicole." He offered Nikki a tired, vaguely impersonal smile. "There are some snack machines at the end of the corridor, Nicole, if you'd like to go and get something to eat while your mother and I—"

"No." She grabbed my hand, holding on with surprising force. "I want to see Rachel."

The doctor looked at me, apparently expecting support. I shook my head. "I told her she could stay home if she wanted to." Although not in the house, dear God, not in the house; not when mold could grow on a ceramic bowl that had already been bleached and boiled. We'd have to burn the place to the ground before I'd be willing to go back there, and even then, I would probably have avoided contact with the ashes. "She said she wanted to see her mother, and I try to accommodate her wishes."

The doctor hesitated again, taking in the obvious physical similarities between Nikki and me, and comparing them to dark-skinned, dark-haired Rachel, who couldn't have looked less like Nikki's biological mother if she'd tried. Family is a complicated thing. Finally, he said, "I don't want to discuss Ms. Riley's condition in public. If you would please come with me...?"

We went with him. For once, I didn't feel like the people still waiting were watching with envy as I walked away: they had to know what it meant when someone arrived and was seen this quickly. Nothing good ever got you past the gatekeeper in less than half an hour.

The air on the other side of the door was even cooler, and even cleaner. The doctor walked us over to a small waiting area, guiding Nikki to a seat before pulling me a few feet away. Neither of us argued. We were both in shock, to some degree, and cooperation seemed easier than the alternative.

Voice low, he said, "Ms. Riley's condition is complicated. We have been unable to isolate the fungal infection. To be honest, we've never seen anything this virulent outside of laboratory conditions. We've managed to stabilize her, and she's not in much pain, but the fungus has devoured the majority of her left arm, and patches are beginning to appear elsewhere on her body. Barring a miracle, I am afraid that we will have no good news for you here."

I stared at him. "Say that again."

Dr. Oshiro visibly quailed. "Ms. Riley..."

"Outside of lab conditions, you said. Is this the sort of thing you've seen *inside* lab conditions?"

He hesitated before saying, "Not this, exactly, but there have been some more virulent strains of candida—the fungus responsible for yeast infections—that have been recorded as behaving in a similar manner under the right conditions. They had all been modified for specific purposes, of course. They didn't just *happen*."

"No," I said numbly. "Things like this don't just happen. Excuse me. Is there somewhere around here where I can go to make a phone call?"

"The nurse's station—"

"Thank you." And I turned and walked away, ignoring Nikki's small, confused call of "Mom?" at my receding back.

I just kept walking.

The phone at the lab rang and rang; no one answered. I hung up and dialed again: Henry's home number. He picked up on the second ring, sounding groggy and confused. "Hello?"

"What did you do?" I struggled to make the question sound mild, even conversational, like it wasn't the end of the world waiting to happen.

"Megan?" Henry was waking up rapidly. Good. I needed him awake. "What are you talking about?"

"*What* did you *do*?" All efforts at mildness were gone, abandoned as fast as I had adopted them. "How much fruit is Johnny's orchard producing? Where have you been sending it?"

And then, to my dismay and rage, Henry laughed. "Oh my God, is that what this is about? You figured it out, and now you want to yell at me for breaking some lab protocol? It can wait until morning."

"*No it can't.*"

Henry wasn't my teenage daughter: he'd never heard me use that tone before. He went silent, although I could still hear him breathing.

"What did you do? How did you slip her the fruit?" I was a fool. I should have realized as soon as I saw the mold…but maybe I hadn't wanted to, on some level. I'd already known that it was too late.

God help me, I'd wanted my last perfect night.

"Maria from reception. We had her meet your wife in the parking lot and say she'd bought too many peaches. It was going to get you to come around to our way of thinking, but Megan, the fruit is safe, I promise you—"

"Have there been any issues with contamination of the samples? Mold or fungus or anything like that?"

There was a long pause before Henry said, "That's classified."

"What kind of mold, Henry?"

"That's classified."

"How fast does it grow?"

"Megan—"

"Does it grow on living flesh?"

Silence. Then, in a small, strained voice, Henry said, "Oh, God."

"Did it get out? Did something get loose in the orchard? Who decided testing genetically engineered food on human subjects was a good idea? No, wait, don't tell me, because I don't care. How do I kill it, Henry? You made it. How do I kill it?"

"It's a strain of *Rhizopus nigricans*—bread mold," said Henry. "We've been trying to eliminate it for weeks. I…we thought we had it under control. We didn't tell you because we thought we had it under control. We didn't want to trigger one of your episodes."

"How kind of you," I said flatly. "How do I kill it?"

His voice was even smaller when he replied, "Fire. Nothing else we've found does any good."

"No anti-fungals? No poisons? Nothing?"

He was silent. I closed my eyes.

"Who decided to give it to my wife?"

"I did." His voice was so small I could barely hear it. "Megan, I—"

"You've killed her. You've killed my wife. She's melting off her own bones. You may have killed us all. Enjoy your pie." I hung up the phone and opened my eyes, staring bleakly at the wall for a long moment before realizing that the nurses whose station I'd borrowed were staring at *me*, mingled expressions of horror and confusion on their faces.

"I'm sorry about that," I said. "Maybe you should go home now. Be with your families." There wasn't much else left for them to do. For any of us to do.

Rachel was in a private room, with a plastic airlock between her and the outside world. "The CDC is on their way," said Dr. Oshiro, watching me and Nikki. Anything to avoid looking at Rachel. "They should be here within the day."

"Good," I said. It wasn't going to help. Not unless they were ready to burn this city to the ground. But it would make the doctors feel like they were doing something, and it was best to die feeling like you might still have a chance.

The bed in Rachel's room was occupied, but where my wife should have been there was a softly mounded gray *thing*, devoid of hard lines or distinguishing features. Worst of all, it moved from time to time, shifting just enough that a lock of glossy black hair or a single large brown eye—the right eye, all she had left—would come into view, rising out of the gray like a rumor of the promised land. Nikki's hand tightened on mine every time that happened, small whimpers that belonged to a much younger child escaping her throat. I couldn't offer her any real comfort, but I could at least not pull away. It was the only thing I had to give her. I could at least not pull away.

The doctors moved around the thing that had been Rachel, taking samples, checking displays. They were all wearing protective gear—gloves, booties, breathing masks—but it wasn't going to be enough. This stuff was manmade and meant to survive under any conditions imaginable. They were dancing in the fire, and they were going to get burnt.

All the steps I'd taken to keep my family safe. All the food I'd thrown away, the laundry I'd done twice, the midnight trips to the doctor and the visits from the exterminator and the vaccinations and the pleas…it had all been for nothing. The agent of our destruction had grown in the lab where I worked, the lab I'd chosen because it let me channel my impulses into something that felt useful. I hadn't even known it was coming, because people had been protecting me from it in order to protect themselves from me. This was all my fault.

Dr. Oshiro was saying something. I wasn't listening anymore. One of the nurses in Rachel's room had just turned around, revealing the small patch of gray fuzz growing on the back of his knee. The others would spot it soon. That didn't matter. The edges told me that it had grown outward, eating through his scrubs, rather than inward, seeking flesh. The flesh was already infected. The burning had begun.

"Mom?" Nikki pulled against my hand, and I realized I was walking away, pulling her with me, away from this house of horrors, toward the outside world, where maybe—if we were quick, if we were careful—we still stood a chance of getting out alive. Nikki was all I had left to worry about.

Rachel, I'm sorry, I thought, and broke into a run.

LISA L. HANNETT has had over seventy short stories appear in venues including *Clarkesworld, Fantasy, Weird Tales, Apex, The Dark* and *Year's Best* anthologies in Australia, Canada and the US. She has won four Aurealis Awards, including Best Collection for her first book, *Bluegrass Symphony*, which was also nominated for a World Fantasy Award. Her first novel, *Lament for the Afterlife*, was published in 2015. Her latest collection of short stories, *Songs for Dark Seasons*, came out in April 2020. You can find her online at WWW.LISAHANNETT.COM and on Instagram @LISALHANNETT.

Sweet Subtleties
Lisa L. Hannett

JAVIER CALLS ME Una, though I'm not the first. There are leftovers all around his studio. Evidence of other, more perishable versions. Two white chocolate legs on a Grecian plinth in the corner, drained of their caramel filling. A banquet of fondant hands, some of which I've worn, amputated on trays next to the stove. Butter-dipped petals crumbled on plates, lips that have failed to hold a pucker. Butterscotch ears, taffy lashes, glacé cherry nipples. Nougat breasts, pre-used, fondled shapeless. Beside them, tools are scattered on wooden tables. Mixing bowls, whisks, chisels, flame-bottles. Needles, toothpicks, sickle probes, pliers. Pastry brushes hardening in dishes of glycerine. In alphabetical rows on the baker's rack, there are macadamias, marshmallows, mignardises. Shards of rock candies, brown, yellow and green, that Javier uses to tint our irises. Gumdrop kidneys, red-hot livers, gelatine lungs. So many treats crammed into clear jars, ready to be pressed into cavities, tissue-wrapped and stuffed into limbs. Swallowed by throats that aren't always mine.

"Delicious," I say as Javier jams grenadine capsules into my sinuses, a surprise for clients with a taste for fizz. "Delicious." The word bubbles, vowels thick and popping in all the wrong places. Gently frowning, Javier crushes my larynx with his thumbs. He fiddles with the broken musk-sticks, tweaking and poking, then binds the voice box anew with liquorice cords. I try again.

"Delicious."

Still not right. The tone is off. The timbre. It's phlegmatic, not alluring. Hoary, not whorish. It will put people off their meals, not whet appetites. It doesn't sound like me.

Javier's palm on my half-open mouth is salty. His long fingers gully my cheeks. I wait in silence as he breaks and rebuilds, breaks and rebuilds. Concentrating on my lungs, my throat. Clearing them. Making sure they are dry. I don't mind being hushed. Not really. Not at the moment. If anything goes wrong, if I collapse this instant, if I crack or dissolve, at least my last words will have been pleasant. Something sweet to remember me by.

It won't be like before, he said. There will be no weeping. No throttling chest-rattle. No thick, unbreathable air.

On Monday, I made my latest debut—I make so many. Served after the soup but before the viande at the *Salon Indien du Grand Café*. My striptease was an enormous success. Fresh and unmarked, clad in edible cellophane, my marzipan dusted with peach velvet. Even the stuffiest top-hat couldn't resist. Javier had contrived a device to drop sugared cherries onto every tongue that probed between my legs. Dozens of gentlemen laughed and slurped, delighted I was a virgin for each of them.

"Marvellous," they shouted, licking slick chops. "Belle Una, tonight you're more divine than ever!"

"Marvellous," I say, calm and mostly clear. Mostly. Close enough.

Sugar-spun wigs line a window ledge above Javier's workbench. Faceless heads, all of them. Now visible, now obscured, as he bobs over me, intent on his work. The hairdos are exquisite. Some pinned up in elaborate curls, some plaited, some styled after Godiva. Glinting honey strands. Carmine. Deep ganache. Exquisite, all of them, despite showing signs of wear.

Between soot-streaked portraits on the walls, wooden shelves support a horde of glass moulds. As one, they gape at me from across the room. Their faces as like to each other as I am to them. High brows and cheekbones, pert mouths, strong jaws, noses so straight we'd be ugly if it weren't for our delicate nostrils. Javier insists we are identical, indistinguishable, impeccable casts of the original. We must be the same, he tells us. We must be. We *must*.

Once people have well and truly fallen in love, he said, *they do not want variety*. They want the same Una they enjoyed yesterday, last week, last month. They want the same Una, now and always. The same Una that Javier, confectioner gourmand, is forever recreating.

For the *hauts bohème* on Wednesday evening, I played the role of limonadière. Stationed behind the bar counter, I wept pomegranate jewels while spouting absinthe verses. Odes to beauty, freedom, love. Javier encouraged this crowd unreservedly. "They've loose clothes, loose hair, loose morals," he said. "And loose purse-strings." Under his guidance, the bohèmes tickled my limbs with the bows of gypsy violins. Scratched me with pen nibs. Trailed paintbrushes along my soft places. With each stroke, swirls of hippocras bled to my surface. Ale, brandy, champagne, rum. One by one, the lushes lapped it all up. They prefer drink to desserts, Javier said. Those with maudlin constitutions cannot keep anything substantial down.

"Una, chère Una," the bohos cried, slurring into their cups. "Promise never to leave us again."

Emotional drunks, I thought. *Glutting themselves into confusion. Muddled on passion and wine. Can't they see I'm here? I am forever here.*

"I feel—" I begin. Javier traps my jaw. Holds it still. Wary of what, I wonder? That it will fall off with talk, no doubt. That I'll run out of things to say before tonight's performance.

I feel solid, I want to assure him. I feel settled. Take it easy now. Easy. I'm going nowhere. I'm right here.

Friday's connoisseurs ate with torturous restraint.

"Pace yourselves," the women said, cracking knuckles with the sharp edges of their fans.

"Sugar is a mere distraction for the palate," said the men. "It will never satiate."

As centrepiece on their ruby tablecloth, I sat with legs pretzelled into Sadean poses. Wearing garters of hardened molasses, nothing more. By the second remove of sorbet, my contorted ankles and wrists had crumbled. I couldn't stand for all the gold in the world. My paralysis thrilled our hosts no end—as did Javier's copper blades. Two daggers per guest. Honed to ravage goodies from my thighs, rump, belly. Tantalised, the feasters took turns at fossicking. At knifing currant ants and blackberry spiders from my innards.

"What an illusion," they moaned, crunching aniseed antennae. "So convincing, so real… And not even a splash of blood! When did you learn such tricks, *chère fille*? Why have you not beguiled us this way before? No matter, no matter. Bravo, chère Una, *et encore*!"

Tips are highest when egos are stroked, my confectioner says. When pomposity is rewarded with flirtation. So Javier slapped their bony backs. He stooped and kowtowed. I bowed as best I could. Waggling my fingers and toes.

Letting them caress me long after the coins had rolled.

Rigged with peanut-brittle bones, my digits made such a gratifying snap when the party finally succumbed. When they gave into temptation. Indulged in wounding and breaking.

Javier ribbons my chin with silk to hold it in place for a few minutes. My neck needs patching; he's made quite the mess of it. He spritzes rosewater to keep me malleable, then shuffles to the stove. Bent over hotplates, he sings quietly as he stirs. His plainchant quickens the pots' ingredients. Sifted flour, hen-milk, vanilla essence. A sprinkling of salty eye-dew to bring his subtleties to life. Over and over, mournfully low, he garnishes the mixture with tears and base notes of my name.

Una, Una, he whispers, adding a pinch of cardamom to freckle my skin. *Una, this time you'll be just right.*

For tonight's outcall, Javier embeds a diadem of Jordan almonds into my curls. "The candied treasure of Priam," he says, chiselling them into my scalp. Content, he moves on to my hazel eyes. Sets them with a stony stare, like Helen's transfixed by the sight of her city ablaze. She's a favourite of Javier's. Peerless Helen. Unforgettable Helen. With that legendary face. All those ships sailing after it. Lately, while assembling and reassembling me, he's worn grooves into her story, worn it thin with retelling. The affair. The abduction. The hoopla and heartbreak. His sunken cheeks gain a healthy sheen as he talks of truces made and broken. Gifts offered, shunned, accepted. The permanence, the stubbornness of young lovers. The tale spills from him like powdered ginger, spicy and sharp, as he presses buttercream icing into my moist gaps.

While he pokes and prods, I make predictable observations. Repeating comments he himself once made. Repeating threadbare conversations. Repeating things he'll smile to hear.

From the shelf, the moulds watch us, unblinking.

"Ignore them," I say, repeating, repeating. "It's just the two of us now."

Javier rubs the scowl from my forehead. Heats a spoon and melts saffron into my eyebrows. Sunshine lilts through the studio's crescent windows as he works. The deep gold of late afternoon adds fire to his story. Promises broken, omens ignored, the grief and wrath of Achilles. Every word igniting, ablaze. But when he reaches the sack of Troy, Javier pauses. Unwilling to narrate the ending, he backtracks. As always, to Helen.

Concentrating, he plunges a series of long plaits into my scalp without letting even a drop of custard ooze out. Carefully, precisely, he stretches them down my spine. I'm half-bowed under the weight of so much hair. He fusses with the braids, fusses.

"Menelaus is furious when his wife returns," he eventually says. "Can you imagine? Almost as furious as when she first left. How dare she have survived so much without him? How dare he remain such a fool in her presence."

I shrug. Javier pushes my shoulders back down, checks for wrinkles. Checks the portrait above the assembly table. Nodding, he reaches up to drape an icing chiton over my nakedness. I am taller than him by a hand, but he is clever as a monkey when it comes to climbing. Hopping from footstool to bench and back, he manoeuvres around me, the long tube of material bunched in his arms. Though the gauze is thinner than faith, the strength of his recipe keeps it together.

That, and his devilish fingers.

They dart in and out, gathering, smoothing, fluffing my garment until it blouses in wondrous folds. Pins appear, disappear. Puncturing, piercing, holding the fabric in place. Javier's lips smack as he thinks, as he tucks. He steps back to take me all in. Steps up, tugs a pleat. Steps back, cocks his head. Steps up, fidgets a cord around my waist. Steps back, smacks, annoyed. Up and back, up and back. Step-ball-change, once more from the top. Up and back in the perfectionist's dance.

At last, he is satisfied. A pendant is the final touch, a mille-feuille heart on a string of rarified gold. "You are a feast," he says, coiling the cold thing around my throat. "You are a picture." Overcome, he smacks lips and hands—and his cufflink catches on my neckline. Catches, and tears.

The robes sigh apart, exposing me from gullet to gut. Javier rushes to fix it. He flaps and gouges, making it worse. Up and back, up and back, he flaps, gouges, wrecks and ruins. Up and back, the necklace snaps. The silver bonbons he'd spent hours spiralling around my cinnamon aureoles are scraped loose. Part of my ribcage concaves. Tiny candies plink to the floor.

But there is air in my chest. There is breath. Surely, this is good?

"And he is ever at mercy of the gods," Javier mutters, smudging my marzipan to keep the custard from seeping out. "We'll have to cancel, Una.

Reschedule for another time. We can't arrive with you in this state—what will they think?"

"You underestimate—" I almost say *yourself*, but taste the error before it's spoken. A confectioner does not reach Javier's standing without resolve. Without ego. Instead, I reassure him with a familiar wink. "Tonight, I'll play the mystic. You know the routine. Smoke, mirrors, communing with spirits. It's only fitting." I look down at my Hellenistic garb. The ragged flaps of material lift easily and, thankfully, with minimal debris. I fasten them on my left shoulder, covering the worst of the mess. Leaving my heart and one flawless breast bare.

Holding his gaze, I curtsey. "A seer should only ever reveal as much as she obscures. *N'est-ce pas*?"

His laugh is a sad little bark.

"And you are a vision," he says.

I am ready to go, but Javier is nervous.

I don't tell him he's being silly. Don't remind him I've survived three vigorous outings this week, mostly intact. He doesn't need to hear it. There's no limit to his talent, no damage he can't reverse. I'm living proof, I could tell him. I'm here because of him. I'm here. But he's heard it all before.

Everything will be fine, I could say. Three faultless soirées in the space of a week. Three journeys, survived. As many trips as Helen made, or more, depending Javier's mood when telling stories. And only a few pieces lost, despite the Sadeans. Nothing important. I'm still together—*we're* still together. Everything is fine.

Even so, Javier is nervous.

"They want to see you, Una. That's all, so they say. After so long. Only to see you." He is speaking to me, but his back is turned. Facing the faded oil painting. "They've got countless portraits, cameos, ambrotypes. Countless memories. *Insufficient*, they say. *It's just not the same*." Javier snorts. "So now, finally, they want to see *you*."

Vacant glass eyes gaze down from the shelves. The moulds sneer at me. Waiting their turn.

"I'll give it my all," I say, the phrase stale on my tongue.

"Yes, of course, *ma chère*," Javier replies to the wall. "You always have."

In the mansion's grand dining hall, dinner is imminent. The sideboard is weighed down with a hoard of gold dishes. Steaming tureens, saucières, bain-maries. The room suffocates with aromas of the meal to come. Fine claret is decanted. Muscat and champagne are chilling for later. Legions of silverware are arranged in ranks beside plates. Crystal stemware gleams. Footmen stand at the ready. Carafes of ice-water dripping condensation onto their white gloves. Poised to begin service, they look out over the room. Vigilant, unblinking.

As always, Madame dominates the table's head while Monsieur commands the foot. Eight rigid people occupy the seats between. Men sporting versions of the same black-and-white suits. Women in lustreless monochrome. All posturing, variations with the same facial features. To my left, Javier folds and refolds his napkin. A cue, perhaps? I await further signals—but like the hors d'oeuvres and drinks, none are forthcoming. For all his anxiety, my confectioner has neglected to give me instructions. Am I the centrepiece this evening? Am I the dessert? Our hosts have offered no guidance. Made no requests. The moment we entered, they simply invited me to sit. To join them at table, like a guest.

They want to see you, Javier said.

They all do, don't they? They want the same Una, over and over. I am always her. Over and over.

But tonight I am also sibyl, oracle, prophetess. Tonight I am breathless from seeing so much. Seeing and being seen.

"A striking resemblance," Maman says at last.

"We had heard," says Papa, moustache bristling. "But, you understand, we needed to see for ourselves."

"Of course," replies Javier. "Of course. Remarkable, *n'est-ce pas?*"

I shiver under their scrutiny.

"How many of these—" says the youngest Demoiselle, *la sœur*, jewelled hand fluttering. Grasping for an explanation. "How long has it been—? How did you reconstruct—? I mean, look at her. Just, *look*. Please tell me this isn't her death mask…"

They look and look and look away.

"Absolutely not," whispers Javier. "Does she look dead to you?"

Of course, I repeat silently. Of course. Remarkable, *n'est-ce pas?*

I reach down. Pull my legs up one at a time. Twist until I'm perched like a swami on the mahogany chair. Mousse leaks from my hips. Cream swills in my guts. I exhale and collect my thoughts. Prepare my premonitions. Summon my ghosts.

"Shall we begin?"

One of the black-ties glares at me. "Una was much more lithe," he says. "Much more vibrant. Such an exquisite dancer, such a beautiful singer. To have wasted her life on vulgar cabaret…"

"Slinking in alleys…"

"Scuffling for coin in dank, decrepit places…"

"Cafés and *folies*." Top-hat shakes, spits. "Damp, even in summer. Small wonder the wheeze got her—"

My joints stiffen as he speaks. Vein-syrup coagulates. Grenadine clogs my nostrils. I exaggerate a cough, swallow fizz. Use spittle and phlegm to demand their attention. "Shall we begin?"

"Heartbreaking," says another. "Clearly, a wife cannot survive on sugar, liquor, and promises alone…"

"A husband should provide more—"

"*Ça suffit*," says Maman. "My daughter made her own choices. What's done is done."

"But this," says Papa, crossing himself. Expression doughy. "She has had no say in *this*."

"Open your eyes," I intone with all the gravitas of Helen on the ramparts. Fire flickers in my gaze. "Open your eyes. Una is here."

Give them what they desire, my confectioner once told me, *and the audience will never forget you.*

Cardamom flakes from my cheeks as I grin, enigmatic. Remember me? Peppermint auras smoke from my mouth, sweet and pervasive. What a show we've planned! What a performance. There will be no weeping this time. No throttling chest-rattle. No thick, unbreathable air. It won't be like before.

Remember?

I am weightless, seeing them here, being seen. I am buoyant.

A fairy-floss spirit spins out of my fingertips. She clouds up to the ceiling, floats down the walls. Shrouds the gallery of portraits hung there. "Una," I say, louder now. At my command, the spectre coalesces. Straight nose, high brows, Helen's fixed stare. She is the mould, the paintings, replicated in floating skeins of cotton candy. "Una is here."

My eyeballs roll back in their sockets. The undersides are concave. Hollow, but not void. Diamond-shaped dragées trickle out. Dry-tears. My pupils turn skullward, but I am not blind. I am Delphic. Past, present, future. All-knowing. All-seeing.

I look and look and don't look away.

Chairs screech back from the table. Heels chatter their exit, but not mouths. Mouths are black lines, firm-clenched or drooping. Mouths are hidden behind satin-gloved fingers, closed behind handkerchiefs. Mouths are quivering disgust. There will be no licks, no nibbles from these. No kisses.

Maman's handmaiden swats the apparition, clearing a path so her mistress can leave. Papa sniffs. Dabs his lowered eyes. Orders servants back to the kitchens. Follows them out. Javier sits rigid as meringue beside me. Will he add this story to his repertoire? Will he tell the next Una what he's told us already, over and over, so many times?

Give them what they desire, he said.

Spectres, spirits, sweet subtleties.

"Wait," Javier says as his in-laws retreat from the room. Indecorous penguins, making their excuses before the entrée. "Stay! You wanted to see—"

New memories to replace the old.

Pulling, pulling, the ghost unspools from my heart. She spills. She aches.

"Is this not her face?" he says, leaning close enough to kiss. "Is Una not right here? Is she not perfect?"

"This is not her face," I repeat. Wrong, try again. My thoughts are muddled, drunk on passion and time. "You wanted to see." Musk falls from my gums. *Bohèmes break brittle bones.* No, wait. Not quite. That's not alphabetical— macadamias, marshmallows, mignardises. Better. My fingers snap, one by one. *Bohèmes bones break brittle.* Sherbet foams from my mouth, grenadine from my nostrils. Custard seeps, melts my delicate robes. My hands find, flail, flounder in Javier's warm grip. Cream gluts from my sternum, splattering the Wedgwood. Shaking, my head teeters. Throbs. Tilts.

"She is not perfect," says the ghost.

Forced skyward, Helen's stony gaze comes to rest on the ceiling rose.

"This is not her face."

Will Javier tell the next Una this story?

Give them what they desire, he said.

New memories.

Remember?

My chest heaves, drowning in buttercream. The ghost breaks its tether, unmoors, dissolves. "This is not her face," she says. Not quite. The tone is off. The thick-glugging timbre. "Javier."

Try again and again.

"Una is not right here."

CAITLÍN R. KIERNAN sold her first short story in 1993, and since then her short fiction has been collected in numerous volumes, beginning with *Tales of Pain and Wonder*, and including the World Fantasy Award-winning *The Ape's Wife and Other Stories*, and most recently *The Very Best of Caitlín R. Kiernan*. Her novels include *The Red Tree* and the Bram Stoker Award-winning *The Drowning Girl: A Memoir*. She lives in Birmingham, Alabama.

Elegy for a Suicide
Caitlín R. Kiernan

This is the story of the hole in the ground.

"Our souls are damned," E said, and she folded open the pearl-handled straight razor. I know that she doesn't believe in souls, and I know, too, that she knows I know. But it's a game, a staple of this pantomime. The stainless-steel blade catches the bathroom light and flashes it back. The razor is one of the lovers she's not yet found the courage to fuck. There are a lot of those, but the razor is the most immediate, the most precious, and, I would say, the most cheated. She taunts the razor at the very precipice of orgasm. It may as well be the soft pad of her index finger pressed against my clit, the way she folds that razor open, then trails vulnerable flesh along metal, almost, *almost* slicing. Only ever *almost*. Only ever until tonight, but I'm getting ahead of myself, and I don't see how that will profit anyone. E studies every minute detail of the blade. She is intimately familiar with its history, knows it like she knows the inside of her eyelids, and I understand this familiarity is crucial to…what? This is a ritual, I suppose. Did I ever suppose that before this moment?

"W.H. Morley and Sons, Clover Brand—" and she pauses to point out to me the tiny clover stamped into the narrow *tang,* there before the deadly-sweet *shank,* sharp as her grey eyes. "—and the handle only looks like old ivory or bone."

The handle is yellowed, like a mouthful of nicotine-stained teeth.

"French Ivory celluloid," she says and shuts off the tap. The water in the tub steams in our cold bathroom. The window above her, the width of a grave, has completely fogged over. Nothing outside worth seeing anyway. "Manufactured in Austria, 1923, between the wars. There on the handle, I believe that's one of the lotus-eaters of, maybe, the Isle of Djerba or the country of the Gindanes." E adds, "A lotophage."

I know she got all that last bit off Wikipedia, because E's a lazy scholar. But, yes, there *is* the figure of a nude woman molded or carved, I don't know which, into the handle. The nude woman's arms are upraised, and above her is a single flower stained red. I don't know if it was stained red when it left the factory. Morley and Sons wherever in Austria. But now there is that splotch of red, rather like an invitation. The woman stands inside the blossom of a second flower, though it *isn't* stained red. The flowers look nothing like lotus.

She's still talking. She doesn't need an audience to listen.

She doesn't need an assembly for her oratories.

"'Why are we weigh'd upon with heaviness,

And utterly consumed with sharp distress,

While all things else have rest from weariness?'"

She holds the razor up to the light and reclines in her hot bath. I sit on the toilet seat while she recites Tennyson. I don't look at her, because then I can't pretend nothing has changed. I can't pretend that we can return to that time back to before the hole. The Hole. And I'm tired of looking at her face, and I'm sick of seeing the razor. I count the filthy, once-white hexagonal tiles of the floor.

"It'll all be a pretty story when you're done," she says, and I shake my head.

"I'm never writing this."

"Of course you will."

"You're seriously fucking deluded."

"Oh, you'll write about it. You'll never see a god again. You'll write about it."

She laughs, and I wince—no, I actually do wince—because I know she's absolutely goddamn right. However this goes, I'll write it down. I'm already composing sentences in my head, sick fuck that I am. I stare at the tiles, and I listen to her razor soliloquy, and I think back on the day it begins, a day faded down almost to twilight, the day when we found the damned thing. That's more than a month ago, far back in January. We're picking our way through the snow-scabbed, brown-weeded wastes on the western bank of the Seekonk River. Near the old railroad leading out to that towering drawbridge that's been raised since sometime in the 1970s. It's a rust cathedral, girders and bolts instead of flying buttresses, but it's still a cathedral. E's looking through the trash, because it's something she does. Me, I'm just along for the ride, freezing my ass off and wishing she'd get bored and announce that it's time to head back towards Gano Street and town.

I'm trying not to shiver. E says only pussies shiver.

We come upon a sheet of corrugated tin or aluminum, and she reaches down and pulls it back to reveal a barren patch of ground. No, not genuinely barren. Better if it *had* been truly barren. It's black, and no weeds grow there, and so at first it strikes me as barren. But, in point of fact, there's pale mold and a riot of tiny brown-capped mushrooms that have grown in the shadow E has now taken away. She leans close, asking herself aloud if maybe they're a psychedelic species, packed with psilocybin.

"Hey, you know, we could pick them, take them back to the apartment and find out," she suggests.

"Of the many ways I would rather not fucking die, poisoning myself by eating toxic mushrooms is high on the list."

E scowls. "Pussy," she says. She's tossed the sheet of tin—or aluminum— aside and is on her knees now at the very edge of that not-quite-barren patch of ground. She begins to pick one of the brown mushrooms, but then something *else* catches her eye. It catches my eye a few seconds afterwards. She's almost always the first to notice anything even just the slightest bit out of place. And this is out of place.

In the tub, E's moved on to James Joyce, episode five of *Ulysses*.

"It's really goddamn tiresome," I say so quietly I'm hardly even whispering. I'm only breathing out syllables. "Do it, or don't fucking do it, but it's really goddamn tiresome the way you go on and on and on."

"You want me to do it," she says.

"I want you to shut the fuck up, that's what I want. I want you to get out of that tub and dry off and throw the razor in the trash and let's never talk about it ever again."

"You don't want much, do you?" she asks. "Think it's going to go away?" she asks and raises her left arm so I have to see what's happening to her. So I have to gaze directly at the corruption eating at her.

Below the sheet of corrugated metal, there in the mold and mushrooms, there is a hole. It can't be more than four inches across. I can't recall how to calculate diameter, but the hole can't be more than five inches across, so it certainly isn't a very big hole. And while it *is* a hole in the ground, it isn't a *dirt* hole. The edges are pink and puckered and fleshy, and its rim puts me more in mind of an enormous asshole than anything else. A sickly shade of pink, like a burn scar, like proud flesh with blue-white veins, and it looks wet and sticky and warm.

Gotta be another sort of fungus, I think. What else would I think?

I tug at the back of her hoodie, like that was going to do any good.

"What the hell…?" she begins and trails off.

I go back to counting the hexagons. "There are these places called hospitals," I say. I say again.

"You seriously think this is anything—"

"I seriously fucking think we don't know whether they could help or not," I say, interrupting her, and she laughs and splashes.

"An apocalypse of the flesh," E smiles. I do not have to look at her face, and the corruption that has also taken hold there, to know that she's smiling. "Do you know the original meaning of *apocalypse*? Not a catastrophe. Not the end of the world. It means revelation, a vision, a sudden insight."

She goes back to describing the razor.

"I have to die to finish it," E tells me. Again.

"I'm calling an ambulance."

"No you're not," she says. She's right.

There in the weedy patch on the bank of the Seekonk, E whispers, her voice filled all at once with awe and curiosity. With, I suppose, apocalypse. She whispers, "Oh my god, what *is* that?"

"One of the nastiest things I have ever seen," I answer, even if I am well aware the question was rhetorical. She doesn't want to know. E never wants to know, because knowing would serve no end but erasing a mystery.

She scoots closer to the hole, smushing mushrooms beneath the knees of her jeans, scraping up the scum of mold with denim.

"Seriously. It's disgusting. Just leave it the fuck alone."

But I'm too late, and she's already touched the outermost edge of the hole, and it quivers like Jell-O. No, I'm not too late, she wouldn't have listened, anyway. Where E touched the hole, a dime-sized crimson blister has formed.

"Jesus," I hiss. "Please. You don't have any idea what that shit is."

"Exactly," E replies, and she almost sounds sensible. "It's warm," she says, so I was right about that. Then she lays her left hand down flat against the pink whatever it is. "It's warm…and it's sort of pulsing. Or throbbing."

For a moment I honestly believe I'm going to vomit.

The mirror on the medicine cabinet door has also steamed over. I wish my eyes could do the same. The pills are in there, the ones she's been taking for the pain, eating them for a week now. Eating them like candy. I have asked her how much it hurts. I only have to see her arm, that patch on her right cheek, and the inside of her thighs to know it must fucking hurt like fucking hell.

She's talking about the razor again.

"They didn't have the nerve, either," says E. "They must have done this, pretty much the same thing as this, trying and unable to make it stop."

"You don't know that."

"I might. The voices are getting louder, and they have an awful lot to say."

"Then stop listening."

"When a god talks, you don't stop listening."

When a god talks. I'm not about to have that argument again. It's not that I lose. You can't lose an argument with a brick wall.

"It's got plans, right? Maybe I'm holding this razor, and maybe I even want to use it. I think that person before me definitely also kept trying, but it has plans."

E put her arm into that hole, and she pulled out the straight razor.

"Zombie ants," I say to her. "I told you about the zombie ants. Maybe they think a god's talking to them, too."

"Fucking ants don't think shit."

Zombie ants.

Ophiocordyceps unilateralis, a fungus that grows in tropical jungles all around the world. Its spores get into an ant, and somehow they force—rewire its fucking tiny ant brain—to clamp down on a leaf, into the a particular vein at a very specific height off the ground. And the zombie ant just hangs there, and the fungus kills it, changes its exoskeleton, until fruiting bodies have filled up its head. The dead ant's head bursts, spreading more spores, infecting more ants, making more zombies.

"Gods don't talk to bugs."

"You think you're anything *more* than a bug to this thing?"

E slides down until only her face is left above the steaming water. A new crimson blister appears below her right eye. I begin to say something that isn't an argument, as if I haven't already tried that, as well. *I love you, and I'm watching while some kind of parasite, some kind of cancer, is eating you alive, and you won't let me help you.*

Why haven't I called an ambulance? Good damn question, right? Is the god from that hole muttering in my ears, too?

I count tiles and listen to the faucet dripping.

She's started in all over again about the razor being like a lotus flower. You eat the flower, and then there's peace. You draw the blade down your forearms and across your wrists, or you cut to the chase and open up your throat, and there's no more pain. Only, of course, that's not what her new god wants. Suicide would interrupt the cycle.

E reaches down into that hole, which is a lot deeper than I would have thought. She reaches in, and something changes about her expression. Just as though somebody flips a switch. But I can't *describe* the change. I've tried. Fuck all knows I've tried. Her face changes, her expression, and, a few seconds later, when she withdraws her hand she's holding the antique Austrian razor. She raises it, opens it, and the blade glints faintly in the last of the daylight. Her arm glistens, wet with whatever that stuff the red blister's secreting.

"Oh my god, it's beautiful," E says. "Who the hell would have just left something this cool lying in a hole?"

I'm supposing that god wasn't talking to her yet.

"You're *not* going to keep that."

"Shit yeah, I am."

E stands before the tall mirror in our bedroom, nude as she is in the bath. Her back is to me, and yet I can watch her eyes. Even scarred, she is as beautiful now as she has ever been. I see her, front and back. I see her, shattered and whole. She says a god is whispering in her ear, but I'm watching Hell devour her. She has become a tiny boat on a vast sea of paradoxes, and I can only watch. Standing here before the tall mirror, she smiles and plays with her left nipple. I don't think I've ever seen such joy in her eyes, such complete delight. The razor is lying nearby, atop the chest of drawers

"Fuck me," she says, but I don't want to. I can hardly stand the thought of touching her, because if I touch her then I'm also touching it.

"Remember that night out on the Cape?" I ask, changing the subject. "The night we watched the Perseids from Newcomb Hollow Beach?"

My iPhone buzzes and I answer it. It's work, wanting to know why I'm late again.

"Star fall, phone call," E smiles at me from the mirror.

Is this all a game to her? Do the zombie ants think that they're playing some sort of game? E says that bugs don't think.

"Tomorrow," I promise the voice at the other end of the line, even though I know the promise is a lie. "I'll be in tomorrow. I'm sure I'll feel much better by then."

A week ago I'd have been terrified of losing my job; now it's something that seems to exist in a time and a place I'll never get back to, not ever again.

If I was *ever* there.

"We should go back there," E says, masturbating for her reflection. "Next July, we should go back there and watch the sky again." The tone of her voice hasn't changed. She doesn't sound like someone masturbating, and I wonder if she knows she's doing it. Maybe this is another compulsive act, like all the baths. Something she's only dimly conscious she's doing, but that the god in her head needs to complete the cycle. I can't turn away. It doesn't matter what she's becoming, what's becoming of her, she's still beautiful, and I still adore the sight of her.

"Yes," I tell her. "We'll go back there."

Her hand stops moving, and she frowns—but only very, very slightly. If I hadn't spent the last two years with her, I might not know she was frowning.

"I don't want to leave," she says, and I say I don't want her to leave, either.

"Maybe," she says, "if I used the razor—"

"You'd be leaving, either way," I reply. "It's only two different doors." And that's assuming that the shit from the hole wouldn't be just as happy with her corpse as with a living host. That's assuming a goddamn lot.

"I can't remember why I did it. Isn't that odd?"

A drop of pinkish slime drips from between her legs and spatters the floorboards between her bare feet. I want to burn the building down.

"All I remember is that it seemed very urgent. Like, all my life had been such a waste right up until then, but if I just reached inside that hole everything would have meaning, finally, forever and forever."

"But you don't feel that way anymore?"

She never answers the question. Her smile comes back, and she turns her back to the mirror. "Fuck me," she says. And that's what I do. Doesn't matter how much the corruption that has taken root on her—*in* her—body disgusts me. I make love to her, knowing that I am also making love to it. I more than half expect, in the moment that we both come, only seconds apart (which never happens), that I'll hear the god inside her skull, too.

She lies beside me on sheets that needed to be washed a month or so ago, and she stares up at the ceiling. Her eyes look glassy. I notice that it's spread to her throat, and I can't remember if it had before we had sex. It's moving fast now. It's impatient to be born, and maybe that orgasm was the last bit of adrenaline it needs to bite down hard on that leaf and hold on. I talk to her, but she doesn't talk back. She only nods a few times, shakes her head once or twice. I ask if it hurts, and she doesn't nod or shake her head, but I go to the bathroom and get the pills from the medicine cabinet. I bring her the pills and a glass of water, and E takes three of them, then lies down again.

"Do you want the razor?" I ask, and E shakes her head. But I go to the chest of drawers and get it for her anyway. I put it in her hands, which are as limp as a ragdoll. Then I get dressed and go out, telling myself there a few things that we urgently need from the market, and that she'll only take a nap while I'm gone.

I can be awfully good at lying to myself.

"I won't be gone long. Get some rest. I'll fix dinner when I get back."

E nods and smiles sleepily.

In the weeds near the Seekonk River, she's already started scratching at the back of the hand she put into the hole. I want to go back and cover up that hole. *We should have,* I think. *We should have left it exactly the way that we fucking found it.*

I'm gone longer than I meant to be, because I run into a friend, and you'd never know from our conversation that this day was any different from any other. It's dark by the time I get back to our street, and it's begun snowing. Fat flakes drifting down to earth like falling stars, like spores, like gods tumbling from imagined heavens. By morning, there will be almost a foot blanketing Providence.

I knew perfectly well that E would be gone, but it still takes me by surprise.

Somewhere soon there will be another hole in the ground.

At least she left the razor lying on the bed, and I sit holding it for a long, long time, staring at that yellowed French Ivory celluloid handle, wishing that the flowers truly were lotuses.

GEMMA FILES was born in England and raised in Toronto, Canada, and has been a journalist, teacher, film critic and an award-winning horror author for almost thirty years. She has published four novels, a story-cycle, three collections of short fiction, and three collections of speculative poetry; her most recent novel, *Experimental Film*, won both the 2015 Shirley Jackson Award for Best Novel and the 2016 Sunburst Award for Best Novel (Adult Category). She is currently working on her next book.

Skin City
Gemma Files

THE STREETLAMP'S GLARE leaks in over her apartment's windowsill, unchecked by blinds, to touch what little furniture remains with a bleak light. Before her, a table—actually, three upturned boxes topped with a plank stolen from the construction site just north of the railway tracks. On the table, a tape recorder. Next to it, an empty cassette case.

Her suit waits, thrown over the end of the bed, for her to make up her mind.

Adage Beck swallows. The bright eye of her cigarette blinks, as ash dots the rug beneath her feet.

Useless even to try and tell you what she looks like. She's naked now, though not as we know the term—naked and red and wet. And it's so comfortable, to be hidden away here in the dark, she almost wishes her cigarette would last forever.

But that's impossible.

Soon the clock will strike, and she'll get up. She'll dress herself, as carefully as she can. And then, when she's presentable, she'll go out. To meet somebody.

Anybody.

Adage takes one last drag. She drops the butt on the rug and lets it lie, smouldering.

She leans forward into the dark, feeling for the "record" button.

A month later. Mike Grell sits by the window nearest the front door, looking out. In one hand he holds a postcard, in the other his Walkman. Outside the bus, Chinatown blurs by, trailing pennants of red lacquer and neon.

The postcard is custom-made. One side's a holiday snapshot: thirteen-year-old Adage tilts her head back, laughing, as the sun bleaches away her face. Mike touches his wallet, where the original lies folded between bank card and expired driver's license.

The other side is a scribble. Deciphered, it reads: *It's happening again. In Toronto. At the Meat Market, there's a girl named Sherri. Ask her where I am. Find me. Please. Adage.*

Below that:

P.S.: If you got the tape, listen to it.

Ahead, a couple with matching Mohawks argues with the cab driver over what currently constitutes exact change. An elderly woman squeezes past, cradling an overweight pug on one hip and a bag of groceries on the other. Somebody drops a dime. Dust motes tremble, caught in mid-flight, as the doors slam shut.

Mike sighs.

He flips the cassette case open and lets the tape fall into place.

A low hiss.

"Testing, one, two, three. Testing. Hello?"

Click.

Rewind, and press play.

"Testing, one, two—"

Click.

Softly: "All right, then."

"July twenty-third, nineteen-ninety. About…quarter to twelve."

Silence. In the background, a distant sitcom's laugh track seeps up through the floor of Adage's apartment like a forming blister.

"Okay," she says, at last. "I'm gonna tell you a story.

"It's a red one, through and through. The words I'll use are stained so deep nothing could wash them clean. They reek and shine. Red the same way the moon would be red tonight, if you could see it. Red the same way the river is red. A red moon, a red rising tide, a red river breaking its banks, and a deep red tale somebody beside me has to hear before the world ends or I do, whichever comes first. And Larry's dead, so it might as well be you.

"Here's how it goes."

Mike hops the curb and stumbles, nearly sprawling waist deep in a puddle. He scans for the Meat Market sign—a steak on a phallic neon stick—as his mind races backwards.

Larry.

Last name—Gurley? Garvey? A skinny kid, bigger even than Adage, who'd spurted to full height that year, the way girls tend to. They spent their summers at the cottage—Mike with his parents, Adage her grandparents—and played in the woods, down by the lake. Always together, but always alone. And not minding, right up until Larry's Winnebago pulled into the vacant lot across the road.

Mike shuts his eyes. Beneath his coat, against his side, he feels the cold iron weight of his father's gun.

"Late July, nineteen eighty. You, and me, and Larry. Out in your Dad's truck, in the woods, before it got light. You wanted to go spot birds, and I wanted to go home. But Larry said no, let's do something different. And he took out the cards. So okay, you said, you want to play gin rummy? And Larry laughed. It's not like that, he said. Now draw.

"So we all took one card.

"And then Larry made us stop the truck, right near the shore. Just before the sun comes up, when all the stars are dead. And the lake was still.

"Now look at your card, Larry said, and I looked down. And my card was just a picture of four sticks, lashed together and hung with some kind of fur, standing in front of a river. Like a door. And underneath it was written the word: *Skin*."

Inside the Meat Market, girls jiggle and sway like parade balloons—white, swollen, shiny as plastic wrap. Strobe lights pulse. Squinting, Mike spots the bartender: a tall skinhead, deep in conversation with an even taller transvestite wearing a lime-green minidress. Next stool over, a yuppie with his shirt open to his waist howls with laughter. Up and down the bar, tattoos bloom, bright as mold.

Mike elbows his way in. "'Scuse me—"

Bottles click together. No reply.

"I said, *'scuse* me?"

The bartender turns, slipping his customary scowl back into place. "Can I help you, buddy?"

Oh, Christ.

"Well, yes," Mike replies brightly. "Actually, you can. I'm looking for a girl—"

Deadpan: "What a shock."

"—named Sherri."

No immediate reaction. The light turns orange. Cheers greet the next number.

"Sherri?" Mike repeats.

The transvestite blows a smoke ring. The bartender jerks his scalp toward the front.

"Back there," he tells him. "In the pink."

Mike turns. One door's propped open, spilling noise. Beyond, shadows move and posture. A faint gleam of rose-colored plastic shimmers, becomes an arm clutching a battered leather bag whose long white fringes seem chewed. Now a profile, once pretty, but equally worn. Between them, couples thrash.

"Thanks," Mike says, pushing off.

"There's nothing on my card, you said. And Larry smiled, like he expected it or something. Nothing on mine either, he said. Then he looked at me.

"Later, you told me Larry said I should stare at the card and try to make the door open. To *want* it to. So I did … think I must have, anyhow. And then you started feeling like there was somebody watching us. Let's go, you said. But Larry, he just said no, wait, something's gonna happen. Like he already knew it would.

"And when he said that, I started to make this noise, deep in my throat.

"So then you got mad, and you said you were going to start the truck, and Larry could go to hell if he wanted but we were going back. But as you reached past me, I grabbed your arm. Hard. And you said it was like my nails were longer or something, because I was hurting you. So you said hey, Adage, let go, hey, what's wrong with you? And then I looked up, I grinned. And you screamed.

"You told me my mouth was full of blood."

"Sherri?"

The girl—fifteen? Thirty?—jumps up, catching Mike's sleeve with her cigarette. A tiny circle of pain stamps itself inside his wrist; she draws back, grimacing. Blurts out: "Oh, man…man, I'm sorry. I—you okay?"

"Fine," he lies, while she beats ineffectually at the damage, making it worse. Adding, through gritted teeth: "Please. No problem."

A shrug. "If you say so." Sherri drops the cigarette, face falling into what seem like far more familiar lines. "Looking for *me,* huh?" she says, turning it on, dim and flickering though "it" might be. "What for?"

Instinctively Mike reaches inside his coat—whether for his gun or his wallet, he couldn't say. "I—I'm a friend of a friend."

Sherri smirks. "Got a lot of friends, baby. Refresh my memory."

Mike swallows, hard; something seems to be caught in his throat, suddenly. It knocks against his tongue when he tries to speak, deforming the words. "A—dagebeck," he manages, at last.

"Come again?"

Much slower, this time: "Adage. Beck."

Sherri recoils, slipping on some stray garbage. When he tries to help her, she avoids his touch. "Get off me," she snarls.

"You knew her, right?"

"Damn straight I *knew* her. That chick was stone crazy. Nuts. And you're her friend?"

"Look, it's important. You know where she is?"

Sherri wrenches away, flattening herself against the inside of the door.

"One time," she says, suddenly clear and calm. "Only one time, and then I don't ever wanna see your face again. Me and Susan, we had a room down in Chinatown. And one night she brings back another chick she found on the street. Your *friend.*"

Adage, Mike breathes.

"So we're doing pretty well here, right? Except our johns start disappearing. And they turn up dead, all over the Strip. It's in the papers. Cops're finding them in pieces. And none of them got any skin, right? Like somebody tore it off."

And—here Mike sees a flash of early morning. 1980, peering through the windshield of his Dad's truck at something. Something small, and nude, and black with flies. Something without a face. As the smell rises and settles, rises and settles, like a tide.

Back to the bar, then. To Sherri, mid-story. Who hasn't even noticed where he went.

"So I start noticing stuff, after that. Like how she smells weird, your friend, like meat that's gone off. And she sleeps all day, and she's always wearing the same clothes. Whatever. And then Susan's gone, and they find another body, out back of Ryerson. And that night I come home early, and your girlfriend's standing there…"

Sherri stops, chokes. *I don't want to hear this,* Mike thinks. *I really don't.*

"She was wearing Susan's—Susan's—"

A nearby streetlamp goes out.

"Sherri?"

Sherri looks up, mascara dripping. "I'm going now," she tells him, and does.

"I was three months in the hospital, but I don't remember any of it. Just a long, red blank, and—the silence. When I resurfaced, they told me Larry was dead. They said it was suicide.

"…likely.

"So I got better, and my parents moved us moved away. You wrote for awhile, and I appreciated it. Then, eventually, you stopped. I wasn't too surprised.

"I went to Toronto, to school, and I was fine for a long, long time. I lived in the waking world, and brushed my teeth twice a day. I thought bright little thoughts which flashed once and were gone, just like everybody else. I did my work. I even had friends. Years slipped by. Until—it happened.

"Again."

Across the street from the Meat Market, Adage leans against a lamp-post, waiting for her evening's prey to reveal itself. It's finally stopped raining. The gutters overflow with light.

At 12:22, a girl in a tight pink plastic slicker finally breaks rank—struggling, briefly, with some unseen partner—and jumps the last two steps, falling into her customary strut as she clicks away.

Sherri, Adage thinks with a little stab. She didn't expect it to be her tonight. Other—worthier—candidates still linger outside the Market's doors: that older woman, whose smile seems penciled on over a lipless slash of a mouth; the boy in the leather jacket, whose ears are fringed with tiny silver rings. The girl with a freshly bloodied nose, whose pendant proclaims her to be a HOT CHICK. *But take what you can get, babe,* she thinks, *and count yourself lucky.*

Adage lets Sherri's footsteps die away before rising to follow.

The moon sees her coming, and narrows, appraisingly.

"Graduation night, I let a boy I barely knew drive me up the hill to that spot we'd all heard so much about. And we sat there, side by side in the car, staring at the city below. He shuffled his feet, and coughed, and finally he put his arms around me. And there in the dark, between the bars of a Depeche Mode song, I felt something change. A key in a lock, turning. A red river rising, a hot red tide finally coming in, high enough to drown us both.

"And when he turned to kiss me, he sniffed the air, and gagged.

"And I just smiled."

Then, in a whisper: "And it was so *sweet,* Mike. Like sex, only so much better. Like Larry must have been.

"And I remember it all."

Pushing her way past the Totally Concerned With Sex Shop, Sherri hangs a right in front of Girls! Live! Girls! Nude!, and disappears. Her scent remains, though, fading fast. Adage swallows, tasting dust.

It'll be over soon enough, she thinks. Walking even faster.

Mike rounds the corner and sees her, up ahead: a slight woman in a long, cloth coat, fashionably cut, with a toque pulled down over her ears. Shabby. Anonymous. Totally unseasonal.

Adage?

She pauses at the crosswalk. Her face is very pale against the dark. White and flat, and oddly limp. Motionless, except for a pair of searching eyes. As she bends to press the signal change button, a lock of hair spills from her hat—

Ad—

Blonde.

Mike feels his heart deflate.

You stupid sucker, he thinks. *She's dead in a ditch somewhere. You blew your education money to get here, and she's dead. Probably died while you were still on the bus.*

The woman reaches up to scratch behind her ear. Maybe to tuck back the lock…

(Stupid, stupid, stupid.)

But instead, instead, she…digs her nails into the side of her neck, and rips. The skin flaps slightly as she shifts weight; the freed lock blows across it and sticks, blonde turning red.

Oh, God.

Delicately, with one too-long nail, Adage reaches further in, to scratch the raw flesh underneath.

The signal changes. Adage spots Sherri on the opposite side—twenty feet ahead and gaining speed. Behind her, a movement; Adage pays no attention, instincts well and truly kicked in. Nothing could deflect her now, short of a bullet. Sherri pauses mid-step, however, nose wrinkling.

The wind has changed.

And the reek of her boils up from Adage like a miasma, so bad even *she* can smell it—an invisible glove of uncured hide, reaching in every direction at once. Prodded by the stench, Sherri turns, just in time to meet Adage's eyes. Her true eyes, staring through the slightly ripped lid-holes of her false face—old now, almost done with. Yet still recognizable.

"Uh," Sherri says. Then asks, timidly: "...Susan?"

Hardly.

And Mike freezes, as Sherri starts to run.

"So why am I telling you all this?"

"Larry was dumb. He wanted power, but he was too lazy to take his own risks. So he tricked me into opening the door, because he thought he could control me, afterward. When what was always inside me finally came ripping up to meet the waking world, all raw and naked and hungry. And...

"...he was wrong, obviously. So wrong, it's kind of funny.

"I live my life the way I was meant to, now. I get up, and I get dressed, and I go out and meet someone new. And then we dance. And then I take what's left of them home and sew it back together, and the whole thing starts over again.

"Winter's better. They can't smell you coming, at least not as well. But summer's okay too, because by the time the cops find them there's very little to even identify, and I'm gone long before they can. I keep my nose clean. I don't get caught.

"I'm lonely, though, and I don't know how long I want to go on like this. But I don't know how to stop, either. Or even if I can. So—

"—find me, Mike.

"And do whatever suits you, when you do."

The parking lot, behind King Fook's. *This is it,* Adage thinks, through her haze. *At last.*

She takes a last step, mainly for effect. Sherri moans, runs straight into the back gate, scrabbles at it for a moment, then bounces back. It holds, locked tight for the night. "God!" she screams.

Adage pauses to remove her coat, which is far, far too expensive to dry clean.

Sherri falls to her knees, sobbing, as much with anger as with fear. And Adage…

…starts to shake.

Sherri looks up, her cupped hands full of snot.

Adage throws her head back. The naked moon, visible at last, ripples in time to her shivering. A red joy cracks her ribs. And Sherri just watches as Adage rears up, full size, the corners of her mouth breaking open. Rips inch towards either ear until, impatient, she thrusts her hands inside, and pulls.

"Adage!"

To her right. From the elevators. Sherri stumbles vertical, using the fence for support. Adage turns, drooling blood. Thinking, in surprise: *Mike?*

(He came.)

The fence's lock explodes.

Sherri shrieks, realizing the possibility of escape; Adage matches her, high and harsh, like a carrion bird sighting a hearse. She lunges.

"Adage—*no!*"

As she turns again, Sherri slips under her arms, disappearing around the corner. Mike and Adage are left, face to face, with only a gun and ten feet left between them. Hesitant, he repeats the name, suddenly less sure.

"…Adage?"

Slouched like a praying mantis, the thing wearing Susan's skin gives a too-dry laugh, coughs a fine pink spray. "See—for—your—self," she says, wetly… indistinctly…as she steps into the light.

Mike's hand—wavers.

Partially stripped, her bloodied skull nods moronically, face a crossfire of nerves. Her nose hangs flat, the torn half-mouth slack. She jerks her head aside and both wounds flap open at once, revealing the craters at their roots. A lipless grin chatters from chin to ear. The nude moon of her left eye bulges and slits, blankly, as its lid smears itself shut.

"I—guess—this—means—you—heard—the—tape."

Mike gulps.

Adage seems to smile. Then the change grips her again. Mike staggers back, gun at knee-level, as blood sprays again, fiercer now: bright red, a slaughter-house sneeze. Adage's borrowed skin snaps at its seams, rucking up like a pair of old tights. She peels herself free. Beneath, the bulge of raw, red flesh; muscles and mucous, thrust center-stage, spurt and writhe and glisten. Gristle follows, flashing taunting little hints of bone; a spine peeps out, vertebrae cracking like a whip as she moves closer. Hands rise, busy with tendons, their nails still growing—slick, and pale, and sharp.

"Oh, Adage," Mike whispers.

An amused croon: "*Miiiike*. What's the matter, baby?"

Almost near enough to touch, now. As she *so clearly* wants to.

"You're like this too, underneath," she says. "Know that? You *all* are."

Half-blind with tears, Mike brings the gun up. "Stay away, Adage."

"Oh, but I can't. Don't you see I'm naked?"

Her hand, reaching. Claws ruffle his hair.

"Adage, *please*."

"You who have so much," says Adage Beck, no longer even faintly human. "Old pal, old buddy, old friend of mine. You who have *so* much, I pray…be lenient, be nice. Be generous enough to lend just me a yard or two of hide, to clothe my awful shame."

And Mike—fires.

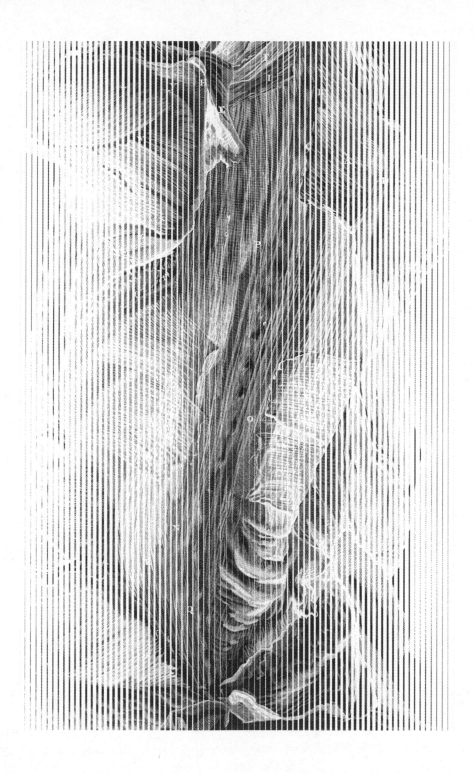

BRIAN EVENSON is the author of a dozen works of fiction, most recently the collection *Song for the Unraveling of the World*, a finalist for the *Los Angeles Times's* Ray Bradbury Prize. Other recent books include the collection *A Collapse of Horses* and the novella *The Warren*, which was a finalist for the Shirley Jackson Award. His novel *Last Days* won the 2010 ALA-RUSA Award for Best Horror Novel. His novel *The Open Curtain* was a finalist for an Edgar Award and an International Horror Guild Award. Other books include *The Wavering Knife* (which won the IHG Award for best story collection) and *Altmann's Tongue*. He is the recipient of three O. Henry Prizes, an NEA fellowship, and a Guggenheim Fellowship. He lives in Los Angeles and teaches in the Critical Studies Program at CalArts.

A True Friend
Brian Evenson

THERE ARE TIMES when it hurts to be alive. Times when the only person who could possibly see how much it hurts lies so far away from the skin into which you are sunken so deeply that they cannot see what you are feeling or that you are even feeling at all. A real friend, a true friend, would not be behind the camera adjusting the shot, making sure everything was in perfect focus, a perfect focus that nonetheless fails to reveal the enormity of your pain. No, a true friend would bring himself very close, would press his ear to your throat and listen carefully, attentively, until he began, finally, impossibly, to hear your voice.

Help, this ear would finally hear you say, *Help, help*. It would not matter to a friend, a true friend, that nothing comes out of your mouth: he would hear the words anyway, would hear how they lodge in your throat, the vibrations buzzing there.

A true friend would not affix a clamp to the back of your head, making it even harder for you to turn and move. A true friend would not direct the glassy eye of the camera so that the light bounced off the lens and into your unblinking eyes. A true friend would, from time to time, moisten your eyes with a little water so that they might continue to work as eyes do, so they would not, as your eyes most assuredly have begun to do, begin to fail.

Above all, a true friend would realize that, despite all appearances, you are not dead.

Paralyzed, can't move, you try to say. *Help, help*, you say, but nothing comes out. Perhaps even if someone, a true friend, say, *were* to press their ear to your throat and hold their breath and listen, really listen, they would hear nothing. Even then, they would not realize you are still alive, that, motionless, you are nonetheless screaming inside.

At least this is what I am counting on. It is right for me, your brother, to preserve this moment, to commission this last remembrance of you before you are buried. It is expected of me, even if my true reasons for having it done are very much my own. Only you and I know you are still alive, and in the end only your mute suffering will be preserved in the photograph, not my pleasure.

I stand discretely to one side, pretending to grieve, relishing the photographer's failure to realize you are still alive, watching the camera's merciless eye record only what is visible on the surface. This will take only a few minutes: the photograph will be completed well before you begin to stir, well before the tincture administered to you wears off. Soon, I will unscrew the clamp from the back of your head and with the help of the photographer carry you back to my wagon and drive you home. Along the way I will rein up and clamber into the back of the wagon beside you, will press my ear to your throat and imagine you screaming inside, and then I will administer a further dose. By nightfall, brother, you will be nailed in your coffin and interred behind your house, and all that you have will belong to me.

But for now the photographer works with care to try to make you appear alive, not realizing that all along you *are* alive. *Help*, you are screaming, *help, can't*, while in my head I am preserving this image, of you helpless and ignored, while I, your brother, but not your friend, watch.

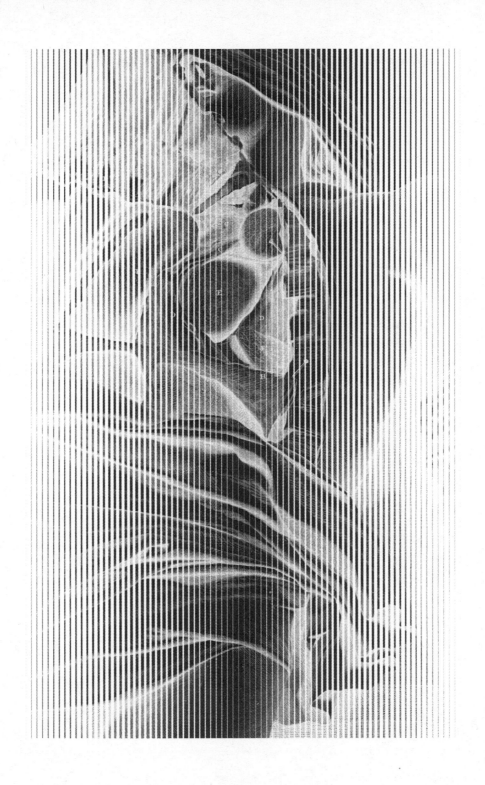

TOM JOHNSTONE's fiction has appeared in various anthologies and magazines, including the *Ninth, Tenth* and *Eleventh Black Books of Horror, Brighton— The Graphic Novel, Wicked Women,* and *Strange Tales V, Supernatural Tales,* and *Shroud Magazine*. In addition he co-edited the British Fantasy Award-nominated austerity-themed anthology *Horror Uncut: Tales of Social Insecurity and Economic Unease* with the late Joel Lane. He lives with his partner and two children in Brighton, where he works as a gardener for the local authority. Find out more about Johnstone's fiction at: WWW.TOMJOHNSTONE.WORDPRESS.COM.

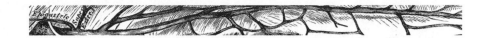

What I Found in the Shed
Tom Johnstone

THAT AUTUMN BROUGHT spider webs that stuck to your face whenever you went outside. One warm Sunday, I was rooting around in the shed at the bottom of the garden. It was full of junk left by the previous tenants: two rusting lawn mowers and a fridge partly wrapped in a black bin bag, as if someone had half-heartedly tried to bag it to put out with the rubbish.

And there was the machine I found under a ragged, blue tarpaulin.

Dad said it must be some sort of printer, but it looked too old somehow. There didn't seem to be a way to plug it into anything. There was a handle shrouded in cobwebs. Unlike the other things in there, it wasn't all brown with rust. It was a sort of mottled grey, speckled with yellow and green flecks, like that stuff you see on old grave stones.

"Is that lichen, Dad?" I asked, trying to impress.

"Lichen, David," he corrected me. I'd said 'lit-chen'. He pronounced it 'lie-ken'.

"What does it say on it?"

"Let's see, shall we?"

He brushed the cobwebs away from the letters carved into the stony surface, scattering spiders and their spongy egg sacs all over the rotten floor of the shed.

"The Quickener," he read. "Quickener," he said again. "Quickens what?"

Above the thing's slit mouth were smaller letters. His finger traced them. Dad's pointing finger was long and sharp, but now it looked blurred by the bits of web sticking to it.

"Feed image in here," he read slowly. "Then wait."

"Look, Dad—those other carvings. What d'you think they mean?"

He frowned then, and said: "I've no idea, David."

"Have you seen it before, Dad?"

"No. Never seen it." His voice was curt.

He stared at the symbols for a bit longer, then said:

"Time for a tea break, I think, mate. All this dust is making me feel rather thirsty."

The chumminess act usually meant there was something he didn't want to talk about.

Over the tea and biscuits, I asked him: "D'you think Mum would like to see it—the Quickener?"

He paused in the act of dunking his digestive.

"No, mate."

"Will she ever come out of her room?"

He put the half soggy biscuit down.

"People respond to grief in different ways, Son. Personally, I prefer to keep busy. Mum's not like that."

"Is that why I'm not allowed in there to see her.?"

He just nodded, then got on with whatever he did to keep himself busy.

I preferred to keep busy too.

So the following afternoon I sneaked into the shed after school with a photo of Emily, taken a month before she died. Dad was still at work. Mum was still in bed. I knew what to do. The Quickener told me. Carefully I fed the picture of my baby sister into the machine's mouth, and waited. The mouth looked dark and wet as it sucked the paper in.

Nothing happened.

Eventually I got cold, hungry, tired of sitting in the damp, dusty shed, and went back inside.

I forgot about it until I awoke to the sound of crying.

Sometimes I thought I heard crying like this from Mum's room, but the sounds were usually faint enough for me to convince myself I was imagining it.

Not this.

It was drifting into my bedroom through the open window, which looked out onto the garden. The warm, still, Indian summer weather had broken that evening, and the wind was bringing in the sound in waves, along with squally flurries of rain that pattered on the panes. It could have been a fox, I suppose. It had that strange, half-human, keening quality. But I knew it was a baby. I knew it was Emily. I peered out through the curtain, and saw the flickering, white line of torchlight in the thin slit left by the shed door in the darkness.

I noticed that Dad's boots were not in their usual spot by the back door. I put my own boots on, and walked slowly out across the darkened garden towards the shed. The noise of crying was a rope guiding me through the wet, howling blackness. It was just the way Emily had screamed, in the days and nights before they took her tiny corpse away. I wondered if Mum was awake and listening to the noise.

"David," he said, when I finally opened the ramshackle, wooden door, his voice hoarse.

But all I could see was Emily, or something that looked just like her, cradled in his arm. By now the screams had reached a fever pitch, enough to wake the dead: it seemed as if the shed's flimsy panels were shaking with them.

And yet there was something not quite right about her, and it wasn't just that her face was red and blotchy from crying. My father could see the confusion and unease in my face. He rocked the baby until it was quiet, then then explained:

"It's not Emily." He paused, sighed. "It's a copy, mate. I might as well tell you now... I tried making a few myself, just after she died. This machine's some sort of weird 3D printer, but it can print things that are alive from 2D images. Or things that *were* alive..."

He must have done the same as I did, then covered the machine up again under the ragged, blue tarpaulin, left it to the spiders' webs, pretended not to know what it was when I found it, said he'd never seen it before.

"I'm sorry," he added. "I should have told you the truth from the start."

He'd lied to me. I'd suspected it from the way he'd been acting when we'd discovered it, but I still remember the empty feeling of disappointment in the pit of my stomach now this was confirmed. It was one thing avoiding certain subjects, leaving certain things unsaid, but this level of deception from him was a new one on me.

"I knew what you'd been up to," he continued, "when I saw the photo was missing."

He pulled the soggy photo from the machine's maw, wiping sticky fluids off it from it with the back of his coat sleeve.

Even now, I still wonder if he meant me to find it.

"Still," he continued, picking up the baby, "you've done a better job than I did. You've obviously got a way with this machine, mate. This is the best one yet. Mum might not even notice the difference."

He was rocking the baby, calming her, shushing her cries. Basking in the rare glow of his approval, my disappointment temporarily forgotten, I asked:

"What do you mean, Dad?"

"Let's take 'Emily' to see Mum, and I'll show you."

I beamed at him. I could tell I'd passed some sort of test, by operating the printer or 'Quickener' or whatever it was, or perhaps by hiding my upset at his dishonesty.

"You mean I can go inside Mum's room now?"

"I think you're old enough now, Son. Here, you hold her."

The baby's alien, black eyes gazed up at me, just like in the photograph.

I was nervous as he led me up the stairs to the door that had been closed to me for a year. What did he mean 'old enough'? The wind was making Mum's bedroom door rattle in the frame now, and it might have been its moaning that I could hear from behind it.

I don't know what I expected to see. But I hadn't expected to see *one* cot, let alone three.

"Hello, David," said Mum, holding something I at first took for an oddly-shaped hot water bottle tucked under her coverlet.

She looked so much older than I remembered. But then I hadn't seen her for a year.

"David's brought someone to see you, Mary. We might be needing another cot."

Only two out of the three cots were occupied, and only one of the creatures inside could be making the mewling I could no longer pretend was the wind or my imagination. The face that had a mouth was kind of lop-sided, as if it was built out of poorly lined-up tiers like a many layered wedding cake that had gone wrong. The other one didn't have a mouth or even a face. It was just a pair of legs really. Beyond these it dissolved into a jumble of fleshy spaghetti, a pink 3D version of the angry, black scribbles I used to draw.

But the third cot was empty.

"Sorry, mate, I should have warned you about this," said Dad, studying my reaction. "Some of the copies I made must have been corrupted or something."

He directed my eyes with his look to where the 'hot water bottle' was writhing under Mum's coverlet. I could just make out a stringy scrap of mouth sucking at her, making rubbery sounds. Her eyes were closed with what looked to me at the time like dreamy bliss, though I now think it might have been exhaustion.

She smiled and listened to Dad explaining how clever I'd been to get the machine working. But when she opened her eyes and looked from the copy I'd made to the glitched versions she'd been nursing all these months, her smile looked more and more thin and wan with every passing minute.

Priya Sharma's fiction has appeared in *Interzone, Black Static, Nightmare, The Dark* and on Tor.com. She's been anthologized in several *Best of* anthologies by editors such as Ellen Datlow, Paula Guran and Jonathan Strahan. "Fabulous Beasts" won the British Fantasy Award for Short Fiction and was nominated for the Shirley Jackson Award. The first collection of her short fiction, *All the Fabulous Beasts* was published by Undertow Publications in 2018 and won the Shirley Jackson Award and the British Fantasy Award, as well as being a Locus Award finalist. Her novella *Ormeshadow* is available from Tor. More about her work can be found at WWW.PRIYASHARMAWORDPRESS.COM

Fabulous Beasts
Priya Sharma

"ELIZA, TELL ME your secret."

Sometimes I'm cornered at parties by someone who's been watching me from across the room as they drain their glass. They think I don't know what's been said about me.

Eliza's odd looking but she has something, don't you think? Une jolie laide. A French term meaning ugly-beautiful. Only the intelligentsia can insult you with panache.

I always know when they're about to come over. It's in the pause before they walk, as though they're ordering their thoughts. Then they stride over, purposeful, through the throng of actors, journalists, and politicians, ignoring anyone who tries to engage them for fear of losing their nerve.

"Eliza, tell me your secret."

"I'm a princess."

Such a ridiculous thing to say and I surprise myself by using Kenny's term for us, even though I am now forty-something and Kenny was twenty-four years ago. I edge past, scanning the crowd for Georgia, so I can tell her that I've had enough and am going home. Maybe she'll come with me.

My interrogator doesn't look convinced. Nor should they be. I'm not even called Eliza. My real name is Lola and I'm no princess. I'm a monster.

We, Kenny's princesses, lived in a tower.

Kath, my mum, had a flat on the thirteenth floor of Laird Tower, in a northern town long past its prime. Two hundred and seventeen miles from London and twenty-four years ago. A whole world away, or it might as well be.

Ami, Kath's younger sister, lived two floors down. Kath and I went round to see her the day that she came home from the hospital. She answered the door wearing a black velour tracksuit, the bottoms slung low on her hips. The top rose up to reveal the wrinkled skin that had been taut over her baby bump the day before.

"Hiya," she opened the door wide to let us in.

Ami only spoke to Kath, never to me. She had a way of ignoring people that fascinated men and infuriated women.

Kath and I leant over the Moses basket.

"What a diamond," Kath cooed.

She was right. Some new babies are wizened, but not Tallulah. She looked like something from the front of one of Kath's knitting patterns. Perfect. I knew, even at that age, that I didn't look like everyone else; flat nose with too much nostril exposed, small eyelids and small ears that were squashed against my skull. I felt a pang of jealousy.

"What's her name, Ami?"

"Tallulah Rose." Ami laid her head on Kath's shoulder. "I wish you'd been there."

"I wanted to be there too. I'm sorry, darling. There was nobody to mind Lola. And Mikey was with you." Kath must have been genuinely sorry because normally she said Mikey's name like she was sniffing sour milk. "Where is he now?"

"Out, wetting the baby's head."

Kath's expression suggested that she thought he was doing more than toasting his newborn. He was always hanging around Ami. *Just looking after you, like Kenny wants*, he'd say, as if he was only doing his duty. Except now that there were shitty nappies to change and formula milk to prepare he was off, getting his end away.

Ami wasn't quite ready to let Kath's absence go.

"You could've left Lola with one of my friends."

Ami knew better. Kath never let anyone look after me, not even her.

"Let's not fight now, pet. You're tired."

Ami's gaze was like being doused in ice water. It contained everything she couldn't say to me. *Fucking ugly, little runt. You're always in the way.*

"You must be starvin'. Let me get you a cuppa and a sandwich and then you can get some sleep."

We stood and looked at the baby when Ami had gone to bed.

"Don't get any ideas. You don't want to be like your aunt, with a baby at sixteen. You don't want to be like either of us."

Kathy always spoke to me like I was twenty-four, not four.

Tallulah stirred and stretched, arms jerking outwards as if she was in free-fall. She opened her eyes. There was no squinting or screaming.

"The little scrap's going to need our help."

Kath lifted her out and laid her on her knee for inspection. I put my nose against the soft spot on her skull. I fell in love with her right then.

"What do you wish for her?" Kath asked, smiling.

Chocolate. Barbies. A bike. A pet snake. Everything my childish heart could bestow.

Saturdays were for shopping. Kathy and I walked down Cathcart Street towards town. We'd pass a row of grimy Victorian mansions on our way that served as a reminder of once great wealth, now carved up into flats for social housing or filled with squatters who lay in their damp dens with needles in their arms.

After these were the terraces, joined by a network of alleyways that made for easy assaults and getaways. This model of housing was for the civic minded when everyone here had a trade, due to our proximity to the city of Liverpool. The ship- building yards lay empty, and the 1980s brought container ships that did away with the demand for dockers. The life inside spilled out into the sun; women sat on their steps in pyjama bottoms and vest tops, even though it was lunchtime. Fags in hand, they'd whisper to one another as Kathy passed, afraid to meet her gaze. A man wore just shorts, his pale beer belly pinking up in the sun. He saluted when he saw Kathy. She ignored him.

I followed Kathy, her trolley wheels squeaking. The sound got worse as it was filled with vegetables, cheap meat shrink wrapped on Styrofoam trays, and bags of broken biscuits.

Kathy stopped to talk to a woman with rotten, tea-stained teeth. I was bored. We were at the outskirts of town, where the shops were most shabby. House clearance stores and a refurbished washing machine outlet. I wandered along the pavement a way until something stopped me. The peeling sign over the shop window read "Ricky's Reptiles." The display was full of tanks. Most were empty, but the one at the front contained a pile of terrapins struggling to climb over one another in a dish of water.

The shop door was open, revealing the lino floor that curled up at the corners. It was a shade of blue that verged on grey, or maybe it was just dirty. I could see the lights from the tanks. The fish were darting flashes of wild colour or else they drifted on gossamer fins. I was drawn in. The man behind the counter looked up and smiled, but to his credit he didn't try and talk to me, otherwise I would've run.

Then I saw it, a long tank along the back wall. I went closer. The snake was magnificent, from the pale skin on her belly to the brown scales on her back.

She slithered closer, eyeing me and then raised her head and the front third of her body lifted up as if suspended on invisible thread. I put my forehead against the glass.

"She likes you," the man murmured.

She moved up the side of the tank. I realised that I was swaying in time with her, feeling unity in the motion. I was aware of her body, each muscle moving beneath her skin, her very skeleton. I looked into the snake's black eyes and could see out of them into my own. The world was on the tip of her forked tongue; my curiosity, the shopkeeper's sweat and kindness, the soft flavour of the mice in the tank behind the counter.

A hand gripped my shoulder, hard, jerking me back to myself. It was Kathy.

"Get away from that thing." Her fingers were digging into me. "Don't you ever come in here again, understand?"

She looked at the snake, shuddering. "God, it's disgusting. What's wrong with you?"

She shouted at me all the way home, for putting the wind up her, letting her think some pervert had taken me. I didn't realise just how afraid she was. That she was looking at me like she didn't know what she'd birthed.

The novelty of motherhood soon wore off. Ami sat in the armchair of our flat, her toenails painted in the same tangerine shade as her maxi dress. She was sunbed fresh and her lips were demarcated in an unflatteringly pale shade of pink. Her hair was in fat rollers ready for her evening out.

"Guess where I went today?" she asked, her voice bright and brittle.

"Where, doll?" Kath puffed on her cigarette, blowing a stream of smoke away from us.

If Ami was slim, Kath was scrawny. The skin on her neck and chest was wrinkled from the lack of padding and twenty-five cigarettes a day. She wore a series of gold chains and her hands were rough and red from perpetual cleaning. Her face was unbalanced: nose too small and large ears that stuck out. Round eyes that never saw make-up. I forget sometimes, that she was only twenty-four then.

"To see Kenny."

Tallulah got up and I thought she was leaving me for Ami but she was just fetching her teddy. When she sat back down next to me, she wriggled against me to get comfortable. Ami bought Tallulah's clothes. Ridiculous, expensive things to dress a toddler in, old fashioned and frilly.

"Kenny always asks after you." Ami filled the silence.

"Does he?" Kath tipped the ash from her cigarette into the empty packet. God love her, she didn't have many vices.

"He never says but he's hurt. It's all over his face when I walk in and you're not with me. You're not showing him much respect or loyalty. All he wants to do is look after you and Lola, like he looks after me and Tallulah."

"I don't want Kenny's money. He's not Robin Hood. He beat a man to death."

"He's our *brother*."

Which was funny, because I didn't know that I had an uncle.

Kath's face was a shutter slamming shut.

"He loves to see pictures of Lola."

"Photos? You showed him photos?" Kath was blowing herself for a fight.

"I only showed him some pictures. He wanted to see her. What's up with you?"

"Lola's *my* business. No one else's."

"Well, I'm taking Tallulah for him to see next time."

"No, you're not. Not to a prison."

"She's mine. I'll take her where the fuck I want."

"You've done well to remember you've got a daughter."

"What's that mean?"

"You're always out with your bloody mates. You treat me like an unpaid baby sitter. She spends more time here than with you and then you've got the cheek to tell me to mind my own."

"So it's about money?"

"No," Kath threw up her hands, "it's about you being a selfish, spoilt brat. I'm your *sister*, not your mum. And it's about how you treat Tallulah."

"At least I know who her dad is."

Kath slapped her face. A sudden bolt that silenced them both. It left a red flush on Ami's cheek. Whenever I asked about my dad, Kath told me that she'd found me in a skip.

"I'm sorry, Ami…" Kath put out her hands. "I didn't mean to. I mean…"

"Tallulah," Ami snapped, holding out her hand.

Tallulah looked from me to Kath, her eyes wide. Ami pulled her up by the arm. She screamed.

"Be careful with her."

"Or what, Kath?" Ami lifted Tallulah up, putting her under one arm like she was a parcel. "Are you going to call Social Services? Fuck off."

Calling Social Services was a crime akin to calling the police.

Tallulah was in a full on tantrum by then, back arched and legs kicking. Fierce for her size, she proved too much for Ami who threw her down on the sofa. She lay there, tear stained and rigid. Ami had started to cry too. "Stay here then, see if I sodding care."

There are times when I feel lost, even to myself, and that what looks out from behind my eyes isn't human.

I'm reminded of it each day as I go to work at the School of Tropical Medicine.

Peter, one of the biochemists from the lab downstairs has come up for a batch of venom. He watches me milk the snakes when he can overcome his revulsion.

Michael, my assistant, tips the green mamba out of her box. I pin her down with a forked metal stick, while Michael does the same, further along her body. I clamp a hand just beneath her neck, thanking her silently for enduring the indignity of this charade. If it were just the two of us, she'd come to me without all this manhandling. I'll make it up to her later with mice and kisses. She's gorgeous in an intense shade of green, her head pointed.

"You have to stop that work when you get too old," says Peter, "you know, reflexes getting slow and all that."

The deaths of herpetologists are as fabled as snakes are touchy. There's no room for lax habits or slowness. Handled safely for years, a snake can turn on you, resulting in a blackened, withered limb, blood pouring from every orifice, paralysis and blindness, if not death.

Peter's a predator. He's been a swine to me since I knocked him back. I turn to him with the snake still in my hand. She hisses at him and he shrinks away.

I hook the mamba's mouth over the edge of the glass and apply gentle pressure. The venom runs down the side and collects in a pool.

What Peter doesn't know is that when my darlings and I are alone, I hold them in my arms and let them wind around my neck. Our adoration is mutual. They're the easy part of my job.

"They like Eliza," Michael is offended on my behalf. There's not been a bite since I've been here.

"Concentrate." I snap at him as he brings the mamba's box to me. I regret my churlishness straight away. Michael is always pleasant with me. He never takes offence at my lack of social graces but someday he will.

Snakes are easy. It's people that I don't know how to charm.

Tallulah trailed along beside me. She looked like a doll in her school uniform; pleated skirt and leather buckled shoes. I didn't begrudge her the lovely clothes that Ami bought her. She jumped, a kittenish leap, and then she took my hand. We swung arms as we walked.

We turned onto Cathcart Street. Laird Tower was ahead of us, dwarfing the bungalows opposite. Those used by the elderly or infirm were marked out by white grab handles and key safes.

A pair of girls sat on a wall. They jumped down when they saw us. School celebrities, these playground queens, who knew how to bruise you with a word. They'd hurt you for not being like them, or not wanting to be like them.

"Is she your sister?" Jade, the shorter one, asked Tallulah.

"No," Tallulah began, "she's…"

"Of course not," Jade cut across her, keen to get out the rehearsed speech. Jade didn't like my prowess in lessons. I tried to hide it, but it occasionally burst out of me. I liked the teacher. I liked homework. I even liked the school, built in red brick, that managed to still look like a Victorian poorhouse.

Jade was sly enough not to goad me for that, going for my weakness, not my strength. "You're too pretty to be Lola's sister. Look at her ugly mug."

It was true. I remained resolutely strange; my features had failed to rearrange themselves into something that would pass for normal. Also, my sight had rapidly deteriorated in the last few months and my thick lenses magnified my eyes.

"Be careful." Jade leant down into Tallulah's face. "You'll catch her ugliness."

Tallulah pushed her, hard, both of her small hands on her chest. Jade fell backwards a few steps, surprised by the attack. She raised a fist to hit Tallulah.

My blood was set alight, venom rising. Water brash filled my mouth as if I were about to be sick. I snatched at Jade's hand and sunk my teeth into her meaty forearm, drawing blood. I could taste her shock and fear. If she was screaming, I couldn't hear her. I only let go when her friend punched me on the ear.

After I'd apologised I sat in the corner of the room while Kath and Pauline, Jade's mum, talked.

"I thought it would be good if we sorted it out between us, like grown ups," Pauline said.

Social Services had already been round to confirm that I was the culprit.

Has she ever done anything like this before?

No, Kathy was calm and firm, *Lola wasn't brought up that way.*

"I'm so sorry about what happened." Pauline lifted her mug of tea, her hand trembling a fraction. She took a sip and set it down, not picking it up again.

"Why?" Kath sat up straighter. "Lola bit Jade. *I'm* sorry and I'll make sure that she is too by the time I'm done with her."

"Yes, but Jade was picking on her."

"That's no excuse for what Lola did. She should've just walked away."

"It's time that someone cut Jade down to size."

"My daughter *bit* yours." Exasperation raised Kathy's voice a full octave.

"She was asking for it."

Kathy shook her head. Then, "How is she?"

Jade had lain on the pavement, twitching. Red marks streaked up her arm, marking the veins.

"She's doing okay," Pauline swallowed. "She's on antibiotics. She's a bit off colour, that's all."

"The police and Social Services came round earlier."

"I've not complained. I'm not a nark. I'd never do that."

"I didn't say you had."

"You'll tell Kenny, won't you? We're not grasses. We won't cause you any bother. I'll skin Jade if she comes near your girls again." We were known as Kathy's girls.

"Kenny?" Kathy repeated dully.

"Please. Will you talk to him?"

Kath was about to say something but then deflated in the chair.

"Ami's says she's visiting him soon, so I'll make sure he gets the message."

Kathy closed the door after Pauline had gone.

"What did you do to her?" It was the first time she'd looked at me properly since it had happened.

"It wasn't her fault." Tallulah stood between us. "She was going to hit me."

"What did you do to her?" Kathy pushed her aside. "Her arm swelled up and she's got blood poisoning."

"I don't know," I stammered. "It just happened."

She slapped me. I put my hands out to stop her but she carried on, backing me into the bedroom. She pushed me down on the floor. I curled my hands over my head.

"I didn't bring you up to be like that." Her strength now was focused in a fist. Kathy had hit me before, but never like that. "I swear I'll kill you if you ever do anything like that again. You fucking little monster."

She was sobbing and shrieking. Tallulah was crying and trying to pull her off. Kathy continued to punch me until her arm grew tired. "You're a monster, just like your father."

We stayed in our bedroom that night, Tallulah and I. We could hear Kathy banging about the flat. First, the vacuum hitting the skirting boards as she pulled it around. A neighbour thumped on the wall and she shouted back, but turned it off and took to the bathroom. She'd be at it all night, until her hands were raw. The smell of bleach was a signal of her distress. There were times when I thought I'd choke on the stench.

The skin on my face felt tight and sore, as if shrunken by tears. Tallulah rolled up my T-shirt to inspect the bruises on my back. There was a change coming, fast, as the shock of Kathy's onslaught wore off.

It hurt when Tallulah touched me. It wasn't just the skin on my face that felt wrong. It was all over. I rubbed my head against the carpet, an instinctual movement as I felt I'd got a cowl covering my face. The skin ripped.

"I'll get Kathy."

"No, wait." I grabbed her wrist. "Stay with me." My skin had become a fibrous sheath, my very bones remoulding. My ribs shrank and my slim pelvis and limbs became vestigial. My paired organs rearranged themselves, one pushed below the other except my lungs. I gasped as one of those collapsed. I could feel my diaphragm tearing; the wrenching of it doubled me over.

I writhed on the floor. There was no blood. What came away in the harsh lamplight was translucent. Tallulah held me as I sloughed off my skin which fell away to reveal scales. She gathered the coils of me into her lap. We lay down and I curled around her.

I couldn't move. I could barely breathe. When I put out my forked tongue I could taste Tallulah's every molecule in the air.

The morning light came through the thin curtain. Tallulah was beside me. I had legs again. I put a hand to my mouth. My tongue was whole. My flesh felt new. More than that, I could see. When I put my glasses on the world became blurred. I didn't need them anymore. The very surface of my eyes had been reborn.

My shed skin felt fibrous and hard. I bundled it up into a plastic bag and stuffed it in my wardrobe. Tallulah stretched as she watched me, her hands and feet splayed.

"Tallulah, what am I? Am I a monster?"

She sat up and leant against me, her chin on my shoulder.

"Yes, you're *my* monster."

I ache for the splendid shabbiness of my former life, when it was just Kath, Tallulah, and me in the flat, the curtains drawn against the world and the telly droning on in the background. Tallulah and I would dance around Kath while she swatted us away. The smell of bleach and furniture polish is forever home. Kath complaining when I kept turning the heating up. Being cold made me sluggish.

Endless, innocuous days and nights that I should've savoured more.

"How was your test?"

"Crap." Tallulah threw down her bag. "Hi, Kath."

"Hi, love," Kathy shouted back from the kitchen.

Tallulah, school uniformed, big diva hair so blonde that it was almost white, a flick of kohl expertly applied at the corner of her eyes.

"I'm thick, not like you." She kicked off her shoes.

"You're not thick. Just lazy."

She laughed and lay on her belly beside me, in front of the TV. She smelt of candy floss scent that she'd stolen from her mum. Tallulah was the sweetest thing.

There was the sound of the key in the door. I looked at Tallulah. Only her mum had a key. We could hear Ami's voice, followed by a man's laugh.

A foreign sound in the flat. Kathy came out of the kitchen, tea towel in hand.

Ami stood in the doorway, flushed and excited, as if she was about to present a visiting dignitary.

"Kath, there's someone here to see you."

She stood aside. I didn't recognise the man. He was bald and scarred. Kathy sat down on the sofa arm, looking the colour of a dirty dishrag.

"Oh, God," he said, "aren't you a bunch of princesses?"

"Kenny, when did you get out?" Kath asked.

"A little while ago." He took off his jacket and threw it down. A snake tattoo coiled up his arm and disappeared under the sleeve of his t-shirt. It wasn't the kind of body art I was used to. This hadn't been driven into the skin in a fit of self-loathing or by a ham-fisted amateur. It was faded but beautiful. It rippled as Kenny moved, invigorated by his muscles.

"Come and hug me, Kath."

She got up, robotic, and went to him, tolerating his embrace, her arms stiff by her sides.

"I've brought us something to celebrate."

He handed her a plastic bag and she pulled out a bottle of vodka and a packet of Jammy Dodgers.

"Just like when we were kids, eh?" he grinned.

"See, Kenny's got no hard feelings about you staying away." Ami was keen to be involved. "He's just glad to be home."

They both ignored her.

"Now, girls, come and kiss your uncle. You first, Tallulah."

"Well, go on." Ami gave her a shove.

She pecked his cheek and then shot away, which seemed to amuse him. Then it was my turn. Kath stood close to us while Kenny held me at arm's length.

"How old are you now, girl?"

"Eighteen."

"You were born after I went inside." He sighed. "You've got the family's ugly gene like me and your mum, but you'll do."

For what? I thought.

Kenny put his fleshy hand around Kath's neck and pressed his forehead against hers. Kathy, who didn't like kisses or cuddles from anyone, flinched. I'd never seen her touched so much.

"I'm home now. We'll not talk about these past, dark years. It'll be how it was before. Better. You'll see. Us taking care of each other."

Georgia's unusual for a photographer in that she's more beautiful than her models. They're gap-toothed, gawky things that only find luminosity through the lens. Georgia's arresting in the flesh.

I hover beside our host, who's introducing me to everyone as though I'm a curio. We approach a group who talk too loudly, as if they're the epicentre of the party.

"I find Georgia distant. And ambitious."

"She lives on Martin's Heath. In one of the old houses."

"Bloody hell, is that family money?"

"Rosie, you've modelled for Georgia. Have you been there?"

"No."

Rosie sounds so quiet and reflective that the pain of her unrequited love is palpable. At least I hope it's unrequited.

"Have you seen her girlfriend?"

"Everyone, meet Eliza," our host steps in before they have a chance to pronounce judgement on me within my earshot, "Georgia's partner."

I shake hands with each of them.

"Georgia's last shoot made waves. And I didn't realise that she was such a stunner."

We all look over at Georgia. Among all the overdressed butterflies, she wears black trousers, a white shirt, and oxblood brogues.

"Don't tell her that," I smile. "She doesn't like it."

"Why? Doesn't every woman want that?" The man falters, as if he's just remembered that I'm a woman too.

These people with their interminable words. I came from a place where a slap sufficed.

"Don't be dull," I put him down. "She's much more than her face."

"What do you do, Eliza?" another one of them asks, unperturbed by my rudeness.

"I'm a herpetologist."

They shudder with delicious revulsion.

I glance back to Georgia. A man with long blonde hair reaches out to touch her forearm, and he shows her something on his tablet.

I'm a pretender in my own life, in this relationship. I know how my jealousy will play out when we get home. I'll struggle to circumnavigate all the gentility and civility that makes me want to scream.

Eventually Georgia will say, *What's the matter? Just tell me instead of trying to pick a fight.*

She'll never be provoked, this gracious woman, to display any savagery of feeling. I should know better than to try and measure the breadth and depth of love by its noise and dramas, but there are times that I crave it, as if it's proof that love is alive.

Ami took Tallulah away with her the first night that Kenny came to the flat.

"But it's a school night. And all my stuff's here."

"You're not going to school tomorrow." Ami picked up her handbag. "We're going out with Kenny."

Tallulah didn't move.

"Mind your mum, there's a good girl." Kenny didn't even look up.

After the front door closed, Kathy locked and chained it.

"Get your rucksack. Put some clothes in a bag. Don't pack anything you don't need."

"Why?" I followed her into her bedroom.

"We're leaving."

"Why?"

"Just get your stuff."

"What about college?"

Kathy tipped out drawers, rifling through the untidy piles that she'd made on the floor.

"What about Tallulah?"

She sank down on the bed.

"There's always someone that I have to stay for. Mum. Ami. Tallulah." She slammed her fist down on the duvet. "If it had been just us, we'd have been gone long ago."

"Stay?"

She wasn't listening to me anymore.

"I waited too long. I should've run when I had the chance. Fuck everyone."

She lay down, her face to the wall. I tried to put my arms around her but she shrunk from me, which she always did when I touched her and which never failed to hurt me.

———

If we were his princesses then Kenny considered himself king.

"Kath, stop fussing and come and sit down. It's good to be back among women. Without women, men are uncivilised creatures." He winked at me. "Tell me about Ma's funeral again, Kath."

Ami sat beside him, looking up at him.

"There were black horses with plumes and brasses. Her casket was in a glass carriage." Kath's delivery was wooden.

"And all the boys were there?"

"Yes, Kenny. All the men, in their suits, gold sovereign rings, and tattoos."

"Good," he said, "I would've been offended otherwise. Those boys owe me and they know it. I did time for them. Do you know the story?"

"Bits," Tallulah said.

"I told her, Kenny." Ami was keen to show her allegiance.

"You were what, twelve?" He snorted. "You remember nothing. We did a job in Liverpool. A jeweller who lived in one of those massive houses around Sefton Park. We heard he was dealing in stolen diamonds. I went in first," he thumped his chest. "At twenty-three I was much thinner back then, could get into all sorts of tight spots. I let the others in afterwards. We found his money but he kept insisting the diamonds were hidden in the fireplace, but his hidey-hole was empty. He kept acting all surprised. He wouldn't tell, no matter what." Kenny shrugged. "Someone grassed. A copper picked me up near home. Under my coat, my shirt was covered in his blood. I kept my trap shut and did the time. The others were safe. Eighteen years inside. My only regret is what happened to Ma. And missing her funeral."

"There were white flowers, everywhere, spelling out her name." Ami said. He patted her arm in an absent way, like she was a cat mithering for strokes.

"I wish they'd let me out for it. Ma was a proper princess, girls. She was touched, God bless her, but she was a princess."

Kath sat with her hands folded on her knees.

"Do you remember what Dad said when he was dying?"

Kath stayed quiet.

"He said, *You're the man of the house, Kenny. And you're the mother, Kathy. Kenny, you have to look after these girls.* Poor Ma, so fragile. When I heard about her stroke, I was beside myself. It was the shock of me being sent down that did it. Who ever grassed me up has to pay for that, too. I should've been here, taking care of you all."

"I managed," Kathy squeezed the words out.

"I know. I hate to think of you, nursing Ma when you also had a baby to look after. You were meant for better things. We didn't always live in this shithole, girls. We grew up in a big rambling house. You won't remember much of it, Ami. Dad bred snakes. He was a specialist. And Ma, she was a real lady. They were educated people, not like 'round here."

The words stuck in my gut. 'Round here was all I knew.

"Happy days, weren't they, Mouse?" Kenny looked directly at Kathy, waiting.

"Mouse," Ami laughed like she'd only just noticed Kathy's big eyes and protruding ears, "I'd forgotten that."

Mouse. A nickname that diminished her.

"What's *my* pet name?" Ami pouted.

"You're just Ami." He said it like she was something flat and dead, not shifting his gaze from Kathy.

There it was. Even then, I could see that Kathy was at the centre of everything and Ami was just the means to reach her.

There's a photograph in our bedroom that Georgia took of me while we were travelling around South America. It embarrasses me because of its dimensions, and scares me because Georgia has managed to make me look like some kind of modern Eve, desirable in a way that I'll never be again. My hair is loose and uncombed and the python around my shoulders is handsome in dappled, autumnal shades. My expression is of unguarded pleasure.

"Let's stay here, forever," I said to her when she put the lens cap back on, "It's paradise."

What I was really thinking was *What would it be like to change, forever, and have the whole jungle as my domain?*

"Do you love it that much?" Georgia replied in a way that suggested she didn't. "And put him down. Poor thing. If he's caught he'll end up as a handbag."

So it is that serpents are reviled when it's man that is repulsive.

I got off the bus at the end of Argyll Street and walked towards home. Kenny was sat on a plastic chair outside The Saddle pub, drinking a pint. He was waiting for me.

"What have you been doing today?" He abandoned his drink and followed me.

"Biology." I was at college, in town.

"Clever girl. That's from your grandparents. I used to be smart like that. You wouldn't think it to look at me."

There was an odd, puppyish eagerness to Kenny as he bounced along beside me. I darted across the road when there was a gap in the traffic. The railway line was on the other side of the fence, down a steep bank. Part way down the embankment was a rolled-up carpet, wet and rotted, and the shopping trolley that it had been transported in.

"Let me carry your bag. It looks heavy."

"I can manage."

"I wasn't always like this. I had to change for us to survive. Fighting and stealing," he shook his head, embarrassed. "I only became brutal to stop us being brutalised. Do you understand?"

The sky had darkened. Rain was on its way.

"We lost everything when Dad died. The house. The money. Your grandma lost her mind. It was the shock of having to live here. We were posh and we paid for that. On our first day at school a lad was picking on Kathy. Do you know what I did? I bit him, Lola. Right on the face. He swelled up like a red balloon. He nearly choked. Nobody picks on my princesses."

Nobody except him.

"Are you special, Lola?"

"I don't know what you mean."

I dodged him as he tried to block my path. Tallulah wouldn't have told him anything. Ami though, she had told him to prevent Pauline and Jade getting a battering.

"I can wait," he didn't pursue me, just stood there in the drizzle. "We have lots of time now."

"We're going for a ride today." Kenny followed Kath into the kitchen. He'd started turning up at the flat every day.

"I can't, Kenny, I've got loads to do."

"It can all wait."

Kenny had the last word.

"Where are we going?" Tallulah asked.

"You're not going anywhere except to Ami's. She needs to get her house in order. A girl needs her mum. She's sorting your bedroom, so you're going to live with her. Properly."

"I don't want to."

"Want's not in it."

Kathy stood between them. He pushed her aside.

"I live *here*." Tallulah wouldn't be moved.

"You live where I tell you." He had this way of standing close to you, to make himself seem more imposing, and lowering his voice. "You act like you're something with that pretty little face of yours. Well, I'm here to tell you that you're not special. You're fucking Mikey Flynn's daughter. And he's a piece of dead scum."

Poor Mikey Flynn, rumoured to have done a runner. I wondered where Kenny had him buried.

"Go home, Tallulah." Kathy raised her chin. "Kenny's right. You're not my girl. You should be with your own mother."

Tallulah's eyes widened. I could see the tears starting to pool there.

"Go on, then," Kathy carried on, "you don't belong here."

"Mum," I opened my mouth.

"Shut it." Kathy turned on me. "I've been soft on you pair for too long. Now help Tallulah take her stuff to Ami's."

"No," Kenny put a hand on my arm, "Lola stays with us."

As Kenny drove, the terraces changed to semis and then detached houses. Finally there were open fields. It felt like he'd taken us hours away but it wasn't more than thirty minutes. We turned up an overgrown drive. Branches whipped the windscreen as Kenny drove.

"Kenny." Kath's voice was ripped from her throat. He patted her hand.

The drive ended at a large house, dark bricked with tall windows. It might as well have been a castle for all its unfamiliar grandeur. Overgrown rhododendrons crowded around it, shedding pink and red blossoms that were long past their best.

"Come on."

Kenny got out, not looking back to see if we were following.

Kath stood at the bottom of the steps, looking up at the open front door. There were plenty of window bars and metal shutters where I grew up, but the windows here were protected by wrought iron foliage in which metal snakes were entwined. The interior was dim. I could hear Kenny's footsteps as he walked inside.

"This is where we used to live." Kathy's face was blank. She went in, a sleep walker in her own life. I followed her.

"Welcome home." Kenny was behind the door. He locked it and put the key on a chain around his neck.

Kenny showed us from room to room as if we were prospective buyers, not prisoners. Every door had a lock and every window was decorated in the same metal latticework.

I stopped at a set of double doors but Kenny steered me away from it. "Later. Look through here, Kathy. Do you remember the old Aga? Shame they ripped it out. I thought we could get a new one."

He led us on to the lounge, waving his arm with a flourish.

"I couldn't bring you here without buying *some* new furniture." He kept glancing at Kathy. "What do you think?"

The room smelt of new carpet. It was a dusky pink, to match the sofa, and the curtains were heavy cream with rose buds on them. Things an old woman might have picked.

"Lovely, Kenny."

"I bought it for us." He slung his arm around her neck. It looked like a noose. "You and me, here again, no interference." His face was soft. "I've plenty of money. I can get more."

"Go and play," Kath said to me.

It'll shame me forever that I was angry at her for talking to me like I was a child when all she was trying to do was get me out of his way.

I went, then crawled back on my belly to watch them through the gap in the door.

Kath broke away from him and sat down. Kenny followed her, sinking down to lay his head on her knee. Her hand hovered over him, the muscles in her throat moving as she swallowed hard. Then she stroked his head. He buried his face in her lap, moaning.

"What happened to us, Mouse?"

Mouse. He'd swallow her whole. He'd crush her.

"You said you can get more money. Do you mean the money from the job in Liverpool?"

He moved quickly, sitting beside Kathy with his thigh wedged against the length of hers.

"Yes." He interfaced their fingers, making their hands a single fist. "I want you to know that I didn't kill anyone."

"You didn't? You were covered in blood."

"It was Barry's son, Carl. He always had a screw loose. The man wouldn't tell us where the diamonds were and Carl just freaked. He kept on beating him."

"But you admitted it."

"Who would believe me if I denied it? I did the time. Barry was very grateful. I knew it would set us up for life. I hated waiting for you. I imagined slipping out between the bars to come to you. I was tempted so many times. I hated the parole board. There *were* diamonds, Kath. I took them before I let the others in. I stopped here and buried them under the wall at the bottom of the garden. I nearly got caught doing it. Then the police picked me up, on my way back to you. That's why I had to do the stretch, so nobody would suspect. They're safe, now. Shankly's looking after what's left of them." He laughed at his own cryptic comment. Every Merseysider knew the deceased Bill Shankly, iconic once-manager of Liverpool Football Club. "Did I do right, Kath?"

Then she did something surprising. She kissed him. He writhed under her touch.

"Mouse, was there anyone else while I was inside?"

"No, Kenny. There's never been anybody else."

He basked in that.

"It'll be just like I said."

I sensed her hesitation. So did he.

"What's wrong?"

"It won't be like we said though, will it?"

"Why?"

"It should be just us two." She leant closer to him. "Lola's grown up now. She can look after herself."

"Lola's just a kid."

"I was a mother at her age." She put her hand on his arm.

"No, she stays."

Her hand dropped.

"Lola," Kenny called out. "Never let me catch you eavesdropping again. Understand?"

"I'll just say goodnight to Lola." Kath stood in the doorway to my new bedroom, as if this game of fucked-up families was natural.

"Don't be long."

I sat on the bed. The new quilt cover and pillow case smelt funny. Kenny had put them on straight out of the packaging without washing them first. They still bore the sharp creases of their confinement.

"Lola," Kathy pulled me up and whispered to me. "He said to me, when we were kids, 'I'm going to put a baby in you and it's going to be special, like me and Dad,' as if I had nothing to do with it. I can't stand him touching me. When I felt you moving inside me, I was terrified you'd be a squirming snake, but you were *mine*. I'd do anything to get him away from us and Ami. I was the one who told the police."

Uncle. Father. Any wonder that I'm monstrous?

"Kenny's always been wrong. He thought it was from Dad, although he never saw him do it. It's from Mum. It drove her mad, holding it in. She nearly turned when she had her stroke. I have to know, can you do it too?"

"What?"

"We can't waste time. Can you turn into," she hesitated, "a snake?"

"Yes." I couldn't meet her gaze.

"Good. Do it as soon as I leave." She opened the window. "Go out through the bars. Will you fit?"

"I don't know if I can. I'm not sure that I can do it at will."

"Try. Get out of here."

Panic rose in my chest. "What about you?"

"I'm going to do what I should've done a long time ago." She showed me the paring knife in her back pocket and then pulled her baggy sweater back over it. It must've been all she had time to grab. "I won't be far behind you."

"What if you're not?"

"Don't ask stupid questions," she paused, "I'm sorry for not being stronger. I'm sorry for not getting you away from here."

"Kathy," Kenny's voice boomed from the corridor, "time for bed."

After she left I heard the key turn in the lock.

I went through the drawers and wardrobe. Kenny had filled them with clothes. I didn't want to touch anything that had come from him. There was nothing that I could use as a weapon or to help me escape.

I'd not changed since the time I'd bitten Jade. I lay down, trying to slow my breathing and concentrate. Nothing happened. The silence filled my mind along with all the things he would be doing to Kathy.

I dozed, somewhere towards early morning, wakening frequently in the unfamiliar room. I missed Tallulah beside me in the bed we'd shared since childhood. I missed her warmth and tangle of hair.

When Kenny let me out it was late afternoon.

"Where's my mum?"

"Down here."

There was a chest freezer in the basement. Kenny lifted the lid. Kathy was inside, frozen in a slumped position, arms crossed over her middle. Frozen blood glittered on the gash in her head and frosted one side of her face.

Kenny put his hand on my shoulder like we were mourners at a wake. I should've been kicking and screaming, but I was as frozen as she was.

One of Kathy's wrists was contorted at an unnatural angle.

"She betrayed me. I always knew it, in my heart." He shut the lid. "Now it's just you and me, kid."

He took me up through the house, to the room at the back with the double doors. There were dozens of tanks that cast a glow. Some contained a single serpent, others several that were coiled together like heaps of intestines.

"My beauties. I'll start breeding them."

There were corn snakes, ball pythons, ribbon snakes, though I had no names for them back then, all of which make good pets. I stopped at one tank. He had a broad head with a blunted snout

"Ah, meet Shankly." Kenny put his hand against the glass. "He was hard to come by. They're called cottonmouths because they open their mouths so wide to show their fangs that you see all the white lining inside."

The cottonmouth must have been young. I remember his olive-green colour and the clear banded pattern on his back, which he would lose as he got older.

"Are you special, Kathy?"

"I'm Lola."

"Yes, of course you are. Are you like me?"

"I'm nothing like you. Leave me alone."

"I'll look after you. Like you're a princess. You'll want for nothing. And you'll look after me because that's how it works."

"Don't fucking touch me."

Kenny pressed my face against the tank. Shankly showed me his pale underbelly as he slid towards me.

"Be afraid of him," Kenny nodded at the snake, "he still has his fangs. I'll make a mint from his venom."

Shankly climbed up a branch in his tank and settled there.

Kenny pushed me down with one hand and undid his belt buckle with the other.

"I'm your daughter." It was my last defence.

"I know."

Then he put his forked tongue in my mouth.

I couldn't move. The place between my legs was numb. I'd already tried sex with a boy from college. I knew what it was about. We'd fumbled and fallen in a heap in the bushes by the old boating lake one afternoon. It wasn't an experience to set the world alight but it was satisfactory enough.

This wasn't just a sex crime, it was a power crime. Kenny wanted my fear. I shrunk into the distant corners of myself trying to retreat where he couldn't follow. His orgasm was grudging, delivered with a short, gratified moan.

Afterwards he sat with his trousers open, watching me like he was waiting for me to do something. I was frozen. I'm not sure I even blinked. That was how Kathy must have felt, forever stuck in that single moment of inertia and shock that kept her in the same spot for a lifetime. She was right. She should have run while she had the chance. Fuck her mother. And Ami, for all the good she'd done her.

Kenny stood up. I thought, *It's going to happen again and then he's going to dump me in the freezer.* Instead, he went upstairs, his tread heavy with disappointment.

"Don't stay up too late, pet."

I think I was waiting for something too, when I should've been searching for something sharp to stick between his ribs. I couldn't summon anything; I was still too deep inside myself.

I was colder than I'd ever been before, even though the summer night was stifling. The room felt airless despite the window being wide open and butting up against the grille. Sometimes, when Georgia's away, I feel that cold.

Get up, get up before he remembers you and comes back down for more.

"Lola." A voice carried through the window.

It was Tallulah, a pale ghost beyond the glass. Her mouth was moving as she clutched at the bars.

I turned my face away, in the childish way of *if I can't see her, then she can't see me*. I didn't want her to see me like this. It occurred to me that she might have been a witness to the whole thing. I turned back but she'd gone, so I closed my eyes.

I should've known that Tallulah would never leave me. The snakes swayed in their tanks, enraptured. Tallulah was long and white, with pale yellow markings. Slender and magnificent. She glided over me and lay on my chest, rearing up. I couldn't breathe because she took my breath away. I could feel her muscles contracting and her smooth belly scales against my bare chest.

Get up, get up, or he'll come down and find her like this.

Are you special?

Her tongue flicked out and touched my lips. I had no choice. I had to do it, for her. There was the rush of lubricant that loosened the top layer of my skin. The change was fast, my boyish body, with its flat chest and narrow hips perfectly suited to the transformation.

I crawled out of my human mantle. Moulting was good. I shed every cell of myself that Kenny had touched.

Both Tallulah and I are unidentifiable among my extensive research of snakes, bearing properties of several species at once. We made a perfect pair for hunting. The pits on my face were heat sensitive, able to detect a variation of a thousandth of a degree, feeding information into my optic nerves. I saw the world in thermal. Kenny's heart was luminous in the dark. I slid up the side of his bed and hovered over his pillow. Tallulah lay beside him on the mattress, waiting.

Look at your princesses, Kenny. See how special we are.

Kenny snored, a gentle, almost purring noise.

It's a myth that snakes dislocate their jaws.

I opened my mouth as wide as I could, stretching the flexible ligament that joined my lower jaw to my skull. I covered his crown in slow increments. He snorted and twitched. I slipped down over his eyes, his lashes tickling the inside of my throat. He reached up to touch his head.

Tallulah struck him, sinking her fangs into his neck. He started and tried to sit up, limbs flailing, which was a mistake as his accelerating heartbeat sent the venom further around his circulation.

Trying to cover his nose was the hardest part, despite my reconfigured mouth. I thought my head would split open. I wasn't sure how much more I could stomach. Not that it mattered. I wasn't trying to swallow him whole. A fraction more and I was over his nostrils completely.

There was only one way to save himself. I recognised the undulations he was making. I could feel the change on my tongue, his skin becoming fibrous. I had to stop him. I couldn't imagine what he'd become.

He was weakening with Tallulah's neurotoxins, slumping back on the bed, shaking in an exquisite fit. He'd wet himself. I stretched my flesh further and covered his mouth and waited until long after he was still.

I woke up on the floor beside Tallulah. We were naked. My throat and neck were sore. The corners of my mouth were crusted with dried blood. We lay on our sides, looking at one another without speaking. We were the same, after all.

"How did you find me?" I was hoarse.

"I had to wait until Ami went out. I found the house details in her bedroom drawer. I didn't have any money so I had to get a bus and walk the rest of the way. I'm sorry that I didn't get here sooner."

"It doesn't matter now."

Tallulah picked up our clothes and then our skins which lay like shrouds. It was disconcerting to see how they were moulds of us, even down to the contours of our faces.

"I'll take these with us. We can burn them later."

I went upstairs. I edged into the darkened room as if Kenny might sit up at any moment. He was a purple, bloated corpse with fang marks in his neck. I fumbled with the chain around his neck, not wanting to touch him.

"Where's Kathy?" Tallulah asked.

I told her.

"Show me."

"No, I don't want you to remember her like that." I seized Tallulah's face in my hands. "You do know that she didn't mean what she said, about you not belonging with us? She was trying to protect you."

Tallulah nodded, her mouth a line. She didn't cry.

"We have to bury her."

"We can't. Tallulah, we have to get out of here. Do you understand? Ami will come for you when she realises you've gone. There's something else."

I put my hand in the cottonmouth's tank. It curled up my arm and I lifted it out, holding it up to my cheek. He nudged my face.

"Lift out the bottom."

Tallulah pulled out bits of twisted branch and foliage, then pulled up the false base. She gasped. Out came bundles of notes and cloth bags. She tipped the contents out on her palm. More diamonds than I could hold in my cupped hands.

We loaded the money into Kenny's rucksack and tucked the diamonds in our pockets.

"What about the snakes?"

We opened the tanks and carried them outside. I watched them disappear into the undergrowth. Except for Shankly. I put him in a carrier bag and took him with us.

There are days when I wake and I can't remember who I am, like a disorientated traveller who can't recall which hotel room of which country they're in.

I'm hurt that Georgia didn't want me to collect her from the airport.

There's been a delay. I won't get in until late. Go to bed, I'll get a cab.

I wished now that I'd ignored her and gone anyway instead of lying here in the dark. The harsh fluorescent lights and the near empty corridors of the airport are preferable to the vast darkness of our empty bed.

Not going is a stupid test with which I've only hurt myself. I've resolutely taken her consideration for indifference. I want her to be upset that I wasn't there, as if she secretly wanted me there all along.

See, I confuse even myself.

The front door opens and closes. I should get up and go to her. She comes in, marked by the unzipping of her boots and the soft sound of her shedding clothes.

Love isn't just what you feel for someone when you look at them. It's how they make you feel about yourself when they look back at you.

Georgia is the coolest, most poised woman that I know. We're older now and our hearts and flesh aren't so easily moved but I still wonder what she sees when she looks at me.

"Do you love me?" It's easier to ask it with the lights off and my head turned away from her.

Everything about us is wrong. We're lovers, sisters, freaks.

She answers in a way that I have to respond to. I glide across the floor towards her and we become a writhing knot. We hunt mice in our grandiose pile, and in the morning we are back here in our bed, entwined together in our nest.

When we wake again as human beings, she says, "Of course I love you, monster."

When we shed the disguises that are Georgia and Eliza, and then the skins that are Lola and Tallulah, we *are* monsters. Fabulous beasts.

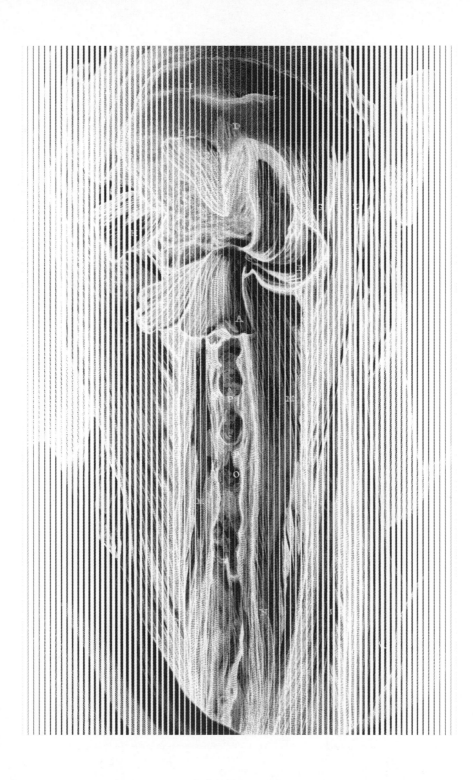

MICHAEL BLUMLEIN, M.D. was an American fiction writer and a physician. Most of his writing is in or near the genres of science fiction, fantasy, and horror. His novels include *The Healer*, The *Movement of Mountains* and *X, Y*. He was nominated for the World Fantasy Award and the Bram Stoker Award. His final work was the novella, *Longer*, which came out in 2019, a few months before he died of cancer.

Tissue Ablation and Variant Regeneration:
A Case Report
Michael Blumlein

AT SEVEN A.M. on Thursday morning, Mr. Reagan was wheeled through the swinging doors and down the corridor to operating room six. He was lying flat on the gurney, and his gaze was fixed on the ceiling; he had the glassy stare of a man in shock. I was concerned that he had been given analgesia, but the attendant assured me that he had not. As we were talking, Mr. Reagan turned his eyes to me: the pupils were wide, dark as olives, and I recognized the dilatation of pain and fear. I felt sympathy, but more, I was relieved that he had not inadvertently been narcotized, for it would have delayed the operation for days.

I had yet to scrub and placed my hand on his shoulder to acknowledge his courage. His skin was coarse beneath the thin sheet that covered him, as the pili erecti tried in vain to warm the chill we had induced. He shivered, which was natural, though eventually it would stop—it must—if we were to proceed with the surgery. I removed my hand and bent to examine the plastic bag that hung like a showy organ from the side of the gurney. There was nearly a liter of pale urine, which assured me that his kidneys were functioning well.

I turned away, and, entering the scrub room, once more conceptualized our plan. There were three teams, one for each pair of extremities and a third for torso and viscera. I headed the latter, which was proper, for the major responsibility for this project was mine. We had chosen to avoid analgesia, the analeptic properties of excruciating pain being well known. There are several well-drawn studies that conclusively demonstrate the superior survival of tissues thus exposed, and I have cited these in a number of my own monographs. In addition, chlorinated hydrocarbons, which still form the bulk of our anesthetics, are tissue-toxic in extremely small quantities. Though these agents clear rapidly in the normal course of post-operative recovery, tissue propagation is too sensitive a phenomenon for us to have risked their use. The patient was offered, routinely, the choice of an Eastern mode of anesthesia, but he demurred. Mr. Reagan has an obdurate faith in things American.

I set the timer above the sink and commenced to scrub. Through the window I watched as the staff went about the final preparations. Two large tables stood along one wall, and on top of them sat the numerous trays of instruments we would use during the operation. Since this was the largest one of its kind any of us at the center had participated in, I had been generous in my estimation of what would be needed. It is always best in such situations to err on the side of caution, and I had ordered duplicates of each pack to be prepared and placed accessibly. Already an enormous quantity of instruments lay unpacked on the tables, divided into general areas of proximity. Thus, urologic was placed beside rectal and lower intestinal, and hepatic, splenic, and gastric were grouped together. Thoracic was separate, and orthopedic and vascular were divided into two groups for those teams assigned to the extremities. There were three sets of general instruments—hemostats, forceps, scissors, and the like—and these were on smaller trays that stood close to the operating table. Perched above them, and sorting the instruments chronologically, were the scrub nurses, hooded, masked, and gloved. Behind, and throughout the operating room circulated other, non-sterile personnel, the nurses and technicians who functioned as the extended arm of the team.

For the dozenth time I scrubbed my cuticles and the space between fingernail and fingertip, then scoured both sides of my forearms to the elbow. The sheet had been removed from Mr. Reagan, and his ventral surface—from neck to foot—was covered by the yellow suds of antiseptic. His pubic parts, chest, and axilla, had been shaved earlier, although he had no great plethora of hair to begin with. The artificial light striking his body at that moment recalled to me the jaundiced hue I have seen at times on certain dysfunctional gall bladders, and I looked at my own hands. They seemed brighter, and I rinsed them several times, then backed into the surgical suite.

A nurse approached with a towel, whose corner I grabbed, proceeding to dry methodically each finger. She returned with a glove, spreading the entrance wide as one might the mouth of a fish in order to peer down its throat. I thrust my fingers and thumb into it, and she snapped it upon my forearm. She repeated the exchange with the other, and I thanked her, then stood back and waited for the final preparations.

The soap had been removed from his skin, and now Mr. Reagan was being draped with various sized linens. Two of these were used to fashion a vertical barrier at the mid-point of his neck; behind this, with his head, sat the two anesthesiologists. Since no anesthetic was to be used, their responsibility lay in monitoring his respiratory and cardiovascular status. He would be intubated, and they would make periodic measurements of the carbon dioxide and oxygen content of his blood.

I gave them a nod, and they inserted the intracath, through which we would drip a standard, paralytic dose of succinylcholine. We had briefly considered doing without the drug, for its effect, albeit minimal, would still be noticeable on the ablated tissues. Finally, though, we had chosen to use it, reasoning— and experience proved us correct—that we could not rely on the paralysis of pain to immobilize the patient for the duration of the surgery. If there had been a lull, during which time he had chosen to move, hours of careful work might have been destroyed. Prudence dictated a conservative approach.

After initiating the paralytic, Dr. Guevara, the senior anesthesiologist, promptly inserted the endotracheal tube. It passed easily for there was little, if any, muscular resistance. The respirator was turned on and artificial ventilation begun. I told Mr. Reagan, who would be conscious throughout, that we were about to begin.

I stepped to the table and surveyed the body. The chest was exposed, as were the two legs, above which Drs. Ng and Cochise were poised to begin.

"Scalpel," I said, and the tool was slapped into my palm. I transferred it to my other hand. "Forceps."

I bent over the body, mentally drawing a line from the sternal notch to the symphysis pubis. We had studied our approaches for hours, for the incisions were unique and had been used but rarely before. A procedure of this scale required precision in every detail in order that we preserve the maximal amount of viable tissue. I lifted the scalpel and with a firm and steady hand made the first cut.

He had been cooled in part to cause constriction of the small dermal vessels, thus reducing the quantity of blood lost to ooze. We were not, of course, able to use the electric scalpel to cut or coagulate, nor could we tie bleeding vessels, for both would inflict damage to tissue. Within reason, we had chosen planes incision that avoided major dermal vasculature, and as I retracted my first cut, pressing harder to separate the more stubborn fascial layers, I was reassured by the paucity of blood that was appearing at the margins of the wound. I exchanged my delicate tissue forceps for a larger pair, everting the stratum of skin, fat, and muscle, and continuing my incision until I reached the costochondral junction in the chest and the linea alba in the belly. I made two lateral incisions, one from the pubis, along the inguinal ligament, ending near the anterior superior iliac spine, and the other from the sternal notch, along the inferior border of the clavicle to the anterior edge of the axilla. There was more blood appearing now, and for a moment I aided Dr. Biko in packing the wound. Much of our success at controlling the bleeding depended, however, upon the speed at which I carried out the next stage, and with this in mind, I left him to mop the red fluid and turned to the thorax.

Pectus hypertrophicus occurs perhaps in one in a thousand; Billings, in a recent study of a dozen such cases, links the condition to a congenital aberration of the short arm of chromosome thirteen, and he postulates a correlation between the hypertrophied sternum, a marked preponderance of glabrous skin, and a mild associative cortical defect. He has studied these cases; I have not. Indeed, Mr. Reagan's sternum was only the second in all my experience that would not yield to the Lebsche knife. I asked for the bone snips, and with the help of Dr. Biko was finally able to split the structure. My forehead dripped from the effort, and a circulating nurse dabbed it with a towel.

I applied the wide-armed retractor, and as I ratcheted it apart, I felt a wince of resistance. I asked Dr. Guevara to increase the infusion of muscle relaxant, for we were entering a most crucial part of the operation.

"His pupils are fixed and dilated," he announced.

I could see his heart, and it was beating normally. "His gases?" I asked.

"O_2 85, CO_2 38, pH 7.37."

"Good," I said. "It's just agony then. Not death." Dr. Guevara nodded above the barrier that separated us, and as he bent to whisper words of encouragement to Mr. Reagan, I looked into the chest. There I paused, as I always seem to do at the sight of that glistening organ. It throbbed and rolled, sensuously, I thought, majestically, and I renewed my vows to treat it kindly. With the tissue forceps I lifted the pericardium and with the curved scissors punctured it. It peeled off smoothly, reminding me fleetingly of the delicate skin that encloses the tip of the male child's penis.

In rapid succession I ligated the inferior vena cava and cross-clamped the descending aorta, just distal to the bronchial arteries. We had decided not to use our bypass system, thus obviating cannulations that would have required lengthy and meticulous suturing. We had opted instead for a complete de-vascularization distal to the thoracic cavity, reasoning that since all the organs and other structures were to be removed anyway, there was no sense in preserving circulation below the heart. I signaled to my colleagues waiting at the lower extremities to begin their dissections.

I isolated the right subclavian artery and vein, ligated them, and did the same on the left. I anastomosed the internal thoracic artery to the ventral surface of the aortic arch, thus providing arterial flow to the chest wall, which we planned to preserve more or less intact. I returned to the descending aorta, choosing 3.0 Ethilon to assure occlusion of the lumen, and oversewed twice. I released the clamp slowly: there was no leakage, and I breathed a sigh of satisfaction. We had completed a crucial stage, isolating the thoracic and cephalic circulation from that of the rest of the body, and the patient's condition remained stable. What was left was the harvesting of his parts.

I would like to insert here a word on our behalf, aimed not just at the surgical team but at the full technical and administrative apparatus. We had early on agreed that we must approach the dissection assiduously, meaning that in every case we would apply a greater, rather than a lesser, degree of scrupulousness. At the time of the operation, no use—other than in trans-plantation—had been found for many of the organs we were to resect. Such parts as colon, spleen, and vasculature had not then, nor have they yet, struck utilitarian chords in our imaginations. Surely, they will in the future, and with this as our philosophy, we determined to discard not even the most seemingly insignificant part. What could not immediately be utilized would be preserved in our banks, waiting for a bright idea to send it to the regeneration tanks.

It was for this reason, and this reason alone, that the operation lasted as long as it did. I would be lying if I claimed that Mr. Reagan was not in constant and excruciating pain. Who would not be to have his skin fileted, his chest cracked, his limbs meticulously dissected and dismembered? In retrospect, I should have carried out a high transection of the spinal cord, thus interrupting most of the nerve fibers to his brain, but I did not think of it beforehand and during the operation was too occupied with other concerns. That he did survive is a testimony to his strength, though I still remember his post-operative shrieks and protestations. We had, of course, already detached his upper limbs, and therefore we ourselves had to dab the streams of tears that flew from his eyes. At that point, there being no further danger of tissue damage, I did order an analgesic.

After I had successfully completed the de-vascularization procedure, thus removing the risk of life-threatening hemorrhage from our fields, I returned to the outer layer of thorax and abdomen. With an Adson forceps I gently retracted the thin sheet of dermis and began to undermine with the scalpel. It was painstaking, but after much time I finally had the entire area freed. It hung limp, drooping like a dewlap, and as I began the final axillary cut that would release it completely, I asked Ms. Narciso, my scrub nurse, to call the technician. He came just as I finished, and I handed him the skin.

I confess that I have less than a full understanding of the technology of organ variation and regeneration. I am a surgeon, not a technologist, and devote the major part of my energies toward refinement and perfection of operative skills. We do, however, live in an age of great scientific achievement, and the iconoclasm of many of my younger colleagues has forced me to cast my gaze more broadly afield. Thus it is that I am not a complete stranger to inductive mitotics and controlled oncogenesis, and I will attempt to convey the fundamentals.

Upon receiving the tissue, the technician transports it to the appropriate room wherein lie the thermo-magnetic protein baths. These are organ specific, distinguished by temperature, pH, magnetic field, and substrate, and designed to suppress cellular activity; specifically, they prolong dormancy at the G1 stage of mitosis. The magnetic field is altered then, such that each cell will arrange itself ninety degrees to it. A concentrated solution of isotonic nucleic and amino acids is then pumped into the tank, and the bath mechanically agitated to diffuse the solute. Several hours are allowed to pass, and the magnetic field is again shifted, attempting to align it with the nucleic loci that govern the latter stages of mitosis. If this is successful, and success is immediately apparent for failure induces rapid and massive necrosis, the organ system will begin to reproduce. This is a macroscopic phenomenon, obvious to the naked eye. I have been present at this critical moment, and it is a simple, yet wondrous, thing to behold.

Different organs regenerate, multiply, in distinctive fashion. In the case of the skin, genesis occurs quite like the polymerization of synthetic fibers, such as nylon and its congeners. The testes grow in a more sequential manner, analogous perhaps to the clustering of grapes along the vine. Muscles seem to laminate, forming thicker and thicker sheets until, if not separated, they collapse upon themselves. Bone propagates as tubules; ligaments as lianoid strands of great length. All distinct, yet all variations on a theme.

In the case of our own patient, the outcome, I am pleased to report, was bounteous; this was especially gratifying in light of our guarded prognostications. I was not alone in the skepticism with which I approached the operation, for the tissues and regenerative capacity of an old man are not those of a youngster. During the surgery, when I noticed the friability and general degree of degeneration of his organs, my thoughts were inclined rather pessimistically. I remember wondering, as Dr. Cochise severed the humeral head from the glenoid fossa, inadvertently crushing a quantity of porotic and fragile bone, if our scrupulous planning had not been a waste of effort, that the fruits of our labor would not be commensurate with our toil. Even now, with the benefit of hindsight, I remain astonished at our degree of success. As much as it is a credit to the work of our surgical team, it is, perhaps moreso, a tribute to the resilience and fundamental vitality of the human body.

After releasing the dermal layer as described, I proceeded to detach the muscles. The adipose tissue, so slippery and difficult to manipulate, would be removed chemically, thus saving valuable time. As I have mentioned, the risk of hemorrhage—and its threat to Mr. Reagan's life—had been eliminated, but because of the resultant interruption of circulation we were faced with the real possibility of massive tissue necrosis. For this reason we were required to move most expeditiously.

With sweeping but well-guided strokes of the scalpel, I transected the ligamentous origins of pectoralis major and minor, and serratus anterior. I located their points of insertion on the scapula and humerus and severed them as well, indicating to Ms. Narciso that we would need the technician responsible for the muscles. She replied that he had already been summoned by Dr. Ng, and I took that moment to peer in his vicinity.

He and Dr. Cochise had been working rapidly, already having completed the spiraling circumferential incisions from groin to toe, thus allowing, in a fashion similar to the peeling of an orange, the removal in toto of the dermal sheath of the leg. The anterior femoral and pelvic musculature had been exposed, and I could see the sartorius and at least two of the quadriceps heads dangling. This was good work and I nodded appreciatively, then turned my attention to the abdominal wall.

In terms of time the abdominal muscles presented less of a problem than the thoracic ones, for there were no ribs to contend with. In addition, as long as I was careful not to puncture the viscera, I could enter the peritoneum almost recklessly. I took my scalpel and thrust it upon the xiphoid process, near what laymen call the solar plexus, and started the long and penetrating incision down the linea alba, past the umbilicus, to the symphysis pubis. With one hand I lifted the margin of the wound, and with the other delicately sliced the peritoneal membrane. I reflected all the abdominal muscles, the rectus and transversus abdominis, the obliquus internus and externus, and detached them from their bony insertions. Grasping the peritoneum with a long-toothed forceps and peeling it back, I placed two large towel clips in the overlying muscle mass, and then, as an iceman would pick up a block of ice, lifted it above the table, passing it into the hands of the waiting technician. Another was there for the thoracic musculature, and once these were cleared from the table, I turned to the abdominal contents themselves.

Let me interject a note as to the status of our patient at that time. As deeply as I become involved in the techniques and mechanics of any surgery, I am always, with another part of my mind, aware of the human being who lies at the mercy of the knife. At this juncture in our operation I noticed, by the flaccidity in the muscles on the other half of the abdomen, that the patient was perhaps too deeply relaxed. Always there is a tension in the muscles, and this must be mollified sufficiently to allow the surgeon to operate without undo resistance, but not so much that it endangers the life of the patient. In this case I noted little, if any, resistance, and I asked Dr. Guevara to reduce slightly the rate of infusion of the relaxant. This affected all the muscles, including, of course, the diaphragm and those of the larynx, and Mr. Reagan took the opportunity to attempt to vocalize. Being intubated, he was in no position to do so, yet somehow managed to produce a keening sound that unnerved us all. His face, as reported by Dr. Guevara, became constricted in a horrible rictus, and his eyes seemed to convulse in their sockets. Clearly, he was in excruciating pain, and my heart flew to him as to a valiant soldier.

The agony, I am certain, was not simply corporeal; surely there was a psychological aspect to it, perhaps a psychosis, as he thought upon the systematic dissection and dismemberment of his manifest self. To me, I know it would have been unbearable, and once again I was humbled by his courage and fortitude. And yet there was still so much left to do; neither empathy nor despair were distractions we could afford. Accordingly, I asked Dr. Guevara to increase the infusion rate in order to still Mr. Reagan's cries, and this achieved, I returned my concentration to the table.

By prearrangement Dr. Biko now moved to the opposite side of the patient and began to duplicate there what I had just finished on mine. The sole modification was that he began on the belly wall and proceeded in a cephalad direction, so that by the time I had extirpated the contents of one half of the abdomen, the other would be exposed and ready. With alacrity I began the evisceration.

It would be tedious to chronicle step by step the various dissections, ligations, and severances; these are detailed in a separate monograph, whose reference can be found in the bibliography. Suffice to say that I identified the organs and proceeded with the resections as we had planned. Once freeing the stomach, I was able to remove the spleen and pancreas without much delay. Because of their combined mass, the liver and gall bladder required more time but eventually came out quite nicely. I reflected the proximal small and large intestines downward in order to lay bare the deeper recesses of the upper abdominal cavity and have access to the kidneys and adrenals. I treated gland and organ as a unit, removing each pair together, transecting the ureters high, near the renal pelvises. The big abdominal vessels, vena cava and aorta, were now exposed, and I had to withstand the urge to include them in my dissection. We had previously agreed that this part of the procedure would be assumed by Dr. Biko, who is as skilled and renowned a vascular surgeon as I am an abdominothoracic one, and though they lay temptingly now within my reach, I resisted the lure and turned to accomplish the extirpation of the alimentary tract.

We did not, as many had urged, remove the cavitous segment of the digestive apparatus as a whole. After consultation with our technical staff, we determined that it would be more practical and successful if we proceeded segmentally. Thus, we divided the tract into three parts: stomach, including the esophageal segment just distal to the diaphragm; small intestine, from pylorus to ileocecal valve; and colon, from cecum to anus. These were dutifully resected and sent to the holding banks, where they await future purpose and need.

As I harvested the internal abdominal musculature, the psoas, iliacus, quadratus lumborum, I let my mind wander for a few moments. We were nearing the end of the operation, and I felt the luxury of certain philosophical meditations. I thought about the people of the world, the hungry, the cold, those without shelter or goods to meet the exigencies of daily life. What are our responsibilities to them, we the educated, the skilled, the possessors? It is said, and I believe, that no man stands above any other. What then can one person do for the many? Listen, I suppose. Change.

I have found in my profession, as I am certain exists in all others, that to not adapt is to become obsolete. I have known many colleagues, who, unwilling or unable to grapple with innovation, have gone the way of the penny. Tenacity, in some an admirable quality, is no substitute for the ability to change, for what in one age might be considered tenacious in another would most certainly be called cowardly. I thought upon our patient, whose fortunes had so altered since the years of my training, and considered further the question of justice. Could an act of great altruism, albeit forced and involuntary, balance a generation of infamy? How does the dedication of one's own body to the masses weigh upon the scales of sin and repentance?

My brow furrowed, for these questions were far more difficult to me than the operation itself, and had it not been for Ms. Narciso, who spoke up in a timely voice, I might have broken the sterile field by wiping with my own hand the perspiration on my forehead.

"Shall we move to the pelvis, Doctor?" she said, breaking my reverie.

"Yes," I replied softly, turning momentarily from the table to recover, while a nurse mopped the moist skin of my face.

The bladder, of course, had been decompressed by the catheter that had been passed prior to surgery, and once I pierced the floor of the peritoneum, it lay beneath my blade like a flat and flaccid tire. I severed it quickly, taking care to include the prostate, seminal vesicles, ureters, and membranous urethra in the resection. A technician carried these to an intermediate room, where a surgeon was standing by to separate the structures before they were taken to their respective tanks. What remained was to take the penis, which was relatively simple, and testes, which required more care so as not to disrupt the delicate tunica that surrounded them. This done, I straightened my back for perhaps the first time since we began and assessed our progress.

When one becomes so engrossed in a task, so keyed and focused that huge chunks of time pass unaware, it is a jarring feeling, akin to waking from a vivid and lifelike dream, to return to reality. I have felt this frequently during surgeries, but never as I did this time. Hours had passed, personnel had changed, perhaps even the moon outside had risen, in a span that for me was marked in moments. I looked for Drs. Ng and Cochise and was informed that they had left the surgical suite some time ago. I recalled this only dimly, but when I looked to their work was pleased to find that it had been performed most adequately. All limbs were gone, and the glenoid fossae, where the shoulders had been de-articulated, were sealed as we had discussed. Across from me Dr. Biko was just completing the abdominal vascular work. I nodded to myself, and using an interior approach, detached the muscles of the lumbar spine, then asked for the bone saw.

We transected the spinal cord between the second and third lumbar vertebrae, thus preserving the major portion of attachments of the diaphragm. This, of course, was vital, if, as we had planned, Mr. Reagan was to retain the ability to respire. It is well-known that those who leave surgery still attached to the respirator, which surely would have been the case if we had been sloppy in this last part of the operation, do poorly thereafter, often dying in the immediate post-operative period. In this case especially, such an outcome would have been particularly heinous, for it would have deprived this brave man of the fate and rewards most deservedly his.

I am nearing the conclusion of our report, and it must be obvious that I have failed to include each and every nerve, ligament, muscle, and vessel that we removed. If it seems a critical error, I can only say that it is a purposeful one, intended to improve the readability of this document. Hopefully, I have made it more accessible to the laypeople that exist outside the cloister of our medical world, but those who crave more detailed information I refer to the Archives of Ablative Technique, vol. 113, number 6, pp. 67-104, or, indeed, to any comprehensive atlas of anatomy.

We sealed the chest wall and sub-diaphragmatic area with a synthetic polymer (XRO 137, by Dow) that is thin but surprisingly durable and impervious to bacterial invasion. We did a towel count to make certain that none were inadvertently left inside the patient, though at that point there was little of him that could escape our attention, then Dr. Guevara inserted the jugular catheter that would be used for nourishment and medication. Dr. Biko fashioned a neat little fistula from the right external carotid artery, which, because we had taken the kidneys, would be used for dialysis. These completed, we did a final blood gas and vital sign check, each of which was acceptable, and I stepped back from the table.

"Thank you all very much," I said, and turned to Mr. Reagan as I peeled back my gloves. He was beginning to recover from the drug-induced paralysis, and his face seemed to recoil from mine as I bent toward him. I have seen this before in surgery, where the strange apparel, the hooded and masked faces, often cause fright in a patient. It is especially common in the immediate post-operative period, when unusual bodily sensations and a frequently marked mental disorientation play such large roles. I was therefore not alarmed to see our patient's features contort as I drew near.

"It is over," I said gently, keeping my words simple and clear. "It went well. We will take the tube from your mouth, but don't try to talk. Your throat will be quite sore for a while, and it will hurt."

I placed a hand on his cheek, which felt clammy even though the skin was flushed, and Dr. Guevara withdrew the tube. By that time the muscle relaxant had worn off completely, and Mr. Reagan responded superbly by beginning to breathe on his own immediately. Shortly thereafter, he began to shriek.

There are some surgeons I know, and many other physicians, who believe in some arcane manner in the strengthening properties of pain. They assert that it fortifies the organism, steeling it, as it were, to the insults of disease. Earlier, I mentioned the positive association between pain and tissue survival, but this obtains solely with respect to ablative surgery. It has not been demonstrated under myriad other circumstances, and this despite literally hundreds of studies to prove it so. The only possible conclusion, the only scientific one, is that pain, apart from its value as a mechanism of warning, has none of those attributes the algophilists ascribe to it. In my mind these practitioners are reprehensible moralists and should be barred from those specialties, such as surgery, where the problem is ubiquitous.

Needless to say, as soon as Mr. Reagan began to cry, I ordered a potent and long-lasting analgesic. For the first time since we began his face quieted and his eyes closed, and though I never questioned him on it, I like to think that his dreams were sweet and proud at what he, one man, had been able to offer thousands.

Save for the appendix, this is the whole of my report. Once again I apologize for omissions and refer the interested reader to the ample bibliography. We have demonstrated, I believe, the viability of extensive tissue ablation and its value in providing substrate for inductive and variant mitotics. Although it is an arduous undertaking, I believe it holds promise for selected patients in the future.

APPENDIX

As of the writing of this document, the following items and respective quantities have been produced by our regeneration systems:

Item	Source	Quantity
OIL, REFINED	Testes: semniferous tubes	3761 LITERS
PERFUMES AND SCENTS	Same	162 GRAMS
MEAT INCLUDING PATTIES, FILETS AND GROUND ROUND	Muscles	13,318 KG
STORAGE JUGS	Bladder	2732
BALLS, INFLATABLE (RECREATIONAL USE)	Same	325
CORD, MULTI-PURPOSED	Ligaments	1.2 KILOMETERS
ROOFING MATERIAL, E.G. FOR TENTS; FLEXIBLE SIDING	Skin: full thickness	3.6 SQ. KM.
PROPHYLACTICS	Skin: stratum granulosum	18.763 CARTONS OF 10 EA.
VARIOUS ENZYMES, MEDICATIONS, HORMONES	Pancreas, adrenal glands, hepatic tissues	272 GRAMS
FLEXIBLE STRUTS AND HOUSING SUPPORTS	Bone	453 SQ. METERS

The vast majority of these have been distributed, principally to countries of the third world, but also to impoverished areas of our own nation. A follow-up study to update our data and provide a geographical breakdown by item will be conducted within the year.

About the editor

ELLEN DATLOW has been editing science fiction, fantasy, and horror short fiction for forty years as fiction editor of OMNI Magazine and editor of *Event Horizon* and SCIFICTION. She currently acquires short stories and novellas for Tor.com. In addition, she has edited about one hundred science fiction, fantasy, and horror anthologies, including the annual *The Best Horror of the Year* series, *The Doll Collection, Mad Hatters and March Hares, The Devil and the Deep: Horror Stories of the Sea, Echoes: The Saga Anthology of Ghost Stories, Edited By,* and *Final Cuts: New Tales of Hollywood Horror and Other Spectacles.*

She's won multiple World Fantasy Awards, Locus Awards, Hugo Awards, Bram Stoker Awards, International Horror Guild Awards, Shirley Jackson Awards, and the 2012 Il Posto Nero Black Spot Award for Excellence as Best Foreign Editor. Datlow was named recipient of the 2007 Karl Edward Wagner Award, given at the British Fantasy Convention for "outstanding contribution to the genre," was honored with the Life Achievement Award by the Horror Writers Association, in acknowledgment of superior achievement over an entire career, and honored with the World Fantasy Life Achievement Award at the 2014 World Fantasy Convention.

She lives in New York and co-hosts the monthly Fantastic Fiction Reading Series at KGB Bar. More information can be found at WWW.DATLOW.COM, on Facebook, and on twitter as @ELLENDATLOW. She's owned by two cats.